The Huguenot Sword

Shawn Lamb

Allon Books

THE HUGUENOT SWORD by Shawn Lamb

Published by Allon Books
209 Hickory Way Court
Antioch, Tennessee 37013
www.allonbooks.com

Cover design by Robert Lamb

Library of Congress Control Number: 2011917328

International Standard Book Number: 978-0-9829204-4-2

Other Books by Shawn Lamb

Young Adult Fantasy Fiction
ALLON ~ BOOK 1
Published by Creation House, a division of Charisma Media

Published by Allon Books

ALLON ~ BOOK 2 ~ INSURRECTION
ALLON ~ BOOK 3 ~ HEIR APPARENT
ALLON ~ BOOK 4 ~ A QUESTION OF SOVEREIGNTY
ALLON ~ BOOK 5 ~ GAUNTLET
ALLON ~ BOOK 6 ~ DILEMMA
ALLON ~ BOOK 7 ~ DANGEROUS DECEPTION
ALLON ~ BOOK 8 ~ DIVIDED
ALLON ~ IN PLAIN SIGHT
PARENT STUDY GUIDE FOR ALLON ~ BOOKS 1-9
THE ACTIVITY BOOK OF ALLON

For Young Readers – ages 8-10
Allon ~ The King's Children series
NECIE AND THE APPLES
TRISTINE'S DORGIRITH ADVENTURE
NIGEL'S BROKEN PROMISE

Historical Fiction
GLENCOE

Dramatis Personae

Arsène LAMONREAUX

PHILIPE BOURDIAS, son of Baron Bourdias, twin brother of Adele

DOMINIC CHARBONIER, Comte de Trevoux, son of the Marquis de Charbonier

ADELE CHARBONIER, Comtesse de Trevoux, daughter of Baron Bourdias,
               twin sister of Philipe

SABRINA CHARBONIER, cousin of Dominic, niece of the Marquis de Charbonier

ROGER, Philipe's servant

JOURDAIN, Marquis de Charbonier

MADELINE, Marquise de Charbonier, wife of Jourdain

CAPTAIN DE LACY, of the Cardinal's Guards

CARDINAL RICHELIEU

KING LOUIS XIII

QUEEN ANNE OF AUSTRIA

PRINCE GASTON, Duc d'Orleans, brother of King Louis XIII

MARGUERITE DE BETHUNE, Duchess de Rohan, wife of Henri, Duc de Rohan

COMTE DE BORCHARD

MARQUIS D'AVALLON

COMTE DE REYNARD

WILLIAM, Duc de Trudeau

HENRI, Duc de Rohan

DUKE OF BUCKINGHAM

JEANETTE CHARISE, lady in waiting

FRANÇOIS TREVILLE, Captain of the King's Musketeers

ELIZABETH PONTINIERE, lady in waiting

BENJAMIN SOUBISE, younger brother of Henri, Duc de Rohan

⚜ Chapter 1 ⚜

A LARGE MAN OF TWENTY-THREE YEARS, dressed in black doublet, breeches and cloak stood by the door. He peeked out the small opening of the door into the dark night. Standing several inches over six feet, he had to look down through the opening. He shrugged the cloak over his shoulder to move for a better view. The black gloves he wore were stretched to the brink of ripping in an attempt to cover his massive hands. Thick sable hair hung like a wavy mane about his face. On the table in the center of the room were a large black hat and mask.

Beside the table stood a young man of roughly the same age, only a head shorter and thirty pounds lighter. His black outfit was almost identical to his companion and he wore the black mask. He held his hat, fingers nervous in clenching the brim. Even with the mask, his blond hair and mustache were in marked contrast to his dark disguise. The lamp on the table burned low, yet danced in his hazel eyes, which changed shades with his mood. His focus shifted from a hallway leading further into the house to the door.

"Dominic," he hissed to get the attention of the other. "Any sign of the Cardinal's men?"

"No." Dominic turned from his vigil to glance down the hall. "What of Arsène?"

"Nothing yet, and they should be ready to leave."

Both became alert at hearing running feet coming down the hall and a harsh call, "Make ready!"

Dominic slammed the opening shut and moved to stand beside his companion.

"Arsène," he said to Dominic upon recognizing the voice.

A third young man dressed in identical clothes appeared, only with black hair, clean-shaven, handsome features and blue eyes illuminated by the candlelight. He removed his hat, tossed it onto the table and withdrew a mask from his doublet pocket to put on.

They mimicked Arsène in donning the masks and placing their hats securely on their heads.

"De Lacy?" Arsène asked Dominic.

"No. Maybe we succeeded in thwarting the traitor."

"Whether we did or didn't, does not change what must be done. Philipe, the west route," he said to the blond man then held out his right arm. "For faith."

"For friendship," said Philipe, taking hold of Arsène's arm.

"For freedom," said Dominic, adding his hand to make a triangle of clasped arms.

After a nod from Arsène, Dominic returned to the door. He waited for Philipe to extinguish the lamp before opening the door enough to poke his head out and look up and down the street. "All clear."

Arsène moved to the hallway and called in the same voice as earlier. "Go!" He turned and waved to Philipe. The latter took the lead in leaving the house, followed by Arsène and Dominic.

At the corner, Arsène stopped and gazed intently down an adjacent alley. Philipe halted across the boulevard when he noticed Arsène stop. Dominic fell in behind Philipe.

"Well?" asked Philipe.

Arsène moved to join them. "They are away."

"Why does he not want us as escort?" asked Dominic.

"He does. After we pass Tuileries we are to rendezvous."

Arsène signaled and once again Philipe took the lead.

Along the dark, quiet streets of Paris they moved fast yet making as little noise as possible for any sound traveled a good distance in such stillness. The quarter moon gave off little light by which to see, but that didn't trouble them as they navigated the pre-determined route.

A few streets later, Arsène pulled up and ducked into an alley between buildings. Philipe followed Arsène, his left hand ready to draw his sword. Dominic took cover in the deep shadow of a doorway across the street. All waited in rapt attention, listening.

"Two men," whispered Arsène to Philipe then made a signal of two fingers to Dominic.

"Will you be able to see them as well as hear them?" said Philipe in mock admiration.

The footsteps came closer. All drew their swords in anticipation of a confrontation. Just as Arsène estimated, two cloaked men stopped at the corner of the intersection. One was stocky and stout, the other a little taller and thinner.

"Did we lose them?" asked the taller one.

Hearing the man's voice, Arsène stepped out to approach them. "Monsieur! What is wrong?"

The stocky one whirled about, sword first ready to confront whoever approached. "Arsène!" he said in relief. "Cardinal's men were waiting."

By now Philipe and Dominic joined them.

"The others?" asked Arsène.

"We chose to be decoys and left Chandler to see them home."

More footsteps, only the sound of many, and accompanied by raised voices.

"Down here!" came a shout.

"Go!" said Arsène, practically shoving the stout man in the opposite direction.

The two men headed east. Arsène, Philipe and Dominic continued on the westerly route. The clock in the watchmaker's window behind the Palais des Tuileries chimed ten as they raced past the shop. But the escape route became blocked when four of the Cardinal's Guards rounded the corner in front of them. The lamplight of the boulevard revealed the distinct shape of their red uniform with extra wide breeches and short tunic. The hats were also differed with a smaller brim and a few feathers instead of ostrich plumes.

Arsène and Philipe pulled up short, but Dominic made a loud war cry and rushed the guards. Caught by surprise of the bold attack they either retreated or stepped aside in avoidance. Dominic's blade sliced open the chest of one guard and soon the battle was fully engaged.

Arsène reacted with cat-like agility, out-maneuvering his opponent, who grew frustrated and finally made a move that tripped Arsène. Rolling away from danger, Arsène sprang to his feet in time to block a thrust aimed at his throat. He returned the favor of tripping by stabbing his dagger in the man's calf. The man yowled, falling backwards, which ripped the dagger from his leg.

Philipe's left-handedness proved bothersome for the guard he fought, as the man used both hands on the hilt to parry the unusual style. Driven back, he bumped into a stoop and felt something against his leg—empty wine bottles. He feinted an attack but instead reached down, seized a wine bottle and swung at Philipe, catching him in the head near the right temple. Philipe cried out and dropped onto all fours.

The guard thrust down at Philipe, who fell aside in avoidance of the blade. He then rolled onto the blade, breaking it and disarming the man. But the move made him dizzy and unable to react when the guard moved to strike him again with the wine bottle. The blow never made it. Arsène's sword passed through the man's chest. He used his free hand to knock the wine bottle from the man's hand and jerked out his blade, which made the man fall away from Philipe.

Arsène knelt. "How bad?"

"Glancing blow from the bottle. But I think I can see straight," he said, blinking to bring Arsène into focus.

"Reinforcement!" said Dominic in warning.

Arsène pulled Philipe to his feet in time to see six more Cardinal's Guards arrive, and this time led by a familiar man. The streetlight revealed him to be of dark gypsy countenance with ebony hair, mustache and small beard. The aquiline nose appeared to have been broken at the tip and he scowled, intensifying his intimidating appearance.

"De Lacy," said Arsène in a low hiss of venom.

"Surrender in the name of Cardinal Richelieu."

"You see our answer," said Arsène in a well-disguised voice, as he motioned to the fallen guards.

De Lacy's response was a predatory grin and command, "Charge!"

Two raced at Dominic. He easily knocked one guard aside then grabbed the other and tossed him at de Lacy. This briefly halted the captain's approach.

Philipe staggered, still recovering from the wine bottle. He used a violent circular parry to disarm his attacker before another engaged him.

De Lacy and a guard charged Arsène. The guard landed a hard blow with the flat of his sword to the back of Arsène's hand, disarming him. Arsène seized the man's sword arm, kicked him in the groin and sent him to the street with a hard blow to the back of the head.

"This night your mask comes off!" de Lacy declared.

"Only if you can get close enough to pull it off." Arsène whipped out his dagger in his right hand to deflect de Lacy's next attack. He dodged under de Lacy's blade and grabbed his fallen sword with his left hand. With a swipe, he stopped the advance, but missed de Lacy.

"Rather clumsy tonight." De Lacy attacked and when Arsène made an awkward riposte, they came together at the hilt.

Arsène smiled, the blue eyes behind the mask mocking. "I know something you don't." He shoved de Lacy back and the captain briefly stumbled, but gave Arsène enough time for him to shove the dagger in his belt and toss his sword to his right hand. "I am right-handed." His attack was more precise and quick and drove de Lacy back into a building. The jarring stop made de Lacy glance back. This made him vulnerable and disarmed by a deep cut to his arm.

De Lacy launched forward and tackled Arsène. Both tumbled backwards with de Lacy ending on top. His minor triumph didn't last long when Dominic pulled him off Arsène and slammed him into a wall. De Lacy sank to his knees, semi-conscious.

Arsène, Philipe and Dominic ran from the square, over a nearby bridge to the far bank and didn't stop until they reached a rundown building several blocks from the river. Philipe stumbled and sat to rest. Arsène knelt to examine Philipe, who hissed and shoved the hand away from his head.

"I'll be all right. Just a slight headache."

"From what?" asked Dominic.

"Bad wine."

"Bottle to the temple," explained Arsène and became more insistent on examining Philipe. "Doesn't feel like he broke your skull."

"Close enough," groused Philipe.

"I think you've had enough for one night. By now the others should be safely home."

"You two leave first. I don't have as far to go," said Dominic.

Arsène helped Philipe to his feet, only to have him push away to stand on his own.

Dominic smiled and said to Arsène, "If you make the remedy strong enough it may cure his ego of refusing help along with the headache."

Philipe flashed a mocking grin to the teasing and began to leave.

Dominic stopped Philipe, his tone serious. "Let Arsène mix you a remedy."

This time Philipe's smile showed reassurance. "I'd never hear the end of it from either of you if I refused. Until tomorrow, old friend."

Dominic watched until Philipe and Arsène were out of sight then headed in the opposite direction. When he passed St. Eustache Cathedral, the bell chimed half past the hour of ten. He turned onto the Rue Réanmur and approached a large, older chateaux built in a bold Gothic style. To reach the rear courtyard one rode through a covered alleyway to an arched gate of heavy wood and iron. The width and height were large enough for a carriage. Built inside the right side of the gate was a smaller door for pedestrians. He used the door.

In the courtyard stood a fountain, marble benches, a terrace, a small back lawn, and finally the stables and carriage house. Three entrances led from the terrace to the chateau; two were double doors flanking a single door in the center of rear wall. He produced a key from his pocket and unlocked the single door. The door made a slight creek upon initial opening, then fell silent. Soft light came from a dying fire in the kitchen hearth and lamp on the table. Beside the lamp was a meat pie and bottle of wine.

Dominic smiled. "Bless you, Adele." He devoured the pie in a few large bites, grabbed the bottle and lamp to head for the back stairs.

At the bottom of the steps he met Adele. She carried a single candle. Soft light reflected off her golden hair and she smiled. Even in the dim light the resemblance to her twin brother Philipe was evident.

"I see you found the treat I left," she said.

He took a drink to help wash down the last swallow of pie. "What are you doing up this late? Is something wrong with child?" He moved to support her about the waist.

"You know I have trouble sleeping when he or she becomes too active." She held her swollen belly and smiled. "But truly, I was concerned and came to see if you returned unharmed."

"Returned and eaten and ready to retire." He began to escort her upstairs.

"Then all is well? No one hurt?"

"I am unscathed."

"Philipe?" When he didn't immediately answer, she stopped on the stairs. "I know what I felt. Do not dismiss my feelings."

"I do not dismiss them. I understand the bond you share. I have seen it since we were children." He took her hand to continue upstairs.

"Do you seek to spare me from horrid news?"

"No," he said with a light chuckle. "Although I rather you were not upset in your condition. Philipe received a glancing blow from a wine bottle, nothing broken or cracked. A dose of Arsène's headache remedy and he'll be fine." He escorted her to her chamber, adjacent to his. "Now, sleep well, for your sake and the child. Philipe will be fine come morning." He moved to kiss her, but she stopped him.

She took off his hat and removed his mask. "I would rather see the face of my husband than the mask of a rogue."

He smiled. "It doesn't change the lips of the one who loves you."

They kissed.

"Oww!" he murmured and backed off.

"You think the kick hurt you?" She held her belly.

"To bed, the both of you." He held the door open for her to enter the chamber but both became alert upon hearing the ringing of a bell.

"The front door? This late at night?" asked Adele.

"It wouldn't be Philipe or Arsène. Wait while I learn who." He proceeded downstairs.

At the same hour, three riders entered Paris. They appeared to be gentlemen of means seated upon fine, but tired horses. The well-made somber-colored doublets and cloaks were covered with the dust of travel while the boots scuffed and muddy. Large brimmed hats decorated with expensive ostrich feathers were pulled low to shadow their faces. Each wore an impressive rapier at the hip. The oldest appeared to be in his mid-thirties, comely and clean-shaven. He rode slightly ahead of the others.

He glanced over his shoulder to check the distance between himself and his companions. Both were younger, fair in feature, one dark-haired and the other blond. The blond youth was smaller in stature than the dark one and rode with shoulders hunched, anxiety etched in the brow and chewing nervously on a pale lower lip. The darker one also showed signs of apprehension, but sat erect in the saddle watching him. He flashed a smile and faced forward only to his hear his name called in a harsh whisper, but even that volume sounded like shouting at night.

"Roger. How much further?" the dark youth asked.

"Once we pass St. Eustache Cathedral we will turn on the Rue Réanmur, then a short distance to Le Petit Châteaux."

"Cathedral," the youth repeated with disturbance, looking to where he indicated.

"Have no fear, you shall be safe soon," he said in a kind, reassuring voice.

Indeed, his estimation proved correct, as barely five minutes passed and he turned onto another street. But he no sooner turned then pulled up and jumped from the saddle and seized the bridle of the dark youth's horse.

"What is it?"

"I saw horses out front."

"At this hour?"

"Have we arrived too late?" asked the blond youth in a light nervous voice.

"Hush!" commanded the other youth.

"We best continue on foot and enter through the back," said Roger.

"What about our horses?"

"I'll fetch them once you are safe." He took the reins of the horse after the youths dismounted and tied them to a hitching post. He did the same with his horse.

At a cautious pace, he led them a few hundred yards to the chateaux. He stopped and, with urgency, ushered them into a shadow of a building.

"D'Algernon's men," he said.

"Dear God, no!" murmured the dark youth

"It may serve your purposes. By arriving before us, they will not find you." He peeked out again. "They have moved around front so the way is clear."

The youth seized him to prevent movement. "But I'll be discovered!"

"There is a secret entrance that leads to the drawing room. We can wait there until they are gone."

"How will we see?" asked the blond youth, still very nervous.

Roger didn't answer, rather went and withdrew a half-used candle from his saddlebag. He checked to see if anyone was in view. Seeing no one, he dashed to a shop outside of which hung a lamp. He climbed up the windowsill and used the lamp to light the candle. Careful to shield the flame, he moved across the street to the chateau where he signaled for the youths.

"Hold this." He handed the candle to the dark youth.

Rather than using the rear pedestrian door, he felt against the wall until he found what he was searching for and pushed. The youths jumped at hearing the brief scraping of stone and a crack appeared in the wall. Roger forced the wall panel open and nudged the youths inside. He pulled a lever on the other side and the wall panel closed.

"How did you know this was here?" asked the dark youth.

Roger just smiled. "My master and the count would sometimes sneak in after some childhood escapade." He took the candle from the dark youth. "Follow me closely."

With a single flame providing the only light, the youths did as instructed. In fact, the blond youth clung to the cloak of the dark youth. Nearing the end of the passage, they heard voices and stopped to listen.

Inside the drawing room, Adele sat, fretful as Dominic glowered at the smaller, lean, older man, who appeared almost anorectic compared to the robust young giant. Clothes hung upon him as on a wooden scarecrow.

"I understand your annoyance, monsieur. But I'm only following the marquis' instruction," said d'Algernon said.

Irate eyes narrowed. "My word should be sufficient!"

D'Algernon swallowed back his intimidation to reply. "Duty compels me to obey. If it was my choice—"

"Yes, I know! My father would not believe me!"

"Dominic," said Adele, trepidation in her voice.

His ire focused again on d'Algernon. "Now you upset my wife."

"Pardon, madame. Monsieur, I—"

Dominic waved him off and drew to his full height when a soldier entered. He bowed to the count yet spoke to d'Algernon.

"We found nothing, monsieur."

"You may tell my father his instructions were carried out. Sabrina is not here!"

D'Algernon bowed. "Again, I beg pardon for this intrusion." He and the soldier withdrew.

"Gérard, make sure all the doors are locked and no more disturbances tonight," Dominic ordered the house steward.

Adele moved beside Dominic. She was pale with concern. "What are you going to do?"

"I don't know, but—" he stopped when part of the wall cracked and began to open. Adele seized him, prompting him to speak. "Only a few know the passageway." He moved closer for a better view as the panel swung into the room. Guarded anticipation crossed his features when the shadow gave way to figures. "Roger?"

Roger didn't immediately reply, guiding the youths into the room. Their appearance placed Dominic on guard.

"Dominic, it is I, Sabrina," said the dark youth and quickly removed the hat and wig. A long, fawn-colored braid fell across her shoulder. Her features were not striking, a gentle oval face, a slender nose slightly up-turned and big brown eyes. The shape of her upper lip was well defined, while the lower lip small and rounded. Her complexion was of a country gentlewoman, amber with fading freckles. In all she appeared exactly as her nineteen years would indicate, the transition of a girl into womanhood.

"Sabrina?"

With tears of relief, mixed with anxiety, she embraced Dominic.

Dominic turned to Roger, both annoyed yet curious. "You have some explaining to do."

"Yes, monsieur."

"Do not be cross with Roger. Because of what happened, he discovered I was to be secretly conducted by the Viscomte d'Algernon to the Convent of the Virgin in Rome! There to be kept in solitude where Uncle hoped you would never find me. Roger orchestrated the whole escape. I brought Angela to protect her from Uncle's wrath." She motioned to the blond youth, her maid.

"It was a harrowing escape, monsieur," said Angela.

Dominic turned his attention from the maid to Sabrina. "We thought nothing when Roger spoke of a family tragedy. If we knew—"

"No! It is good you did not."

"I hold myself responsible for your misfortune."

"I do not blame you. Yet you've been successful in hiding your conversion for so long. How could this happen?"

Dominic snorted with a faint smirk. "Not all things are within my control. And let's not forget, my father had a hand in this unpleasant incident."

Sabrina looked confused. "I realize his abrasive and stubborn character has lead to many disagreements, but whoever this Lamonreaux is, I question his character for such indiscretion."

"That's not the issue at present. What to do now that you are here is the issue."

Her head fell. "I didn't know where else to go."

He lifted her head. "You did right. I'll think of something. I promise."

"You must be exhausted," said Adele.

Sabrina balked when addressed by Adele, but Dominic kept her from withdrawing.

"Adele knows everything. In fact, she too has embraced the faith, along with Philipe."

"And you are all still allowed at Court?"

"No one knows we are Huguenots."

"But Uncle pronounced such vehement curses I thought it was a known fact."

Dominic shook his head. "Like yours, our faith is a matter of the heart, that is what my father discovered. Fortunately, we have avoided making it known publically."

"And the viscount?"

"Will report you are not here."

"For how long?"

"I don't know, but I will shield you as long as I can. I promise."

"Now, come," said Adele, taking Sabrina's hand. "You must rest."

Dominic spoke to Roger after the women left, his voice firm in addressing the servant. "Why did you not tell us the truth rather than lie?"

"It would have been too dangerous, monsieur. It is fortunate the marquis did not kill Sergeant Lamonreaux. To expose you and my master to his spleen was unthinkable. If action were not taken, she would be en route to the convent as we speak. I'm sorry if I offended you or acted inappropriately, monsieur."

Dominic pursed his lips then shook his head. "No, you did well." He held fast to Roger's shoulder for a moment of consideration. "Inform Philipe and tell him I wish to speak with him first thing in the morning."

"Yes, monsieur. What of Sergeant Lamonreaux?"

"Leave him to Philipe and I."

"Yes, monsieur."

At first light, Dominic dressed and moved to the private study. He had a fitful night, his mind racing to find a solution to the situation. His warring thoughts went between recalling the past events that brought Sabrina to live with his family and the present dilemma.

She was only nine years old when she survived the fire that killed her family. It occurred during Michael's attempt to reconcile with his older brother Jourdain. Guilt over the tragedy prompted Jourdain to bring Sabrina into his home. However, the gesture was not totally selfless. Jourdain tried to drive the *heretical religion* from her. He bribed, cajoled, condemned and threatened; but through it all Sabrina held fast to her faith. Dominic became naturally curious at her behavior, so he and Sabrina often spoke in secret concerning God. The more he learned about the Protestant faith and witnessed her fortitude, the more he questioned his Catholic upbringing.

He knew he couldn't keep his conversion a secret forever, but how it was discovered and the subsequent consequences were nothing like he imagined. Many times he thought of different scenarios of how his father would learn the truth and always with the same dismissal outcome, rejection and renouncement. He hoped to secure Sabrina from his father's control before being discovered by discreetly finding her a suitable husband, preferably a well-known noble Huguenot his father could not reject. Now what? He and Adele managed to play the dangerous game of Court intrigue well, but full revelation could lead to ruin, something he must prevent.

A brief knock, followed by an entrance drew him from his pondering. "Philipe."

Philipe flashed a smile of greeting. This morning his eyes shifted from the darkened hue to the normal olive green. "Arsène's headache remedy made me sleep so soundly, Roger couldn't wake me until this morning."

"What of Arsène?"

"He knows nothing, I came here straightaway. How is Sabrina?"

"Still asleep, but Adele will see to her."

"You told Adele already?"

Dominic smiled. "The child sometimes gives her fitful nights. She was awake when d'Algernon made his search and Sabrina arrived. Have you given any thought to our dilemma?"

"Naturally, but it is not a simple problem. We must act quickly but without causing further trouble. There is one person who can help us."

Dominic pursed his lips in thought. "That may prove hazardous, for it would openly announce our conversion and nothing would incite my father more than public scandal."

"That leaves us with little option since she is unknown in Paris. If she were known, the situation could be a bit easier—"

Dominic smiled with sudden pleasure. "Philipe, you're a genius! How does one become known in Paris?"

"By introduction at Court ..." Philipe smiled with understanding. "The Spring Festival in two days."

"Yes! The debut of the niece and ward of the Marquis de Charbonier might just prove the thwarting we need."

"It can protect both Sabrina and our reputation. What of Arsène? He must to be told."

Dominic nodded. "Tell him at your discretion. Only warn him to be careful."

Sabrina felt someone shaking her on the right shoulder, but the last thing she wanted to do was wake up. She had not slept in a comfortable bed in nearly a week. The persistent shaking was becoming annoying. She groaned and buried herself further under the covers. That didn't help. The blankets were ripped off, exposing her to the cool morning air. She bolted up at the violence and chill.

"Adele?" she squealed in surprised indignation.

Adele signaled Angela to open the drapes. "I tried to be gentle, but you wouldn't wake."

"It's cold!" Sabrina reached for the covers, but Adele prevented her from grabbing them.

"You'll be warm enough in a dressing gown for the time being."

Angela held a dressing gown so Sabrina stood and wrapped the gown around her and put on slippers. "Is something wrong?" she asked Adele.

"There is much to do and you can't lay about all day. My seamstress is waiting in antechamber." Adele nudged Sabrina toward the door.

"Seamstress? What for?"

"You can't go to Court in men's clothes."

Sabrina paled with fright and stopped. "I can't go to Court! I'm not supposed to be in Paris!"

Adele prodded Sabrina to keep moving. "You can and you will. The Spring Festival is in two days. Dominic will make the introduction and hopefully stay the marquis' hand."

Sabrina was slow to comprehend. "What? How?"

"Simple. Once you have met Their Majesties, the marquis will be careful in taking any action in response to your flight."

Sabrina grew fretful. "I still don't understand. I'm a Huguenot. I will not be accepted."

Adele smiled. "That's just it. No one knows you are a Huguenot. As the Comte de Trévoux and son of a royal favorite, Dominic freely associates with the King. Being his wife and daughter of the Baron Bourdias, I enjoy the privilege of attending the Queen. Without question, you will be accepted as the niece of one of the most staunch Catholic nobles in France."

For a moment Sabrina considered the advice. Adele spoke so easily of being at Court, but she grew up isolated in the country. "I don't know if I can."

Adele became forceful in speech and expression. "You must! Our success depends upon you. Including our child's future." She placed a hand on her belly.

"Oh my," said Sabrina, taken back. "I hadn't noticed. Are you well?"

Adele smiled. "I am well."

Sabrina gave Adele a gentle hug and kiss on the cheek. "Does Uncle know?"

"Dominic meant to tell him when in Reims, but that never happened." With tender sympathy she touched Sabrina's cheek. "You know Dominic would do nothing to harm you."

"I know, but seeing you with child, I regret I came."

"No!" she insisted, seizing Sabrina's hand. "There is no time for regret, we must act, swift and decisive."

Sabrina squared her shoulders with determination and rose to her full height. She frowned, placing a hand on her stomach at gurgling sounds. "Can I at least have breakfast before being poked with pins and needles?"

Adele laughed. "Angela will fetch you food while you are being fitted."

❧ Chapter 2 ❧

GOLDEN SUNLIGHT OF LATE AFTERNOON BATHED THE CHÂTEAU Vieux de Saint-Germain-En-Laye. The Royal residence stood on the site of the old fortress that protected Paris from the west. The building had five connecting sides enclosing a private courtyard. The bottom floor was situated several feet below the surrounding grounds. Accessibility to the first floor meant crossing one of four bridges over a dry moat. Due to the unique construction, carriages stopped at the end of the main bridge. In uniforms of white and gold, Royal footmen greeted the arriving guests.

When the gilded carriage of the Comte de Trèvoux arrived, Philipe emerged first. He wore a suit of dark green yet retained the high polished boots of a soldier. Since he despised the fashionable wigs, his blond hair was pampered for the night. He offered his hand to Sabrina and helped her from the carriage.

Her gown of gold silk was interwoven with a small green fleur-de-lis pattern. Her hair was curled and pampered while her entire appearance enhanced by the sweet fragrance of newly bloomed roses.

Dominic and Adele followed. The heavy russet and gold brocade suit could not hide his broad shoulders, muscular chest and brawny arms. In gallant fashion the coordinating cloak hung over his right shoulder, exposing his baldric and sword. Even with child, Adele appeared angelic in her peach gown with the trimmings and toiletries of high nobility.

Sabrina gripped Philipe's arm as they made their way inside the grand ballroom. Large marble columns stretched up to the balcony. Magnificent paintings decorated the ceiling. A floor of Italian marble, painstakingly cut and inlaid, brilliantly shone underfoot. Massive portraits of kings and queens hung along the wall between gold gilded mirrors. Enormous crystal chandeliers with hundreds of candles illuminated the room. Two mammoth staircases rose to the balcony and second floor.

As they waited in line to be announced, she noticed the room crammed with people, all elaborately dressed and decorated. Women wore ornate dresses trimmed with lace, jewels or other extravagance. Some were more highly cosmetic than others, with pale faces of powder and false beauty marks and smelling of an exotic fragrance or wild flower. The men caught Sabrina's attention. Many of them were more embellished than the women being arrayed in the finest suits and using the most expensive toiletries available. Long, black, curly wigs were popular since King Louis XIII wore one as he turned prematurely bald.

Tables of food and drink lined both sides of the room. The fabulous display and tempting aromas tantalizing the taste buds. Ingeniously designed fountains flowed forth with limitless wine.

"Are the King and Queen here?" she asked Philipe.

"Not yet. They arrive later and make a grand entrance."

Comte de Trèvoux and party were announced and several pairs of eyes surveyed the arrival.

"Now we begin." Dominic took Sabrina's arm to steer her toward an interested group, which included Gaston, brother to the King. "Monsieur." Dominic made a nodding bow.

"Monsieur le Comte. Comtesse," said Gaston in regal greeting.

Adele curtsied and Philipe bowed. Sabrina tightly held Dominic's arm as she mimicked her companions in paying respect to the Prince Royale.

"Who is this charming young lady?" asked Gaston.

Dominic smiled and would make good the opportunity. "Monsieur, I have this night the honor to present my cousin, Sabrina Charbonier. His Royal Highness, Prince Gaston, Duc d'Orleans."

The Prince was two years older than Sabrina and quite handsome with his black hair and dark eyes dashing against his smooth, fair-skinned face. The long, lean, noble Bourbon nose and stout chin were clearly visible. His regal apparel shone forth in a suit of crimson, gold and black. The sleeves of the crimson doublet were in a slashed pattern, revealing the lily-white silk shirt beneath. Diamonds were used for buttons. Black velvet ribbons tied the stiff, laced collar and held up the gold stockings. The black shoes were thick high-heeled with crimson and gold bows. He wore no cloak or sword, though retained the hat tailored to his costume.

In gallant fashion, Gaston kissed her hand. "A pleasure, mademoiselle." His eyes surveyed Sabrina, drinking in every detail of her appearance. "I don't recall Jourdain mentioning a niece," he said aside to Dominic, but his eyes remained on Sabrina.

"My father did not wish to make mention of her until Sabrina's formal introduction."

Gaston widely smiled. "I can see why the marquis chose to keep such a lovely secret for as long as possible."

Sabrina blushed, a nervous smile on her lips.

"Is the marquis in Paris?"

"Unfortunately, my father was detained in Reims. Not wanting Sabrina's debut to be delayed, he sent her on with instructions for me to take charge of her introduction."

"Monsieur!" a voice called from behind to Gaston chagrin.

"Duty calls, I fear. I hope to have the honor of a dance, mademoiselle."

"I'd be delighted, Monsieur." Sabrina modest blush deepened under the royal glance.

"Until then." Gaston withdrew.

"Excellent. To meet the Prince the first moment we arrive," said Dominic.

"True, but his actions confirm the rumor," said Adele in discretion.

"Fortunate for us, a pity for the King. She kept him out of trouble."

"Now he seeks another," said Philipe.

"Who?" asked Sabrina.

"The Prince's wife recently died in childbirth," replied Philipe.

Further conversation was halted by a fanfare of trumpets. The King and Queen arrived amidst a flurry of pomp and circumstance. Sabrina watched the arrival with awe and anxiety. At age twenty-six, Louis XIII looked plain and sickly. The lean, long and straight nose appeared oversized for his face.

His countenance appeared washed out in his silver and white suit. Tales of constant ill health gave reason for him remaining on the thin side. In fact, rumors claimed he suffered from various aliments ranging from tuberculosis to an embarrassing speech impediment. But for now, Sabrina watched Louis bedecked in royal splendor.

Her gaze passed to the Queen, Anne of Austria, a beautiful woman with dark red hair and emerald eyes. Her complexion was pale, almost white without any cosmetics. She moved with the bearing of a Queen, regal and proud. Uncle Jourdain told her how the Queen's beauty and charming character found many admirers both near and abroad.

Being close to the entrance and in the path of the royals, Dominic said, "Your Majesties." He and the others bowed and curtsied to the couple.

"Trèvoux! Tell me, is the marquis here?" said Louis with pleasure.

"Alas, Sire, he is once more detained."

Louis scowled. "He keeps himself too long from Court. You tell him that for me the next time you correspond with him."

"Yes, Sire. However, he sent an ambassadress, my cousin Sabrina Charbonier. She arrived from Reims the other day with the expressed purpose to make herself known to Your Majesty and extend his deepest regrets at missing another Spring Festival."

Sabrina curtsied when royal eyes fell upon her. She felt her knees weaken, but maintained her balance and found enough of her voice to speak. "Sire, I bear warm greetings from the Marquis de Charbonier. My uncle often speaks with great remorse at being so long detained. Until now, I never fully understood his glorious description of Court. Being here, the wonder is even beyond his words."

"Well said, mademoiselle." Louis smiled.

The Queen surveyed Sabrina. "Welcome, Mademoiselle Charbonier. In your uncle's absence, I hope you shall attend us while in Paris."

"I would be honored, Your Majesty."

All bowed when the King and Queen moved on.

Sabrina trembled, her face now pale. "My mouth and throat are so dry I need something to drink and a place to sit."

The men obliged, leading the women to a bench beside a terrace door. As Adele and Sabrina sat, the foursome overheard three gentlemen standing nearby conversing about recent events.

"I learned this morning the Duc de Rohan is back in Paris. I suspect the Huguenots will be secretly assembling," said one man with a sneer.

"They already have. The Huguenot Sword once again made a fool of de Lacy, sending him on a wild goose chase all over Paris," said another.

"And may they be blessed for doing so," said a third man.

"You speak of heretics!"

"Who cares if they trouble de Lacy? None of us want him at our door."

"Here's Trèvoux. He can tell us about de Lacy," said the second and indicated Dominic.

"Gentlemen, I keep my comments private where the captain is concerned," said Dominic.

"Very wise, but who would you rather tangle with, de Lacy or the Huguenot Sword?"

"Neither. And I dare say, you wouldn't want to see the Huguenot Sword at your door any more than de Lacy."

"No. I'd rather deal with the rebels at La Rochelle. We may face civil war if Father Joseph has his way."

"You mean if he convinces Richelieu," stressed the third.

"Since when does the mentor have to convince his protégé of anything?"

Sabrina clenched her hands to contain rising distress at the conversation. She was now paler then when she sat.

"A bit warm and stuffy in here. Don't you agree, cousin?" asked Adele.

Sabrina's head snapped around in surprise at the address. "A bit."

Dominic offered Sabrina his hand. "Some fresh air will help. Stay inside with Philipe, my dear. It's too nippy out this evening for you," he said to Adele. "Gentlemen, excuse us."

The men bowed to Dominic and Sabrina.

On the terrace, a refreshing breeze came from the north. The moon and stars shone bright in the cloudless sky.

"You did well," began Dominic. "In truth, with God's grace, the evening is turning out splendidly. My plan was to introduce you to some important people, but I did not dare hope to encounter the King, Queen or Prince."

Sabrina absentmindedly nodded, concern etched on her face.

Dominic leaned closer and lowly spoke. "Forget what you just heard."

"How can I? They speak of my—"

He stopped her protest by drawing her further away from the open doors. He grew stern in warning. "You must. The situation is tenuous enough. Don't make trouble by displaying emotion over a religious conversation. At Court you cannot have such feelings."

"Is this the price of freedom? To deny myself and my heritage?"

"Trust me in this."

She bit her lip and shook her head. "I don't understand. Does this talk have anything to do with what happened between you and Uncle?"

"This is not the time nor the place to be having this discussion."

"Then when?"

"After the outcome of tonight is known," he said brusquer than intended. He flashed an apologetic smile. "I promise I will explain in time, but for now regain your composure and persevere through this evening."

"Who is this Huguenot Sword?"

"I said enough talk!" He took a deep breath to regain his temper when she recoiled. "Enjoy the crisp night air while I fetch wine to steel your nerves." He left.

Sabrina followed his suggestion and moved toward the terrace railing. She tried to will the disturbing conversation from her mind. So much happened, causing her head and heart to swarm with emotion. To honor the memory of her parents and their belief, she endured her uncle's attempts to drive the "demon heresy" from her. However, at the threat of being taken to a convent she had to flee! Yet impulse laid aside reason in coming to Paris. What did she expect Dominic to do? Only now she understood she placed him in a position of defying his father. Alas, if she left now, her uncle would vent his spleen on Dominic and Adele. No, she could not turn back or grow weak in her resolve. They must play their parts and leave the outcome to God.

Occupied in thought, a close sudden sound startled her and she turned. She came face-to-face with a man, a soldier from the look of his black and silver uniform. He wore a steel blue embroidered tunic with the silver Royal Cross surrounded by lilies and tongues of fire.

"Forgive me, mademoiselle. I did not mean to startle you. Simply making my rounds," he spoke in gallant manner, but with an unfamiliar provincial accent.

She studied him. At first she was startled by his appearance then intrigued. She reckoned him to be a year or two older than she and of a good height with a lissome athletic body. He was very handsome with clean-shaven features. The nose was straight with a slight square hook at the end. His hair was as black as the uniform he wore. Yet in all his good looks, his eyes captured her attention; a vivid blue; most striking against his dark coloring and with a fluidity of passion that twinkled when he smiled.

"Mademoiselle?"

She realized she stared and replied in demure voice. "I'm recovered."

His smile livened at her modesty. "I shan't keep you from your gentleman."

"He's my cousin," she spoke impulsively when he turned to leave.

"Your cousin? The Comte de Trèvoux?"

"Yes." She blushed at his look, but returned the gaze.

His smile took on a rakish quality, his eyes making a survey of her. "Monsieur is fortunate to have such a beautiful and charming cousin."

Despite having initiated the conversation, she mistook his expression for impudence. "You are bold to speak to me so, monsieur!"

"You misunderstand. I am well acquainted with the count."

"Are you also in the Cardinal's Guards?"

He laughed, a melodic laugh, one used to mirth and gaiety. "No. I am of His Majesty's Musketeers."

"Lamonreaux, where are you?" an angry voice called from behind.

His smile vanished, replaced by wariness of her. "Forgive me, mademoiselle. I have stayed too long from my duty." When she made no reply, he touched his hat and withdrew.

She didn't speak because the name stunned her mute. She leaned against the terrace rail in perplexity, watching him disappear into the shadows. Is this the same Lamonreaux her uncle cursed? The one whose action would send her to a convent? So handsome and gallant, not at all like she imagined him under the circumstance.

She jumped in fright when a cup was placed in front of her and she heard, "Your wine." Dominic returned, accompanied by Philipe. Her eyes darted in the direction Lamonreaux left, then to Dominic.

Neither noticed her distraction. In fact, Philipe asked, "The dancing is to begin. May have the honor of the first dance?"

"Yes, that would be nice," she replied, though preoccupied and this time, it was noticed.

"Sabrina?" inquired Philipe. He tossed a questioning look to Dominic, but the latter shrugged ignorance.

She flushed. "Of course. Only I'm not well practiced."

"I shall be patient." Philipe smiled, offering his arm. Dominic followed them back inside.

Marguerite de Bethune, the Duchess de Rohan, moved from the other side of the terrace intent on intercepting Arsène after he took his leave of Sabrina. Even in her early forties, she retained her good looks, however skewed by her caustic smile.

"Preparing to make another conquest, Lamonreaux?" she asked, her acidic tone enhanced by the matching smile.

He mirrored her tone and expression. "No, madame, tending to my duties of protecting His Majesty's guests."

She made a short mocking laugh. "You would have me believe the offer of protection genuine after usurping a father's affection so much as to keep him from his natural child?"

Arsène bristled and stepped closer to speak. "I do not prevent such a union. Look to yourself, madame. We both know the real person keeping them apart. But for his sake, I will treat you better than you do him."

She flushed in anger. "Insolent braggart! I can have you whipped and discharged for speaking to me thus."

"And admit to even speaking to a Gascon solider? The usurper of your pretended family tranquility? I'm certain Monsieur du Morte, your *escort du jour* will disagree." She stood mute with fury so he touched his hat in salute and flashed a triumphant grin. "Madame. Enjoy this evening, safe and secure, compliments of His Majesty's Musketeers."

She turned on her heels to go inside and he went his way.

Sabrina and Philipe took their position on the dance floor when Gaston approached.

"If I may beg your indulgence in yielding the young lady, Lieutenant."

"Of course, Monsieur." Philipe gave a formal nod and passed Sabrina's hand to the Prince before bowing and departing the dance floor. He joined Dominic and Adele.

"Usurped, I see," said Dominic.

"I could hardly refuse."

"A pretty young woman. Who is she?" A fat nobleman appeared beside them. The Comte de Borchard was near forty years of age. If it was not for the extra weight that made his face wide and rounded, he might have been an appealing man. His hair ash blond, the eyes light blue and a healthy rosy complexion. The double chin was made larger by the stiffness of the laced collar. No cloak could conceal his girth, so he wore none.

"My cousin Sabrina, Monsieur le Comte."

Borchard's gaze changed from Dominic to Sabrina dancing with the Prince. "I say she is about twenty-one or twenty-two years of age."

"Nineteen," said Dominic. He cast Philipe a side-glance of annoyance.

"Mature for her age."

"She's new to Paris, monsieur," Dominic continued in a guarded tone.

"Perhaps some refreshment?" said Philipe.

"A wonderful idea," said Adele, taking Dominic's arm. "Excuse us, monsieur."

"Of course," said Borchard with a nod but not looking at them.

"I detest that fellow," said Dominic between clenched teeth.

29

"You're not the only one." Philipe glared at Borchard, who still watched the dance. "We must keep him away from Sabrina."

"That will be rather difficult," said Adele. They reached the refreshment table.

"I don't want Sabrina becoming involved with us," said Dominic.

Philipe shrugged, accepting a glass of wine from a servant. "Another difficulty considering the circumstances."

"She can't return to Reims," began Adele. "Sooner or later she must be brought in our confidence. She knows us all too well and may soon suspect something."

"She questioned me about the incident with father. I confess I am curious as to what he told her, but dare not ask." Dominic took a long drink.

Philipe shook his head. "Then she should be told. A wondering and idle mind could prove worse than one confided in."

"She has never betrayed my confidence. You know that, Philipe."

"We are no longer children playing children's games."

When the dance ended and Gaston took his leave, Dominic waved Sabrina over to where he stood with the twins. He saw her glance at the terrace before joining them.

"Dominic—" she began but the sound of trumpets caught everyone's attention.

"His Most High Eminence, Cardinal Richelieu!" the herald announced.

Sabrina's gaze became transfixed on the powerful priest. Armand-Jean du Plessis of the House of Richelieu was a man plagued by illness. At forty-two years old his hair turned gray and balding. The eyes were sunken and dark from ill health, but not dulled in sharp intellectual gleam. His glance was thoughtful and interrogating at the same time, and the hollowed cheeks made more dramatic by the shape of his Van Dyke-type mustache and goatee. Like the majestic bird of prey, the Cardinal's hawk-like nose was long, lean and noble. In his withered hands and thin fingers, the devastating effects of sickness were seen.

The sight of the Cardinal proved awesome enough, but the man accompanying him caused alarm. Sabrina seized Dominic's arm, her face instantly pale in horror. Walking beside the great Cardinal was the Marquis de Charbonier.

Jourdain did not age well. Circles formed under the light brown eyes, but still held a virile and keen look. His nut-brown hair thinned with age so, as was fashionable, he wore a wig of long curly brown locks. He was an unusually large man both in height and frame, six feet tall and two hundred pounds, still two inches shorter and twenty pounds lighter the Dominic. His rounded nose and thick lips were well proportioned and did not appear awkward. He sported the fashionable thin mustache but not the goatee many noblemen fancied. Despite the festive dress, his face showed his foul mood.

Dominic held Sabrina's arm in support when Jourdain caught sight of them and separated from the Cardinal. "Stay calm," he said to her.

Adele clenched her hands in an attempt to hide her anxiety and Philipe braced himself.

"This is a bold surprise." The sharp edge in Jourdain's voice tempered due to the environment.

"No more so than seeing you this evening, sir," said Dominic.

Jourdain's disapproving eyes passed to Sabrina. She shrank back a step, but held onto Dominic. "My compliments on your resourceful escapade, young lady. However, this evening you will leave with me for the intended journey."

"I think not," said Dominic.

"I beg your pardon?"

"After relaying to Their Majesties a most excellent greeting from you, Sabrina received a Royal invitation to attend Court."

The marquis became rigid, his face flushed with anger.

"Jourdain?"

Richelieu approached and all bowed to the mighty minister. De Lacy accompanied the Cardinal. Richelieu smiled in cordial greeting. "Now I see what distracted you. Monsieur le Comte. Comtesse. Lieutenant Bourdias. Who is this?"

"My niece, Sabrina Charbonier, Eminence," said Jourdain with a voice of great restraint. His eyes darted flames of displeasure at his son.

Richelieu extended his hand upon which he wore the ring office. Sabrina kissed the ring. "Mademoiselle is new to Paris?"

"I arrived only two days ago, Eminence."

"I hope you find your visit with us an enjoyable one, mademoiselle."

"Thank you, Eminence," she replied, her eyes distracted by the dark man.

"Where are my manners? May I present Captain de Lacy of my Guards. Mademoiselle Charbonier."

De Lacy bowed. "Paris is delighted to be graced with your fresh young beauty, mademoiselle."

"Thank you, Captain."

"If the marquis would not think me forward, I would be honored if I may be permitted the next dance," said de Lacy.

"My niece is a trifle pale, Captain. The excitement is proving too much. I suggest she retire early," said Jourdain with enforced politeness.

"Not at all, Uncle. I would be delighted to dance with the captain."

De Lacy beamed when Jourdain forced a smile. "Then I give my consent."

Sabrina accepted the captain's arm. She may have felt uncertain about dancing with de Lacy, but was certain of what she avoided by doing so.

"By the heavens, Jourdain!" said Louis, moving briskly to greet the marquis. "Your charming niece said you would not be here."

"A sudden change in plans my niece was unaware of, Sire. One that afforded me a long awaited opportunity to return to Your Majesty."

"Splendid. And the marquise?"

"In Paris, but incommode this evening."

"Excellent. We shall hunt and game as before. Not to mention become familiar with your niece. You never spoke of her," said Louis, taking Jourdain's arm. "I see why." He pointed to Sabrina and de Lacy on the dance floor. "Such an innocent young beauty could incite jealousy among Paris' eligible bachelors. We can take care of that. Cardinal." He chatted on about various people and marriage while drawing Jourdain and Richelieu away from them.

When they bowed to the departing King and Cardinal, Philipe saw Arsène appear at the terrace door, careful in his observance. Philipe slipped away and exited to the terrace by way of another door.

Outside, Arsène scowled at seeing Sabrina dancing with de Lacy. He tried to withdraw unnoticed when— "Arsène?"

He darted into the shadows until he identified the caller. Annoyed, he drew Philipe into his concealment. "I don't need to be found here. I'm supposed to be on guard duty."

"I know that, but do you remember is the question?"

"I was curious about Dominic's cousin. She's a pretty young woman."

"Of all the times for you to pop up unexpected. Don't cause trouble tonight. The marquis is here."

"He is? I haven't seen him."

"He just arrived with Richelieu."

"Don't fret. I won't cause trouble. I just wanted to see her and assess the situation." His smile grew as he peeked inside. "To my surprise, she's too attractive to have her angry with me on our first meeting."

Philipe glared at Arsène, who watched Sabrina dance with de Lacy. "Mind yourself, and remember why she fled to Paris. She is also unaware of our situation."

Arsène leaned against the building, smiling at Philipe. "My friend, you sound jealous. I simply stated she's pretty, and I wouldn't want anger to furrow such a lovely brow."

Philipe's scowl made Arsène laugh aloud. Philipe covered Arsène's mouth and only when Arsène ceased laughing did he let go.

"You are jealous."

"I am not! I confess Sabrina is as dear to me as Adele. She needs time to adjust to Paris. If she remains."

"Oh, but she must. This is amusing."

"Sometimes, Gascon, you try my patience!"

Such an angry reference to Arsène's county of origin normally offended him, but from Philipe, he tolerated much, especially in his present good humor. With a hearty pat, he placed an arm about Philipe's shoulder. "I would never interfere with a liaison, my friend."

"This is not a liaison."

Arsène looked back inside. The dance ended. "If it were me, it would be a nice liaison."

Philipe shoved Arsène's arm off his shoulder. "Get back to duty, Sergeant. And, for heaven's sake, stay out of sight! It could undo everything if the marquis discovers you."

"Yes, Lieutenant." Arsène saluted and smiled before leaving.

Philipe went back inside.

The King kept Jourdain occupied the remainder of the evening and this pleased Dominic. Near one o'clock in the morning, they left the palace. Utterly exhausted, Adele rested against Dominic for the ride home. Sabrina gnawed on her lower lip, gazing out the carriage window. Dominic noticed her preoccupation.

"Sabrina, is something troubling you? The evening went well and Father thwarted."

"It's not Uncle Jourdain," she replied with distraction.

Dominic noticed Philipe's signaling smirk. "Oh, please tell me he didn't."

"He did."

Sabrina sat up. "Then I heard his name right. He is the Gascon, Lamonreaux."

Dominic averted his gaze, suggesting an unwillingness to answer.

Philipe spoke. "Yes, the man you saw this evening is Arsène Lamonreaux."

Sabrina frowned at the affirmation. "The way Uncle spoke of him I imagined him an ogre. Does he have anything to do with this Huguenot Sword?"

Despite his initial reticence, Dominic rebuffed, "I said forget what you heard!"

She didn't take his rebuke well. "Am I also to forget the way Uncle looked at you? It is the same angry, hateful expression that overcomes him when my father is mentioned. That frightens me."

"When people are angry they often distort the truth to suit themselves."

"I want to know the undistorted truth. Unfortunately, I don't even know if I can get it from you. You're as bitter and angry as he."

Wounded, Dominic turned away. His brooding profile showed his warring attempt to maintain his temper.

Adele shook her head at Sabrina and Philipe gripped her arm, both acts of warning. Subdued, Sabrina reclined with a thwarted grunt.

The following morning, an anxious chamberlain roused Dominic from sleep. "The marquis is here! He waits in the private drawing room."

"What about Sabrina?"

"He made no mention of her. Please hurry, monsieur, he is quite vexed!"

Dominic tossed aside the covers and donned a dressing gown and slippers before heading to the private drawing room. From the moment his father arrived at the festival, he knew confrontation was not far off. The true test of how well his hurried plan worked would now be learned.

He paused in the drawing room threshold to watch his father pace, the tapping of the riding crop against his leg in time with his agitated movement. His father was dressed for travel, the cloak floating behind him as he moved. When Dominic entered and spoke, Jourdain halted.

"You wish to see me, sir?"

"You defied me once before, and I gave you fair warning of doing so again!"

"Sabrina came to me for protection. I will not turn her away."

"Protection indeed! You should have thought of that before committing such a disgraceful act."

Dominic's anger propelled him to accost his father. "You wish to vent your spleen, then do so against me and not Sabrina."

"Years ago such venting nearly destroyed this family. I vowed to my dying father it would not happen again. God be thanked, he is not alive to see the shame his grandson now brings up this house!"

"Who brings shame? The one whose heart is pricked by injustice or the one who seeks to extinguish an innocent life for pride's sake?"

Jourdain slapped Dominic. The violence prompted a female outcry. Sabrina stood near the door, pale with fright and trembling hands covering her mouth.

"The vixen dares to emerge." Jourdain moved towards her but Dominic intercepted him.

"You won't take her from this house!"

"You would dare to defy me and bring not only yourself, but your wife into ruin?"

The threat to Adele made Dominic wince, but he could not back down. "Not I. Or did you forget how the King expressed interest in Sabrina? Take her now, and it is you who causes questions to be raised."

Jourdain stared at Dominic with sudden understanding. "You planned this."

"I had no choice!" declared Dominic, a quiver of regret creeping into his voice. "I know how vicious your temper can be. You won't believe me, but I never meant for my decision to disgrace our family. Soothe, if you look beyond your hatred you would see by our behavior no one knows or suspects. We have been nothing but models of courtesy and respect to the King and Cardinal. Our beliefs are private matters of the heart, not open rebellion," he argued. Alas, by Jourdain's hardened expression his words fell upon deaf ears and a hard heart.

Jourdain jerked away from Dominic and lashed out at Sabrina. "Flesh and blood by hanged! I curse the day I brought you into my home."

In terror, she backed into the hall to let him pass on his march from the house. "He'll destroy you," she cried when Dominic came alongside her.

"No. To do so would destroy the Charboniers."

"He said so!" she clamored, beside herself with despair.

He snatched her arms and tried to calm her. "He spoke in anger. Reality will temper his harsh words."

"No! You made an enemy of your father, and it is my fault! I should never should have come to you," she bitterly cried and tried to break free, but he held fast.

"Father's hatred stems from the past, not you or me. He and Grandfather disowned Uncle Michael for embracing the Protestant faith. The discovery of my conversion reopened old wounds."

In vehement disagreement, she shook her head. "I thought we managed to stem his hatred. That he may have some feeling for me other than disdain."

His featured showed his reluctance to pursue the matter. "Sabrina—"

"No more excuses! Tell me what happened to renew his hatred." Despite her tears, her expression told of determination.

He paused to consider. "Under the circumstances, it may be best."

Adele arrived, flushed and fearful. "I thought I hear a row."

"Father confronted me about Sabrina."

Adele paled and sat in a nearby chair to compose herself. Sabrina went to aid Adele and cast a prompting irate glance at her cousin. "Dominic was about to tell me what happened to make Uncle so angry."

Dominic tried to keep his voice level. "As I said when you arrived, not all things are within my control. The situation was unexpected and unfortunate. We met many times before in secret. Needless to say, we were surprised when Father burst in upon us."

"Does he know this Arsène Lamonreaux?"

He nodded. "He learned of him because of his position as Philipe's platoon sergeant. Which is also how I met Arsène, through Philipe. Being a low country-born Gascon incited Father, who made it known to Baron Bourdias he disapproved of Philipe's association. The thought of me, *his* son, associating with such an individual is an abomination. Apparently, after witnessing us together, Arsène's background warranted further inquiry. Father discovered he is sponsored by the Duc de Rohan."

"Rohan?" she said in consideration. "The name sounds familiar."

Adele's concern made Dominic give her a short shake of his head.

"Never mind him." His speech drew Sabrina's attention from her pondering. "It is common in Paris for a soldier to have a wealthy or noble benefactor, regardless of politics or religion. Still, Father took umbrage. His unexpected arrival at a late dinner surprised us. He confronted Arsène with bitter and spiteful speech, accusing him of all manner of evil. When Arsène protested, Father struck him. That's when Arsène lashed out about Father's treatment of his brother and warned about doing the same with his son."

Sabrina listened, with concentration but took in a sharp breath when Dominic spoke of her father. "What did Uncle do then?"

"He went for his sword, but I stepped between them and Philipe urged Arsène to leave. He did so, and with tremendous regret. Father assumed the worst about my conversion, which I neither denied nor admitted, rather tried to reason with him but he wouldn't listen."

Sabrina tugged at her fingers; fret on her face and in her voice. "Aunt Madeline and I were in the salon when he returned. I saw the old animosity and realized something dreadful happened. He jerked me out of my seat and drug me to my chamber, spouting horrible accusations against Huguenots." She then spoke with certainty, "He will seek to destroy you."

Adele covered her mouth to stifle a gasp.

Dominic moved to comfort his wife but spoke to Sabrina. "He won't. He hasn't destroyed you because of Uncle Michael."

She shook her head in rebuke. "We were children when my father died trying to reconcile. He could not hold me accountable then. But now we are adults, and he *does* hold me responsible for your change of heart! He told me when he locked me away before making arrangements for the convent."

He chewed on his lower lip with consideration before asking, "What do you remember of Uncle Michael's visit?"

"What does that have to do with this?"

"Everything!"

Her brows knitted in recollection. "After we arrived in Reims, my older brother, Jacques pressed Father for answers. He told us some very important business brought him to Reims. Little did we realize it was like Jacob returning to Esau. Although he never displayed fear, he was unusually tense and short-tempered, not like himself at all."

"Did he ever answer Jacques' questions?"

"No, my entrance at hearing raised voices gave him the excuse he needed to leave. Jacques told me afterwards what I interrupted." She paused with a lamenting sigh. "Speaking of my family makes me miss them. Jacques would be your age by now, though not as large."

"I believe my father made a mistake in not reconciling."

"Although a devout man, my father acted reckless at times. On one occasion, I overheard him speaking to a gentleman named Maurice and bemoaning several errors in judgment. He spoke of Henri and William in dealing with those errors." Her voice grew shaky at the end.

Adele's sympathetic glance turned from Sabrina to Dominic and asked, "Must we pursue the matter?"

"No." He touched Sabrina's shoulder to get her attention. "Since Father knows you are here we must be careful. You cannot be left home alone."

"I will obtain permission for her to attend the Queen," said Adele.

Dominic nodded his agreement, eyes direct on Sabrina. "You must be more resolute and guarded in your behavior at court."

"I will."

✤ Chapter 3 ✤

THE FOLLOWING MORNING AT AROUND NINE-THIRTY, Sabrina and Adele sat in the morning room partaking of breakfast. Adele was wide-awake and eating as a woman in her condition normally did. Sabrina barely touched the food on her plate. She appeared fatigued, her hair loose and a bit unkempt from sleeping.

Philipe joined them, only dressed in his formal uniform complete with silver gorget and gray gloves. His hat and gloves were tossed in a nearby chair as he sat to eat.

Dominic arrived, also bright-eyed and awake like Adele and Philipe. He was dressed casual, his doublet opened and shirt not completely laced closed. He kissed Adele on the cheek and spoke a good morning to Sabrina, who nodded an acknowledgment as she yawned.

Dominic chuckled and reached to help himself to the food. "How long did you sleep, cousin?"

"Not long enough it appears," said Philipe, a chuckle and wink at Sabrina. She smirked and tried to eat.

"What about you? I thought you were going to stay for a visit," Dominic asked Philipe before proceeding to eat.

Philipe took a drink to swallow what he was chewing to answer. "Apparently du Pree didn't appreciate the fact I attended the festival; a low ranking noble lieutenant hobnobbing with royalty. I'm to report to duty at Saint Germain for some event the King is hosting this afternoon."

While Philipe spoke, Gérard entered and handed a note to Dominic. He frowned at reading the note. "It seems we'll be doing the same in returning to Saint Germain."

"Oh?" asked Adele.

Dominic addressed Sabrina and indicated the note. "Father orders us to attend this event; an afternoon of lawn tennis followed by dinner."

"Go back to Court? After last night?" asked Sabrina, with the most emotion she displayed all morning, trepidation.

"Your presence is requested by the Queen. Father can hardly refuse and we can't refuse him." Dominic passed her the note and went back to eating.

Sabrina read, her head shaking, both dismay and uncertain on her face. "I don't think I can."

"You must. Besides, such a request and your continued involvement at Court will help to assure your independence. Father dare not interfere and risk provoking Royal displeasure."

"It probably galled him to write that note," said Philipe.

"You'll be there," she said.

"On duty, but supporting you in spirit." He squeezed her hand.

"You'll be there in person and not on duty," said Dominic.

"Du Pree won't like that."

"Tell him to speak to the count." Dominic took the note and held it up.

Philipe grinned. "It does help to have well connected in-laws. Gérard. Send for Roger to bring my blue suit. It won't do to return in the same clothes from last night, or my uniform."

The valet bowed and left.

"Will *he* be there again?" asked Sabrina, trying to be discreet in questioning Philipe.

"By *he,* I take it you mean Arsène."

She nodded, covering her flush by taking a drink.

"More than likely." He took hold of her hand. "Don't fret. Arsène is always diligent when on duty."

"Indeed, he is. We are instructed to arrive by noon," said Dominic.

"Noon?" Sabrina looked across to Adele. "Can you be ready so quickly?"

Adele chuckled. "I'm well practiced at being ready on a moment's notice. You, on the other hand, are on a steep learning curve. Come." She rose and extended her hand to take Sabrina's arm.

41

"But I haven't eaten."

"Food will be sent up."

At the palace, they joined the marquis and marquise near the main entrance. Jourdain wore a fixed expression, so no words were necessary, even those of greeting. Dominic did greet his mother, Madeline, with a kiss on the cheek. She was a woman of great beauty for her age of forty-five and well proportioned for being so tall and slender, but fragile in health. Her eyes were large dark chestnuts that looked out onto the world from a face of pale complexion. The noble cheeks and lips were only beginning to show signs of relaxing with age. Her nose was too small, but graceful and straight. Curls of graying honey colored hair were meticulously arranged in the latest fashion.

The palace steward escorted them to the back lawn where the royals and guests gathered.

The Prince de Condé, Comte de Turenne, Monsieur de Fontaine and Gaston were already present. The wives of the first two were with the Queen who, like the King, sat in a pavilion built for shade. Charlotte Talbert, another lady-in-waiting, attended Her Majesty. Monsieur Fontaine was Mademoiselle Talbert's lover and the wealthy Keeper of the Royal Mews and Falcons.

Turenne and Gaston were playing lawn tennis, much to the amusement of the noble onlookers. Both were stripped of their doublets with sleeves rolled up. The Comte de Turenne was Gaston's contemporary and a fair man with wavy flaxen hair and light brown eyes. The immaturity of youth was still evident in his smile and the lean shape of his head.

Turenne wore a kerchief about his forehead. Lawn tennis was a combination of badminton and tennis. The net was short and each player held a long thin racket. The French used their version of the English shuttlecock. A white cord marked off the playing area. On the far side of the net, stood a high-ranking household servant, serving as judge for the match.

Turenne missed a return by Gaston, making the score thirty to love, Gaston getting the better of his contemporary.

The King did not notice the Charboniers' arrival as he was doing some good-natured bantering with Monsieur Fontaine over the betting. Today Louis looked in better health, or perhaps it was the colorful suit of lavender and mulberry. His skin reflected the hue of the cloth and helped his pale complexion. No one could out shine the King or Queen in rich apparel or decorations, thus Louis was bedecked from head-to-toe with jewels and silver.

Condé was the closest and greeted the new arrivals with a simple nod, to avoid interrupting the game. Henri de Bourbon, the Prince de Condé was a plain man of thirty-nine years His naturally dark brown long locks were curled and pampered. He wore the usual mustache and pointed goatee. The classic Bourbon nose was not as prominent as on his cousin, the King and he was fit and vigorous in health compared to Louis. Like most of those at Court, he flaunted his wealth by wearing it. Diamonds and amethysts were embroidered upon the rich amber velvet doublet using real gold thread. A wide purple sash encompassed his waist, while the bejeweled matching baldric hung over his right shoulder. About his neck he wore his symbol of office, a large gold and purple chevron of the highest financial advisor.

Upon hearing the judge call set and match to Gaston, there was a mixture of reactions. Fontaine lost one hundred gold pieces to the King for betting on Turenne, who only twice before defeated Gaston. Not a sound bet to make.

Taking an elaborate bow to his audience, Gaston shook Turenne's hand in a friendly competitive manner. But the exchange with his opponent was short-lived as he spied the new arrivals.

"Mademoiselle Charbonier!" he called to Sabrina as she politely applauded with the others. She curtsied to his approach, but he took her hand and kissed the knuckles. "Forgive my gamely appearance. Did you enjoy the match?""

"Unfortunately, we arrived too late to see most of it."

"The day is not over. There will be more games in which I may display my athletic prowess. Perhaps your cousin will consent to a match?"

"Monsieur, your reputation as an excellent tennis player is widespread," said Dominic.

"You would decline a challenge before your cousin?"

Dominic smiled. "I did not refuse, Monsieur. I merely referred to your reputation."

"After we have dined," said Gaston, giving his racket to the lackey, who stood ready with a basin of water and towel.

"My dear marquis!" Louis jingled some money in his fist. "The bounty from betting on my brother."

"Glad to be of service, Sire," said Gaston with a slight edge to his voice. He stepped back to freshening up.

Louis spoke. "It is good to have you back, Jourdain."

"Not being in your magnificent presence has been a sorrow to me, Sire. Alas, great sacrifices must be made if a person is to continue in his livelihood."

Louis chuckled. "Marquise. You are looking well."

"Thank you, Sire."

Louis took Jourdain's arm. "Come. The noon feast awaits us yonder." He pointed to a pavilion of sumptuously filled tables.

While Louis engaged the marquis and marquise, Dominic reintroduced Sabrina to the remaining nobles, mostly the wives of the men present. Turenne's wife, Éleonore was a comely woman for being a foreigner, specifically from Germany and displaying all the common features with blond hair and plump frame, yet reserved in nature.

The atmosphere about the noon feast was casual, so Sabrina managed to carry on general conversations with natural grace and charm. Gaston made particular effort to pay her compliments. A few times Jourdain commented on Sabrina, but in all focused his attention on the other guests. That's not to say he ignored his niece, quite the contrary. His seeming distraction was actually means by which to observe her interaction.

Philipe made good on his offer of lending support to Sabrina, but often found himself usurped by Gaston. Since Gaston and Dominic were to compete immediately after luncheon and both left to make ready, Philipe escorted Sabrina and Adele back to the tennis area. Sabrina chanced to see

Arsène and several other soldiers standing guard about the grounds. Discreetly he acknowledged her with a smile and nod. She flushed and turned away, but dared a second glance. Feeling someone take her arm she turn to Philipe.

"Why would he take such a risk?" she asked, though not good at hiding her feelings of flushed anxiety.

"Guarding royal guests is his duty. Remember I was to report to do the same. He has been watching since we arrived."

"Really?" When she started to glance back, he stopped her.

"Nobles at Court ignore soldiers with an arrogant indifference."

"Indeed, and you must do the same," said Adele. "Still, I will inform Dominic."

"He knows," said Philipe.

Despite his confidence, Adele moved to join Dominic. He stood to one side of the pavilion preparing for the game. To the casual observer she seemed to wish him luck, a warm smile on her face. He paused after stripping off his doublet, to listen, but recovered and rolled up the sleeves of his shirt. He smiled and winked at her before taking the racket held by a lackey. She proceeded to her seat in the pavilion. The Queen invited Sabrina to sit next to her during the match. Adele sat on the other side of Sabrina.

"If you'll permit me, Sire," began Gaston approaching Sabrina. She shyly smiled when he took her hand. "I wish to salute our newest arrival to Court and present her with the fruits of my victory."

Dominic chuckled at the boastful statement.

"Providing the fruit is not too heavy on the Royal purse," said Louis lightly.

"An invitation to the ballet next month, Sire."

Jourdain fought to contain his ire, yet made no vocal objection as the King replied. "Done. Unless, mademoiselle objects?"

"Oh, no, Sire! I am overwhelmed by such an offer."

Louis smiled and nodded. "Proceed with the game, gentlemen."

As the players took their places, polite wagering began. Louis graciously gave odds of 3 to 1 in favor of Gaston. The odds for Turenne were only 2 to 1.

For civility's sake the marquis wagered on Dominic. To Louis' pleasure, Fontaine bet another hundred gold pieces on Dominic. Condé and Louis favored Gaston of course. Turenne declined partaking in the wagering after being so soundly beaten by the Prince.

Gaston allowed Dominic to serve first. With a shuttlecock the service is underhand. Since the cock could not go as far as a ball nor allowed to bounce, the court was shortened. They exchanged several volleys before Dominic scored the first point.

As the heat of the afternoon increased, three lackeys with large ostrich feathered fans provided a breeze for those in the pavilion. Wine and pastries were served the observers and soon conversation began.

Condé spoke to Louis. "Your Majesty, I know this is to be an enjoyable day, however, I learned this morning the Duc de Rohan is back in Paris. I suspect the Huguenots will be secretly assembling very soon." He watched the match as he spoke. Dominic lost his serve to Gaston.

"There has been news from La Rochelle. The rebels are again raising arms," said Turenne.

"It sounds like the Huguenots no longer value the Treaty of Montauban," said Jourdain.

Louis scoffed. "As I said, my dear marquis, you have stayed away from Court too long. The treaty was broken nearly a year ago. The rebels trade openly with pirates and England." Louis scowled when Gaston lost the first game to Dominic. The players switched sides for the next game.

"They also defy Royal orders to surrender Catholic property," said Fontaine.

"Could there be another civil war?" asked Madeline with some disquietude when Jourdain glared at Dominic, who just won back the serve.

"There must be if France is to be rid of those Protestant rebels," said the Queen with pride, though ignorant of the private tension.

Whereas the Queen was ignorant, the King observed Jourdain's sudden silence. "Does the game disturb you, Marquis?"

As one thoroughly schooled in the ways of Court, Jourdain softened his expression at his sovereign's question. "Not the game, Sire; the news of the Huguenots. My son and I fought to bring that treaty into existence."

"Important news does have a way of missing the provinces," said Condé with seeming indifference.

Jourdain made a quick piercing side glance to Condé, but rather than comment on the slight, asked, "What steps are being taken to confront the situation?"

"Richelieu is formulating a plan of attack with Father Joseph as his advisor."

To the remark several of the women made a cooing noise of apprehension. To Sabrina, the name meant nothing. It was the reaction that caused her trepidation. Her good humor faded long ago, while the icy look of her uncle to Dominic distressful. As talk of the Huguenots turned into bitter name calling and gloating, her uneasiness grew.

The Princess de Condé sat beside Sabrina and noticed the girl's pale countenance. She laid a gentle hand upon Sabrina's shoulder and whispered. "Do not let all this political talk upset you. Men can think of nothing else more pleasant to discuss. Unless of course, it is a new conquest or victory in a battle."

"Conquest?" asked Sabrina with large innocent doe eyes.

The Princess lightly laughed. "If you stay in Paris any length of time, you will understand what I mean, and get used to it. We all do."

Sabrina was grateful the tennis match ended, for so did talk of the Huguenots.

To their surprise, Dominic beat Gaston. He tried not to defeat the Prince, but his size and strength prevailed even when not trying. The King grumbled, but paid his debts. Fontaine smiled in triumph since Dominic unwittingly avenged his earlier loss. Gaston profusely apologized to Sabrina. She did her best to hide her disquietude when he insisted she attend the ballet next month.

While receiving accolades, Dominic noticed Sabrina's change in mood and demeanor. He caught Philipe's glance, conveying something was amiss. He gave a short nod of understanding and went back to his admirers. Gaston handed him a glass of wine with the compliment of their match being the best he played in a long time.

Turenne did not take the slight well. He did his best playing against Gaston, and here comes Charbonier beating him with little effort. "Gad, the big galoot is barely sweating!" he mumbled into his drink.

In twilight's glow, the Royals and their guests retired to the château for dinner. Adele, Philipe and Sabrina lagged slightly behind. Dominic walked with them, donning his doublet as they moved along.

"Talk of the Huguenots and La Rochelle," said Philipe in a low voice.

"No, it was the way Uncle leered at you during the match, with his same hateful glare. When he looked at me, I shuddered!"

Dominic took hold of her arm as they crossed the bridge over the dry moat. "Again, you must not react to any news. We still have dinner, and Father is already angry enough. Don't make him more so by any display."

She frowned but acquiesced with a curt nod.

The small dining hall was large enough to seat fifty people. The tile floor gleamed and reflected the beautifully set table. A lace tablecloth adorned the mahogany table upon which sat three large silver candlesticks. Fine china, silverware, glasses and goblets were precisely set for each guest. To one side of the room stood a serving bar from which a dozen royal waiters would bring the food to the honored diners. At the other end of the room, musicians played a soothing violin concerto.

At dinner, a clean and refreshed Gaston presented himself to Sabrina. Condé kept a keen eye on the Prince. Condé was not the only one watching Gaston; Dominic did as well. Those associated with the young Prince paid a heavy price as attested to by the banishment of Madame Chevreuse and the death of the young Marquis de Chalais. They tried to help the Prince conspire against Richelieu's wishes for him to marry. It was a shame the poor girl died in childbirth. Gaston was a risky, irresponsible and egotistical friend to have.

Gaston acted uncharacteristically chivalrous after being beaten. But listening to Prince's speech, Dominic realized this act was for Sabrina's benefit, to impress the young and vulnerable woman. He became her constant companion and that made Dominic nervous. Then again, by the admiring glances from Turenne, Gaston was not the only one wanting to be favored with Sabrina's attention. Turenne was supposedly happily married. As crass as it sounded, her innocence had the same effect as teasing hungry lions with an unblemished lamb; so Dominic thought.

After dinner, they adjourned to the golden salon. Attention continued to be paid to Sabrina, who held up surprising well for being unpracticed in the ways of Court. Adele helped on the occasions she became flustered by an off-color comment. The few times Dominic and Philipe attempted to intervene on Sabrina's behalf they were brushed aside by Gaston or Turenne. However, they were gracious when Adele spoke. So Dominic and Philipe deferred to her, but stayed in close proximity.

Philipe and Dominic were fetching more brandy and overheard Fontaine's comment to the marquis.

"Your niece is causing quite a stir, Jourdain. Why didn't you warn us of her fresh, charming innocence?"

Before a piqued Jourdain replied, Condé spoke in an obvious dig at Fountaine. "Perhaps that is why he kept her a secret, to shield her from being overwhelmed by your radiant flamboyance."

Fontaine flushed with outrage, prompting Jourdain to intervene.

"Gentlemen, my niece appreciates all considerations with a grace becoming one of her years."

Condé laughed. "Meaning she is tolerant of fastidious old men making fools of themselves."

Fontaine huffed and marched out of the salon.

"Oh dear. I say something to offend him?" Condé flashed a perverse grin and moved to join another group to converse.

Jourdain downed the remainder of his brandy. His displeasure found his niece only to be intercepted by his son moving into his line of sight. For a moment Dominic and Jourdain stared at each other. Loud laughter and Gaston's address to Jourdain interrupted the tense visual exchange.

"Your niece is charming, Jourdain. With artful words of retort she disarms a Prince."

"In this, I must agree with my brother," said Louis. "I hope you will remain in Paris for quite some time, mademoiselle. It is not often such simple charm is seen here."

"With my uncle's permission, I would like to remain, Your Majesty."

"If the old stiff neck will not allow it, I shall give him a Royal command."

Jourdain forced a grin and replied. "If it brings Your Majesty pleasure, I shall not refuse my niece the privilege of being in your divine presence."

Louis laughed, pressing Jourdain's hand but speaking to Sabrina. "See, he is not so difficult to deal with."

"Thank you, Sire," said Jourdain, again with forced grace. "However, after your gracious hospitality of yesterday and today, I can tell by her countenance, my niece is fatigued. Although she would not deprive you of her company, pray excuse us so she can rest to be so favored by you another day."

Louis feigned a pout then kindly smiled. "Indeed, the child looks a trifle tired. Another day, my dear, and very soon."

"Of course, Sire." Sabrina stood and paid her respects to the King and Queen.

Dominic escorted Adele and Philipe held the marquise's arm as Jourdain had Sabrina by the arm in leaving. No words were spoken in exiting the chateau and crossing the main bridge to wait for the carriages.

Madeline finally broke the silence. "I thought the visit went well." When Jourdain didn't respond she continued. "She captured the Prince's attention without a hint of trouble, that should please you."

Jourdain's glance shifted from his wife to Sabrina. "There is always intrigue where the Prince is concerned."

"But favor also, as told by Louis. Sabrina behaved most adequately."

"Thank you for your encouragement, Aunt."

"How long can you keep up your manners is the question," said Jourdain with a brusque tone and suspicious sneer. Conversation stopped since the marquis' carriage arrived and he ushered Madeline inside.

Dominic leaned close to Sabrina. "Mother's right, you did well."

In turning to reply, Sabrina noticed Arsène carefully make his way among the shadows to watch the departure.

"Is he always so brazen and bold?" she asked in annoyance.

Dominic frowned.

"At least your father didn't see him," said Adele.

"The carriage," said Philipe. He was the last to enter and made a careful gesture for Arsène to depart.

❦ Chapter 4 ❦

THE LOUVRE STOOD IN THE CENTER OF PARIS JUST OFF THE SEINE on the left bank. Each mammoth pavilion was symmetrically shaped with high-pitched roofs cut off at the apex. The buildings were fixed together at right angles in the Baroque style with a series of pavilions centered on a courtyard extending the length of the plaza. The main pavilion housed the Royal Family. Flanking pavilions served as various offices of the government or military.

The Palais des Tuileries stood across from the Louvre. Tuileries' grand arch of ironwork opened to the Louvre and boasted of the largest and most beautiful gardens in Paris. A high block wall enclosed the garden and tall trees obscured the view from buildings across the boulevard. The garden bloomed like a paradise on earth, vibrant with colors and scents to entertain the senses. Water cascaded or sprung up from various fountains, sparkling and dancing in the sunlight. Stone statues in the Florentine style overlooked the recreated Eden.

The gardens were a favorite place for the Queen to stroll on mild sunny afternoons. Three days passed since the tennis match and Adele gained permission for Sabrina to attend. They walked a respectful distance behind the Queen.

In this lovely and inspirational setting Sabrina noticed the Queen's somber mood. "What ails Madame?" she asked Adele.

Adele tried to keep a scowl from her face. "She is ill."

"Should not the Royal Physician be sent for?"

Adele laughed with cynicism. "Not a physical illness, but of the heart and mind. One, which causes great fear and anxiety and no medicine can cure. Despite our difference, I have her confidence on occasion."

"What does the Queen have to fear?"

"Things too numerous and dangerous to mention."

Sabrina turned her attention ahead toward the Queen, but instead, noticed three gentlemen and an older lady watching from the terrace. "Who are they? I don't recall seeing them before."

Adele fought to keep the annoyance from her face both in looking to the people and in replying. "The fat one is the Comte de Borchard. His companions are the Marquis d'Avallon, and the Comte de Reynard. Rumor says Borchard gained his title by shrewd accounting and cunning devices shortly after King Henri's death. None are proven, and he is faithful to the Cause. D'Avallon was once a good friend of the Comte de Turenne. On occasion I have seen them together. Alas, you met the catholic Princess he married against his family's wishes. His actions placed a great barrier between he and d'Avallon."

"And the lady?"

"Duchess de Rohan."

"Rohan. Each time I hear the name I'm certain I know it beyond what scorn is attached to it—and certain beliefs." She tried to be discrete, though her voice betrayed irritation.

"She is another person to avoid."

"Why? Because she keeps company with those men?"

Adele shook her head, her features turning sympathetic. "More complex than her male companions, though she uses them to constantly humiliate and degrade her husband the duke."

"I don't understand why husbands and wives so viciously disgrace each other in public. Still, I had no idea so many Hu—" she stopped at a hard grip on her arm from Adele.

She steered Sabrina away from the terrace; her voice low and filled with warning. "There are many who occupy high positions, and with those positions comes danger."

"Are you and Dominic in danger?"

"Less than others, more than some; but such is the nature of Court." Adele tried to answer in a matter-of-fact tone. "In this time of unrest only a few known Huguenot nobles dare to attend Court, and only ones who are powerful or well connected. Those on the terrace are among them."

Sabrina dared a glance back to the terrace. "The name Reynard is also familiar."

"The count is a nasty man, arrogant and vain, who has bad taste in women. Madame Fontaine is his mistress and she is a staunch supporter of the Cardinal."

Disturbed, yet disgusted Sabrina said, "I don't understand this unashamed contempt of marriage."

"Having a mistress or lover is commonplace in Paris. Monsieur Fontaine is the lover of Mademoiselle Charlotte Talbert, whom you met at the tennis match. Court is filled with ugly vices and little, if any, virtue."

"Then why do you remain? Oh, what of Philipe?" added Sabrina in a sudden and unpleasant afterthought.

"Philipe is wise. Any liaisons are discreet and not connected to Court."

"You mean he has lovers?" the question slow in asking.

"Not in the plural or permanent sense. There was a woman, a short affair, from which he learned a valuable lesson. There's no joy in sordid liaisons. There's been no one else."

Sabrina bit her lip, discommoded by the answer, but after a brief pause asked, "And the other? His sergeant?"

Adele looked curiously at Sabrina upon her question. "His reputation is more known than Philipe. But in truth, much exaggerated, and he is a good friend, dependable and loyal."

"Sounds nothing like what I was told."

Adele grinned. "No. His birth and reputation malign his good qualities. However, caution is advised. Oh, and three people to avoid in any form of entanglement, are the Comte de Turenne, the Prince de Condé, and Monsieur."

"Prince Gaston? Why? He is most attentive and kind."

"He schemes and plots with anyone to undermine the King and Cardinal. Those within his scope pay a heavy price for their association, no matter how remote the connection. He tried to rebel against his State arranged marriage, but Richelieu quelled that."

"Uncle Jourdain said it was a good marriage."

"It was. This was simply one of his fits. His attention to you is cause for concern. Although the marquis may not see it that way, Dominic and I do. And for reasons you should understand. Thus, I advise you to be courteous but aloof in accepting or returning his overtures."

"Very well. I shall heed your advice. Still, if my marriage is arranged, I pray it does not carry such heavy consequences, rather be as blissful as you and Dominic."

Adele smiled in genuine fondness. "We are blessed with one of those rare marriages. The child shall double our joy."

Sabrina hooked arms with Adele and smiled. " I shall be in Paris to see the child born."

"Oh, my dear Sabrina, it is good to have you near again. Your good humor is contagious and gives me hope."

"Since when were you without hope, my dear Adele?"

"Court dims one's views. Keep your good humor for us all, and we shall be well."

Sabrina smiled one of those winning smiles of an unpretentious soul. "I shall."

"Come, the Queen is far ahead, and I would be within voice if she has need of me."

The rest of the day passed in pleasant company and conversation until Gérard arrived at four o'clock with the carriage. He acknowledged Adele's explanation of remaining at Court for dinner so only Sabrina would be returning home.

In the midst of the hustle and bustle of Market Square sat an elderly scruffy beggar with ragged gray hair, long shaggy beard, and a wart on his nose. From his seat on the curb he begged for alms, yet his eyes shifted about, scanning the crowd. His gaze narrowed when a large cloaked man with a partial mask on his face entered a building across the street. The old man stood, but a nobleman emerged from the shop and collided with him.

"Filthy beggar!"

The old man spoke in a gravel voice. "Pardon, monsieur. Have you alms for a poor old man?"

The noble shoved him aside before continuing on his way, not seeing he caused the old man to stumble into a cart of potatoes.

"Here now! Stop bothering my customers!" The shopkeeper seized the old man, cuffed him and booted him into the street where he fell face first.

The old man felt some warm liquid at the right corner of his mouth. Blood oozed from a cut. He snarled at the shopkeeper. "Why you—" The gravel voice gone and he began to rise when a female shouted.

"Stop!"

The old man and shopkeeper saw Sabrina move from the carriage. The old man stayed down when she knelt beside him.

"Why did you strike him?" she accosted the shopkeeper.

"Why trouble yourself, mademoiselle? He's only a dirty beggar."

"That is no reason to strike him down." She gasped at seeing his face. "You hurt him! Gérard, help me get him to his feet. Or, can you not stand?"

"I can try, sweet lady." He was a bit wobbly.

Sabrina placed a supportive arm about his waist. "I can hold you. Now, sit on the step."

The shopkeeper gave a disapproving grunt and returned inside.

"Thank you for your kindness, sweet lady."

She simply smiled and pulled out a handkerchief from her sleeve. She pressed it against the old man's face. "Does it hurt?"

"No." He placed a hand over her hand holding the handkerchief.

For the first time their eyes met. Under the bushy gray brows shone a pair of bright blue eyes. The color rose to her face and she shied, removing her hand, but leaving him to hold the handkerchief against his cut.

"Mademoiselle, we should go before the count worries," said Gérard.

"A moment. Will you be well?" she asked the old man.

"Yes. I'm afraid I got blood on your handkerchief."

She smiled, kind and gentle. "You keep it."

"For now. Someday I will return it to you, sweet lady," he spoke in all sincerity, blue eyes fixed upon her.

She did not shy from his gaze, but when his smile grew roguish she blushed. "Take care." She stood and entered the carriage.

The old man watched Gérard climb onto the driver's seat and the carriage leave. He gazed at the handkerchief, turning it over and saw the initials SC embroidered on a corner. He smiled, looked up again to stare after the carriage, but the man he watched left the building. He stuffed the handkerchief up his sleeve and hurried to follow, no longer bent or limping.

He tried to keep a discreet distance but the man stopped and looked directly at him. He played the beggar again. When the man moved on, he continued the pursuit. The man darted around a corner, forcing him to push through the crowded street, but alas, the man was gone. Frustrated, he left Market Square.

He made his way to a building owned by a prosperous tailor. Above the shop were two apartments for rent. He climbed the outer steps to one of the apartments, which consisted of three modest sized rooms.

"I've been waiting for you," said Philipe.

"You needn't have bothered." Arsène removed the hat and wig, wet black hair falling around his face. He crossed to a table with a basin in front of a mirror and poured water from a pitcher for cleaning. He removed the beard before speaking again. "I lost him in Market Square."

"You lost him?" teased Philipe. "Did you at least get a look at him?"

Arsène removed the fake wart then washed off the makeup before replying. "He was disguised in a massive cloak, large hat, and silk mask, yet was of considerable girth."

"That describes just about everybody at Court. Most are fat and pompous."

Arsène toweled off his face then looked in the mirror to examine the cut by his mouth. The bleeding stopped and showed nothing more than a small line and slim abrasion.

Philipe poured wine into cups. "If this keeps up, the traitor will get away."

"I know," groused Arsène. He sat opposite Philipe "We must find some way to bait a trap."

"Perhaps a meeting with some bogus information."

"Most of Court gossip is bogus information. Whoever he is, he is cunning. By his disguise and stealth he acted as if he knew I was following him. That does not bode well. I need to maintain my reputation."

"Narrows the list to a mere two dozen."

Arsène scowled in dispute. "Less than a half a dozen were aware of my assignment."

Philipe grew guarded. "You don't mean what I think?"

Arsène shrugged. "When does Le Resistance meet?"

"Rohan hasn't said." Philipe closely watched Arsène during his pondering. "What is brewing in that Gascon mind of yours?"

"Nothing solid yet, but give me time. I would discover this man who thwarts me. It's the only explanation."

"I hope you're wrong." Philipe took another drink.

"So do I. Otherwise the traitor is closer to the bosom of Le Resistance than Rohan thought; which distresses me greatly." His expression grew hard and icy.

In warning, Philipe touched Arsène's arm. "Do not let your feelings about the duke make this become blind vengeance."

Arsène flashed a smile of reassurance. "You know I always keep my wits."

Philipe grinned. For the first time he noticed a red line by Arsène's mouth. "Your face? Is it a cut?"

Arsène smiled in remembrance. "Nothing. An irate shopkeeper."

"You took the abuse?" asked Philipe in disbelief.

"I had no choice. Reacting would give me away." Arsène took a drink, which exposed the handkerchief up his shirtsleeve.

"And this?" Philipe pulled out the handkerchief. "A beggar wouldn't carry about such a fancy handkerchief."

Arsène snatched the handkerchief before Philipe read the initials. He tried to appear nonchalant. "A kind lady stopped to help an old man struck down by the shopkeeper."

"Who might his gallant lady be?"

"Philipe, you ask me betray such delicate information?" He rose and placed the handkerchief in the top dresser drawer. "I intend to return it to her."

Philipe flashed a wry playful grin. "In disguise or as your true self?"

Arsène shrugged and returned to the table, also smiling. "I have yet to decide. Either way, I am indebted to her for such kindness. If not for her, I would have struck the shopkeeper."

Philipe laughed. "I knew it! You take a blow? Never. Your Gascon pride would not allow it."

Arsène did not reply rather took a long drink. The clock in his apartment struck five.

"I nearly forgot, I'm to meet du Pree at half past five. I'll see you tomorrow." Philipe rose and departed.

The next day, Sabrina returned to Market Square, and this time shopping with Philip. Roger accompanied them in dutiful attendance. She spied the old man sitting on the curb and left Philipe, who examined the open wares of a silversmith and ignorant of her departure.

"Are you better today?"

Her inquiry startled him. "Sweet lady! Much better, thank you."

"Sabrina?" called Philipe.

When Sabrina turned, the old man quickly disappeared. "Wait!"

Philipe and Roger hurried over at her call. "What is it?" Philipe helped her stand.

Sabrina sighed with disappointment at finding the old man was gone. "Nothing."

"Are you sure?"

"Yes. Now where is this inn you mentioned?"

"This way." He offered his arm and they began walking away from the shop. They barely walked two blocks when a soldier ran up to Philipe.

"Lieutenant Bourdias, Captain du Pree sends for you."

Philipe frowned, turning from the soldier to Sabrina. "I hate to leave you unescorted."

"You can't ignore your duty. Besides, I'm safe with Roger."

"Very well." Philipe went to speak to the soldier, but he left. "Have her home before dark," he instructed Roger before leaving.

"The food at the inn is good, mademoiselle. We've eaten there quite often," said Roger, motioning for them to continue.

"Perhaps, but this afternoon was to be an outing. At least at the château I could dine with Adele."

Passing under an archway, Roger was attacked from behind and someone seized Sabrina. She let out a partial scream before being silenced by a hand over her mouth.

"Leave off!" a voice commanded, knocking away her assailant.

The momentum of the intervention sent Sabrina to the pavement. More hands grabbed her and she fought back, biting one of the hands. A short outcry escaped but the hands were persistent in holding her.

"Easy, sweet lady!"

The old man aided Sabrina to her feet. He gingerly used one hand, the one she had bitten. Shouts and running feet drew closer.

"Whoever wants you is determined. Roger!" he called over his shoulder before ushering her away.

Roger managed to throw off his attacker to follow.

The old man's speed and strength surprised Sabrina. He half-dragged, half-propelled her along their flight. When they paused around a corner, she surveyed this once bent and hobbling individual. He, on the other hand, was more interested in the sights and sounds of pursuit. "You're no beggar!"

He silenced her by covering her mouth, but after being manhandled, she kicked his shin in an attempt to break free. He seized her and pinned her against the wall, preventing her from moving or crying out.

"You've bitten me and kicked me when all I'm trying to do is rescue you. Now be still and silent!"

They were pressed so close together she could barely breathe. Although he held her, his blue eyes were reassuring. The brief assuage of the moment disappeared at hearing running feet drew closer. She tensed, then relaxed at seeing Roger.

"Sergeant," he said to the old man then, "Are you all right, mademoiselle?"

"Sergeant?" she asked in confusion.

"No time to explain. Take her. I'll hold them off." Arsène nudged Sabrina toward Roger just as two men appeared.

Roger and Sabrina only moved halfway down the alley when two more men blocked their escape. By the looks of their good quality clothes, these were no ordinary thieves. The men charged and Roger drew his sword. Sabrina shrank into the safety of a doorway.

Arsène fought two assailants. He threw off his ragged cloak to distract them. One man came at him in an awkward manner, trying to avoid the cloak but fell under a thrust from Arsène's blade. Hearing a muffled scream, he turned to see a fifth man begin to drag Sabrina away. Employing a quick deception and parry, he sent the second assailant's sword flying then knocked him to ground with a left cross. He raced to Sabrina's aid and a slice to the man's back stopped the abduction.

An unexpected blow from behind slammed Arsène into the wall. It was the man he downed to help Sabrina. A struggle ensued and Arsène tried to break free of the vise grip about his head and neck but the man held on. He ripped away from the hold, leaving the false beard, mustache and fake nose in the man's grasp.

"The solider from the terrace!" said Sabrina in surprise.

"Nice of you to remember, but rather inconvenient." Arsène dodged to one side when the man threw the disguise at him and moved to retrieve his weapon.

Roger did not fair well and suffered a wound to the left shoulder. The attackers pressed their advantage, but an intervening violent circular parry knocked the blades aside. Given the element of surprise, Philipe sent the assailants back a step. He also had the advantage of being left-handed. The oddity proved a troublesome obstacle for many right-handed swordsmen. A high slash from his dagger cut one man across the face while a sword thrust put more distance between the men and the wounded Roger. Philipe now become the focus of their attack.

"It's about time you showed up!" said Arsène.

Philipe gave a snort of annoyance as acknowledgment. He shoved one man aside just as the other came at him in a daring move of both dagger and sword. He had no choice but to repel the attack using both weapons. This gave the opponent he shoved aside a clear swipe at him. Philipe ducked and his hat sliced off his head. The men rushed at him. Again using a fast circular parry, Philipe halted them, then lunged with his dagger, burying it into the nearest man's pelvis. A swipe from his blade sent the other retreating. The odds were now even.

Arsène backed away from a dagger thrust. The man lunged, which forced Arsène to parry. This gave an opening for the man's knee to come up and into Arsène's stomach. Winded, Arsène staggered back, dropping his dagger to clench his abdomen. The man attacked. Fighting off the pain of the blow, Arsène tried to avoid the sword, but sustained a cut below the right ribs. Already incensed at being unmasked, the wound let forth an explosion of fury and he went on the offensive. The man fell, mortally wounded. Arsène stepped back to examine his ribs. Not too serious, just a painful scratch that bled a good deal. He reached for a handkerchief to hold over the wound.

Sabrina rushed over. "Sergeant?"

Arsène flashed a gallant smile. "A scratch."

A distraught cry escaped her lips at seeing he used her handkerchief to hold his wound.

"Hush, I'm not killed," he said, surprised by her reaction. His gentle touch upon her shoulder made her look at him. He balked at seeing her large brown eyes filled with tears of concern and turned his attention to the fighting.

Philipe used his dagger like a toreador, coming under the blade to deflect it upwards. A savage sword slash cut the man's right side. A dagger thrust to the body sent the last attacker to the street. In all, six men lay dead or wounded.

"Arsène?"

"A cut along the ribs." Arsène raised the handkerchief for Philipe to examine the wound. This also made the initials *SC* visible.

Philipe made no comment rather asked Sabrina, "Are you hurt?"

"No. Who were those men?" she said in a shaky voice.

"I don't know. Brigands, I suppose."

"Master, I saw someone." Roger cast a hesitant look to Sabrina before continuing to Philipe, "Merrill Chanute."

"Viscomte d'Algernon's man? Are you sure?"

"Yes, master."

Sabrina felt weak and leaned upon Arsène. He held her for support.

"Who is the Viscomte d'Algernon?" asked Arsène.

She regained herself to stand and answer. "The man my uncle sent to fetch me back to Reims. I ran away when I learned of his plan to send me to a convent in Rome after discovering Dominic's conversion."

The anger and disappointment in her eyes made him recoil. "I'm sorry, sweet lady. I never meant for any such thing to happen to you or Dominic."

Warring emotions played across her face as she regarded him and demanded, "What did you expect, Sergeant?"

"I don't know!" he snapped in frustration. The excitement caused his side to ache.

Seeing his pain made her bite her lip.

"Now isn't the time for argument. The Cardinal's Guards will learn of this and come to investigate," said Philipe.

They limped from the alley to Arsène's apartment a few blocks away.

Sabrina balked at the bottom of the steps. "Take me home, Philipe."

Greatly frustrated, Arsène lashed out. "Have you ever made a mistake you deeply regret? *Zut!* I offered Dominic satisfaction, and would more tolerate his sword through me than hear myself say what I did!" He struck his left breast.

His fervor confounded her. "I'm sorry, Sergeant," she murmured, tugging on Philipe's arm to leave.

Arsène turned to Philipe, anticipation on his face made Philipe reticent.

"I'm sorry," he said and left with Sabrina.

A long downcast sigh followed Arsène as he sat on the bottom step. "Oh, Roger. What has my Gascon temper done this time?"

"Come, Sergeant. Let's attend to our wounds and I'll tell you the whole tale."

Chapter 5

RETURNING TO LE PETITE CHÂTEAU, SABRINA AND PHILIPE WERE MET by Dominic. He gave a casual greeting, but she ran to her chambers, upset and in tears. This made Dominic press Philipe for answers. He paced the drawing room in an attempt to curb his irritation in listening to the tale of near kidnapping.

"I can't imagine my father causing more disruption by ordering this!"

"After the tennis match, the marquis might be capable of anything."

Dominic gave a stout rebuttal. "No, not so bold as to let men be recognized. Remember, he wanted to move her to the convent in secret. D'Algernon is more likely to act singularly in hopes of pleasing my father. Especially since hearing of her arrival after his search."

"Whichever scenario it is, the danger is increasing. Adele maybe right, Sabrina should be brought into our confidence."

"Exactly why she shouldn't be. However, there are personal answers she needs and I can provide those. Although this is not the circumstance under which I hoped to pass them along," he said in regret. "Please wait. I may need some moral support when I'm done."

Dominic left the drawing room and went upstairs to his bedchamber. From a box on his dresser, he took out a small, oddly shaped bauble, crossed to a writing desk and used it to unlock a large hidden compartment. From the compartment he withdrew two books. The first was a thick leather journal with the Charbonier coat of arms embossed on the cover. The pages were brown with age and some fraying on the edges. The second book was smaller in size with gold-gilded words and decoration on its leather cover. The words were in French: "Holy Bible."

After locking the hidden compartment and replacing the strange-looking key, Dominic made his way to Sabrina's room. At the door, he heard soft sobbing. Whereas he desired different circumstances, her distress convinced him of his choice. He didn't knock just entered.

Sabrina bolted up from lying on the bed where she wept. "I don't want talk to anyone!"

"I bring answers I should have given you when you first arrived. But in my attempt to shield you, I made a wrong decision. These will help you understand what is happening and why."

Sabrina became astonished at seeing the books. "Father's Bible! Where did you find it?" She took it from him.

"Trèvoux. It was buried in a trunk in one of the boarded-up rooms. I found it along with this: the last volume of Uncle Michael's journal." He handed her the other leather book.

"You defied Uncle and went to Trèvoux?"

He sat on the bed beside her. "Like you I needed answers, so when Adele and I left for our honeymoon, I made a detour. According to Tullies, the steward of Trèvoux, my father found the Bible among the rubble of the fire and brought it back to Trèvoux, locked it in the trunk and ordered the room sealed." He smiled and looked at the Bible. "The only Scripture I knew was written in Latin at the cathedral, the Common Book of Prayer and Catechism. Not that I can read Latin well. You know my tutor always complained about my lack of interest in the Holy Language." He grinned. "To read the Scriptures in French brought a new understanding of God." He opened the Bible and pointed to the feminine handwriting. "This is most touching."

He read aloud:

"My dearest Michael, on this our wedding day I give you not only my heart and soul but this Bible also. As our sacred vows shall seal our love on earth, may these Holy Words seal our souls together for eternity.

Your ever-loving,
Elizabeth
September 17, 1602."

She wept. "I thought it was destroyed in the fire!"

He tapped the journal. "This, more than the Bible, gave me the answers I needed. Not only about the rift in our family, but great insight into the thoughts, actions and faith of a man I wish with all my heart I could have known as his words mirror my own." He lifted her face to meet his gaze. "But I see his faith reflected in you. Where he tried to convince Father and Grandfather with words, your unwavering belief to withstand the cruelties of life and attacks upon your faith bring a reality to his words." He kissed her forehead. "I'll leave you to read."

The door no sooner shut then Sabrina opened the journal. For an hour she read, wiping tears from her eyes to clear her vision. Toward the end of the journal, the handwriting became unsteady and parts of pages were smudged and stained, perhaps by tears for the words were those of a tormented heart yearning for understanding. He quoted Scripture to aid his lament. The most difficult pages to read were those dealing with his father's renouncement and his brother's scorn. Oh, how he loved his father and Jourdian, and wept at their inability to accept his decision. Over and over again he wrote how it was not a matter of turning away or disavowing his heritage, rather a compulsion to follow his heart and faith. He could do nothing else. His last entry was dated two nights before the fire, and he declared how he would not give up seeking reconciliation even though his brother was stubborn at their first meeting.

Sabrina couldn't read any more for great weeping. How could one brother love so much but the other hate in the same measure? She used her handkerchief to wipe her eyes but stopped, gripped by fear at seeing her initials. She turned it over.

"No blood," she murmured in some relief. "He still has it—to cover his wound!" She fought back new tears of concern for Arsène. Her emotions shifted between anger, sympathy and gratitude. His thoughtless betrayal of Dominic's conversion caused another dangerous rift that almost sent her to a convent. Yet, their encounter on the terrace showed a different man than she imagined according to her uncle's description. He was handsome and charming. Then today he became wounded while rescuing her from a terrible fate. He knew her identity, but risked his life anyway.

Her gaze moved between the clean handkerchief and her father's Bible. "Until now, I had not even considered that you too are Huguenot."

Adele's earlier assessment of Arsène echoed in her mind: *he is a good friend, dependable and loyal.* Dominic's explanation also came to mind of how his father was predisposed against Arsène solely for his heritage, and the thoughtless words were in response to a violent assault and not a purposeful act.

She studied the handkerchief. "Uncle's hatred drove him to confront and assault you, just like he wanted to shut me away." She picked up the Bible. "Oh, Father, may the words in your most prized possession guide me now as I face the same hated you did then."

Downstairs Dominic explained his visit to Philipe. A note arrived for Dominic.

> *H.S.*
>> *Ten o'clock, baker's house. Prayer.*
>>> *L.R.*

He tore the paper and flung it into the fire. "Of all the nights."

"It's only a prayer meeting. And those who employ us were once powerful friends of your uncle. Perhaps we can use them to our advantage in dealing with d'Algernon."

"We shall speak to them this evening."

"Why not bring Sabrina with us?"

"I don't want her becoming involved!"

Dominic's outburst did not intimidate Philipe and he spoke in calm reply. "A little late for that. You just gave her the journal and Bible, so why not attend a prayer meeting? When was the last time she sat among her own people? Ten years ago?"

"Those are to explain my father's actions and behavior in respect to our situation, not to involve her. Despite claiming familiarity with the name, she didn't remember Rohan when I questioned her."

"She was a child. I scarcely recall the names of my father's friends from childhood. You've told me all these years how you wish to help her. Here's your chance."

Dominic scratched his mustache in thought. "Very well, she will come."

At nine o'clock, Sabrina sat in a dressing gown at the vanity preparing for bed. There came a knock at the door followed by Dominic's voice inquiring if she was awake. She didn't reply, hoping by being silent he would go away. She wasn't ready to speak yet. Instead of departing footsteps, the knob turned, unsuccessfully since she locked the door for privacy.

Neither her silence nor the locked door helped as she heard a jingling and realized he was using his key. She stood ready for confrontation. He barely entered when she accosted him. "I locked the door to be left alone!"

"All day I have allowed you time to read and digest the truth of the past. But the evening grows late and our time to depart is near, so I grow bolder."

"I'm not going anywhere at this hour of the night." For the first time she noticed he was fully dressed and wore a hat, cloak and sword.

"Don't take an attitude with me, my little rascal. You will find this venture interesting and rewarding. Now put on a plain shift and cloak."

"I will not!"

"You will if I command it," he said, being just as stubborn.

"Command—" she couldn't finish for surprise.

"Get dressed. Unless you want me to dress you," he said with a smirk.

Much to her chagrin, Sabrina did as instructed. Her displeasure turned to surprise when she found Philipe and Adele waiting downstairs. Gérard also wore clothes for a night's outing.

"We're all going?" she asked.

Adele just smiled and took Sabrina's arm.

Being unfamiliar with Paris, adventure into the night caused Sabrina apprehension; especially considering the earlier encounter. The men surrounded the women, who walked with hoods up hiding their faces. After twenty minutes they reached their destination. With each new revelation,

Sabrina found herself growing more curious instead of fearful. A bigger surprise awaited in the basement of a bakery—people assembled in what appeared to be a makeshift church.

"A Huguenot prayer meeting," Dominic whispered in her ear.

Emotions muting her, she took hold of his hand. Her eyes scanned the assembly. Across the room stood Arsène, clean of makeup and wearing normal clothes. She was glad to see his wound did not incapacitate him. However, his countenance appeared pale and pensive. He didn't acknowledge her, perhaps because he didn't recognizing her under the hood. She went to remove it but Dominic stopped her.

"Not just yet." He motioned to a bench. "Sit and I'll tell you when."

Sabrina obeyed, still watching Arsène, who remained on his side of the room.

Three men appeared before the gathering. One was a minister by the look of his simple somber garments. The other two were high-ranking by their bearing and rich tailored dark suits. One nobleman had a ruddy complexion with red hair, beard and green eyes, and stout and stocky build. The second was a most elegant and handsome gentleman with graying black hair, more slender and slightly taller than his companion.

Sabrina regarded the two gentlemen.

"Henri and William," whispered Dominic.

With more determination, she studied the men, especially the red man. Not until he spoke a greeting to the crowd did a glimmer of recognition appeared as she muttered in wonder, *"Papa Ours!"*

"What?"

"We called him *papa bear* because of his scruffy beard."

Dominic smiled. "The man you called *papa bear* is Henri, Duc de Rohan. The other is William, the Duc de Trudeau."

"I vaguely remember William."

"They remember you. We have spoken of you and uncle on occasion. That is why I want you to keep your hood up until the meeting is over."

They fell into silence, giving their attention to Rohan. His zeal for the Huguenot cause was as fiery as his red hair. He spoke with deep conviction and an air of superiority and manner demanding of attention.

"Dear Brethren, our cause has become a desperate one. Not satisfied with trying to silence us, they wish to send us into oblivion without so much as a memory that we ever existed in France! The Catholic missionaries conscript our men for service; confiscate our lands and possessions while teaching our children their false doctrines! Dear Brethren, this can no longer be tolerated. Your brothers in the south and on the coast are ready to raise their voices in protest. Yea, in rebellion if necessary! The Duc de Trudeau and myself are calling upon the brethren throughout France for their support by prayers, fasting or any other means to contribute. You here in Paris are examples of true faith. For by living in the great shadow of this Roman priest you endure much grief and suffering."

Rohan offered a short prayer of strengthening before Minister Le Suer began a twenty-minute sermon of encouragement and perseverance.

Sabrina only heard bits and pieces of the sermon, her mind and attention shifting between Rohan, Trudeau and Arsène. Finally her attention went back to Le Suer when he began his conclusion.

"My brethren, remember the words of Our Lord in His Sermon on the Mount. '*Blessed are ye, when men shall revile you and persecute you and shall say all manner of evil against you falsely for my sake. Rejoice and be exceedingly glad for great is your reward in heaven. For so persecuted they the prophets which were before you.*' So while we are forced to take up arms to defend ourselves let us do so in a spirit of humility, supplicating God for strength and deliverance while remembering those who cause us grief and pain are also God's children gone astray. For once ye were no better than the sinner and although now forgiven and are cleansed by the blood of Christ, you still seek His forgiveness when you do err."

Sabrina bit her lower lip and gazed across the room. Arsène paid attention to Le Suer, but shifted uncomfortably in his seat, touching his right side. Seeing him turn his head, she faced forward. His discomfort proved difficult enough to witness, she could not meet his gaze. She let out a low sigh of thanks when the minister called for all to bow in prayer.

After the *amen,* Philipe went forward to speak to a fourth man at the front of the room. The man nodded and began ushering people from the basement. Philipe approached the dukes. Arsène joined Rohan and Trudeau.

"Messieurs, we have a surprise. One requiring Chandler to clear the room," said Philipe.

"Does this pose any danger?" asked Arsène.

"No danger for messieurs. It is for another individual's sake."

Arsène turned to where Dominic sat with the women.

Rohan followed the interest. "A lady?"

"Yes, monsieur," said Philipe.

Both parties kept their distance until the room was clear and Dominic rose to escort the women forward.

"Dominic, Philipe tells us you've brought a guest," said Rohan

Sabrina removed her hood. "*Papa Ours,*" she said, her voice choked by tears.

Rohan's eyes widen in momentary surprise. "Dear child!" He embraced Sabrina, speaking words of wonder and endearment. He held her at arms length to survey her. "William! Look at her! All grown."

"Indeed! What wonder brought this about?"

"Not a wonder, messieurs. An unfortunate set of circumstances." Dominic cast Arsène a side-glance before explaining the unpleasant history that brought Sabrina to Paris and the meeting.

During the explanation, Arsène fidgeted, but kept silent. Occasionally he caught Sabrina's sympathetic gaze, but also Rohan's fatherly frown of disappointment.

"You took a great risk with the Spring Festival, but bravo, for succeeding," began Rohan, a hearty clap of Dominic's arm. "Yet I agree, I don't believe Jourdain gave d'Algernon leave to kidnap Sabrina. He maybe pigheaded, stubborn and narrow-minded, but he is too noble and honest to resort to such base means. Just a word of this incident, altered of course," he added to Arsène, "reaches him, d'Algernon will be dealt with by the marquis."

"I thought it best to tell you and Monsieur Trudeau in case my father does seek to take Sabrina from my house."

"You did the right thing. However, to keep up the pretense we can do nothing openly. You understand?" said Rohan with some regret.

"Of course. My only objective was to make you aware of the situation."

Rohan's arm encircled Sabrina's shoulders, an affectionate smile appearing. "If only Michael could see the beautiful young woman you've become."

"Monsieur," said Chandler in a tone suggesting impatience.

Rohan scowled. "Yes, yes. Perhaps one day soon we can dine together," he said to Sabrina.

"I'd like that, monsieur."

"Always *Papa Ours* to you, my dear. No one else," he added at hearing Arsène snicker.

Arsène forced the smile from his face. He fell in behind Rohan and Trudeau, intending to leave with them when Sabrina's voice halted him.

"Sergeant Lamonreaux. A word please."

"I am at your service, mademoiselle."

A moment of silence followed as they waited for the dukes to depart. Sabrina spoke again. "We have some unfinished business, Sergeant."

Arsène stiffened as Dominic appear stoic, Adele placid, and Philipe wore a fixed expression. "If I am to be rebuffed in public then I ask to speak in my defense."

"Who said you were going to be rebuffed, Sergeant?"

"That is where our last conversation ended, mademoiselle."

"No, Sergeant. It ended with you reciting your passionate offer to my cousin for satisfaction at the offense."

"To which your response was to leave."

"Sabrina, what is the point of this?" asked Adele.

"To apologize to the sergeant for my ghastly behavior and offer my gratitude for his valor."

Her answer surprised all, especially Arsène. "Sweet lady, my deplorable actions nearly sent you to a foreign convent."

"No. My uncle's hatred nearly did so. A hatred stemming from the past, is that not so, cousin?"

73

"Yes," said Dominic, though a bit baffled.

"Further you have forgiven Sergeant Lamonreaux for his offense, have you not?"

"Yes."

"Philipe," she proceeded. "From my observations and limited knowledge, you are more than the sergeant's lieutenant; his good friend perhaps? He commands your servant and you fight together."

"You are correct. We are good friends."

Sabrina returned to Arsène. "We are Huguenots, born and reared. Anger, bitterness and hatred follow us wherever we go. Many times for the simple reason we are different. Our enemies are the same, and our struggles the same."

Her generous speech brought Arsène to one knee, taking her hand and kissing the knuckles. "Sweet lady! You overwhelm me."

Moved by his gallant gesture, she blushed and balked. "Your posture is not necessary, Sergeant."

Dominic coughed to clear his throat.

"I ask pardon for my forward behavior, Monsieur le Comte," said Arsène, rising.

"Perhaps. Yet, my cousin has clearly described the situation."

"It grows late, and we should be leaving," said Adele.

Sabrina replaced her hood. "Forgive me, Sergeant. I forgot to inquire about your wound."

Arsène grinned; gallant and warm like the first night they met. "A scratch. I should be healed in a few days. Roger, on the other hand, has a nasty hole and need to be watched for infection."

"He shall be," said Philipe. He took Sabrina's arm to depart.

"Sergeant." Chandler beckoned from a corner under the stairs.

Arsène turned from watching the others depart to approach Chandler. "Have they left?"

"*He* insisted on waiting for you," came a terse reply and curt motion upstairs.

Arsène made certain the others were gone before bounding up the stairs to find Rohan and Trudeau at the rear door. Chandler followed close on his heels.

"I'm sorry for the delay, monsieur. I didn't realize—"

Rohan's smile and clap on Arsène's shoulder stopped him. "Chandler is a worrywart."

Trudeau coughed to cover a surprised reaction, making both Rohan and Arsène look at him and Chandler to frown.

Arsène led the way from the house, Rohan and Trudeau behind him with Chandler guarding the rear. After seeing Trudeau safely to his chateau, they proceeded to Rohan's home. For security reasons, they entered by a hidden side door rather than the main entrance.

"Turn down my bed then retire, I have some business before sleep," said Rohan to Chandler and steered Arsène down the hall to his study.

"What business, monsieur?" asked Arsène.

"Wanting a report on your assignment and to tell me more about the incident with Sabrina. Is that how you were wounded?"

"Yes," began Arsène, frowning. "I lost him in Market Square two days ago, and returned each day since trying to find him again. That is how I happened to be around when the Viscomte d'Algernon's men tried to kidnap her. Philipe was her escort, but drawn away by a false report of being summoned to duty. I'm uncertain whether my wound occurred before or after his arrival, but Roger suffered worse than I."

Arsène fidgeted, prompting Rohan to ask, "Is your wound troublesome?"

"No. The fact he eluded me is bothersome. I believe he knows me."

"Can you be sure?"

"Forgive me if I appear boastful, yet I have been successful in surveillance for years. His disguise and defensive actions made me suspicious. When I followed him, he turned and looked directly at me. I made pretense of not watching, and when next he moved, I quickly followed, but he disappeared around the corner."

Rohan studied Arsène in consideration of the young man's report. "Only a handful of people were told of your assignment."

"That's why I came earlier to the meeting in hope of informing you, but Mademoiselle Charbonier's arrival delayed me," he said with some distress, but tried to pass it off when Rohan appeared curious. "Since the incident I have racked my brain, but nothing."

"You did right, my boy. Speaking of Sabrina, you are disturbed concerning her. Your earlier behavior and tone betrayed jealousy."

"Monsieur," stammered Arsène, but Rohan's grip stopped further words and he hung his head. "I have no right to be. You are a great man and I, a Gascon—"

"Arsène," he began in tender parental rebuke. "After all these years you know I bear the heart of a father towards you. Cannot a man love more than one child?"

"Forgive me."

"There is nothing to forgive. You two are not much different. Even in her youth, Sabrina was an independent and stubborn girl." He drew a long breath of remembrance. "I wept when word reached me of how Michael and his family perished in a terrible fire. He was a good kind-hearted man, a dear loyal friend, and strong in the faith. Until I met Dominic, I didn't know she survived. If I had, she would not have gone to live with Jourdain and be treated with such animosity! Alas," he said with a deep sigh, "there isn't much I can do now—publicly without endangering everyone."

"What if the marquis chooses to expose his son?"

"Then I will act to protect them. But, I doubt Jourdain will."

"She is a remarkable and beautiful young lady," said Arsène with a hint of adoration.

This intrigued Rohan. Arsène possessed a cavalier indifference toward noble women, often finding amusement in the flirtations of the frivolous and frustrated women of the French Court, but never anything serious. As for ambition, if he ever had need or desired a position, he only need ask, but content in his present employ. The possibility of Arsène being smitten made Rohan smile.

Seeing the reaction, Arsène changed subjects. "My humble apologies for failing, monsieur."

"No, son. If this person does know you, then you are at the disadvantage."

"Son? How quaint," said Marguerite. She stood in the threshold. "Another late night, Henri?" She sent Arsène a withering, predatory glare as she passed him to approach Rohan.

The duke's posture and features turned rigid. "Madame, what are you doing here?"

"I live here."

"No, you plague this house!"

"You turn your attention to vermin!" She motioned to Arsène. He recoiled a step, more to appear inconspicuous than cowering in fear.

"Better an honorable man than a scheming, ambitious wife who beds every man in Paris!"

She slapped him, making Rohan seize her wrist, fury on his face.

In a voice full of warning and unction, but level in volume he spoke. "Madame, I have endured years of ridicule, scorn and your attempts to keep me from my daughter, but be warned, accost me again or do anything to Arsène and, as God is my witness, I will cut you off and leave you destitute!"

His determined and merciless expression made her tremble. "You mean that."

"Have you ever known me to say anything I did not mean?"

She nodded and forced a reply. "Very well, you have my word. I will not accost you again nor insult—your favored one."

"You can't even say his name," he scoffed, shoving her away. "What of *ma chère*? Is she in Paris?"

"No. I left her Pontivy."

"Good. She is too young and innocent to be continually subjected to her mother's outrageous behavior."

"What of her father's rebellion?"

"Forgotten my warning already, have you?"

She gripped her hands and pressed her lips together to maintain her composure.

He crossed to the wall and pulled the rope bell.

Chandler appeared, still fully dressed, like any good servant who did not retire before his master. "Monsieur."

"Escort madame to whatever place she wishes to pass the night."

"You would turn me out at this hour?" she asked in outraged shock.

He flashed a caustic grin. "I'm certain one of your paramours would be more than accommodating. Du Morte perhaps?" He waved for Chandler to take charge of her. When the door closed upon the departure, he stopped Arsène from speaking. "Do not be upset at her display."

"My concern is for you and little Marguerite, not myself."

Rohan smiled, genuine, which turned melancholy. "Where she thwarts me in protecting my daughter, I will not allow her venom to touch you."

"Can you not order her to yield the child to you?"

Regret filled Rohan's face and voice. "I fear the child's choice of parents is not an easy one. Her mother cavorts and her father stirs rebellion. At least she is kept safe form Paris, for now. Until she is of age." He grew sullen. "Enough. The hour is late and we must both put this behind us so we can lay our head to pillow and rest, or else tomorrow will be more difficult to contend with than today." He escorted Arsène to the side door. "Bonsoir, son."

"Monsieur."

The bells of Notre Dame tolled one in the morning when Arsène returned to his apartment. A late night thunderstorm prevented him from sleeping or rather the confusion racking his brain was as noisy as the storm. Blessed with keen ingenuity, he normally could reason out any problem, but wondering who thwarted him and if there was a connection to the attempted kidnapping of Sabrina mystified him. He recalled her tears at his wounding and the look of sincerity in her eyes when apologizing and expressing her gratitude at the meeting.

A close and loud thunderclap startled him from his introspection. He chuckled under his breath at the brief fright. "Think, stupid Gascon, think!"

He pushed his mind to concentrate on the man he followed. The thought of the traitor being an inner member of the Huguenot leadership plagued him. It could mean danger to Rohan, and he would not allow anything to happen to his beloved mentor.

He and the duke met by chance, when as a lad of fourteen he came to Paris to become a soldier. He fled the poor, provincial life of Gascony, hoping to make a new start for himself. Being an orphan and raised by his grandfather and two older sisters didn't offer much hope, thus his decision to strike out on his own.

Paris proved overwhelming at first, but he determined to stay. Having only elementary skill with a sword, he was passed over for the Royal Army. Being Huguenot, he didn't even consider seeking admittance into the Cardinal's Guards and serve the Catholic Church. True, he didn't practice his Protestant upbringing, but he wouldn't betray the heritage. Leaving the Louvre in dejection, he literally ran into Rohan, who was mounted and barely kept his horse from trampling the lad. Fearing severe injury, Rohan ordered Chandler to bring Arsène to his chateau for treatment. For a week, Arsène remained at the chateau recovering and spent long hours of conversation with the duke. At the time, Arsène was ignorant of Rohan's identity or significance to the Huguenots and France, but a kinship arose that neither expected.

Rohan set about instructing Arsène in matters of religion and arms. After two years serving in Rohan's household, the young protégé was ready. The duke secured him a position in the King's Musketeers.

For his part, Arsène considered Rohan as a father, and loved him dearly. His real father died when he was five and his grandfather an old man when he and his sister went to live with him. Rohan was the only true man of faith and integrity he ever met. If even the slightest danger threatened the duke, he acted. Except with the duchess. Toward her, he had to curb his temper, but her constant goading and numerous liaisons infuriated him. He aided

Rohan by maintaining a watchful eye on her activities whenever she came to Paris. He only met Rohan's daughter once.

The current situation with a possible traitor proved more frustrating than the duchess living up to her old tricks and behavior. He knew the danger existed but he didn't know how to combat it until he could determine the source.

This night's consideration took on a different and uncharacteristic cloudiness to his thinking. Each time he pursued an avenue of thought, he became distracted by—"Sabrina," he murmured.

His curiosity became aroused when Philipe told him she fled to Paris for protection. The meeting on the terrace showed she was a pretty young lady, but even that did not impress him to the point of interest. He was concerned of a possible threat to Dominic. No matter the personal danger he protected his friends thus he went to festival and tennis match.

He went to the dresser and pulled out the handkerchief. He sat at the table gazing at the initials. He turned the handkerchief over in his hand. Upon seeing the original bloodstain his mind recalled Sabrina's kindness in helping who she believed to be an injured old beggar. He smiled.

"Truly, in his hatred the marquis only sees your religion, for your soul is gentle and courageous. I don't know you well yet you are never far from my thoughts—" He laughed. "Gad, I sound smitten! Sabrina Charbonier, in all your innocence, you may have done what I thought no woman could, though some have tried. Their names and faces I have forgotten, but yours, I won't forget."

He blew out the lamp and went to bed holding the handkerchief. Within moments he fell asleep.

Chapter 6

EVERAL NIGHTS LATER AT A QUAINT HOME ON THE EDGE OF PARIS, the shutters were secured to obscure any curious eyes. All appeared still and quiet from the outside, but within a large oak hearth dominated the living room with a fire well underway.

When the high leadership met, Rohan utilized the Huguenot Sword as guards. Nothing was left to chance since the League of Princes—those of royal blood—agreed to meet with Le Resistance. They were Rohan's comrades among the Peers of France, Nevre, Bouillon, Bourbon, and de Longueville.

Rohan stood gazing into the fire, thoughtful and pondering as the others seated themselves at the table. He disliked the idea of open discussion knowing what he did, but to change plans may alert the traitor to his suspicions and something he did not want to do. No, to snare the sly fox everything must appear normal.

His focus changed from the fire to the men arranging themselves around the table. He took careful note of each individual, trying to determine who and why? All stood the chance of losing much, but the Princes were at greater risk should their cause fail. Cousin to the King, Bourbon took his involvement most personally. Four members of Le Resistance were not among the elite, the Comtes de Borchard and Reynard, the Duc de Trudeau, and the Marquis d'Avallon. They were more likely to succumb to threats or temptations.

Although William Trudeau bore the title of duke, he did not rank among the peerage elite, but a cavalier in every sense of the word in honor. A quiet man and devoted Huguenot, and a dear friend of Rohan before the latter was knighted and made a peer by King Henri IV in 1603. No, Rohan could not imagine any duplicity from Trudeau.

Borchard and Reynard were shrewd and ambitious men, yet loyal to Le Resistance for many years. Of the two, Reynard's refined and gallant manner reflected in his dress and deportment. His face did not show his girth like Borchard. He suffered a case of the pox as a child that left some marks upon his placid complexion. His dark eyes were piercing and keen.

Rafaelle Leon, the Marquis d'Avallon, was the youngest of the group at thirty-five and a man of a serious brooding nature, careful in speech and action. He fought hard during the uprising in 1620 and 1621 and bitterly disappointed with the Treaty of Montauban.

How can it be any of them? Rohan's mind searched for any clue. *Perhaps one who recently left our faith?* One believed to be stoutly loyal, was Condé, First Prince of the blood, cousin to the King. Condé was a key figure against the Treaty of Fontainebleau that arranged the marriage between the King and then Infanta, Anne of Austria. However, years of imprisonment softened Condé and he took advantage of King's mercy by publicly denouncing the Huguenots, thus securing his release and return to Royal favor. *But Condé has not been in our confidence for years. He wouldn't know about Arsène's recent assignment.*

His considering glance passed to de Bouillon, a Prince among Princes, hailing from a long lineage of Royal blood and commanded the powerful province of Sedan. Bouillon never forgave Henry of Navarre for renouncing the Protestant faith and embracing the Roman Church after being crowned King. Nor did he seek Royal forgiveness for his part in the assassination plot of the late King. He had personal reasons for revenge upon this present King. His son, the Comte de Turenne, made a mockery of his family by his associations at Court.

Such humiliation Rohan understood since his estranged wife frequented Court and scorned him in everything, making a mockery of fidelity and spending lavishly. Fortunately, he had the unflinching support of his mother, sister and brother. In fact, Benjamin moved to London to act as Rohan's liaison to King Charles.

Rohan became roused from his consideration by a touch on his shoulder. Dominic leaned close and whispered. Rohan brows became furrowed with surprise. "You say he is here?"

"With Arsène, who is making the necessary arrangements for later."

Rohan approached the table, his voice and face deliberate in speech and expression. "My friends, the original purpose for this meeting has changed due to a most extraordinary and singular occurrence. A prominent visitor waits in the antechamber. One we dare not keep waiting—his lordship the Duke of Buckingham."

Stunned murmurs arose from the men.

"By God, let him in!" exclaimed Bouillon.

Rohan waved to Dominic to admit Buckingham.

George de Villiers' entrance was inconspicuous under the circumstance, but his appearance and mannerisms spoke of a man high in quality and station. At the peak of manhood, his handsome and the forceful character made a lasting impression upon all those he met, both friend and foe.

"Monsieur, this is an unexpected, pleasant surprise," said Rohan.

"An opportunity presented itself and I thought best to take it, monsieur," Buckingham spoke in perfect French. "You received a correspondence from your brother the distinguished Seigneur de Soubise?"

"Yes, monsieur. Any further developments?"

"Parliament is being stubborn. It is because of their lackadaisical attitude I have paused in Paris on my way back to London from Geneva. I want to convey my deepest assurances that Charles is as willingly disposed to aiding our French Protestant Brethren as his father. Only Parliament hinders us."

"Does Richelieu know you are in France?" asked d'Avallon.

Buckingham scoffed in disdain. "What the insufferable priest knows or doesn't is of little concern! See how boldly I defy his banishment to come before you."

"Your banishment was ordered by King Louis," said Reynard.

"Are we here to discuss the fate of the Huguenots or my dispensation?"

"Gentleman!" Rohan intervened. "My lord Buckingham, I can assure you we appreciate the dangers you face on our behalf. Unfortunately since your last visit the islands of Ré and Oléron have fallen into Royalist hands. They are key to securing La Rochelle from the sea."

"How is La Rochelle holding out?"

"Mayor Gertion reports the fortification are almost complete. His concerns are the possible tactics the Royal forces may throw against the city; shy of all out war, he hopes."

"I suggest we each pour a large glass of wine. This could be a long evening, gentlemen," said Longueville.

Rohan signaled to Chandler. The valet stepped forward bringing several large scrolls and unrolled them on the table before stepping back. One item was a map of La Rochelle, and the other a sketch of the surrounding countryside and St. Martin's harbor. Some shifted in their chairs to see, while others rose and moved to view the maps.

"Other than the islands, the surrounding area is clear of Royalist forces," said Rohan.

"How is our navy?" asked Bourbon.

"I've not learned much past the rumors of rebuilding."

"England fears no other naval forces," said Buckingham with pride.

"What of this town? On the seaward side of La Rochelle?" asked Nevre, indicating a tiny spot on the larger map. "La Pallice. If Richelieu gains command of the town, he can control the channel with the help of the garrison on Ré."

Trudeau leaned over the map to measure the distance. "Barely two miles across the channel. Cannonade from land will deter shipping supplies."

"I'll send word to Geriton to secure La Pallice," said Rohan.

"How?" asked Buckingham.

Rohan slyly smiled. "The mayor is a master of persuasion. I'll leave it to his discretion; but money is usually the fastest way. To that point we can more easily obtain funds than Richelieu; who needs the King's permission to take any sizable sum from the Royal coffers."

Buckingham snickered and returned to studying the map.

"What about the army at Langerdoc?" asked Borchard.

"That is another option we have if Richelieu chooses to move against us, which I have no doubt will happen sooner or later," replied Rohan.

Skeptical, Reynard shook his head and surveyed the map. "The plain fact is we don't know what Richelieu is planning! We can sit here and speculate all evening; but until we learn by some word or action on the Cardinal's part, I advise we move slowly. Secure La Pallice but leave the army in Langerdoc."

"Sound advice, monsieur. We should not tip our hand before it is necessary," said Buckingham to Rohan.

Rohan stroked his beard in silent contemplating.

Nevre glanced at his watch. The time was nearly midnight. "Well? It grows late."

Rohan forced himself from his pondering. "If we adopt Reynard's suggestion, this meeting can adjourn, for we remain as we are."

"That would serve us no purpose," said Trudeau.

"Agreed, but what? Gentlemen, I'm open to suggestions."

The debate began. Not all held with Reynard's view. Bourbon was anxious to resolve the matter, along with Bouillon, d'Avallon and Nevre. Borchard and Longueville sided with Reynard. To everyone's dismay, Trudeau saw both sides of the issue and gave the military advantages and disadvantages to both.

Finally, at one-thirty in the morning, Rohan suggested adjournment until he received more intelligence from Geriton about La Rochelle. He expressed his personal gratitude to Buckingham before bidding the English duke farewell and signaling Dominic to escort Buckingham. Little progress was made concerning English involvement or their strategy against Richelieu. Nor was Rohan any wiser as to the traitor's identity. He hoped and prayed Buckingham would leave Paris safely, and the traitor would not take action against their most needed ally.

Only the occasional sound of nocturnal creatures broke the deep stillness of the late night. Suddenly a hurried form invaded the silent street behind the Palace de Royal. The cloak whirled about when he turned to look back. Satisfied at seeing nothing, he paused to lean against the wall and pushed up the hat to wipe his brow. He was a young man in his early twenties with a straight squared off nose, thin mustache and small beard. The short waist English doublet was loose fitting as if a size too large. The stiff collar was an annoyance and he tugged at it to breathe. Although he paused, his right hand held the hilt of a bloody sword.

The splashing of water caused him to turn. Two of the Cardinal's Guards appeared with drawn swords.

"Halt in the name of His Eminence, Cardinal Richelieu!" called a guard.

My God, how much longer must I run? The young man's mind shouted as his legs ached and lungs demanded oxygen. In desperation he turned into an alley. It ended. Frantic, he searched for an escape route through a door or window, but the doors were locked and windows too high. The sounds of pursuit dew closer and he darted behind several crates and barrels just before an all too familiar voice reached his ears.

"We have you now, Milord!" de Lacy spoke in English.

The young man's hand nervously flexed. He watched de Lacy move closer to his concealment. He tried to calm his labored breathing by holding his breath but his heart beat so he thought he would suffocate.

"How pleased Richelieu will be when I report your untimely demise!"

A guard kicked at the crates. The sound of clashing steel resounded in the alley as the young man grunted with exhaustion when the swords came together. He managed to shove the guard aside.

"He's mine!" de Lacy shouted.

The young man barely had the strength left to make defense, and when de Lacy lunged, he fell backward to avoid the lethal blade. The blade plunged downward and he rolled away, narrowly escaping the deathblow.

"The game is over, my Lord Buckingham. You have eluded me for the last time! What? No cry of mercy from the great English duke?"

"Never!" Landing a swift kick, he knocked de Lacy to one knee and jumped to his feet in preparation for the captain's riposte.

The blades met in a clash. This time the captain's blows were more of anger than those of a skilled swordsman.

"Lost your composure, de Lacy?" the young man taunted in English.

"Prepare to die, English dog!" De Lacy wildly came at him.

An opening! Avoiding de Lacy's sloppy attack, he lunged, piercing the captain below the right collarbone. De Lacy retreated, reaching for his shoulder. The guard rushed to aid de Lacy. Summoning what was left of his stamina the young man gripped the hilt of his sword like a club, batted aside the guard's blade and kicked him in the groin, sending him sprawling to street. He raced from the alley.

Meanwhile, near the waterfront, a large rat found a morsel of food but darted away when Philipe stepped on its meal. The clouds concealing the moon drifted aside. He would have to wait for darkness before proceeding. He pulled down his hat and wrapped the cloak about him to blend with the shadows. Eyes shifted about for any signs of danger as he waited for another cloud to cover the moon. He motioned to someone behind him. Dominic and Buckingham joined him. They ran across the street to the top of stairs leading down the river.

"Stand guard while I escort the duke to the boat," said Philipe to Dominic.

He and Buckingham crossed the street and descended dark steps to the water's edge. Below a middle-aged man sat in a boat slumped over the oar snoring. Philipe kicked the oar and the man bolted up. Buckingham took a seat then Philipe helped to launch the boat. Having completed his task, he joined Dominic.

"That was easy," said Dominic.

"Almost too easy. We better hurry to meet Arsène at the rendezvous."

Arsène was not at the rendezvous. Though he wounded de Lacy and doubted pursuit, he ran as far as he could until he tripped and fell on all fours. Winded and laboring for breath, he rose to a sitting position and leaned against a wagon wheel to rest. He lost the hat and the hair disheveled from running. Upon recovering his breath, he looked about to get his bearings. Satisfied at recognizing the area, he turned onto the street leading to Dominic's home.

At the chateau he went to the rear entrance where he knocked twice, thrice, and twice again on the single door. After a brief silence, he heard the shuffling of skirts and footsteps from inside. He squinted when the door opened and candlelight momentarily blinded him. "Adele? It's Arsène."

Adele opened the door just enough for him to enter then quickly closed it. "Where are Dominic and Philipe?"

Arsène pulled off the hot wig before answering. His black hair wet and matted from activity. "They maybe waiting for me at the rendezvous, but after my narrow escape from de Lacy, the house was closer. If they haven't returned in an hour, I'll search for them."

"Wash up. I'll fetch you food and drink."

He pulled off the stiff lace collar. "I don't know how the English tolerate such confinement," he complained and unfastened the top two buttons of the doublet. He carefully removed the mustache and small beard before washing at a water basin. He slicked back his wet hair and sat at the table.

Adele served him leftovers from dinner. She sat across from him with an annoyed grunt. "This happens every time Buckingham comes to Paris!"

"How did you know Buckingham was in Paris?" he asked, a small smile appearing.

"Does he ever come to Paris without contacting the Queen?"

He chuckled. "Did she see him this time?"

"No! Since the incident in her bedchamber it is extremely dangerous. Richelieu's eyes are everywhere, only *he* doesn't seem to care what anxiety he causes her, whether declaring his love in private, in public or demanding a secret rendezvous!" she bitterly complained.

"Men in love are not deterred by a little danger."

Adele frowned with irritation at his flippant attitude. "As if you three didn't do enough for Rohan and the cause! To be bodyguards for an English dandy."

He raised his shoulders in a noncommittal shrug. "Negotiations are delicate matters. More so when involving an English dandy."

"You laugh, but I don't find his advances towards our Queen amusing."

"I never said I approved of his romantic activities. However, we need English military and financial aid if we are to be successful. That means negotiating with this dandy. As Buckingham controlled his father James, he controls King Charles now."

"I don't trust him."

"Why? Because he's English, or a dandy?" he asked, smiling.

"You are incorrigible!"

Arsène laughed.

A sudden sound at the back door brought Arsène to his feet and grabbing his sword. Adele stood behind him as the door opened. Dominic and Philipe appeared.

"Here you are! We waited at the rendezvous for nearly half an hour," complained Philipe.

"I'm not the swordsman you are, I ran for my life," quipped Arsène, returning to the table. "My flight brought me within a block of the château. Did Buckingham get off safely?"

"Yes. And no sign of the Cardinal's Guards."

"Cardinal's Guards?" A new voice from behind startled them and sent the men reaching for their swords.

"Sabrina!" exclaimed Dominic when she stepped into the light. She wore a dressing gown, her hair falling about her shoulders. He let his sword fall back into the sheath, trying to appear nonchalant. "What are you doing down here?"

She folded her arms, smirking in obstinate suspicion. "I live here, remember?"

Philipe put up his sword up, frowning at the retort and Dominic. Arsène grinned and sat at the table to resume eating.

"It was foolish of you to come down alone in the middle of the night," Dominic scolded in clumsy manner.

"A pounding woke me. Then I kept hearing voices. I wondered who was up at this hour. I went to your chamber, but you weren't there and your bed not slept in. Neither did Adele answer me, yet her bed was slept in. I grew concerned for her condition and came down to see if she was well. I didn't expect to find this gathering."

Dominic fidgeted and continued his flimsy argument. "Paris is not like Reims. It's dangerous. We could have been thieves—"

"Or intriguers."

"You're imagining things."

"Really? Dominic Charbonier, I may be new to Paris but I know you. Since being here you have acted vague and clandestine. Not to mention my near kidnapping and being rescued by your chameleon friend here!" She motioned to Arsène and picked up the wig off the sideboard. "Who were you this evening, Sergeant?"

"You can be infuriating!" Dominic growled with deep displeasure.

Adele ushered Sabrina toward the back stairs. "Return to bed and forget what you think you know. It's for your own good. You're too young."

Sabrina stopped moving, her temper getting the best of her. "You were not so old and wise when you left Reims," she said to Adele then turned to Dominic. "I may be naive in Court affairs, but I know when something is amiss! Or have you forgotten intrigue murdered my family?"

"What?" his response was quick and sharp.

She bit her lip as his astonishment turned to anger. He could be fierce and intimidating when provoked and his eyes narrowed, searching her face.

"The fire was accidental, wasn't it?"

She shifted uneasily under his heavy, relentless gaze. She shied away and shook her head.

Dominic seized her so hard by the shoulders that a small cry escaped. "What are you saying?" he demanded.

The surprising violence brought Arsène and Philipe to intervene. Philipe grabbed Dominic's arm as Arsène tried to draw Sabrina away.

"Dominic!" snapped Philipe.

90

Bewildered, Dominic turned from Philipe to Sabrina. At stark realization of what he'd done, he released her, turning away to regain his composure.

Arsène steadied her after the rough release. Bashful, she stood on her own after regaining her balance.

Despite his effort to control his temper, Dominic lashed out. "Did you learn this recently or is it a secret you kept from me all these years?"

"I always suspected it," she lowly replied.

"Good Lord, Sabrina!"

Arsène again took up a defensive position of Sabrina, but Dominic moved no further. Although a wellspring of emotions played crossed his face in an effort to contain his fury.

Sabrina's eyes filled with tears of shame. "I did not mean to wound you by my thoughtless outburst. Forgive me."

He remained rigid but this voice level, though forced. "What made you suspicious about the fire?"

She took a deep breath before proceeding. "I'm not certain how, but my father was involved with the Huguenot resistance."

"That is not something a father tells a child."

"No. From my observations I drew that conclusion."

"You witnessed him involved with some intrigue?"

"A secret meeting and hushed conversations."

"How? Intrigues are closely guarded."

"A meeting took place at the house we rented in Reims. You know I sleep lightly. I woke to shouting and terrible arguing. I crept downstairs and found a group of men gathered in the living room. Father tried to calm someone as they talked of the war and religion. Things I didn't fully understand then."

"How long did you listen?" asked Dominic, his anger replaced by curiosity.

She shrugged. " Long enough to realize the dreadful seriousness of their discussion. I can still see them now." Her voice quivered so she paused to compose herself. "After a while I heard horses and went to look out the window. The local magistrate arrived and the men scrambled to leave."

"Must have been a sight when he discovered you," said Philipe.

"He never knew," she droned. "I became frightened and hid in a cupboard so I wouldn't be seen. He had a heated argument with the magistrate. I only heard the influx of voices and occasional words then a crashing or breaking of something."

"They came to blows?" asked Dominic, now concerned.

"Father showed no signs of injury the following morning. Then again, he was a large powerful man." She gazed directly at Dominic. "You look very much like him. Perhaps Uncle sees the resemblance."

Dominic somberly nodded.

She continued, "The magistrate left and it took Father a long time to calm down. He paced, muttering under his breath things I couldn't understand. Even after he retired, I stayed in the cupboard, trembling and wondering what to say or do. I thought best to say nothing. The following night—the fire happened!" Her voice cracked with emotion.

"Why didn't you tell me this before?"

She shook her head, reluctant to answer but he insisted.

"What prevented you from confiding in me? My father?"

"No—yes, indirectly," she admitted. "As children we became close, but, forgive me, you were not a Huguenot then. I feared you'd tell Uncle—," she broke down and wept.

He held her. "I would never betray you!"

She forced herself to speak, her words thick and anxious. "I said what I did because your actions have brought back frightful memories with startling parallels to the past! Although you try to deny it, I know intrigue in involved. Some secret you refuse to tell me."

He touched her cheek. "I did not want to place you in further jeopardy and did everything I could to keep you from becoming suspicious."

Sabrina wiped her eyes and replied in a stronger voice. "I'm Huguenot. By nature I have one eye on God and the other looking out for trouble. From what I've seen tonight, I believe you have joined the resistance. More rightly, this Huguenot Sword I heard about."

A cough of surprise escaped Arsène. Philipe bit his mustache and an overwrought Adele sat at the table. Her reaction made Dominic leave Sabrina to comfort his wife.

"I guessed rightly," she said to the reactions. "Don't you think I want to fight for my beliefs too? For years Uncle suppressed my freedom. Why are you now doing the same?"

He winced at the accusation. "I never meant that! While you lived under his authority, I dare not say or do anything to cause alarm. I knew I couldn't keep up the pretense indefinitely. It was unfortunate how, but some good may come yet."

"Will I need to make redress for the rest of my life?" snapped Arsène.

"No. Your apology was sufficient; your gallantry on my cousin's behalf extraordinary."

Subdued, Arsène bowed to the compliment.

"As for your involvement, that will have to progress over time. We are not an independent entity and work in accordance with a higher authority, which is all I am at liberty to say. The secret is not mine to reveal. Now, we best retire. It's been a long and difficult night, and I am weary of making a jack-ass of myself," he said. But when Sabrina moved to object he raised a hand for silence and she complied.

Arsène gathered his things and bade Sabrina good night with gallant gesture of kissing her hand. "Mademoiselle."

Philipe went one better and kissed Sabrina's cheek. He also kissed Adele before leaving with Arsène.

Sabrina was grateful for the low light as she blushed under the attention.

❧ Chapter 7 ❧

THE IMMENSE PALAIS DE CARDINAL CONSISTED OF NUMEROUS connected buildings with massive ornate columns. The first grouping contained the main apartments and offices where all the daily activities occurred. The second group, still under construction, would house three small theaters, a chapel and the Galerie des Hommes Illustres to celebrate the accomplishment of past French kings. The rear wall of the buildings used ironwork screens to view the gardens Richelieu enjoyed. A great patron of the arts, he admired such contemporaries as Rubens, Van Dyck, and Titan. The palace showed a side of the "Red Eminence" not often seen by the world, a side of beauty and romance.

When Richelieu came to power, France was like an abused woman in need of loving care and gentle handling. In the past few years of declining health, from France Richelieu drew his strength. He dedicated his life to the country's unity and detested the Huguenots for their rebellion, but legally forced to tolerate them because of the Edict of Nantes. Rohan's was a cousin by marriage and close companion to the late King Henri and played a major part in the decision to grant the Huguenots freedom of worship and the right to maintain their independent cities and towns. The two strongholds were Montauban and La Rochelle.

Unfortunately, after King Henri's assassination those more vehemently opposed to the Huguenots sought to undermine the Edict and provoked Rohan to fight back. Alas, in the ensuing battle, the Huguenots lost Montauban and other smaller towns, leaving only La Rochelle as their place of refuge. With civil war again threatening his beloved country, Richelieu threw his energy into destroying those who brought such a state to France.

Still, with Rohan he had to be careful. Although a staunch Catholic, Louis respected Rohan due to the relationship to his late father. Rohan also served well in military campaigns for Louis in the early years of his reign.

This morning the Cardinal sat in his main chamber, a cavernous room with a high ceiling and large terrace doors on two sides. One side opened to the courtyard, the other to the garden. Each door was draped by red velvet curtains, which were drawn aside to permit sunlight into the room. A Persian carpet lay atop the Italian marble floor. The mahogany desk was situated to look out into the garden. Behind the desk stood a carved marble hearth. A rich embroidered tapestry combining the French fleur-de-lis with the symbol of the Roman Catholic Church hung over the hearth. Two large iron candle stands flanked the desk.

Richelieu glanced up from his writing when de Lacy entered. The captain appeared pale, holding his right arm in a sling. "Did you meet with some misfortune, Captain?"

"A hazard of the job, Eminence."

"Any news from our weasel?"

"Yes, Eminence. He has recruited one of the others, but assures me all is well, though he did not mention his name."

Richelieu eyes narrowed. "So he has found someone foolish enough to share his danger. I doubt voluntary. Only now there is twice the money to pay. Did he tell you how much it would be this time?"

"The usual."

"The danger must be getting to him if he does not increase his price."

De Lacy grunted and cradled his arm. "Buckingham was in Paris last night."

Richelieu grew red-faced. "He dare defy a Royal edict? What of the Queen?"

"Not at the palace; he met with the Huguenots. They intend to secure La Pallice, a town—"

Richelieu put up an abrupt hand. "I know everything about La Pallice. Tell me of Buckingham."

Sheepish, de Lacy glanced at his wound when replying. "He escaped, Eminence."

Scowling in great annoyance, Richelieu tossed his pen onto the desk. "Don't tell me! The Huguenot Sword once again lured you from your main objective. How many times does that make this month, Captain?"

De Lacy couldn't look at the Cardinal while replying, "Three."

Richelieu snarled. "Did you at least find out what I asked for?"

"No, Eminence. For some twisted reason of loyalty he refuses to betray them. Although, I suspect this false Buckingham and the man our weasel claims to be following him are one in the same. And I would know him!"

Richelieu closely studied his proud captain. "I'm sure you would. Patience is one of the Cardinal virtues, Captain."

De Lacy spoke with a slight edge to his voice. "I find it strange he so easily betrays secrets vital to the Huguenots, but not individuals."

Richelieu sat with elbows on the arms of the chairs and fingers steepled together before his lips. "By keeping his compatriots identities, he can more easily betray their secrets. Once their confidence is betrayed, the peril would increase tenfold. Have your men keep a sharp eye for anyone with the talent and wherewithal for disguises and intrigue. This man could even be a noble, but that matters not. Understand, Captain?"

"Yes, Eminence." De Lacy saluted and began to depart.

"De Lacy," said Richelieu with an afterthought. "Pay particular attention to the Musketeer Rohan is fond of. The name escapes me, but he is country born."

"Lamonreaux, and he is a Gascon. I have watched him on occasion, but if he is involved with anything, he's good at keeping himself hidden."

"If you keep a close enough watch and apply some intimidation, even the good ones are inclined to make mistakes, Captain."

"Yes, Eminence," de Lacy said with a predatory smile.

By way of orders issued to officers in the Guards, Dominic learned of de Lacy's intent and warned Arsène. Thus, during the next three weeks, Arsène limited his contact and visibility to only the most important of appointments. He continued his afternoon escort of Adele and Sabrina from Court to Le Petite Chateau. There was nothing usual in this since Lieutenant Bourdias was the countess' brother, thus to the public, he was acting on his lieutenant's behalf. In private, he looked forward to those times. He delighted in their diverting conversations as Sabrina's unspoiled demeanor and optimism seemed to repel the pollution of Court. As a result, he found himself drawn to the Huguenot prayer meetings more frequently.

At first he wanted to continue enjoying her company, but in worship she displayed unsophisticated humility and reverence that captured his interest even more. Once before he witnessed such dedication from his sister, Gabrielle. Being the eldest of three orphans, she needed to be devout. She was instrumental in his accepting God's mercy at age ten by explaining the sacrifices of Christ. Eager to learn more about God, he listened to Gabrielle read Scripture at night. When leaving for Paris and the Académie de Militarie, she gave him an old Bible and warned him about the vices of Court. She said she would pray for him daily. He thanked her and went on his merry way to Paris. He tried to maintain his faith in private, but eventually the energy and enthusiasm of Paris gave way to the intrigues and delights of city life.

At the latest prayer meeting, he sat beside Sabrina as usual and he recognized the old Bible she began carrying. Dominic showed it to him and Philipe and told them about discovering his uncle's Bible at Trevoux. Only this time he caught a glimpse of something unusual on the pages of Scripture.

"What is this?" He pointed to some handwritten words.

"My father often made careful notations in the margins or underlined a special or meaningful passage."

"I didn't think anyone would dare to mar the Holy Book."

"Not mar, personal notes. This is a living book one takes to heart and uses, not a sacred relic to be stored and never touched." She turned to the front page. "This was a gift from my mother to my father on their wedding day."

He read the endearing inscription and was about to speak when Dominic cleared his throat and indicated Le Suer, who concluded his sermon by calling for prayer.

After escorting the others home from the meeting, Arsène returned to his apartment. The clock on the hearth mantle in the main room chimed one o'clock in the morning. Although tired, the inscription in Sabrina's Bible prompted him to look for the Bible Gabrielle gave him as a lad. He hadn't read it in years and thought it was in his small dresser, but no. The only other place he kept his meager possessions was in his trunk, but that contained mostly military supplies or costume accessories. He became concerned at not finding it easily and pulled everything out of the trunk. Underneath and pushed into a back corner, lay the Bible. It was actually a small leather book of the Psalms and New Testament. The cover was bent and edges of the pages frayed a bit from being piled on.

He sat on the floor with his back against the trunk, brushed the dust off the cover and tried to flatten out the curved corners. After some repair he opened to the first page. The phrase was not as long, but just as sentimental.

> To Arsène,
>> My beloved brother on earth and for eternity.
>>> Your sister in the flesh and in Christ,
>>>> Gabrielle.

For several moments he stared at the words, tears welling. He had not seen Gabrielle or his other sister Mallory since leaving Gascony. Gabrielle was the eldest and Mallory closest in age at five years older than Arsène. However, Gabrielle was the more motherly of his sisters. She was eleven years old when Arsène was born, which made her sixteen when their father died and they went to live with their grandfather. Her latest letter came five months ago. He couldn't remember the last time he wrote Gabrielle. He reasoned not maintain correspondence was to protect his sisters from danger since he became involved with the Huguenot resistance. But in his heart, he knew the truth. It was also why he avoided fully embracing Rohan's counsel, it meant coming face-to-face with a past commitment he failed to live up to.

True, meeting Rohan rekindled the zeal for his faith, yet he remained easily swayed where women and adventure were concerned. Although he refused to take advantage of this new life, or more truthfully, the women who found him attractive. Sabrina's appearance unearthed the forgotten ten-year-old boy who wholeheartedly embraced God.

He thumbed through the pages, and to his surprise, he noted underlined passages. He stopped to read:

> *For this people's heart is waxed over and their eyes have closed: lest at any time they should see with their eyes and hear with their ears and should understand with their hearts and should be converted and I should heal them. But blessed are your eyes for they see and your ears for they hear.*

The words struck him for those were the exact actions he did, shut his eyes and ears to what he knew was right. Hearing the clock chime and distant church bells startled him and he listened to determine the time was now two o'clock.

His eyes weary with sleep and blurred by emotions he spoke to the Bible. "I will read more of you when I can concentrate. I need to get some sleep for duty tomorrow and further discussion with Sabrina." He grinned at saying her name. He replaced everything in the trunk, only this time, laid the Bible on top before closing the lid and locking it.

The following morning, Arsène woke just in time to get dressed in his full uniform with tunic and musket, grab a quick breakfast of day old bread and cheese before reporting for duty. Philipe kept a tight schedule and Arsène's watch at the palace usually ran from noon to three o'clock in the afternoon. Exceptions were those days the palace sent word of a change in plan or special event. He was pleased to see the schedule remained. He learned Philipe was making his rounds, so Arsène went to his normal station at a palace gate. From here, he could see the terrace overlooking the palace garden and all those who came and went.

It was common to find a group of nobles gathered on the terrace. These were the ones who did not receive royal invitation to stroll the garden. They congregated in hopes of receiving an invitation, to exchange gossip or just to be seen. Such a group appeared during Arsène's watch. He saw the usual suspects of those who dealt with gossip, Mademoiselle Charlotte Talbert, Bridgette Charteaux and Monsieur Fontaine. A few particulars among the group caught his attention, the Duchess de Rohan, the Comte de Borchard, and Comte de Reynard. He would make note of their activities and consider them against the recent events.

Perhaps the one he took the least pleasure in seeing was Jeanette Charise. She was the youngest of the group at fifteen years old. Her yellow hair and alabaster skin gave her an appearance of an angel. Her round almond-colored eyes flirted with every man, while her full ruby lips invited kisses of passion. Her dresses were as revealing as Paris society permitted without being tasteless. Arsène's spurring of her mother's advance last year became a hot topic for gossip. It nearly led to his dismissal from the Musketeers when Madame Charise sought vengeance by fabricating how he accosted her. Only Rohan's intervention quelled the situation and he kept his rank of sergeant. He tried to ignore Jeanette's glances at him.

On the terrace, Borchard spoke to the duchess. "Madame, you cannot believe every rumor. He is a mere soldier." On this blustery day he wore a cloak while the sword was more for fashion than practicality.

"I assure you, monsieur, his reputation is well-founded," said Marguerite.

"Rumors say he has a steady lover," began Charlotte, her eyes opening in coquettish surprise on the duchess. "Is it true?"

"Far be it from me to spread rumors, only to state facts as I have them." Charlotte and Bridgette exchanged shameless glances and giggled.

"Ladies, what you find attractive in this Gascon soldier is beyond me," groused Fontaine. "His is a country bumpkin with crude manners."

"Perhaps it is his crude manner that is so appealing," said Reynard.

"I, for one, wish he would leave the women of Court to the men at Court."

Jeanette's eyes narrowed with determination. "I shall learn just how much he has changed." She left the group.

"Do you think she will succeed where her mother failed?" asked Charlotte.

"No. Jeanette is worse," said Bridgette.

"If you ladies will excuse me. Messieurs." Borchard took his leave.

"I wonder where he's going?" mused Charlotte.

"To spy, perhaps?" said Bridgette with a smirk.

Charlotte giggled in wicked delight. "That might be fun."

The younger women followed Borchard. The duchess smiled in private triumph and left the terrace in the opposite direction.

Sabrina arrived on the terrace to wait for Adele as the group dispersed. Adele was dismissed at three to prepare for supper. Sabrina was a few minutes earlier than usual. Arsène stood at his post, but he wasn't looking at the terrace so she acted with discretion. Huddled at a rail nearest Arsène's position, Charlotte and Bridgette giggled.

"Mademoiselle Charbonier. A lovely day, isn't it?" said Borchard, diverting her attention from the women.

"Indeed, monsieur."

"Any sign of the Queen?" he asked, looking into the garden.

"She was over by the fountain not long ago."

Borchard's fat face smiled, eyes surveying Sabrina. "You have been in Paris a short time but made many admirers, including myself."

Sabrina flashed a retiring smile. "You flatter me, monsieur. I often feel inadequate among so many noble ladies."

"Your fresh young modesty delights us all. It is quite refreshing. Oh, is that Jeanette Charise by the gate?"

Sabrina followed Borchard's indication to see Jeanette approach Arsène.

Arsène checked his watch and read two-forty. Sabrina was punctual so he pocketed the watch. At sight of Jeanette, he fought to curb a sneer. Since the incident with her mother, she had not spoke to him and he hoped she had forgotten. Her countenance and saunter told him differently.

"Sergeant Lamonreaux," she greeted him with a purposeful smile.

Formal in speech and decorum, Arsène returned her greeting. "Mademoiselle. Is there a reason for your presence?"

"I never do anything without a reason, my dear Arsène."

Arsène raised a rebuking brow to use of his Christian name. "What do you want, mademoiselle?"

"No need to be formal. I came to discuss some distressing rumors about you."

"Distressing?" he dryly questioned more wary than when she first approached him.

"They say you are no longer available," she said with a fake pout, touching his arm and drawing closer.

"I never recall being available to everyone."

"Distressing to those of us from whom you were available."

He removed her hand on his chest. "Mademoiselle, I wasn't available to your mother, so what makes you believe I would be available to you?"

"A simple misunderstanding." She continued in her unabashed attempt, caressing his face.

"There was no misunderstand then, and there is none now." He seized her hand. "Need I remind you I am on duty and we are in plain view? You're making a spectacle of yourself."

"Arsène, are you serious?"

He spoke low and firm: "I will not suffer a flogging for the likes of a spoiled child." He pushed her away.

Her eyes blazed with anger. "Rumors say you have a lover who has bewitched you into fidelity!"

His temper began getting the better of him. "That is a word you should take heed of; for at your age and with your background you would intimate any man with the insane notion of becoming your husband!"

She raised her chin, shoulders squaring with offended pride. "You know what my mother did when you refused and insulted her, Sergeant Lamonreaux!"

He clenched his fists to contain his anger. "I do not take threats lightly!"

"You treat me cruelly, Sergeant!"

"No more so than you, a mere child, insulting me with threats of scandal if I do not bed you!"

She slapped him.

Arsène's blue eyes flashed with rage making her recoil. He smiled with hauteur. "I suppose that is the only appropriate response for one so chided. But a good spanking is what you need."

Jeanette flushed with outrage, stomped her foot and turned away. A white object caught her attention. On the terrace, Borchard used his handkerchief as if covering his mouth after coughing. Sabrina's gaze was transfixed at them and appeared ignorant of Borchard's gesture. The delay was brief before she turned back to Arsène, her arrogance restored.

"I suggest you reconsider, my proud Gascon. Her noble rank won't shield her from the scandal I can create!"

He seized her arm. "I won't tolerate your venomous lies to touch her!"

"You have an alternative if you wish to protect her." She wrapped her arms about him, pressing herself hard against him as she kissed him.

Even under threat, he could not stomach her kiss and pushed her away.

She smiled, wicked and triumphant. "Too late. Try explaining to her." She pointed to the terrace.

Arsène's breath caught in his throat when Sabrina turned and left the balcony with Borchard. The duchess stood about ten feet away from Sabrina and Borchard. She smiled at him and used her fan in a discreet motion toward Sabrina. His anger flared at discovering her involvement, but Jeanette's loud mocking laughter diverted his attention to her departure.

"Filthy slut!" he snarled under his breath. "Someday you will receive your dues and I hope I'm around to see it." He looked back to the balcony, his expression growing forlorn. "Oh, Sabrina."

Jeanette rounded the corner from Arsène when a hand seized her and drew her into the shadows. Her startled outcry stopped by a hand over her mouth. She became irked at de Lacy and hit his arm to release her mouth.

"You shouldn't frighten people like that, Captain."

De Lacy ignored her rebuke. "What did you say to Lamonreaux?"

"A private conversation and none of your concern."

His grip tightened on her arm, making her wince. "Everything at Court is my concern. And the Cardinal's."

A look of fear passed over her face. "What do you want?"

"Any information you learn from Lamonreaux, you are to tell me."

"What if I choose not to do this?" She tried to sound brave.

"There is no choice, my dear."

She paled at seeing his cold black eyes and merciless expression. "Very well; if I can learn anything. What do I get in return?"

De Lacy smiled. "The eternal gratitude of His Eminence, with perhaps a token of thanks from me." He kissed her hand with a devilish gleam in his survey of her. "You have your ways of prying things out of men. Use them to the fullest." He shoved her away.

Sabrina's mind raced in turmoil. She could not hear what passed between Jeanette and Arsène, but the immodest scene and kiss caused enough distress.

"Shameful the way he carries on with women. For some insane reason the Duc de Rohan took the Gascon under his wing, but such reckless abandon can only lead to trouble," said Borchard.

A gasp escaped and she bit her lip.

"Mademoiselle?" He reached to stop her. "May I take you some place more suitable for recovery?"

His touch on her arm made her balk. "Monsieur le Comte, forgive me. I'm not feeling well," she murmured, fighting from become emotional.

"My dear mademoiselle, how can I leave you in such distress?"

"Please, monsieur, do not be offended. I do appreciate your concern. Excuse me." She hastened from the terrace. In a rush she drew near one of the palace gates and saw a friendly face on the other side, but walking away. "Philipe!"

He motioned the guard on duty to allow him to pass. He became surprise by her tears and drew her away to speak privately. "Sabrina, what's wrong?"

"How could I be such a fool?"

He gave her his handkerchief. "Take a deep breath, dry your eyes and tell me what troubles you."

"I don't know where to start."

"The beginning is always a good place."

Shy and uncertain, she tugged at the handkerchief. "You are his friend."

"Whose friend?"

"Arsène."

"Yes, I am his friend," he said with perturbed sigh.

"You speak with regret?"

"Solely in response to your inference he has upset you."

"Then you are as good of friends as I thought?"

"Most assuredly. Now what did he do?"

She again became bashful. "Is he always so open - I mean indiscreet?"

"Arsène indiscreet?" Philipe couldn't help a snicker.

She grew angry at his amusement. "He kissed a woman on guard duty! Oh, how could I be so foolish in my ignorance?" She began to pace, trying to restrain her emotions.

"Sabrina, I met Arsène my first day as a Musketeer five years ago. Despite his faults, he is an honorable man. He would not be so crass toward you, nor derelict in duty." He stopped her to search her flustered face. She shied at his interest. "Have you feelings for Arsène?"

"He was ignorant of observance until after. She sauntered up to him, and he pushed her away." She didn't make eye contact while speaking, but his prolonged silence made her venture a glance at him.

"Then Arsène did not instigate the encounter, did he?"

"No."

"This maybe a simple misunderstanding. I shall speak to him."

Her head snapped up in surprise. "No! I mean, have I any right to be so angry with him?"

The giggling voices of three women reached their ears. The group walked passed the gate, unaware of their attention. Charlotte Talbert was among the women.

"You saw them kiss?" one asked of Charlotte.

"Yes. And little miss country girl turned green with jealousy."

"So they are lovers!" said another.

"I daresay her prim and proper upbringing didn't last too long. Lamonreaux made certain."

Sabrina clenched her hands to maintain her anger and upset. Philipe seized her hands in an effort to divert her attention from the women back to him.

"I will escort you to the carriage."

She held onto his arm with both hands, not daring to speak. At the carriage, the servant opened the door for her.

Philipe touched her cheek to make her look at him. "Think no more about it. I shall speak to him."

"Dear Philipe, you are a true friend." She kissed him lightly on the cheek.

"Yes, ... well." He flashed an awkward smile and helped her into the carriage. He shut the door and ordered the driver to go. He remained watching the carriage, a ripple of confusion crossing his features.

A nearby clock chimed three, rousing Philipe from his stupor. Arsène's watch was over and he more than likely left the compound. Thus Philipe left the palace.

Arsène barely entered his apartment when the door burst open. He snatched the pistol from under his tunic, whirled about and aimed. "Philipe! Be thankful I'm not trigger-happy. You would be dead."

An angry Philipe stood in the threshold, but Arsène didn't notice, relieved at not having shot his friend and placed the pistol on the table.

"Next time don't come in so fast, you might not be so lucky," he said as lit the lantern on the table. "Now—," he turned to Philipe, but his words cut short by a left fist sending him backwards into the table then to the floor.

"You better have a good explanation, Gascon!"

Arsène gaped in hurtful surprise. He touched the right side of his jaw and flinched in pain. Nothing appeared broken, but painful and his lower lip bled. "Why did you strike me?"

"Don't play the fool! You know why."

"If I did, would I let you get away with hitting me?"

"You deny it?" Philipe accused, the darkened eyes narrowing.

Arsène touched his lip again and stood. "Deny what?"

"The scandal with Sabrina!"

Arsène growled and swore. "*Zut!* She's as vindictive as her mother!"

"I knew you were lying."

Arsène seized Philipe by the collar. "I'm not lying! I endured your blow and your scorn, my friend, but don't press me with your mockery!"

"Explain yourself."

Arsène released Philip. "Jeanette Charise made advances to me on duty. When I refused, she threatened me with scandal concerning Sabrina. She kissed me, not I her! *Auggh!* Her kiss is poison and I could not stomach it. Sabrina is a victim of spite because Jeanette believes she and I are intimate."

"Where did she get that idea? Your handkerchief perhaps?"

"Philipe, please! Upon my word, I told you the truth!"

Philipe's expression softened at noticing blood from the wound his blow caused. "Jeanette is a devilish girl who beds every man she comes across. She's tried to seduce me."

"I would be a better conquest since I refused her mother. And the duchess was privy to it all, maybe even an instigator." Arsène wiped the blood from his lip and crossed to a cupboard. He took down a bottle of wine and two cups.

"Will you tell Rohan?"

"No. She vexes him enough. What of Sabrina? I tried to find her, but she left in the company of Borchard." He poured the wine, setting the second cup across from him for Philipe. A plate of bread and cheese were already on the table next to the lantern.

Philipe sat, eyeing the cup, biting his moustache. Without hesitation, Arsène offered him a drink.

"Well?" pressed Arsène, watching Philipe.

Philipe snatched the cup and took a drink before answering. "I didn't see Borchard. Sabrina was alone and upset." He looked at Arsène. "Are you aware she has feelings for you?"

107

Arsène nodded, his despondence evident. "Believe me, Philipe, she is the last person I want to hurt. On the contrary, because of her I want to change my reputation."

"You have a strong reputation."

"Plague take it! It's all false! Well, a good deal of it anyway."

Philipe took a drink without comment.

"In my attempt to change, I made it worse. And included someone I wish it never touched." He sighed. "Were we not once as innocent and blameless as Sabrina, or have we been so demoralized by this accursed Court we cannot yearn for our lost innocence? Are we to become like those twice our age, devoid of hope because they are so far in there is no way out? Oh, my dear friend, everything is so confusing." He took a bite of bread. "Aaah!" he moaned in pain, spitting out the bread and massaging his jaw.

"I'm sorry."

Arsène studied Philipe, the hazel eyes dark and he chewed on his mustache, something he did when vexed or troubled. "You would have done more to me if your conscience allowed. Be honest. You have more than brotherly feelings towards Sabrina."

"You're imagining things." Philipe drank and refilled his cup.

"I didn't image this." Arsène pointed to his jaw and lip.

"I already explained! I would act the same for Adele." Philipe's movements grew agitated and he drank more.

Arsène watched the nervous action. "Then you refuse to admit it?"

"There is nothing to admit. I hit you because I thought you compromised Sabrina." Philipe tried to act nonchalant in his reply, but his agitation was told in his darkened eyes and shifting in his seat.

Arsène shook his head in disbelief. "No, you are afraid of something. Is it confrontation with me, or refusal from Sabrina?"

Philipe bolted up. "I won't sit here and be interrogated! I gave my reason. Let that satisfy!" He stormed out.

Arsène stared at the door in concern over Philipe's strange behavior. In truth, he found the whole afternoon disturbing. Snatching his hat, he left his apartment to make his way to Le Petite Chateau. More than likely Dominic would be home and informed of what happened. Of his two dearest friends, he most respected and admired Dominic. Philipe was a comrade-in-arms, gallant companion, and stalwart confidant but Dominic a true nobleman in character and rank. For his mammoth size, he possessed an even-temper and fair mind. Yet a mere glance of annoyance or growl of anger when aroused could intimidate any man. Dominic cared a great deal for Sabrina and would jealously protect her. The first problem was how to approach him in respect to this incident. Although Dominic never condemned or reproved Arsène's lifestyle, he now unwittingly compromised Sabrina. This confrontation would be a true test of their friendship.

In the private study, Arsène found Dominic tending to paperwork. At the stern look from his friend, he removed his hat. "Good evening, Monsieur le Comte."

Dominic said nothing in reply to the formal address.

"Is Mademoiselle Charbonier at home?"

"Yes, but I don't think you should speak to her."

Dominic's aloof behavior and answer stung Arsène, and frustration came out. "You don't believe the rumor too? Gad, Philipe bust upon me like an enraged bull and knocked me to the floor!"

"He did what?" asked Dominic in surprise, observing the injury.

"Well, I didn't get this bruise on my jaw from walking into a door!" Arsène forgot his humble posture and straightened.

"You deserved it for involving Sabrina in one of your sordid affairs!"

"No! Jeanette Charise tried her wiles and I refused. I didn't know Sabrina was nearby until Jeanette pointed her out. And the duchess witnessed everything. Although my guess is she prompted Jeanette, who ignored me for year. Why suddenly seek to humiliate me now unless incited? This is all a terrible misunderstanding. Please, Dominic, I need to speak to Sabrina."

"I wasn't told of Jeanette or the duchess."

"I doubt Sabrina knows of the duchess' machinations, or Jeanette's history. Nor is this the way she should find out."

"Agreed. Only Sabrina doesn't wants to see you."

Arsène winced, the pain on his face intense. "Then how can I apologize?"

Dominic tilted his head in uncertainty. "I'll speak to her on the matter and let you know."

Arsène fingered the brim of his hat, his earlier reticence returning. "This scandal is an unfortunate repercussion of my past for which I am sorely trying to make amends and somehow alter. In truth, I'm very fond of Sabrina. More so than any other woman. In an honorable way, I assure you! Please believe me, I would not trifle with her affections or harm her. Soothe, I would give my last drop of blood to protect her from injury."

An awkward silence fell during which Arsène tried to withstand Dominic's scrutinizing gaze. He began to wonder if he could make amends. He turned to withdraw but when he reached the door he heard Dominic say, "Sabrina's in the family salon." Arsène turned, not certain of what he heard.

"I maybe foolish to let you speak to her but—"

"You won't regret it! I swear!" Arsène flashed a smile and headed for the salon.

Dominic followed Arsène into the hall but stopped when Adele hurried around the corner heading for the front door. Gérard followed. "Where are you going?"

"To Philipe."

"Is he hurt?"

"Not physically, but he's in need."

"If you feel so strongly I shall come too."

"No. This is not be the first time I go out alone at night. I shall be safe with Gérard."

"Arsène is here. He explained how Jeanette Charise did this in vengeance for refusing her and the duchess added her machinations. I agreed to allow him to speak to Sabrina. I believe they share feelings for each other."

Adele's glanced back toward the salon and touched her husband's arm. "Stay near. I sense a fragile blossom about to be pricked."

"Summon me if something is wrong."

"Of course." Adele left with Gérard.

110

The salon was the smallest room in the house, designed for intimate family gatherings. An intricately carved and sculptured mantle dominated the room. A fire burned in the heath. Above the mantle was a portrait of the first marquis in full armor and seated upon his charger. Since the hearth was the focal point all furniture centered on it, from the red and gold brocade upholstered sofa to the embroidered side chairs. The heavy coordinating drapes were closed. Large iron candleholders stood in the four corners of the room. Each successive marquis modernized the interior of the old château. This room was paneled with mahogany and accented with gold gilding. Several displays of medieval weaponry hung upon the wall. The decorator had definitely been a male. Other rooms of the château reflected a more feminine and genteel nature than the drawing room.

Arsène stood just inside the door for a moment to watch Sabrina sitting in chair near the hearth doing needlepoint with a hoop. She did not look up. Either she was unaware of his presence or ignoring him. He cleared his throat in gathering his thoughts.

She began to speak. "Domi—What are you doing here?" she demanded in a cool voice.

"I needed to speak to you about this afternoon."

"I observed nothing unusual, from what I'm told." Her manner was cutting.

"Sabrina, please! To hear you speak falsely wounds me deeply."

"Lies wound *you*, Sergeant?"

"When it comes from one so honest, yes. At Court lying is an art."

"Perhaps I should go to Court more often and learn this art! That way I too shall have as smooth a tongue as you."

He sighed in doleful resignation. "Unlike yourself, I cannot claim purity in affairs d'amour. Yet, what you witnessed is not what you think."

"You were indiscreet all the same."

"She kissed me—!" began Arsène in passionate defense.

"You don't owe me an explanation, Sergeant! Your affairs are a personal matter," she interrupted, returning to her needlepoint.

"I do, sweet lady. Because I would not bed her she sought vengeance upon me by wounding you."

"Why would she do so? How did we become an item of gossip? Certainly not by my actions, Sergeant!" She bolted to her feet, the needlepoint falling from her lap to the floor.

"Neither did I given anyone reason to think such. I respect and admire your chastity and will not allow anyone to speak a cross word against you. If I had agreed, none of this would have happened."

"Is that minor point of gallantry supposed to excuse your folly?"

"Not an excuse!" He fought to contain his vexation. "I have experienced the Charise spleen before. A destructive and self-serving device used to get their way. If you doubt me, ask Dominic, Adele or Philipe. Much of my sordid reputation is false."

"Reputations usually begin with some facts."

"Yes," he droned in agreement. "Until now I never gave much thought to that *one* fact or the subsequent reputation it fostered. I had no reason."

"Is not your immortal soul a good enough reason?"

He drew a steadying breath at the pleading in her eyes. "Others tried to counsel me on faith. However, at Court the virtues of one's upbringing are sorely tested. I thought, I'm young and have enough time for faith when I'm older."

"Think of the times you could have been killed. What would that do to your timing?" Her words were cynical, but a faint quiver of passion in her voice.

Arsène noticed the weakening and became hopeful. He grinned. "They say a good woman could sooner turn a man than words."

She became flustered. "Your affairs are your own concern, Sergeant Lamonreaux!"

"I don't want affairs!" he said in exasperation. He stepped forward, tossing his hat aside to seize her hands. They were cold and trembling but he made no mention of it. "Oh, sweet lady, to ask for your love is too much for the wretched man I am. But upon my honor I swear, I never would do anything to hurt you."

For a moment she couldn't speak.

He grimaced at her silence, perhaps he had been impulsive, but he couldn't give up not since he admitted his feelings. "Reputations be cursed for their ugly and twisted maledictions!" he swore. "I beg you, say you believe me and I pledge from this day forth to do all within my power to change my reputation! If you cannot, then Jeanette has succeeded." She shied, glancing down. His heart sank at her avoidance and he murmured, "I'm all the more wretched than when I came."

She still did not speak and his heart sank, thus he lowered his head to gather his emotions.

"Sabrina, don't be so quick to judge," began Dominic. He entered unnoticed. "Yes, a folly occurred, but not intentional."

"Thank you for the confidence," began Arsène. "Alas, when a rumor is believed as fact for any length of time it is hard to reverse without someone not liking or not wanting it so."

"You just have to want it more."

"I do!" declared Arsène, tightening his hold on Sabrina's hands. "I admit weakness in failing to stifle those rumors, or more rightly, manly pride in allowing them to grow. However, I cannot control the actions of others. Without your faith in me, there is no purpose."

"Why?" was her simple question.

"Why?" he echoed with uncertainty. He sent an apprehensive glance to Dominic. A short benevolent nod told him frankness would be met with favor. Arsène turned back to Sabrina. "You not only showed me kindness, but for the first time given me a reason to fight this devil of abandonment. True, you spoke of my immortal soul, as others also, and though I believe in God, the idea of living such a chaste and faithful life seemed almost impossible for me. Thus I lost my innocence."

"Such a life is impossible if we attempt to live our life in our own strength. Relying on God's strength, nothing is impossible."

Arsène grinned. "With my intellect I acknowledge that. Alas, my heart and emotions are not well grounded enough to withstand temptation. Your moral strength and chastity brings clarity and tangibility, more so than at any other time in my life. I beg your forgiveness and seek your encouragement. Please, say you believe in me."

Her response was barely above a whisper "I do."

He kissed her hand in relief. "Thank you." He turned to Dominic, his Gascon smile appearing. "I don't know which was harder, dealing with you two together or Philipe alone."

She noticed the bruise on his jaw and touched it. "What happened to your face?"

He flinched in pain, but covered his reaction with a gallant smile. "An accident."

Dominic chuckled but a stern glare from Arsène stifled him.

Her suspicions were aroused by the exchange. "Accident? Philipe said he would speak to you."

"He did."

"The bruise?"

"An accident."

She stiffened, glancing askew at him. "Very well. If that is what you wish to tell me, I believe you."

"Oh, sweet lady, you cut me to the quick!"

"Some wine to ease the pain?" said Dominic with a smirk.

"No, thank you. I already pressed upon your hospitality. I bid you both good-night." In ardent respect, he kissed her hand then fetched his hat and withdrew.

"He cares deeply for you, Sabrina. I never saw him so humble and sincere. Not that he is an arrogant lout, rather carefree. But a man of his word and I believe him."

"I care for him, which is why I became jealous."

Dominic embraced her and kissed her forehead. "I know and so does Arsène."

Adele became apprehensive at the darkness of the Bourdias house.

"Maybe he's not home, madame," said Gérard.

"No, he's here." Adele knocked.

Roger opened the door. "I knew you would come," he said to Adele with a smile of relief. "He's in the study."

By the light of a dying fire, Philipe sat in a chair before the hearth, staring at the embers. He almost jumped out of his seat when Adele touched on his shoulder. "I didn't hear you come in."

He had been drinking, as evident by an empty wine bottle and cup on the side table. His baldric was removed, the doublet opened and the shirt untied about his throat.

She sat on the footstool to better see him. "You're deeply troubled. Why?"

Confounded, he shook his head. "I have raised my sword in battle and been forced to kill. But today I did something I never did before, and pray to God will never do again!" He clenched his left fist. "I lost my head and raise my hand in anger against a dear friend."

"Arsène."

"Yes, Arsène, *mon frère esprit*. Oh, the horrible hurt look on his face after I hit him! I'll never forget it."

"Why?"

His response was slow and uncertain. "I don't know. That's not true. I mean I'm not sure. Arsène asked me to be honest but how can I when I'm uncertain of my own heart? When I learned of the rumor about he and Sabrina, I became enraged that scandal touched her. She was distraught and I promised to speak to him. I went to his apartment with every intention of learning the whole story. Yet when I saw him, a strange anger overcame me and my fist went without giving him a chance to explain!" He snarled in disgust at his left fist clenched so tight the knuckles turned white and the nails dug into the flesh of his palm.

Concerned, she held his fist. Not only was his hand clenched, but his entire body rigid and taut. "What really happened?" she asked, hoping to divert the rage his of self-reproach.

"Jeanette Charise acted out of spite after Arsène refused her this afternoon. He said the duchess was there also and believes they staged it to entrap him and wound Sabrina. But regardless, I struck a dear friend in anger. Perhaps, more honestly, a jealous rage," he admitted in slow painful words. In doing so, his whole posture changed. The rigid muscles and sinews almost sagged as the hot fuel of passion drained from him.

She was grateful, but still concerned. "What are you going to do?"

"I've been sitting here for hours trying to decide. Arsène asked me what I was afraid of—confrontation with him or rejection from Sabrina. After how horrible I felt striking him, yes, I'm afraid. As for Sabrina, she treats me like a brother. *Zut!* I don't know!"

She touched his cheek. "Would you prefer I speak to Arsène?"

He heaved a futile shrug. "To what purpose? He confessed he's trying to change because of Sabrina. Despite it all, they appear so natural together. She has taken to him in a way I could only hope for. To tell her is out of the question." He turned back to the dying embers.

"You must have given Arsène some explanation."

"He didn't believe me."

"If he already suspects, why not tell him so?"

"How do you tell a friend you love more dearly than a brother, and for whom you have risked your life, as he has for you, that you are in love with the same woman? The one for whom he is struggling to redeem himself?" He shook his head. "I believe the confession would be a deadly blow to him, and I would sooner perish than strike another blow, verbal or physical."

"There seems no solution to your dilemma."

"At present, no. For now, leave them believing my affection is platonic. Only you will know the truth." He looked up at Adele. "Are you well?"

"Just weary, which is natural."

He stood, pulling her to her feet. "Go home. You need to take care of yourself and the child."

"You're as much a part of me as this child."

"So is your husband, who I'm certain is not pleased with your coming here at this hour of the night," he scolded, escorting from the room to the front door.

"Gérard is with me."

"Nevertheless get home before Dominic worries." He turned to Gérard. "See she gets home safely."

✦ Chapter 8 ✦

SEVERAL DAYS LATER, SABRINA PUT ON HER CLOAK and pulled up the hood as she left Court. Since the incident on the terrace, she asked for Gérard to come with the carriage to drive her home. Not that she was completely avoiding Arsène, rather wanted time to think and consider their relationship and for the gossip to subside.

Just beyond the gate, three men were engaged in a heated conversation and blocked her path. She recognized Captain de Lacy, whose angry countenance intensified his dark formidable features. Even in the early twilight, the others were familiar but both wore heavy cloaks so she could not see them clearly from her position. They did not see her, so she hid behind a gatepost to avoid trouble.

The voices were muffled, and the taller of the two-cloaked men did most of the talking. The conversation sounded more like a scolding and de Lacy did not agree with the taller man and kept tossing disagreeable looks to the third gentleman. When the conversation appeared over, Sabrina waited until the path clear before stepping out from her concealment to make her way to the carriage. Upon reaching the carriage, she heard a voice from behind.

"Mademoiselle Charbonier."

Startled, she whirled about. "Arsène!"

He noticed her nervous, disturbed pallor. "Is something wrong?"

She didn't immediately reply, looking past him, but no one was there. She spoke low and hurried. "Two men in cloaks had an argument with Captain de Lacy over there."

He followed her indication. "Between here and the gate?"

"Yes. They're gone now."

"Did you hear what was said?"

"No, more tone and expression that suggested a disagreement. It may be nothing and I'm over reacting."

He shook his head. "Not where de Lacy is concerned. Which makes my arrival all the more pertinent."

"Why are you here?"

"I miss escorting you home. I came to ask for that privilege again."

Sabrina balked. Since his apology, he acted most courteous, only she made excuses due to conflicting feelings. She tried to convince herself the avoidance to the gossip, but now faced with the direction question what should she say?

Arsène mistook her reticence and spoke with an effected sigh. "You have not missed our walks and conversations as much as I."

"No," she said, quickly looking up.

"No?" he continued his prodding, adding a tiny frown.

"I mean, yes."

His frown gave way to a grin.

She became annoyed. "You have a vexing way of flustering people, Arsène Lamonreaux!"

He smiled. "Perhaps. However, after what you have told me, it is prudent I escort you home."

"And if I choose not to?" she said in sharp reproach. "The carriage is here."

His face fell, deflated by the challenge. "Then I shall be properly chastised with a wound to the heart."

She bit her lower lip at a shadow of despair in his voice.

"My sweet lady." He took her hands. "Through no fault of either of us there has been a terrible misunderstanding. I beg you, do not allow any more time to pass. For each day the hurt can fester deeper and possibly destroy a cherished relationship before it truly begins."

"I don't want that. But my feelings ..." her voice failed her.

"I can lay to rest those feelings of jealousy if you let me. If not, jealousy can become doubt, and doubt, mistrust, and possibly hatred." He lifted her chin to gaze into her eyes, his voice pleading and urgent. "Are you brave enough to face that? I know I am not."

119

No, she had not been brave, not by avoiding him and not now in response to his heartfelt plea. A reprieve to gather her feelings was granted by Adele's arrival. She too pulled up the hood of her cape.

"Sorry I'm late, Sabrina. Hello, Arsène. Is everything all right?" she asked at seeing their guarded expressions.

Sabrina's expression changed to congenial and she took hold of Arsène's arm. "Yes. I just accepted a gracious offer of escort."

He smiled, wide and pleased.

Adele quelled a grin to give him a mock tone of stern warning. "Don't tarry, Arsène, take her straight home. The Queen invited us to dinner."

"As you say, Countess," he said, touching his hat with nod.

Gérard helped Adele into the carriage then climbed onto the driver's seat. The carriage moved off in one direction while Arsène and Sabrina walked off in another direction.

A brief traffic snarl of several carts and a carriage delayed their arrival at the chateau. Gérard opened the carriage door for Adele. Before alighting, she glanced at her watch.

"We shall need the carriage in two hours, Gérard."

"Very good, Countess."

Adele just stepped out when an armed man jumped Gérard from behind. The struggle was brief, a knife between the shoulder blades killed Gérard.

Adele screamed and ran into the house. The man followed, blocking her path to the closest room, forcing her to take flight up the stairs but he intercepted her.

Meanwhile, Arsène and Sabrina were joined by Philipe and near enough to the Charbonier residence to hear a female scream.

Philipe's eyes widened with horror. "Adele!" He raced to the house. He passed the carriage and barely took notice of the fallen Gérard for hearing another scream from inside.

Arsène knelt to examine Gérard. "He's dead," he said to Sabrina's horror.

"No!" came Philipe's shout from inside.

Arsène responded to his friend's distress call by rushing inside. Philipe was at the top of the stairs, running; Adele lying in an awkward position on the foyer floor. The butler, André, knelt beside her. Arsène moved to examine Adele.

"She fell! Down the stairs," the butler rushed to explain. "Is she alive?"

Arsène touched the side of Adele's neck to feel for a pulse and she groaned. "Adele."

Her eyes fluttered open. "Arsène—"

"Hush, don't speak. André, Fetch the surgeon!"

Sabrina stood with her hands covering her mouth, fearful as she watched them with Adele.

"She's alive. We need to get her to bed." Arsène carried Adele upstairs with Sabrina following.

Philipe burst in the room. The man tried to elude him by entering a bedchamber. Before the man reached the window, Philipe seized him and with a hard left to the jaw sent him to the floor. He immediately pounced upon him, grabbing him by the collar.

"Who are you? What do you want with my sister?"

The man gaped in terror. "I'll be killed if I tell!"

"You'll be killed if you don't!"

The man gasped at the pressure upon his throat and shook his head.

Whether out of sheer terror or insistence, Philipe did not care. "Answer me! Who sent you and why?"

"Not—Adele!" The man tried to breathe.

Philipe released his grip enough so the man would not faint. "Speak!"

"I was sent for Sabrina Charbonier. I thought she was in the carriage!"

"By whom you were instructed?"

"No, please! He'll kill me!"

Philipe whipped out his dagger. "You have more to fear from me!"

The man gaped at the menacing blade inches from his throat. "I didn't see his face! He wore a large cloak, mask and hat. That's all! I swear!"

"Where were you supposed to take her?"

"To a house on the Rue de St. Germain. Oh, if I had known—but she got into the carriage and I thought—!"

Philipe jerked him to his feet and dragged him from the room. In the hall they met Arsène.

"Who's he?"

"The one who assaulted Adele!"

Arsène gave the man such a loathsome glare that he cringed. Arsène spoke to Philipe. "I took her to her room and sent André for the surgeon."

"Mercy, messieurs! I didn't mean to harm her! It was a mistake!"

"Our cloaked friend sent him for Sabrina. He mistook Adele for her."

"Here now! What's this?" Dominic bounded up the stairs.

Arsène snatched the fellow from Philipe. "How many times have I told you, Maurice, never bother the lieutenant unless it is important!" he shouted, leading the man downstairs.

"Monsieur, my name is not Maurice," the man protested.

"No more excuses, Maurice!" shouted Arsène to drown the protest.

From the top of the stairs Philipe watched Arsène drag the man to the front door. Dominic went to speak, but Philipe put up a sharp hand to stop any questions as Arsène shoved the man outside.

"Now good night!" Arsène remained in the threshold staring after the man then gave a curt nod to Philipe before vanishing out the door.

"Where is Arsène going? Who was that man?" insisted Dominic.

"Our Gascon is going to do what he does best. Trust him." Philipe placed a steady hand on Dominic's shoulder. "There's been an accident and the surgeon sent for."

"Accident? Gérard is dead from a knife in the back! The truth."

"I don't know the details, but—Adele fell down the stairs—"

"Good God! How bad is she hurt?"

"Nothing appeared broken."

"And the baby?"

Philipe shrugged ignorance. "The surgeon can tell us."

Ten minutes later, the surgeon arrived. Sabrina made Dominic and Philipe wait in anteroom. Dominic didn't like waiting and the longer they waited, the more agitated he became, pacing the room.

"I don't know what I'd do if anything happens to her."

"Steady, old friend."

Dominic stared at Philipe, but the latter could not meet his gaze. "What are you not telling? For mercy's sake, hold nothing back!"

"It is best to wait until we learn of Adele's condition and Arsène returns."

The door opened, and a sniffling Sabrina appeared escorted by a grim surgeon. Dominic's breath caught in his throat and Philipe bit his mustache so hard he flinched.

"Adele?" Dominic barely uttered her name.

"She is alive. The fall killed the baby," said the surgeon.

Thunderstruck, Dominic fell into a nearby chair trying not to weep. Sabrina went to him, but could offer little comfort.

"I'm sorry, monsieur."

"What of my wife?" he asked in choked voice.

"Rest is what she needs now, but she should recover. Only time will tell if she can bear another child. I have already taken care of the baby so you need not concern yourself."

"Can I see her?"

"Wait until morning. I gave her a sleeping draught. You too should rest, monsieur. I'll return in the morning." He touched Sabrina's arm. "You did well, my dear."

She spoke a muted thank you before the surgeon left. "Who would do such a thing? The poor child," she sobbed.

Philipe embraced her. "You've been very brave though all this." He stroked her hair and kissed her cheek.

Sabrina wiped her eyes. "I'm better now." For the first time she realized someone missing. "Where's Arsène?"

Philipe winced at the question and shrugged. "I'm not sure. The full explanation of this tragic affair must wait for his return."

"And no more excuses, Philipe! Tell me." Dominic stood.

"Dominic, don't upset yourself any more," she said.

"No, Sabrina," began a contrite Philipe. "Let us retire to the drawing room and not disturb Adele."

Once in the room, Philipe poured wine and went to give a glass to the others. Sabrina accepted the wine but Dominic refused, expression fixed and heavy.

Philipe took a long drink before speaking. "Our cloaked friend sent a brigand to kidnap Sabrina and mistook Adele for her."

Sabrina paled with horror and sat. "I didn't think anyone saw me."

"What?"

"Earlier—two cloaked men argued with Captain de Lacy. I told Arsène and he insisted on escorting me home. Adele took the carriage."

André entered. "This note just came, monsieur." He handed it to Dominic and withdrew.

Dominic waited for the door to close before reading. "Rohan's back."

Philipe flashed a smile. "Do you realize what this means? We may be able to unmask our traitor tonight!" He began to leave.

"Wait! Where are you going?"

"To find Arsène. By the look of the buffoon he'll head straight to our cloaked friend!" He hastened out of the room.

Dominic ran after Philipe calling from the top of the stairs. "How will you find him?"

Philipe paused at the front door and flashed a cunning smile. "I know the street. Finding the house is Arsène's task." Without further explanation, he raced off into the night.

The bustling streets of day gave way to the stillness of night. Arsène took advantage of the elongating shadows to hide his pursuit, but by the way the man moved he was unaware of being followed and headed straight for a house on the Rue de St. Germain. Arsène ducked into a doorway when the man looked about before entering the house. Arsène moved closer and squatted down beside a front window. The shutters were closed but light came through the slats. There was a shuffling of feet. From what he could see, he counted three men according to feet and legs. The door to the room burst open.

"Monsieur!"

Arsène recognized the voice of the man he followed. He tried to peek inside for a better view than feet, but had to content himself with listening and memorizing voices.

"Barcarté, where's the girl?" a deep bass voice asked.

"She was the wrong one, monsieur!"

"Wrong one?" another low voice quickly asked.

Arsène tried to match the voice to those he knew.

"It was not her, but one called Adele," said Barcarté.

"What is going on, monsieur?"

To this voice, Arsène started, then scowled in recognition.

"My urgent summons was to inform you we were observed by Mademoiselle Charbonier. I sent Barcarté to fetch her for questioning. He failed!" the first said. "How did you escape?"

"I didn't, they let me go."

"What? And you came hither straightway? Stupid fool, you could have been followed!"

"*Pardieu!*" the second exclaimed. "You don't think?"

"Yes! Why else? His task is to follow people."

Arsène bit his lip in surprised concern. This man knew him.

"Monsieur, if we are discovered—" the familiar voice protested.

"Silence! I have listened to your protests once today. Search the perimeter for spies!" the first commanded.

Philipe paused at the corner when Arsène crouched outside the window. Before he could join Arsène, the Gascon bid a hasty retreat from the window. He stepped out to follow when the front door of the house opened. He pressed against the shadow of the building. Two men stepped outside. Both wore swords and one held a club, the second a pistol. Philipe's pulse raced and he dared not breathe. Only the shadow of the building veiled him from their view fifteen feet away. Without warning, a hand covered his mouth while another hand dragged him off balance backwards and around the corner. He struggled, but the firm grip swung him about and pinned him hard against the building. He lowly groaned when the back of his head struck the wall.

"Shhh!" hissed Arsène, retaining his hold of Philipe.

Philipe's relief was cut short at hearing a familiar voice. "Dead or alive, I don't care. But find him!"

Arsène said nothing to Philipe's surprise rather tugged on him to follow. Not until they traveled a safe distance did they stop.

"You must be more careful. I saw you take up position at the corner."

"I came to find you and tell you Rohan is back in Paris."

"He will be interested in this evening's events, considering there are now two traitors."

"Two? Did you see who they were?"

"No, but you heard their liaison. Come."

On his part, Rohan expected a visitor. He always sent a note to each of his agents upon returning to Paris. Arsène responded by promptly calling upon him. He worked in his private study when Arsène and Philipe arrived.

"You returned at a very appropriate time, monsieur. Our suspicions are confirmed in respect to the liaison," said Arsène.

"De Lacy."

"Yes. This evening he met with two men at a house on the Rue de St. Germain."

"Two?"

"The second must be new, for until now I only followed one, and the same man. I'm sure of that."

Rohan scratched his beard. "What brought about this discovery?"

126

Philipe took up the explanation. Rohan was saddened by the news of Adele and Dominic's misfortune yet swore when Arsène mentioned de Lacy during his part of the story.

"The mistaken identity must have occurred when Sabrina left with me and Adele took the carriage."

"Why? What could they do with Sabrina after the interrogation?"

"Hold as hostage to gain time by thwarting our investigation. Who better than one unfamiliar with the intrigues of Court, and a relative of one of those trying to seek him out?"

Rohan slapped at the mantle. "All this tragedy in an attempt to use an innocent girl as a pawn! How is Dominic taking all this?"

"Grim. Though probably anxious for our return," said Philipe.

"Give him my condolences, and promise to help in any way I can."

Arsène's blue eyes grew intense under level black brows. "By using Sabrina these traitors can be secure at both ends. Especially after the difficulty with the marquis."

Rohan placed a supportive hand on Arsène's shoulder. "At least we know half the conspiracy. De Lacy will be the one to watch."

"Monsieur," began Philipe. "I maybe speaking the obvious, but only five men remained in Paris while you were away; and all aware of Arsène's talents and your instructions. Focusing on Lacy will arouse Richelieu's suspicions and give the traitor a reprieve."

"My dear Philipe, like most people you accept the illusion Richelieu creates for himself; that he is invincible. His position is only as secure as the King allows. Their relationship is out of fear and mutual need, not affection."

"Hard to imagine Richelieu acting out of fear."

"Fear makes him dangerous. Powerful emotions make powerful men."

"What about the traitors?"

"You think Arsène will not be more diligent in his surveillance?"

"Of course. I mean what action will you take? Summon a meeting of Le Resistance?"

Rohan shook his head. "Not until I hear from my brother or Lord Buckingham. As you don't want to arouse Richelieu's suspicion, I don't want to tip my hand to any traitor. For the present, do not keep Dominic waiting."

At the chateau, Dominic listened in fury about de Lacy and Arsène's theories. Sabrina was ashen and her hands clenched and knuckles white.

"Unfortunately, this implicates some members of the Huguenot leadership. Somehow there is a connection to the man who escaped me and this incident," said Arsène in conclusion.

"This has to do with the secret you won't tell me," she chided.

Dominic was slow to answer, tossing looks of consideration to Philipe and Arsène before finally answering, "Yes."

With a hard gaze at each man she said; "So I was right. You are the Huguenot Sword." She turned to Dominic, her voice mixed with anger and frustration. "I understand your concern, but if you told me I would have been forewarned. Perhaps this avoiding this tragedy."

He became rigid and flushed with anger. "Don't use such a argument with me! If I sent you to Trèvoux rather than attend the Spring Festival I would not have lost my first child!" He turned and called, "André!"

She recoiled at his rebuke and summoning of the butler.

"Escort mademoiselle to bed and secure the house for the night."

Although Arsène and Philipe were sympathetic, further words were useless and she left with André.

❧ Chapter 9 ❧

THRICE DURING THE NEXT COUPLE OF WEEKS, Sabrina came to the Palace at the request of the Queen to report on Adele's condition. Sabrina didn't like or approve of lying and Arsène's statement *at Court lying is an art* gnawed at her brain. However, under the circumstances, discretion was needed to protect the others. She accepted the truth behind the entrapment of Arsène by Jeanette. The killing of Adele and Dominic's unborn child in a case of mistaken identity during an attempted kidnapping upset her greatly. Despite the fact she was the intended victim, an innocent suffered in her place. Thus she spoke the words agreed upon with the others when summoned by the Queen.

Those in attendance of the Queen during Sabrina's third audience included Charlotte Talbert, Bridgette Charteaux, and the Prince de Condé.

"I'm glad to hear the countess is doing well. It greatly distressed me to hear of her misfortune. What of your cousin, is he well?" inquired the Queen.

"As well as can be expected, Your Majesty."

"Such tragedy as the result of some scandal is horrifying," said Charlotte.

Sabrina's features grew firm. "Pure misfortune. The man was a thief." Seeing Charlotte exchange skeptical glances with Bridgette, Sabrina fought to contain her anger at their scoffing. Charlotte's involvement with helping to spread the gossip infuriated her, not to mention the woman's pomposity.

"Are you betrothed to anyone?" asked the Queen.

Sabrina became baffled by the question, turning her focus from the ladies to the Queen. "What does that have to do with this?"

"Your understanding is not important. Her Majesty asked you a question, mademoiselle," Condé's husky bass voice rebuked.

"Forgive me, monsieur," she timidly said then addressed the Queen. "No, Your Majesty, I am not betrothed."

The Queen regally nodded. "Thank you informing us of our lady's progress. Express my good wishes for a speedy recovery. She is missed."

Sabrina understood the dismissal, curtsied and withdrew. She wondered about the brief yet strange conversation. The question of betrothal gave her pause for consideration. The thought of marriage was not one she seriously considered under the circumstances. Arsène's attention notwithstanding, numerous obstacles remained before she could entertain any thoughts of a future husband.

Sabrina returned to the carriage to find Philipe speaking to André. "A short visit," he said.

"I thought you were going to intercept Dominic and delay his return home."

Philipe grinned. "I was on my way to do just do when I saw the carriage and asked André the reason. I assume you were unable to speak to the Queen since he said you only left a few moments ago."

"No, I did, but it was a brief conversation which included an odd question if I was betrothed."

Philipe shook his head with a wry smile. "The Queen is—how shall I say—a woman in need of a hobby and tends to meddle."

She gave him a frustrated scowl. "I hope she doesn't meddle with me. The rumors have waned and I don't want them to start again, not when all is going better."

"Yes, Arsène is behaving himself so don't dwell on it." He opened the carriage door. "Besides, we have a surprise birthday party this evening."

She returned his smile only with an impish edge. "Indeed. But it won't happen if you don't go delay Dominic. So shoo!" She nudged his shoulder.

Philipe chuckled. "After you leave." He helped her into the carriage.

The surprise birthday party was a scheme Sabrina devised with Philipe to help Dominic and Adele recover from the loss of their child. Twenty invitations were sent, mostly to friends from Court. However, since the nasty rumor made Arsène's association with Sabrina more public, a degree of discretion was maintained for decorum and security. She expressed disappointment but understood the reason for his exclusion.

The château's Grand Chambre accommodated a hundred people, so the nearly forty guests fit comfortably within its walls. Three golden chandeliers illuminated the room. The inlay marble tile floor alternated in a pattern of white and gold. On one side of the room, French doors led to the terrace and in turn, a step down to the garden. On the far wall, opposite each door stood a mirror shaped like a window. Between the mirrors were white painted panels with gold gilded trim. The mirrors gave the room a larger appearance. Above the doors and mirrors was gold and carved crown molding from which an arched, marble white ceiling rose with gold trim. On the mirror side, and at each end of the room were white paneled and painted doors leading to other parts of the house. One door opened to the elegant formal dining room. The spacious rooms paled in comparison to the splendor of the Charbonier's Le Château Magnifique in Reims.

Half an hour after the guests arrived, Philipe escorted Dominic home. He took the surprise with a gracious smile.

"I wondered how he would react, considering all he spoke about was how terrible we are at keeping secrets," said Philipe to Sabrina as they watched Dominic with Adele. Philipe chose to wear the same suit he did for the Spring Festival, a dashing dark green suit with gold trim and fancy white lace, his sword at his right hip.

Sabrina's silk brocade gown gleamed in rosy opalescence. Rubies accented the gown and ornamented her hair and throat. She wore a scooped collar, but kept her shoulders covered. She flashed a plaintive smile. "Keeping secret is something I never thought we would do to each other."

Philipe took her hand. "Now, this is night for celebrating. I won't tolerate any remorse or gloominess." A cavalier smile appeared. "We haven't danced since the Spring Festival." When she smiled in agreement at hearing the music, he led her to the dance floor.

As the party went on, she found herself the object of Philipe's constant attention. They danced and dined together, yet her mind wandered elsewhere. She tried not to appear too preoccupied, but even the acrobats and jugglers only served as a brief distraction.

Arsène couldn't stay away yet waited until later in the evening. Around midnight, he made his way to the back of the chateau and discreetly entered the courtyard. Someone exited the house so he hid in the shadow. Sabrina. He smiled when she paused by the fountain and sat on the rim, her hand tracing the water.

"A lovely night."

Sabrina bolted up. "Arsè—!"

He placed a gentle finger over her lips and smiled. "Shh. Don't want to draw attention, now do we?"

She took his hand, her voice a low, hurried whispered. "What are you doing here?"

He heaved a casual shrug. "I suppose I could leave, if you insist."

"No," she said, giggling.

"Then you are glad to see me?" It was more a statement than question. His lips smiling and eyes roguish.

"Very glad."

The moonlight silhouetted her face and night beams danced on her hair and shined in her eyes. He drew her close and kissed her for the first time. He longed to kiss her, but never expected a mere kiss to send intense flames of passion through his veins. Mews of ardor escaped her lips. For both their sakes, he forced himself to stop and held her close.

"My dearest Sabrina. In all your charming innocence you did what I feared no woman could." He tilted her head toward him. "When we're apart you are constantly in my thoughts. I yearn for the next time I can see you, even just a passing glimpse when on duty. We've known each only a few months. Perhaps I'm presuming. I do have a reputation."

She smiled. "Since our encounter on the terrace, I knew there was something different about you. Something that makes me feels wonderful. My difficulty arose from conflicting feelings about the situation with my uncle. But each time I see you those feelings don't matter."

"I love you," he confessed. They kissed.

Philipe began to pass the courtyard doors and by sheer chance he saw them. He heard Arsène's declaration of love and observed their kiss. Not the way Sabrina kissed him, and he winced, his left hand clenching. He looked to his fist and turned away, disappearing inside the house.

From another doorway Dominic emerged and was seen by Arsène and Sabrina. His admonishing glance found Arsène. "I wondered if you would pop up this evening."

"I'm sorry. I couldn't help myself."

"Is there something you need?" she asked Dominic, diverting his focus from Arsène.

"Adele is asking for you. Some more guests are ready to depart."

"I better go. Excuse me."

Arsène bowed to her departure.

Dominic cleared his throat to get Arsène's attention. "What are your intentions toward my cousin?"

"My intentions are honorable. I love her."

"Strange for you to admit being in love."

Arsène scowled with annoyance. "I'm sorry if you find it difficult to believe a Gascon can have the same honorable feelings as a noble." He moved to leave but Dominic stopped him.

"You misunderstand. In truth, I suspected as much. However—"

"My reputation follows me like a plague! So this Gascon is good enough to be your friend, but not a relative?"

"Besides Philipe, there is no one else I would rather claim as kin."

Arsène caustically laughed. "He denies it to me, but confesses to you!"

"Confess what?"

At Dominic's ignorance, Arsène waved off his comment. "I would marry her if possible."

"I don't have the ultimate authority."

"Would Philipe be any better in the marquis' opinion?"

Dominic curiously regarded at Arsène. "What a strange question."

"Not so. What Huguenot would be good enough, noble or not?"

"Father is unaware of Philipe's conversion. Still, she is under my roof, but whether it is wise for you to continue seeing each other is another question."

"What does that mean?"

Dominic studied Arsène and replied in carefully chosen words. "My statement is protective of you and Sabrina. For now, let us take one day at a time. I must return to Adele. Try to leave unobserved."

Philipe called to Sabrina her from the threshold of a nearby room. "May I speak to you? In private?"

"Adele is in need of me."

"This will only take a moment. Please."

Sabrina smiled. "Of course."

Entering the room, Philipe's mind reeled in an attempt to find the words to speak and he bit his moustache.

"Philipe, is something troubling you?"

"Yes. Only I'm uncertain how to start. Something happened this evening to cause me to make a difficult decision. One that may come as a complete surprise to you." He gave a short cynical laugh and murmured, "Not may, will."

"Pardon?"

He swallowed back his emotions at the familiar eyes studying him with concern.

"Philipe?" She touched his arm, her gaze compassionate.

At her touch, he gave into his emotions, seized her and kissed her. Not a brotherly kiss and a muffled exclamation of surprise escaped and she stiffened. He released her. The expression of astonishment caused him distress.

"Forgive me, I didn't mean for it to happen like that!"

Sabrina remained speechless, attempting to recover.

"I owe you an explanation and apology, though you probably guessed the reason. Only recently my feelings changed. Tonight—in the courtyard—Arsène—" He grunted in frustration. "The kiss wasn't meant to happen! And by your reaction, I have my answer. Forget my folly!"

"How can I forget I hurt a dear friend?" she found voice to speak.

"It's not your fault. Neither is Arsène to blame. When he confronted me, I denied it."

"That's when you hit him."

He nodded and averted his eyes in shame. "I thought he compromised you. Only after striking him did I learn truth." He met her sympathetic gaze. "You love Arsène and he loves you. I needed to be sure, but not the way I wanted to find out."

"Dear Philipe, I'm sorry. You will always be a special friend to me."

He again averted his eyes to gather his emotions. "Tell no one of this. I made a fool of myself!" He rushed from the room.

His exit from the house stopped when Elizabeth Pontinière hailed him. Although no longer in a social mood, he could not be rude to a lady and especially a woman he once knew well. She wore her cloak also making ready to depart.

"I gave up hope. You were so preoccupied with Mademoiselle Charbonier, I thought to go home," she said.

"Forgive me. I didn't realize you wished to speak to me."

"Speak," she said with a downcast frown. "And dance. And socialize. Like we once did." She raised her eyes to him, her look unmistakable.

He smiled. "Yes, we did. I'm sorry I was preoccupied."

She took his arm. "I'm sorry your preoccupation has disturbed you. Can I help to improve your mood?"

He caught a glimpse of Sabrina with in the room behind Elizabeth. She did not see him since she conversed with Adele and another guest. His mood instantly changed.

"I would be grateful for your help." He took Elizabeth's hand to kiss her knuckles. They left.

❧ Chapter 10 ❧

ADELE RETURNED TO COURT TWO DAYS AFTER THE PARTY. She and Charlotte sat in private attendance of the Queen in Her Majesty's apartment. Adele occupied the chair nearest the window reading aloud. Charlotte and the Queen sat playing cards. Adele stopped reading at the announcement of Richelieu's arrival. She and Charlotte exchanged guarded glances for the relationship between the Queen and Cardinal was strained at best.

Richelieu greeted them in a cordial manner. "Your Majesty. Ladies."

The Queen regarded Richelieu, some trepidation in her eyes, but coolness in her voice. "Thank you for coming so promptly, Eminence."

"When Madame commands, all else ceases."

The Queen addressed the ladies. "Please excuse the Cardinal and me."

Adele tried to hide her discomfort at hearing Richelieu responded to the Queen's summons, but with the dismissal she closed the book and moved to one side of the room. Charlotte joined her a respectful distance away.

The Queen spoke first. "I received a response to your request. The terms have been accepted and shall be handled by the benefactor."

"How generous of monsieur. He comes to Paris then?"

"He should arrive within a week. Is that satisfactory?" she replied with an underlying tone of displeasure.

"A just boon for services rendered to the Crown, Madame."

"It better be for this goes against my better judgment to so intervene." The Queen darted a glance to Adele and Charlotte. The women tried to be discreet and appear disinterested.

Richelieu noticed the gaze and turned to see their reaction. Whether he approved of their presence was hard to tell. His stone cold features rarely betrayed any emotion, but when his eyes fell on Adele, he raised an eyebrow. A mere glance from the Cardinal unnerved even the most innocent of people and Adele shied away.

Richelieu returned to the Queen. "More is at stake than who a young lady's husband should be."

"I'm well aware of ramifications, Cardinal, which is why I agreed."

Richelieu bowed to the rebuttal. "Anything else, Madame?"

"In the future, if this gentleman has a further request, the Crown shall not give heed. Tell him so along with his good fortune."

"As Your Majesty commands." Richelieu bowed. "Ladies." He withdrew.

Adele tried to erase from her mind the Cardinal's unsettling look. What lay behind those eyes one could only hazard a guess. Finally, she approached the Queen.

"Madame, I know how difficult it is for you to speak to the Cardinal. Can Charlotte and I be of any assistance?"

The Queen's smile was faint and thin. "Perhaps *you alone* could act."

Adele took note of the emphasis on the words *you alone*. This visit became mysterious and alarming, but she kept her wits when the Queen continued to speak.

"You are still fatigued and recovering. Attend me tomorrow. Give my regards to your cousin and ask her to attend me the rest of the week."

More was conveyed in the Queen's eyes than the words she spoke and this heightened Adele's concern. "I will, Majesty. I'm sure my cousin will be honored."

Adele paused in the corridor to consider the situation. In a cryptic manner, the Queen tried to tell her something about Richelieu's visit and the boon, but what? *Did it involve Sabrina? Or is it simple courtesy to include her? Dominic! He should be home by now.*

Home is where she found him, sifting through business papers. Concerned for her excited state, he offered her a chair to sit, but she refused, and in hurried words, related the Cardinal's visit.

"Dominic, this frightens me! By the Queen's own words, I could possibly do something to stop this disagreeable boon. Do you think Sabrina is somehow caught up in all this?"

"I hope not."

"What about Arsène?"

Dominic shook his head and frowned. "He is under heavy surveillance by de Lacy. And if our Gascon suspects any person of conspiring against Sabrina, his impulsiveness may cause trouble."

"Philipe harnesses his impatience."

"True," he said with a faint smile. "But Philipe's duties occupy him so he may not be the effective counterbalance we need. No, we best keep them ignorant until we know if this mystery has direct bearing upon us. We should know in next few days."

During the week Sabrina attended Court, Adele kept alert for anything to suggest an answer to the riddle. The Queen said nothing specific yet a few times gazed at Sabrina with great sympathy. This disturbed Adele more, but she could not speak openly.

On Friday, André ran from the house when the carriage returned from Court and Adele was the first to emerge. In agitation he announced, "Oh, madame, the marquis is here!"

Sabrina's breath caught in her throat. "Uncle Jourdain?" She turned to Adele, who grew pale and appeared on the verge of fainting. "Adele?"

She ignored Sabrina, focusing on André. "When did he arrive?"

"Nearly three hours ago."

Her shock turned to anger. "Why did you not send word to me at the Palace?"

"Monsieur forbade me. He said he had some business before seeing anyone. He is very interested in mademoiselle's welfare."

Adele made an impulsive gasp and Sabrina seized her arm. "Adele, what is it?"

"No time to explain." Adele turned to André. "Where is he?"

"In the family salon."

Adele drew a deep steadying breath and took Sabrina's hand. "Come. We should not keep the marquis waiting any longer."

In the salon, Jourdain made himself comfortable. He stood before the hearth smoking a pipe. The rich black doublet of the traveling suit was unfastened.

Adele masked her nervousness behind a large smile of greeting. "Monsieur, what a surprise. If I knew you were coming, I would have arranged a proper greeting."

"Some unexpected business brought me to Paris." Jourdain's pleasant manner continued to Sabrina. "How are you, dear niece?"

Sabrina's was guarded in her response. "I'm well, Uncle. Is Aunt Madeline with you?"

"No, she will be along in a few days. It is good to see you again. I miss you in Reims, as does your aunt. How do you find Paris?"

"Not as quiet as Reims."

Jourdain chuckled and sat on the sofa. "No, it's not." He beckoned Sabrina to sit beside him. "Come, what have you been doing with yourself?"

She spoke after sitting. "Well, there are parties and the theater. Her Majesty has been most gracious. I spent this entire week with her."

Jourdain's jovial tone turned sullen. "Where the Queen is concerned dangerous political intrigue abounds. Mind you, I'm loyal to Her Majesty, yet politics sometimes must take precedent over personal preference."

"Uncle, you sound cryptic and ominous." Sabrina casting a side-glance to Adele, who sat in a chair opposite them, her face drained of all color.

Jourdain rose and returned to the hearth. He snatched a backward glance at his niece.

"Uncle, is something wrong?"

He turned to face her. "You are young and many things can happen to change the life of one so young. Not to mention middle-aged or older, but the young adapt more easily to change."

Adele's apprehension grew at his unusual civil and gracious behavior. Thus she asked a direction question. "Monsieur, what is the reason for this visit?"

"I came to Paris upon request. The task asked of me is a difficult one, but as I said earlier, the powers that be can change one's life; thus my decision."

"You are commanded by the King or Queen?" She waited in rapt attention for the answer.

Jourdain's usual firmness instantly returned. "By whom is of no importance. It is the decision that must be addressed."

Despite the rebuff, Adele did not back down and bravely countered. "Surely, the person is the reason for the decision."

He nodded to the rationality. "You are keen in the ways of Court, daughter; but my answer is the same."

The conversation unsettled Sabrina. "Uncle, what decision?"

He ignored her to ask Adele, "When does Dominic return?"

"Half past six."

The clock on the mantle read six o'clock. He turned to Sabrina. "The decision concerns you. The course of action is not totally to my liking, however personal feelings are laid aside for a better cause. Distressing rumors concerning you—"

"Are untrue!"

He put up a hand to stifle her protest. "True or false, scandal will not again touch this family. Though a closely guarded secret, it is a shame I bear concerning you and my son."

"Uncle!" she stammered with fright.

He then declared, "You are betrothed to the Comte de Borchard."

Sabrina's gasped in horror at the declaration.

The name staggered Adele for a moment before turning to fear concerning the marquis' connection to the boon the Cardinal and Queen spoke of—a marriage contract! How shrewd the marquis acted in telling them without his son present. Dominic would not accept the decision, no matter the consequences. If he succeeds in convincing Sabrina, Dominic will be pre-empted in any attempt to interfere. Were she to act on Sabrina's behalf, what little communication she had with the marquis would be destroyed. Thus she held her tongue in agonizing silence as he continued.

141

"In two weeks you shall become the Comtesse de Borchard."

Utterly broken in despair, Sabrina cried, "No!" and ran from the room.

Adele hurried after Sabrina, only to discover the front door stood open. "No, Sabrina!" she shouted, stepping out into the street. She looked up and down the street, but no sign of Sabrina. Fear turned to anger in glaring back at the salon. "André!"

The streets of Paris grew dark as the western skyline faded into twilight. Sabrina gave no thought to where she ran, and several times collided with people. All she knew was she must find Arsène, and would run until she did or collapsed from exhaustion. Tears blurred her vision and her breathing became labored, forcing her to stop lest she faint. She fell to her knees against a building, her heart pounded and she gasped for air. Her hair was disheveled and her face streaked with tears. She closed her eyes in an attempt to slow her racing heart.

Nearby a cat screamed, startling her. She looked at the surroundings and didn't recognize any buildings. Using the doorway, she pulled herself up and tried to retrace her steps to find a more familiar landmark. Fear gripped her when she heard footsteps behind her. Her blind haste may prove dangerous. She was alone at night on the streets of Paris somewhere unknown to her. An allusive shadow could be anything from a robber to a murderer and she was defenseless and lost. Someone grabbed her and she screamed.

"Sabrina! It's Philipe."

She sagged in relief, embracing him and weeping.

"What's the matter?"

"I must find Arsène!"

His face grew stern. "Is that why you're out here alone? What has the Gascon done now?" There was a cutting sarcasm to his voice.

"It's not what you think! Please, take me to Arsène!"

He could not refuse her tearful plea. "I was on my way home to meet him and Dominic when I saw you. Why do you seek Arsène in such haste?"

"I will only be able to explain once."

"Hush. I can wait to be told till then." He tightened his supporting arm about her waist.

At Philipe's house Adele rushed in, startling Dominic and Arsène. She barely spoke when Philipe arrived escorting a distraught Sabrina.

"It was foolishness to run off," scolded Adele, but half-hearted, more concerned for Sabrina's state.

"I had to." Weary, she collapsed into the chair

Arsène knelt by the chair, troubled. "What happened?"

"Arsène!" Her voice broke and she fell upon his neck, bitterly weeping.

He held her, his questioning glance found Philipe, who shrugged ignorance.

Adele spoke to Dominic. "Our mysterious benefactor has been revealed, your father. He told us in your absence."

"*Mon Dieu!* How?"

Adele woeful gaze passed to Sabrina. "The Comte de Borchard.

Dominic's brows rose in disbelief. "Father would not?"

She nodded, choked by emotions.

Dominic's whole body went rigid, his nostrils flared with anger.

"What about Borchard?" demanded Philipe.

"Sabrina is to marry him in two weeks," said Adele, but barely finished for the horror in Arsène's eyes.

"No!" he exclaimed.

"By order of the Queen and Cardinal."

"What do they have to do with this?"

"Last week Adele learned of a boon for services to the Crown that Richelieu pressed upon the Queen to arrange," said Dominic.

Philipe turned to Arsène in sudden comprehension. "Le Resistance."

Arsène's jowls tightened and he stood, fists clenched and glaring at Dominic. "You knew of this a week ago and didn't tell us?"

"There's so much intrigue at Court we were uncertain this boon dealt with us! My father clarified the mystery."

"He said due to the rumors of scandal this marriage was pressed upon him." Sabrina's grief turned to anger and her voice grew bitter. She stood. "Merciful heaven. He said he could no longer keep the family secret!"

"Blackmail? Your marriage for Borchard's silence? I'll kill him!" Dominic swore.

"No!" cried Adele in terror.

"Do so and all is lost," said Philipe.

"Philipe's right," began Arsène, his voice bitter. "They couldn't take her by force. So one, or both, approached the Cardinal with certain demands while blackmailing the marquis." His jowl's tightened and blue eyes grew virulent. "I'll kill him."

"No, Arsène!" Sabrina seized him. "His death may save me, but you will all be exposed and condemned as traitors! I can't let that happen."

"I won't let him have you!"

"I fear you will have to," she said with new mounting tears.

"We'll flee! Leave the country. Yes, to the New World," he said in desperation.

"No!" she said, forcing him to turn back to her and meet her eyes. "What fate would await the others if we fly? For all our sakes, I must marry him." She wept.

Arsène held her close, his own anguish giving way to tears.

In distress, Philipe turned aside and swore under his breath.

Dominic's expression shifted between anger, sorrow and determination. "Is my father still at the house?" he asked in a thick whisper.

"He was when I left," said Adele with care. "But you can't—"

His stern expression stilled her protest and stopped Philipe's intervention on her behalf. Dominic left and Adele hurried to follow.

"Rohan," said Arsène, hopeful. "He may know what to do, for this exposes Borchard as our traitor."

"Only one of them," said Philipe.

"We can't let this mockery of a marriage take place!"

Deliberate and somber, Philipe said, "We have to. Any action otherwise may prove dangerous, even fatal to any one of us or all of us."

144

"Please, Arsène! For my sake," she pleaded.

"What of you? Throwing your life away on some political marriage."

"I'm not throwing it away if I can save those dearest to me." She caressed his face. "Promise me to do nothing to endanger yourself."

With agonizing heartache he lashed out, "I cannot!" and ran from the room.

Sabrina screwed her eyes shut to fight back the tears. At a touch on her arm, her eyes opened. Philipe stood before her, sympathetic. She gripped his hand. "I beg you, dear friend, look after him for me."

He didn't reply and she grew fretful at his silence.

"Philipe, you are the only one I can depend on. Arsène and Dominic are too passionate to think and act clearly."

"Do you think I lack passion where you're concerned?"

"No, but if you too fail me then I will be throwing my life away."

Once again he stood mute with indecision.

"You hesitate? Why? I thought Arsène was your *frère esprit*. Can you stand by and let him be destroyed?"

"Of course not." He nodded with a sigh of resignation. "I will watch over our hotheaded Gascon. But heaven help me if he finds out I promised this. I will be the one knocked flat."

"Thank you."

Philipe patted her hand in response to her gratitude before leaving.

Dominic and Adele arrived home to find Jourdain ready to depart. His doublet was closed and hat on.

"I would speak to you, monsieur," began Dominic firmly.

Jourdain pulled on his gloves, ignoring his son. "Did you find Sabrina, daughter?

"Yes. She is with Philipe. He will bring her home after she composes herself."

"Did you hear me? I would speak with you upon this matter!" Dominic spoke louder.

Jourdain glared at his son. "Do not raise your voice to me, I am still your father."

"You came to my house when I was absent for the sole purpose of distressing my cousin and wife with horrid news!"

"When duty and honor demand attention, personal feelings are set aside. I will not tolerate your interference in this matter."

"Duty and honor be hanged! You were commanded to do this."

Jourdain squared his shoulders and straightened to his full height, still a few inches shorter than Dominic. "When those in authority command there can be no hesitation. Need I remind you all else is treason?"

"Queen or not, do you have any idea what you've done?"

"Monsieur," interrupted Adele when the marquis became suspicious at Dominic mentioning the Queen. "This is a difficult subject for my husband to keep his temper. I believe you should leave before further anger leads to an undesirable conclusion."

Jourdain's steady gaze never left Dominic as he replied: "You are a very wise woman. Sabrina will stay with me until the wedding. I will send a carriage for her in the morning." He snatched his riding crop and marched from the house.

"*Zut!*" swore Dominic. "Thank you for your intervention. I fear I made him all the more suspicious when I mentioned the Queen."

"What of Arsène? Will he kill Borchard?"

Dominic pursed his lips in worried contemplation. "I don't know. He can be impulsive but his mind is normally quick and clever. Let's hope Philipe can dissuade him from folly."

Philipe first went to Rohan's home, only the duke was not there and Arsène had not called. Foolhardy, but the only other place he thought to look was Borchard's chateau. He raced from Rohan's hotel to the count's home on the Rue Caquilliere and paused a few doors down to contemplate the situation. Going to the front door to inquire was out of the question. Looking about, the merchants closed for the evening and streets clearing. It shouldn't be too hard to find Arsène, if he were nearby. A hard hand clapped down on his shoulder and he reached for his sword, only stopped when Arsène demanded,

"What are you doing here?"

"Looking for you. Have you seen Borchard?"

"Rest easy. He's not home; but he will be."

"Hopefully not before I talk sense into you. His death may save Sabrina from the marriage, but you are not the only person this affects."

Arsène studied Philipe, whose darkened eyes became ill at ease under his steady gaze. "Do you still refuse to admit it?"

Philipe shook his head. "No. You were right, but I had yet to admit to myself I was jealous. Oh, the look on your face when I struck you! I would more tolerate your sword in my heart than such a look."

Arsène's hand clapped the back of Philipe's neck. "My sword will find Borchard's heart and end this misery for all."

"Confounded, Gascon! I agree Borchard is a loathsome beast and deserves full justice for his treachery, but not the way you want, at least not yet," he said with an emphasis catching Arsène's attention. "The wedding is in two weeks. Time enough to act without dangerous bloodshed. Use your quick mind to find a solution. I not only spoke of me, but Dominic and Adele also. We depend upon you. It may mean our lives if you fail us now!"

With a heavy sigh of torment, Arsène sat on an empty barrel before a closed wine shop. "Why, Philipe? Why, when I'm trying so hard to change and do right, is God punishing me?"

Philipe tilted his head with uncertainty. "I'm not the one to ask about such things. But I don't believe God is punishing you since He would be including Sabrina, who does not deserve such chastening. She would say this is a test of character. God can do no wrong in her eyes," he spoke the last sentence with a slight bit of sarcasm.

Arsène's wrath became renewed at seeing a carriage stop in front of the chateau. He reached for his sword but Philipe pulled him around the corner.

It wasn't until nine-thirty that Roger escorted Sabrina home. Dominic and Adele waited.

"Was Uncle Jourdain here when you arrived?" she asked.

"Yes, and we had words," he paused with hesitation, but her prodding look made him speak. "You are to remain with him until the wedding. He's sending a carriage in morning."

Sabrina fought back the tears and just nodded.

He took her hands, his voice and face urgent. "You are in my house and if you don't wish to leave I won't force you. On the contrary, I'll stop anyone who tries to take you against your will!"

"Except my new husband."

Her words were a heavy blow to him and he repined.

"I'm sorry. I know you would if I asked but this is my burden."

"No. This decision affects us all," said Adele.

Sabrina shook her head. "There is no decision to make. I must obey. To do otherwise—" her voice trailed off. Although she spoke truth, her countenance and nervous posture betrayed her inward battle to deal with the situation. She felt his touch upon her arm and continued, not looking at either of them. "I'll be ready to leave in the morning." She ran from the room.

Dominic followed, calling as she rushed upstairs. "If there is way to stop this wedding, God help me, I'll find it!"

✤ Chapter 11 ✤

RICHELIEU RARELY ROSE BEFORE TEN IN THE MORNING, yet he was to accompany the King on the hunt thus he wore a red velvet-hunting outfit. His boots were shiny and spurred. As always the large gold cross-adorned the chain around his neck. He wore no sword, for who would dare to draw upon the most feared man in France. A coordinating cloak flowed behind him as he was admitted to the King's private salon.

Louis was not dressed for riding and in a foul mood, making Richelieu curious, but the Cardinal's face twisted in displeasure at seeing the Captain of the King's Musketeers, François Tréville. Jealousy ran deep between the Cardinal and Captain. Tréville was a few years older, but compared to the maladies that plagued Richelieu, looked the younger of the two. Richelieu was forced to tolerate the captain due to Louis' affection for him since Tréville was a close friend of his late father. In matters of combat, Louis tried to model himself after the famed King of Navarre and often sought Tréville for guidance and comradeship.

"Has some mishap cancelled the hunt, Sire?" asked Richelieu.

Louis snatched several pages from off a table. "I received this report from Chevalier de Torais concerning the deteriorating situation at La Rochelle. The Huguenots received supplies from England and there is rumor of an armada led by Buckingham to support the rebellion."

Tréville nodded in agreement. "Late last night I received a most distressing report about the dwindling number of troops in the Fifth Regimental Musketeers and Third Regimental Guard due to rebel attacks and encounters with Huguenot smugglers."

"Sire, we must act swift and decisive," began Richelieu. "I therefore remind Your Majesty of the dike I proposed to block La Rochelle. With it, I can guarantee a fool-proof plan in six months time."

Tréville laughed in ridicule. "You jest? Dam the harbor, indeed!"

Richelieu eyes narrowed in contempt. "Mind your tongue, Tréville," he warned under his breath.

Louis did not hear the Cardinal's warning nor see Tréville's flush of rage as he took a seat to consider the suggestions.

Richelieu pressed his argument. "Sire, we must face the Huguenots with all our forces. These skirmishes are not only chipping away at our troops but the treasury also. It is more costly than a full campaign."

"I disagree," began Tréville. "We must wait for Buckingham's next move. To utilize all our forces before we know the enemy's strength is sheer folly."

"Captain Tréville!" snapped Richelieu.

This time Louis heard. "You realize what you just said, Tréville?"

"Sire, if the Cardinal wishes to play with trees and make paper plans so be it. But let us not put those plans into action until we are fully informed of the enemy's situation. Buckingham is a puppet with Rohan and Bouillon pulling the strings. We must not overlook the dangers within our own country."

Louis glanced to a red-faced Richelieu. "His reasoning is sound, however impertinent. Yet, refresh my memory of this dike."

"Sire, if you will permit me, I shall return this afternoon with detailed plans. Seeing them would more clearly describe the dike, than I can verbally."

"Do so, and recall Admiral Montmorency."

Richelieu was pleased, and looked for Tréville's reaction. The Captain's mood soured.

Louis addressed Tréville. "What of the request for reinforcements?"

"Another battalion is all I can spare. I still advise caution until our course is decided upon, dike or no."

"Then a battalion is all Torias will receive. Make the arrangements."

"By your leave, Sire." Tréville bowed.

"Allow me to accompany you as far as my carriage, Captain," said Richelieu.

Howbeit reluctant, the captain submitted. After all, Richelieu was the Prime Minister.

"Well, my dear rival, perhaps you will not be so smug when certain matters come to light," said Richelieu as he and Tréville left the Louvre.

"If you refer to the dike, I have my doubts you will succeed."

"I refer to a matter close to your heart and soul."

Tréville stopped. "Do not mince words, Priest. Speak plainly."

"Do not use that arrogant tone with me, Captain. It should be obvious I refer to your Musketeers. The blood that courses through your veins."

"I asked you to speak plainly, Your Eminence." Tréville added the title in a deliberately antagonizing tone.

"There is one Musketeer in particular: Sergeant Lamonreaux. He is becoming a nuisance to certain plans. See he stays clear or suffer the consequences."

"What has he done?" asked Tréville, now interested.

"He interferes with an affair of State by becoming too close to a certain young lady of Court. His reputation is well known, as is his association with the Duc de Rohan. A fact, you seem all too willing to overlook."

Tréville clenched his fists at the hostile and accusatory tone. With great restraint, he spoke. "I do not ignore my men or their associations. However, Sergeant Lamonreaux has done nothing to warrant my suspicions despite his association with the Duc de Rohan. As for his *affair d'amour*, each of us has had a dangerous liaison or two in our time, Eminence. All the same, I shall pass along your warning. Yet heed this. I will not tolerate any fabrications against my men."

Richelieu's chest heaved with contempt. "I do not need fabrications where treason is present, captain!"

"Do accuse Lamonreaux of treason?"

"When I accuse someone, I do so with swift efficiency. At the moment Lamonreaux interferes by his liaison. If that turns into treason, I shall act accordingly, whether you approve or not!" Richelieu turned on his heels and stormed off.

All night and morning, Arsène brooded over the marriage contract. For the first time in his life, he experienced true love. Alas, he never suspected such depth of emotion to swing from ecstasy to utter despair in an instant. His initial impulse was to lash out and strike down what caused the hurt, but Philipe proved wise in his counsel to utilize his sharp imagination. Unfortunately, as the hours past, he began to fear his ingenuity would fail amidst the emotional turmoil. The first thing he had to do was get a grip on his emotions. A sharp rap at the door startled him.

The knocking was persistent, so with annoyed grumbling Arsène opened the door. To his surprise, a woman in a hooded cloak stood before him. The hood hid her face, but by the smaller stature and posture she was not Sabrina. "Who are you and what do you want?"

"Why else does a woman call upon a man?" She removed her hood.

Arsène snarled at seeing Jeanette. "I'm in no mood to play your game, so be gone!"

She looked about. "You would let a woman stand at your door where all eyes can see? Gossip does have a way of spreading."

He pulled her inside and shut the door. "State your business."

She surveyed him. He had not slept and his appearance was that of a man whose heart and soul were in torment. "Such a pity. A most handsome and virile man brought to such a wretched state."

"My state is none of your concern. So if that is your purpose, you can leave." He went to open the door.

She grabbed his arm and spoke in earnest. "Do you hate me so much or love her so deeply?"

The question pricked him, but could not let Jeanette see his pain. "Love is something you know nothing about."

"You could be wrong."

He gave a halfhearted grunt, but did not look at her. He was in such a weakened and desperate state he dared not trust his feelings.

"You and I are cut from the same cloth, my proud Gascon. We are people of passion."

"Then the cloth is wrought with tears and imperfections! Now, be gone before I become angry." He seized her arm and reached for the door but Philipe entered.

Seeing Jeanette, Philipe slammed the door behind him, barring the exit.

"It's not what you think," refuted Arsène.

"It might have been," she sneered at Philipe.

"Have you not one ounce of decency?"

Enraged, she turned to Arsène. "It is not your love for her that keeps you chaste, but a tight leash from the priggish Bourdias."

Arsène waved Philipe aside to drag her to the door, ignoring her protests of his rough handling and shouts of anger at Philipe for his interruption. Arsène had difficulty fending off her physical attacks so Philipe opened the door. One of Jeanette's blows caught Philipe in the face, her nails leaving two small claw marks on his lower left cheek. Outside, they heard her screaming curses.

"Remember, all eyes can see you," said Arsène through the door.

Her voice trailed off and soon could not be heard.

"A regular wild cat." Philipe dabbed his injury with a handkerchief. "Need some salve?"

"No. When did she arrive?"

"A moment before you. In truth, I thought it was you. Then again, you wouldn't knock rather use your key. I wonder what made her come here?"

"News of the marriage contract is spreading. Apparently some at Court already knew of it before Dominic."

Arsène leaned against the door with a deep throaty growl, "Slut."

"That is not why I came. Tréville is looking for you."

"Why?"

"I don't know, but he is furious. You are to report to him immediately."

Arsène murmured a curse under his breath. "Give me a few moments to get into uniform." He disappeared into his bedroom.

In the six years as a Musketeer, it was not often Arsène was called before his captain in so harsh a manner. He searched his mind for a possible answer as he stood at rigid attention in the captain's office waiting for Tréville to speak.

"I won't mince words with you, Sergeant. His Eminence instructed me to give you a warning, *'stop interfering with an affair of State'.*"

Arsène's became puzzled; this wasn't what he expected. "What?"

"According to the Cardinal your liaison with a lady of Court is interfering with some scheme of his design. Does that refresh your memory, Sergeant?"

Arsène inwardly trembled, not from fear, rather anger. Tréville confirmed what was suspected of the marriage contract. "Captain, if I interfered it was unintentional."

"Then you know of what the Cardinal speaks?"

"I am acquainted with the lady of whom the Cardinal speaks, and can tell you, she was also unaware of any interference. This arrangement only came to her knowledge last evening."

Tréville grunted in annoyance. "Then you both know more than I. What are you mixed up in, Lamonreaux?"

"I'm not entirely certain, Captain," said Arsène with all truthfulness. " I fell in love and pursued that love. The affair of State is a marriage contract. As for the Cardinal's accusation, I claim innocence to prior knowledge of his plans."

Tréville regarded him and took notice of the proud shoulders, high head, and sincere blue eyes. "You always had a quick intelligence and great insight for one so young. However, you also possess one weakness not uncommon to a soldier: the ladies."

Arsène colored. "I admit having a reputation. However, that does not make me a party to intrigue and scheming."

Tréville snorted. "Don't play the fool, Lamonreaux; you're too smart for that. As am I!"

Arsène again inwardly trembled, this time for fear. He must play his part with truth and shrewdness. "I meant no offense, Captain. It is true where ladies of Court are concerned intrigue and scheming follow in some form or another. I endeavored to stay clear of them. I do not need to take advantage of a woman to better myself or further my income."

"No, you have the Duc de Rohan as sponsor. Another person the Cardinal mentioned you have a close relationship with."

"A fact known for years. Why should the Cardinal question it now?"

"You cannot ignore the fact he is a Huguenot leader."

"Yes, Captain. However, the custom of a soldier accepting patronage is usually done without question. Many soldiers have a noble or wealthy sponsor who could be considered nefarious or ill-regarded."

Tréville arched a brow. "Richelieu's interest is not easily captured."

Arsène palms sweated inside his gloves. "I don't know how to say I am innocent of what the Cardinal claims than to simply say so. Upon my honor, Captain, I did not intentionally interfere with the Cardinal's plans. I was ignorant until last night, when the distraught young lady in question told me. You can imagine what a blow this is to young love."

Tréville stood with arms folded studying Arsène, a young man in his early twenties valiantly defending himself against the greatest man in France. "Will you give your word as a Musketeer you did not seek to thwart the Cardinal's efforts in respect to your lady love?"

Despite his secret Huguenot activities, Arsène was thankful for his innocence in this affair and sincerely replied. "I give you my word not only as a Musketeer, but also as a Gascon, I did not purposely meddle in any plan of the Cardinal's making concerning this young lady."

To Tréville this was a double reassurance, for he too was a Gascon. "I believe you. And I warn you. I can keep the Cardinal at bay for the present, but if you seek to obstruct him in this, I cannot promise so favorable an outcome a second time."

"I am in your debt, Captain." Arsène bowed in grateful respect.

In a fatherly gesture, Tréville clasped Arsène's shoulder. "Heed my warning and that shall be payment enough."

"Yes, *Mon Capitaine*," said Arsène with relief. After a salute, he withdrew.

In the lobby, Philipe waited, anxious and pacing. He hurried over when Arsène emerged. "Well?"

Arsène waved Philipe from headquarters before relating the interview. By the end, Philipe's eyes turned dark with concern.

"Will you heed his warning?" he asked.

"I'm not sure. I need to think long and hard before deciding. There is much at risk with Richelieu suspicious of me."

"Dominic will need to be told."

"Of course. Adele may have heard some rumor at the Palace. I wish Rohan were in Paris. I could use a mighty ally."

"Dominic won't let you fall prey to Richelieu."

Arsène shook his head. "Any action on his part would provoke the marquis and place he and Adele in danger. I will not allow it."

"Will it be less dangerous for Rohan?"

"The marquis doesn't have authority to refute or stand against Rohan, while Richelieu needs unquestionable proof and redoubtable witnesses to accuse him of anything. But the marquis will not dispute the Cardinal if he chooses to act against Dominic. All the more willing since it deals with me, the corrupting devil." He chuckled in irony. "I'm in love with his niece."

"Promise me you will think hard about Tréville's warning."

Arsène grinned. "I promise I shall consider it. Who knows what the next two weeks will hold? You said to use my mind to discover a solution."

Hearing his own words thwarted any further argument from Philipe.

"Now, come, I need something to eat." Arsène drew Philipe from the building in search of breakfast.

⚜ Chapter 12 ⚜

TWO DAYS LATER, ROHAN RETURNED TO PARIS and called an immediate meeting of Le Resistance. He notified the Huguenot Sword to secure the inn they frequented on the outskirts of Saint-Germain-Des-Pres.

Outside, Philipe was posted at the rear door to admit the members. Dominic sat at the gate pretending to be a groom. He shed his cloak, hat and baldric, though a sword was hidden within arm's reach. He wore the oldest and plainest suit he could. Being in plain view, Arsène supplied him with a gray beard and added white powder to his hair to make him appear older. Dominic was not good at whittling, but did so for appearance sake.

Arsène sat inside among the customers at a table next to the short hall leading to the secret room. He donned the disguise of a red-bearded middle-aged traveler, wearing dusty clothes ten years out of fashion. The innkeeper made certain to treat him like a normal customer.

In the back room, Rohan began the meeting.

"My friends, I thank you for coming on such short notice." He took out a folded paper from his doublet. "I received a letter from my brother. King Charles agreed to Buckingham's plans and requests an envoy to England to make final arrangements, and as a show of good faith on our part. The swiftness of the envoy will determine the date Buckingham will sail. This, gentlemen, is the reason for this meeting, to determine who will go to England. I am unable to do so, yet this opportunity cannot be allowed to pass."

"Is this wise for any of us to undertake a journey? Richelieu is keeping close watch for any suspicious activity," said d'Avallon.

"By tomorrow he will know of this meeting, if he doesn't already," chided Longueville.

"Richelieu employs many spies, we must act prudently," said Reynard.

"Let us leave the future in God's hands and concern ourselves with the present. We would not have come this far if all the little possibilities influenced everything we did," said Trudeau.

"What of our agents?" asked Bouillon.

Rohan shook his head. "No. The very life of our cause depends upon on this. Although I trust them with my life, as we all do," he looked at each man, the thought of treachery on his mind and heart, "this is a mission for a noble, not a messenger."

Borchard cleared his throat. "I must decline. A bridegroom has much to do before a wedding. All the heads of state shall be in attendance. Perhaps this will give whoever goes some extra time."

The announcement peeked Rohan's interest. The others offered various excuses for not going, but he leaned to Bouillon and asked, "What is this about a marriage?"

"To Charbonier's niece. It was announced two days ago."

The answer stunned Rohan since he immediately realized the implications.

"I shall be honored to lend my services," said Trudeau.

Rohan's reaction was a slow nod, as he tried to draw his attention back to the issue at hand. "I leave at dawn to meet with the elders in Amiens. You can accompany me, then proceed to Calais."

With the important matter of England settled, they proceeded to examine all military options opened to the Royal Forces concerning La Rochelle and an English armada. Rohan's mind kept drifting back to Borchard's wedding. In his haste to get the meeting under way, he ignored Arsène's attempt to speak to him. In hindsight, he recalled Arsène appeared unusually grim and pale. He swore under his breath at his thoughtlessness and determined to set it right when the meeting ended. Alas, that didn't happen until one o'clock in the morning.

After the others left, Rohan sent for Arsène. He appeared still in disguise. In regret, Rohan surveyed his protégé. Had nine years past since he

158

met an energetic, intelligent fourteen-year-old boy from Gascony? A boy who quickly filled the emptiness of a heart longing for a son?

"Monsieur, are you ill?" asked Arsène.

"Sick at heart, my boy. Sick because you wished to speak to me earlier and I ignored you. I regret my thoughtlessness, for I learned what you wanted to tell me. Sabrina's upcoming marriage to the Comte de Borchard."

Arsène was crestfallen. "Boon for services to the Crown."

"I feared the connection." Rohan studied a downcast Arsène. What he must say to the young man weighed heavy on his heart. "I wish there was something I could do, but I'm only in Paris tonight. I leave for Amiens on the morrow."

"She's to marry in less than two weeks!"

Rohan winced, pained and stricken, for in that moment, he no longer saw the man his protégé had become, but a frightened son looking to his father for help. "There is little recourse at present. Unless," he began, gripping Arsène's shoulder, "you both flee with the means I provide."

A hint of agreement rose in Arsène's eyes, but soon faded. "Monsieur, I will never desert you. Besides, Richelieu approached Captain Tréville not only concerning my relationship to Sabrina, but you also. I cannot flee without causing worse trouble."

"What did Tréville say?"

"After convincing him I did not deliberately meddle in Richelieu's plan, he gave me his assurance of protection and warned me against entertaining thoughts of interference."

"He's right. The marriage must take place."

Arsène screwed his eyes shut and pressed his lips together.

"I share your pain, son. All I can say is remember what I have taught you. God is faithful and will not give you a burden you cannot bear." Arsène went to speak the contrary but Rohan stopped him with a squeeze on his shoulder. "I know the situation feels unbearable, but look to God, son. From Him you must draw strength or the pain will devour you!"

"I don't know if I can."

"You must! Those who depend upon you will suffer if you fall."

Philipe and Dominic's arrival ended the conversation and Arsène turned aside to regain his composure.

"All is secure, monsieur," said Philipe.

Rohan acknowledged Philipe with a wave, his attention focused on Arsène. "As for Borchard, my faithful Gascon, watch him tonight. The information imparted at this meeting is of vital importance. I do not dare say more save I will not be alone when I leave in the morning. That part of the undertaking must not fail!"

"He won't so much as sneeze without my knowledge."

Arsène began to leave but Philipe grabbed his arm to stop him and said, "For friendship."

"For freedom," added Dominic, also gripping Arsène's arm.

Arsène hesitated in speaking his part of the parting pledge thus Rohan said, "For faith," and clapped Arsène's shoulder.

"For faith," said Arsène in a hushed and lackluster voice. He left.

"Tell me, has his spirit been so severely injured?" asked Rohan.

Philipe met the duke's worried gaze, his reply sober. "If you saw him two days ago, you would wonder what keeps him alive. A piece of him was mortally wounded, and I have not been able to counsel him."

"Then, all we can do is pray." He turned to Dominic. "This must be difficult for you too."

"I failed in my promise to keep her safe," he droned then asked in desperation, "Can anything be done?"

Rohan murmured an exclamation at the entreaty. "How you look like Michael when he asked me the same about Rodrique's renouncement. Alas, powerful though I am, events happen I cannot control. God in heaven knows my heart is torn! Please understand our cause is at a critical juncture. Although I cannot help at present, I must depend upon all of you as never before. The slightest miscalculation now and all is lost."

"Sabrina said much the same thing. Perhaps she saw the inevitable and accepted it before we did," said Dominic in muted resignation.

"Sabrina is an exceptional young woman and it pains me I cannot help her. Encourage her while you can." He turned to Philipe. "With the heart of a father I ask you, don't let Arsène falter. We need him too much to let this destroy him."

"I will, monsieur."

"If need arises, send word to me in Amiens."

In heavy silence, Philipe and Dominic watched Rohan depart.

Late the following afternoon, Dominic was leaving the Palais de Cardinal when he spied someone entering Richelieu's audience chambers. From behind, the face was obscured, but the large stature, dress and carriage was familiar.

Perhaps Borchard is making his move, he thought and moved to follow. He stopped and glanced about for signs of anyone before listening at the door.

Richelieu spoke. "It must be important for a personal visit."

"This news cannot be trusted to a messenger, Eminence."

Dominic furrowed his brows at the familiar voice, but it did not match what he recalled of Borchard's speech, too deep in tone.

"Your price?" asked Richelieu.

"To be determined by Your Eminence after hearing the news."

"You are in a gracious mood, monsieur."

"Always when dealing with Your Eminence."

"*Peste!* Enough of this false flattery," said Richelieu with impatience.

"The English have agreed to send a armada in support of La Rochelle. The Duc de Trudeau left for England at dawn to meet with Buckingham and finalize plans. He rides with Rohan, who is on his way to Amiens and a meeting with the Huguenot elders."

Astonished, Dominic glanced over his shoulder but saw no one. Whether this person was Borchard or the second traitor he would memorize this voice and returned to listening.

"Is this not news worth the price of a Cardinal's hat?"

"Impertinent, little man!"

"Perhaps," he said undaunted. "The price, Eminence?"

There was a pause during which Dominic heard the scratching of quill on paper.

"There," said Richelieu. "Is that satisfactory?"

"Most agreeably. However, there is only one way to prevent such a loyal and brave man like Trudeau from reaching England."

Another pause followed the statement, during which Dominic bit his lip in anticipation.

At length, Richelieu spoke. "I leave the matter to you. I shall have no part. If any word of this conversation is brought up I shall deny it. Understand?"

"Yes, Eminence. I shan't fail."

"For your sake, you better not. Now, go."

Hearing footsteps approach the door, Dominic concealed himself in the shadows. Every muscle in his body tensed when the door opened and the man passed him. Though still unable to see a face, he became certain he knew him.

For a moment, he contemplated what to do. Rohan and Trudeau were somewhere on the road between Paris and Amiens. He, Philipe, and Arsène agreed to meet at Arsène's apartment and dine out, so with hurried steps, he took the shortest route to the apartment.

At seven o'clock the purple haze of summer's twilight faded. By a prearranged signal of a turned drape, Dominic knew Arsène wasn't home yet. He and Philipe each had a key. Inside, the faint light of the day cast long shadows. Being familiar with the layout, he walked to the middle of the front room to the table. A lantern with a match and flint beside it was always on the table. He started to light the lamp when two figures jumped him from the shadows.

He shouted in surprise when cold steel passed through his clothes, scratching his right shoulder. With almost no effort, he heaved his shoulders and threw the assailants back. He turned in the direction from which the dagger came. The man struggled to his feet and raised the dagger to strike again. Dominic caught the man's wrist and twisted the weapon from his grasp. The second man jumped on Dominic's back, wrapping his arms about his neck. He gritted his teeth at the pressure on his throat and shoved the first man away to deal with the man on his back. He elbowed the man in the ribs several times until he let loose and fell to the floor winded. He had to take a moment to recover his breath.

This allowed the first man to get to his feet, retrieve the dagger, and lunge at Dominic. The blade sliced open Dominic's right side, staggering him. The man pressed the attack. Dominic tried to avoid him, but lost his footing and fell, striking the right side of his head hard on the table. He lay motionless on the floor. The first knelt next to check for signs of life, but voices came from outside. The men left by the inner stairs.

Arsène and Philipe arrived. "Dominic?" Arsène dropped beside Charbonier.

Philipe crossed the room in two bounds and looked through the interior open door down the hall. Stairs lead to the shop below. He swore at seeing no one then closed and bolted the door. He joined Arsène.

"They're gone. How is he?"

"Still alive. Help me get him in bed."

They carried Dominic into the bedroom and laid him on the single wooden bed with a thin mattress. Dominic's face was pale and drawn in pain. Philipe sat on the edge of the bed and used his handkerchief to wipe away the blood and get a clearer view of the dagger wound.

"The wound isn't mortal but he's unconscious," he said.

Arsène fetched a basin of water and his box of herbal medicine. "There was blood on the floor near his head."

Philipe searched for and found the laceration over the right temple. "They either struck him or he hit his head falling."

Arsène handed the box to Philipe and placed the basin on the small table beside the bed. "I'll get the bandages."

Philipe opened the box and found the salve. "Phew! What's in this stuff?"

Arsène answered over his shoulder while getting down his only other sheet from a cupboard. "Herbs, mustard paste, water—"

"Enough!" said Philipe, sickened from the smell. "If the wound doesn't kill him the smell of this stuff will."

Arsène tore the sheet into strips and watched Philipe make faces to cope with the foul smelling ointment. Dominic groaned.

"Perhaps this stuff is better than smelling salts." Philipe waved the ointment under Dominic's nose.

Dominic weakly batted away the jar and woke. He grabbed Philipe in an effort to sit up but swayed and fell back.

"Easy, you may have a concussion."

Dominic swallowed back the sickness before speaking. "We are betrayed! I overheard one of the traitors telling the Cardinal that Trudeau rides with Rohan to Amiens then to England to meet with Buckingham. The traitor has Richelieu's blessings to assassinate Trudeau!"

"Borchard?" asked Philipe.

"He didn't leave his château," said Arsène.

"I didn't see him but his voice was commanding and gruff. Somehow familiar, but I could not place it with a face."

"You heard them the night you followed that buffoon. Can you tell which one by Dominic's description?" asked Philipe.

Arsène screwed his lips in recollection. "Doesn't sound like Borchard, other than that, no. But we can't sit here comparing voices. Time is wasting and they ride further with each passing moment." He went to a trunk near the window. Inside were a musket, a pistol, powder, balls; all equipment a soldier needed for a campaign. He stuffed the pistol in his belt, pulled out a saddlebag and put a powder canister and bag of balls into it. He closed the trunk, leaving the musket behind.

"The traitor may not be aware of his discovery, but the moment you leave Paris, de Lacy will be alerted," said Dominic, watching Arsène arm himself.

"There can be no hesitation; not with Rohan and Trudeau in danger. The choice is yours and Philipe's. I will not force either of you to join me since it could mean discovery and possibly death."

"I will not abandon you," declared Philipe, making Arsène grin in relief. He turned to Dominic. "You know me well, old friend. If I were to die I would rather do so fighting than at the end of a hangman's noose. What of you? Our departure leaves you vulnerable. And Adele—" He could say no more in regard to his sister.

"My sentiments are the same. So are those of my wife, your sister," said Dominic with reassurance. "We shall manage; only inform André of my condition. Now, go, before you lose more precious time and our traitor gains the advantage."

Chapter 13

AFTER LEAVING THE APARTMENT, ARSÈNE AND PHILIPE went their separate ways; Philipe to gather his equipment and fetch the horses and Arsène to Musketeer headquarters' to gain urgent leave to prevent arousing further suspicion. Tréville was occupied at the palace so Arsène told du Pree how Philipe's grandmother lay on her deathbed in Reims. The old woman sent for her only grandson and he played upon du Pree's sympathies to obtain the request. With written security in hand, Arsène left.

When he arrived at the Bourdias residence, Philipe and Roger finished saddling two coal black Prussian battle steeds. Each horse was pure black with no markings. The manes and tails were kept long like their ancestors, the Arabians. The special mounts were bred just for elite military units and famed for their speed and endurance.

Not until after eight o'clock at night did they leave Paris. Rohan and Trudeau had a twelve-hour head start forcing them to ride through the night to gain lost ground. Neither wanted to think about the dangers with Richelieu's agents everywhere.

Four hours into the journey, a menacing storm unleashed its fury. Thunder roared and lightning flashed. Rain beat heavily upon the ground turning the earth into a quagmire, making any gait of speed difficult. At one point the rain was so dense they could not see ten feet ahead.

In an effort to find shelter, they spied a cottage a short distance off the main road. Upon approach, it appeared deserted and rundown. Philipe dismounted and pushed open what remained of the door. The interior was difficult to see, but several flashes of lightning helped with quick visibility. Grass and weeds partially consumed the floor but the roof appeared intact with only a few small holes. They found no wood to use for light or to warm their chilled bodies. Rain pounded the roof and fell in heavy streams through the holes. Still, the cottage served as protection from the worst of the storm.

After tethering the horses inside by the front door, Arsène sat against the back wall. He was soaked to the skin and spattered with mud. He removed his hat and gloves before trying to wipe some mud from his face. He slicked back his wet hair from his forehead. Underneath the muck and perspiration the blue eyes showed great weariness. He sneezed a few times.

Philipe untied the food pouch from his saddle and joined Arsène. He tried to clean himself off and gently pulled the caked mud from his mustache. He also tried rubbing his numb legs and feet back to life before removing two baguettes and cheese from the pouch. He handed a baguette and a chunk of cheese to Arsène. They ate in silence. After finishing his portion, Philipe wrapped his cloak closer about him to lie down.

"We should try to get some rest. We'll catch them tomorrow."

"If we don't die from a chill first," grumbled Arsène, running his fingers through his hair.

Philipe noticed the familiar fretful action. "It's not the cold rain troubling you."

Arsène shook his head. "Somehow Dominic's attack is my fault."

"What? You can't blame yourself."

"No? A dear friend is almost killed in my apartment! Perhaps a case of mistaken identity and those men meant to attack me."

"Dominic may be wrong, and the traitor knew of his discovery; followed him and launched the attack. We don't know."

Arsène crossed to where the horses stood grazing. "Call it intuition, a premonition, or what you will, but your theory doesn't make sense. Dominic would have realized he was being followed and not gone to my apartment. They had to be waiting."

Philipe sat up. "Then how do you explain Trudeau?"

"Trudeau is something else. This was a trap for me."

"Borchard?"

"Yes, Borchard!" Arsène slapped his horse's withers in anger. The horse lifted its head then returned to grazing. "He's not content with marrying Sabrina. He wants me dead! He should be afraid of me, the cur."

"You're forgetting a very real threat: the one taking on the road to possible oblivion."

"Yes, yes, the second traitor. I did not forget," he said with impatience. "I was making a point. At first glance, this appears to be a singular incident, but in actuality two separate events that crossed paths."

Philipe leaned back against the wall with an annoyed grunt.

"Forgive me. My words are harsher than I intended."

"But always correct," groused Philipe.

Arsène cocked a grin. "Keen intelligence can often be a hindrance when speed and action are necessary. That's where your strength lies. While my mind is in Paris dwelling on the past, yours is moving toward Calais and the future. Put those minds together and you have an unbeatable force."

A sudden crash of thunder, furious and loud, roared overhead.

"Against men. The weather is a different enemy."

Arsène snickered. "Now, let's get some rest."

The delay lasted two hours, which was fine for the horses. Refreshed, the animals easily navigated the muddy highway. By first light, Arsène and Philipe had been in the saddle nine hours and traveled forty miles. They decided to stop for a good hot meal and replenish their dwindling supplies. They consumed a hearty meal of eggs, bacon, potatoes, bread, cheese and local cider.

"If only we knew how far ahead they were," said Philipe, leading the horses from the shelter. "Delphina was unsteady the last few miles."

"Ranger also; but we can't leave them here. These two Prussian beauties are the Musketeer's trademarks. Discovery will tell them we went this way rather than Reims as I told du Pree." Ranger gave a mild protest when Arsène mounted.

"If we ease off and walk them on occasion they won't die out from under us. By midday, I want to be back at full speed."

168

In forty minutes they traveled one league. From behind a blind bend, two men came riding hard at them. One collided with Philipe, sending men and horses to the ground.

Arsène jerked hard on the reins to keep Ranger from trampling Philipe. The horse skidded and reared, throwing Arsène backwards where he landed flat on his back, smacking his head on the ground, knocking him senseless.

"Arsène?" Philipe scrambled to his feet and began moving toward his friend when a harsh voice stopped him.

"Never mind him! How dare you run into me like that?"

"Me?" Philipe's eyes darkened with rage when confronted by a naked sword. "You ran into me!"

"You mock me and call me a liar, you son of a sow!" He swung at Philipe, who ducked and drew his sword in time to parry the second swing. He snarled at seeing Philipe was left-handed. "You're an oddity."

"Withdraw, if you're frightened."

"Never!" The man came at Philipe.

Arsène groaned to Ranger's nudging, but his eyes remained closed. The second man dismounted, took a pistol from his belt and approached Arsène. A shadow loomed over Lamonreaux. At the pistol cock, Ranger lifted his head and made a loud whinny.

Arsène rolled aside as the weapon discharged. The ball plunged into the ground. Immediately another shot was fired. The man fell to the dirt clenching his chest. Arsène lay back on his elbow with pistol in hand. The sudden movement made him dizzy and nauseated. He closed his eyes.

The shots distracted the first man, giving Philipe the advantage. A thrust to the abdomen ended the duel. Uncertain of what happened, he saw Arsène and another body lying on the ground. He raced over and dropped to his knees.

"Arsène?" He became frantic at no response and seized Arsène by the shoulders and shook him. "Arsène!"

Arsène's eyes snapped open at the rough rousing. "Ranger?"

Philipe's shoulders sagged in relief. "No, it's me."

"Ranger woke me before. Lucky I had my pistol." He looked to the weapon still in his hand. "My head and neck. The fall."

Philipe helped Arsène sit up. Upon examination, he found a lump and a cut on the back of the head.

"I think I'm going to—" Arsène fainted.

Philipe laid him on the ground. With Arsène in no mortal danger, he tethered the animals then dragged the bodies off the road behind a hedge. He noticed a piece of paper partially concealed in one of the dead men's doublet. His eyes widened in astonishment and a soft cry escaped his lips upon reading the letter. Once the shock wore off, he stuffed it into his pocket.

He fetched his canteen and made his way back to a sleeping Arsène. He wiped the dirt from Arsène's face then cleansed the wound and bandaged it. When finished, he stretched out on the grass with his hands behind his head. His stomach growled, but he was in no mood to eat. The events of the past few days boggled his mind. Were those men waiting for Arsène and mistook Dominic for him in the dark? Who is the second cloaked traitor? Poor Sabrina. They would not return to Paris before she marries Borchard. He bit his mustache, recalling the pathetic look of both she and Arsène. His feelings for Sabrina remained strong, yet thought of the marriage possibly being their ruin overshadowed any lingering jealousy.

He glanced to his injured friend. He had known Dominic since childhood, yet developed an instant relationship to Arsène from the moment they met five years ago; a kinship of souls as Rohan described it. Philipe wasn't certain about the comparison to the biblical story of Jonathan and David, but over the years shared adventures and clandestine activities brought a new and deeper meaning to the word *friend*.

At a passing glance, their relationship seemed strange. Philipe was more pragmatic, yet with a hidden, reckless spirit his pragmatic self repressed for sake of decorum. To him, a gallant cavalier was serious in nature, intelligent and not given to flights of fancy that led to the ruin of lesser men. Arsène Lamonreaux was his own man, and definitely not of lesser mettle. He possessed joviality, wit and intelligence that sprang from a secure self-confidence. In the wily Gascon, Philipe discovered a true and loyal friend.

"These men will pay, I promise," he said to the sleeping Arsène.

Fatigue overcame him and Philipe fell asleep yet uncertain for how long he slept when something moved close by him. He bolted up and reached for his sword but to his pleasure Arsène woke. "How are you feeling?"

"I have a headache and a stiff neck. How long was I asleep?"

Philipe glanced at his watch. "An hour." He gave Arsène the canteen. "Drink slowly."

After drinking, Arsène asked, "What happened?"

"Dead. I hid them off the road behind the hedge. I found this on one of them." He showed Arsène the paper. "A letter from Father Joseph promising a reward for our deaths."

Arsène ignored his injuries and snatched the letter from Philipe to read. "Do you know what this means?"

"Our days as Musketeers are numbered."

"Perhaps, but if we stand before Tréville with this—"

"He'll demand to know why and what we've done."

"Remember my interrogation?" asked Arsène, calmly proceeded, much to Philipe's annoyance.

"Of course, but what does that have to do with this?"

"I can explain this as a repercussion of the incident."

"Well and good for you, but my name is mentioned. Explain that."

"No need. When have we done anything separate?"

Philipe gave a short cynical laugh. "Purely through association."

"You would not avenge me if I were killed?"

Philipe frowned in mild offense. "You know the answer."

Arsène's wry expression turned into a kind smile. "There is your explanation. Richelieu already approached Tréville concerning me. Since Richelieu is his protégé, Father Joseph acts on the Cardinal's behalf. For your own safety you should not associate too closely with me." He spoke the last sentence with a wide smile.

"Obstinate Gascon. You have a head for figuring things out, but I hate the way you do it. Even when injured."

Arsène laughed and stood, but swayed when he became dizzy. "Thinking and activity are different."

Philipe steadied him. "Can you ride?"

"I don't have a choice."

At midday, the horses' heads hung so low they almost dragged on the ground. Eighteen hours and seventy-five miles had passed since they left Paris. Arsène drew rein to study a group of four riders a quarter mile ahead. Rohan's bulky frame was unmistakable. He dug in his spurs and Ranger protested, lurching forward.

Arsène called to Rohan, making the duke stop in wary observation of approach. "Thank God we found you in time!"

Rohan was surprised at the sight of Arsène wounded and both he and Philipe exhausted. The animals trembled with pink froth dripping from their mouths where the bits cut after so many hours of hard riding. "Good heavens, you're wounded! What happened?"

"Dominic overheard one of the traitors betray your journey to Richelieu, and obtain authority to assassinate Monsieur Trudeau."

Trudeau swore. "Was it Borchard?"

"Dominic never saw him yet became wounded by assailants, but he'll live," said Philipe.

"Borchard didn't leave his chateau that night," said Arsène.

Rohan regarded their weary and injured condition. "You wasted no time."

"Twenty-five leagues in eighteen hours."

Trudeau reacted in amazement. "A wonder the beasts didn't die under you."

"Chandler, you and Marshall lead these worthy animals at whatever pace they can manage and meet with us at the appointed inn." Rohan then said to Philipe and Arsène, "You can ride double on Chandler's Auvenge. Do not let her size fool you. She maybe small but can bear much weight. Tonight we rest at Amiens. On the morrow William continues to Calais. You can go with him," he continued speaking while his instructions were carried out.

For a country inn, this one was large and well constructed. Wood beams helped support the large plaster walls. The windows were beveled glass with shudders instead of curtains. The door was cut in half and could be opened individually or together when bolted one to another. Rohan, Trudeau, Arsène and Philipe ate a hot and plentiful meal of beef stew, chicken, bread, cheese and wine. When finished, Philipe and Arsène retired.

Despite the daylight, Philipe fell asleep easily. Arsène lay awake tossing and turning. His body was stiff, sore and tired. Alas, his mind would not permit him to rest. He moved to sit on the windowsill and gazed at the horizon. By the way the inn was situated he reckoned the room faced toward Paris. He shuddered at the thought of Dominic and the endless possibilities surrounding the ambush. His heart sank when Sabrina came to mind. What would happen to her now? Would she still be forced to marry Borchard? What if he did not return to Paris in time?

Time: a word that racked him with a cold shudder. In Paris he gave no thought of riding out to warn Rohan and Trudeau, but Rohan's order of he and Philipe accompanying Trudeau to Calais wasn't something he even considered. If they left Amiens in the morning and returned to Paris directly, they would arrive in time to stop the wedding. But, if they ride with Trudeau— He screwed his eyes shut against the pain of how his effort to save a life lost him the possibility of rescuing Sabrina. Maybe if Philipe continued with Trudeau, he could return to Paris.

He moved from the window as to speak, but stopped. Philipe hadn't moved and laid in the same position. He already risked everything by agreeing to the false story of their departure. The die was cast. Arsène left the room.

Several other guests arrived for the evening meal and Arsène avoided them in making his way to the stables. The air smelled of liniment. Chandler took good care of the horses. Ranger barely noticed Arsène, greedily eating the hay and oats. A soft neigh caught his attention. Delphina hung her head over the next stall and nudged his doublet.

"Sorry, I don't have a carrot. Philipe will bring you one in the morning." He laughed at hearing Ranger neigh. "And one for you, my jealous steed." He felt a hand upon his shoulder.

"Is all satisfactory with your horses?" asked Rohan.

"Ranger eats like always and Delphina wants a carrot."

"God made a wondrous creature when he created the horse. Majestic and powerful, yet submits to bridle and spur, willing to go anywhere and face any dangers men can think of. Since the horses are taken care of, why are you not resting?"

"Philipe is asleep."

"That's not what I asked. What keeps you awake?"

Arsène hesitated, twirling some of Ranger's mane in his finger. "This whole business. The woman I love is to marry another, and a traitor." His voice thick was with pain and angry restraint.

"The marriage contract is highly suspicious. Howbeit, after much consideration, I don't see Borchard as the instigator rather the pawn. An unwitting scapegoat for the real traitors."

"Scapegoat or not, she marries him! You want me to go to Calais and by doing so, I lose her." Arsène's voice cracked with passion.

Frustration exploded and Rohan looked up and shouted. "With all my wealth and power I can raise armies and navies to battles kings and cardinals, but I can't raise a finger to help those I love! Why, Lord?"

Arsène's head became crestfallen.

Rohan's anguish deepened. "I'm sorry I failed you, son." He left.

Arsène leaned against the stall and wept.

❧ Chapter 14 ❧

TRUDEAU, ARSÈNE AND PHILIPE TRAVELED THE SEVENTY MILES from Amiens to Calais at a good steady pace. Calais was the most important harbor on the northern coast of France and many battles were fought over the centuries for control of the city. Guardhouses and city police kept watch over the busy port. Gothic homes stood close together and in some places, attached in rows. The most congested and oldest part of Calais was the wharf. Here the stone houses were small with tiny windows and narrow doorways. The strong stench of salt and low tide filled the air. Loud shrilling cries of the sea gulls rivaled the shouts of the merchants selling their wares.

They dismounted at the wharfinger's office. Inside, Trudeau approached the man at the counter.

"When does the next ship sail for England?"

The man squinted at the paper in front of him. Remembering he did not have his glasses on, he took them off his head and placed them on his nose. "On the evening tide at five o'clock, monsieur."

Trudeau pulled out his watch: three-thirty. "I'll take one passage."

"Do you have orders from either the Cardinal or the King?"

Trudeau tossed a quizzical glance to his companions. Philipe stood inside the door, hand resting on the hilt of his sword. Arsène gazed out a window a few steps away from Philipe.

"I'm sorry, monsieur, but unless you have orders you cannot sail. Due to the war all ships to England are stopped. Only by special permission can I allow such a crossing."

"My good man, this is urgent business concerning France!"

"Your orders then, monsieur." The man held out his hand.

Arsène touched Philipe's elbow to get his attention and whispered. "This calls for indiscretion, Lieutenant."

"You there," the man said to Arsène. "If this is some intrigue I'll call the constable!"

Philipe approached the counter and addressed the man in a low harsh tone. "I commended your for performing your duty, but in doing so you cause a dangerous revelation. If you observe my suit and that of my companion are identical. Uniforms to be precise, King's Musketeers, and this gentleman is charged to us upon a secret mission. I suggest you write the passage or face imprisonment for interfering with the King's business."

He gaped at Philipe. "Please, forgive and forget the unfortunate mistake. I shall write the passage immediately!"

Arsène became alert to a group of five ruffians paying attention to the wharfinger's office. A man with a scarred face spotted him and with a word and gesture dispersed the men. Arsène watched the scarred man until he disappeared into the growing crowd on the wharf. He glanced back to see the clerk was writing passage. He caught Philipe's eye and cocked his head toward the window.

Philipe mumbled under his breath, "Nothing can be easy."

Trudeau snatched the pass when the clerk finished and tossed several coins on the counter. Philipe and Arsène were at his heels in leaving the office. "I appreciate your aid, Philipe. I do hope it won't cause you adversity."

"I didn't mention my name or rank. Maybe that will be my saving grace."

Once mounted, Arsène moved his horse close to Trudeau. "I suggest we be very discreet until departure. We're being followed."

"I know just the place to pass the time in relative safety."

They arrived at a tavern on the opposite end of the wharf across from the fish market. Inside the dimly lit tavern, the smell of the sea mingled with the aroma of food. The proprietor must have been an old seaman by his taste in decoration using fishnets for curtains, grappling hooks for hanging one's cloak and worn down galley tables. Arsène inspected the tavern. Although no signs of pursuit they sat a table in the corner with Trudeau next to the wall, Arsène beside him and Philipe opposite, with a pistol next to him, concealed from view.

A burly man with a large apron tied about his belly approached the table. The rolled up sleeves revealed muscular arms capable of crushing any normal size human. "It is good to see you again, monsieur!"

"And you, Parquette. We need the usual for about an hour. Of course, your silence is always appreciated," said Trudeau with a wink and smile.

"Monsieur! How many times have you honored my humble tavern and I failed to provide you with those things you require?" He spoke passionately for there was no other way for such a brawny man to behave.

Trudeau chuckled. "No. Now, your finest meal, we are famished."

Indeed it proved to be the finest meal the innkeeper could provide.

Philipe leaned across to Arsène. "Any sign of our followers?"

Arsène swallowed before answering. "No. If they are around then they are masters of the shadows."

"I thought you were the master?"

"Precisely my point. If I can't detect them, they deserve my title. I can feel them, close."

"Parquette will signal us if they should appear. He helped me before and knows all Cardinalists in this area," said Trudeau.

"Then he would be known to them as well," said Philipe.

"Perhaps, but we're safe within these walls."

Philipe snorted, caustic and tore off some bread. "Is any place in France safe from Richelieu? His agents lurk in the shadows with assassins at every crossroads."

"We have guardian angels."

"Providence watches from its lofty perch as men play out their deadly scenarios. Only once in awhile does it reach down to enter the game."

"Poetic but untrue," refuted Trudeau. "Providence has a greater role in world events than you portray. Christ's life being the greatest evidence. No matter what you believe or don't believe, no one can deny that His coming to earth had a profound effect on human history."

"If only He had the foresight of what was to come."

"What makes you think He didn't know?"

Philipe cast a sour frown. "There has always been hypocrisy in the Church. Throughout history men like Richelieu have hidden behind robes of the priesthood to obtain their goals with blood. I cannot tolerate such falsehood!"

Trudeau nodded in agreement. "What you say is true, men have corrupted the work Christ began. Yet that doesn't make Christ the cause or the sanctifier of unrighteousness. If anything, the evil in men deserves scorn not the Holiness of Christ."

Philipe took a long drink to cover his annoyance but to his chagrin, Trudeau would not let the subject pass.

"You are an intelligent and brave man, Philipe. Thus I find myself confused. You pledge to fight for the Huguenots, but are hostile and sarcastic towards faith. Why? To battle injustice or for vengeance?"

Arsène paused in eating at Trudeau's challenging question. His eyes darted to Philipe, who spoke in surprise, "Vengeance?"

"Yes. You fight for a cause in which you do not believe with all your heart. What other name is there for levying your own justice than vengeance?"

Philipe slumped in his seat and gazed at Trudeau from under perplexed brows. "I never thought of it in quite that manner. I assure you, monsieur, I am loyal to Le Resistance."

Trudeau smiled. "I don't question your loyalty or courage, Philipe. Notwithstanding, you must understand the heart of our cause is faith. Something Henri has tried to instill in Arsène, who remains strangely silent during this conversation."

Arsène colored, flashing a timid smile and shoved a piece of bread in his mouth. He could not look at either of them.

Trudeau continued. "Our time on this earth is short. From here we pass to eternity. The decisions we make and the actions we take here will affect where and how we spend that time. My advice, Philipe, is for you to give greater consideration to Providence in the future when deciding upon a cause to embrace or a path to take."

Philipe nodded and ate rather than reply.

Arsène sighed in relief at seeing Philipe subdued; a man of the sword and not much inclined to religious matters. Yet Trudeau spoke truth, for Philipe did harbor some hidden hostility toward religion. Why? Only Philipe could provide the answer and Arsène never pressed him, also being a man of the sword. He believed in God and miracles, only youth and adventure kept him from pursuing matters of faith further and not cynical indifference. But when prodded by Trudeau, he became reluctant to speak.

They consumed the remainder of the meal in silence. At time to depart, Trudeau signaled Parquette. The big man spoke in a loud exuberant voice to other customers, turning his back to them. Such a large and boisterous man, all attention turned to him. Quiet and unseen, they slipped out of the tavern.

The waterfront was now crowded, making it easy for an assailant to move unseen and launch an ambush from almost anywhere. Trudeau led the way behind the many shops and houses to avoid the crowds. They caught peeks of the wharf through narrow alleyways.

From a dark side alley the ambush was launched. One assailant jumped at Arsène, dagger first. The force of the leaping man slammed Arsène hard against a wall. He grunted, using all his strength to stay the dagger hovering inches from his throat. He managed to get a knee up and into the man's abdomen. He loosed his grip upon Arsène, but retained the dagger. After a second kneeing, the man took a step back and slashed at Arsène, who leapt aside, narrowly avoiding the blade. He grabbed the man's arm holding the dagger. The struggle was short as both lost their balance and fell forward. Being at an awkward angle, Arsène released the man. There came a death groan as the blade buried itself deep in the man's chest upon impact with the street.

Hearing Trudeau's cry, Arsène started to rise, but was struck from behind and fell to the street unconscious. A fifth man held a broken board, his scarred face smiling.

Philipe and the man who jumped him, fell to the ground, struggling. They parted and the man pulled a knife from his belt, grinning in savage mockery. Philipe rolled to one side and the blade broke upon striking the cobblestone. The man tossed aside the useless weapon and they wrestled again. Philipe managed to place his feet against the man's abdomen and thrust him off. He scrambled to his feet and reached for his sword. From behind, someone grabbed him, pinning his arms, rendering him unable to move. The blade fell back into the scabbard.

The other man recovered and swung his fists at the defenseless Philipe. The first blow caught him in the stomach followed by an upper cut to the jaw. Philipe kicked in defense, but missed and cried out in pain at his arms being twisted. All his efforts to escape only made the beating worse. Blood flowed from his lips and nose. One punch hit him squarely in his face and he fell into unconsciousness.

Trudeau proved no match for two men. He made a valiant effort, but couldn't reach his sword. The thrust of cold steel pass between his shoulder blades and another assailant thrust a dagger into the duke's belly. Trudeau died before he reached the street.

The scarred man smiled. "Good work. Now let's collect our reward."

"What about them?" another asked pointing to Philipe and Arsène.

He shrugged with indifference. "We've done our job."

"And Carpè?"

"The more for us to divide." He laughed and they departed.

For a while the alley remained silent, then Arsène stirred. He reached behind his head and winced. Removing his hand, he found fresh blood on his fingers. The wound from the road reopened. He sat back on his heels and saw Trudeau. He staggered over and dropped to his knees beside the duke. Both sides of the doublet were stained with blood.

"Oh no," he lamented in a sob of painful regret.

A groan from behind made him look down the alley. Philipe lay in a crumbled heap, hands clenching his midriff. He moved to his friend. Blood trickled from the upper lip and nose while the cheeks were bruised. "Philipe?"

He reached for Arsène to help him sit up but movement hurt his ribs so he leaned on Arsène. "Trudeau?"

"Dead."

Philipe groaned in pain and anger. "I wonder why they didn't kill us?"

"Does it matter? My thickhead is saving me on this adventure." Arsène's hair lay matted to head.

180

"And you're holding me up?" Philipe began to rise but needed Arsène's help to stand. "What now? We can't tell the magistrate. Too many questions."

"They must have known—Rohan! We must warn him."

"What about Trudeau?"

Arsène bit his lower lip, a pitiful look back to the duke. "We'll leave him with Parquette. He was a good, generous man. It will be difficult to tell Rohan about his friend."

After leaving Trudeau with Parquette and receiving supplies and medical aid, Arsène and Philipe set out for Amiens. By the time they reached the city and the inn where Rohan stayed, Philipe was in intolerable pain from his ribs. Arsène ignored his headache to assist Philipe inside. The duke's whereabouts were unknown, but the innkeeper said he should return later in the evening.

Arsène fetched the necessary medical items leaving Philipe in the room. When he returned, Philipe was stripped to his breeches, examining his right side. Several bad bruises discolored his torso and were tender to the touch.

Arsène mixed a powder into the wine. "Here, this will lessen the pain."

Philipe coughed down the drink. "First some hideous smelling salve and now this poison," he protested to Arsène, who wrapped his ribs. "Careful!"

"It wouldn't hurt so much if you'd be quiet and stop complaining."

Once finished, Arsène yawned and sat in a chair next to a writing table upon which lay paper, pen and ink. In thought, he glanced from the paper to Philipe. "Can you forge your father's hand?"

"I did a few times as a boy, to avoid trouble with my schoolmaster. Why?" He gingerly put on his shirt, then doublet but left it unbuttoned.

"After what happened in Calais, we'll need a reputable alibi to verify our traveling to Reims."

"Tréville may recognize my father's hand."

"Yes, but under the stress of his mother dying—"

"His mother died before I was born. Tréville might know that. My mother's mother would be best. She lives in Navarre and is near eighty."

"Either way, in a time of stress the handwriting could be nervous." Arsène held the pen out to Philipe, who took the pen and sat at the table.

"What about our injuries?"

"The Capuchin's letter."

Philipe snickered in remembrance. "What should I write?" He wrote a passable forgery that Arsène dictated.

Rohan and Chandler arrived. "*Mon dieu*," said Rohan in surprise. "What are you two doing here? Did William sail already?"

Arsène hesitated so Philipe said, "I'm sorry, monsieur, he is dead."

Rohan's breath caught in his throat. "William? Dead?"

"Ambushed in Calais. They knocked Arsène unconscious and I laid low with a few cracked ribs. We hurried back in fear for your safety."

Rohan could not speak for absorbing the sorrowful news.

"What of Buckingham?"

Rohan shook his head trying to regain his voice. "I'll think of another way to reach him. My going is out of the question. And yours," he said, stopping Arsène before the young man objected. "I don't know how you both managed this much. I can see your injuries are painful."

"Forgive our failure, monsieur," murmured Arsène.

Rohan clapped Arsène's shoulder. "My grief is for my friend not disappointment in you. Get some rest. We leave for Paris in the morning."

❧ Chapter 15 ❧

WITH THE SITUATION GROWING MORE DESPERATE AND DEADLY with each passing day, Sabrina buried herself in prayer and reading her father's Bible and journal. Slowly she came to accept that if anything were to change the situation, it would be of divine making. News of Arsène and Philipe's departure to warn the Duc de Trudeau was a clear sign the marriage must take place. If the man she loved could so readily place himself in danger on behalf of another and her Savior willingly go to His death, she could do no less in protecting those she loved. At times her spirit sagged under the weight of the personal burden, but never did her resolve lessen.

However, when Adele told her about Dominic, Sabrina cringed. To the rest of Court, his absence was due to illness, but she determined to find a way to visit him before the wedding. She needed to speak to him, to reassure him on her behalf and to be reassured in respect to his condition. With the help of Roger and André, she arrived at Le Petite Château unnoticed.

In the elaborate master suite, Dominic sat in bed propped up by several pillows. Seeing him sitting up was good, however, when their eyes met, she lost her composure and rushed to the bed, weeping.

"I'll be well in a few days," he soothed.

"Adele assured me you will recover, but I had to come and see you."

"What about Father?"

"He believes I'm at Court. Roger met me behind the palace and brought me here."

"You're taking a great risk."

"I had to come to reassure you about the necessity of this marriage." She stopped him from speaking. "I am convinced it is the only way.

However, I don't know for how long I can keep Uncle from taking further action against all of you."

He winced, more in emotional than physical pain. "I wish to God I could find a way to prevent this marriage."

Adele hurried into the room. "Your parents are here!"

"I'm supposed to be at Court!" exclaimed Sabrina.

"Exit through the anteroom then down the back stairs," said Dominic, before turning to Adele. "Give her a moment then let my parents come up."

Nervous, Adele tugged at her fingers waiting for Sabrina to depart. At Dominic's signal she left to fetch the marquis and marquise.

Dominic tried to appear ill, which was not too difficult in his injured condition. He lay back on the cushions. "Sir. Mother. To what do I owe the honor of this visit?"

Jourdain surveyed his son, scrutinizing every detail. "You appear pale."

"A sudden onset of influenza." His gaze shifted between his parents. His mother seemed uneasy.

"I told you the rumor was untrue," she said to Jourdain and sat on the bed to feel Dominic's forehead. "Are you terribly ill?"

"Having never been ill, I suppose anything would be terrible." He looked to his father. "You heard something concerning me?"

"Your absence from duty the past few days is being questioned."

"Why? Adele told Captain de Lacy of my illness," he said, coughing for effect. "It has caused concern."

"If Captain de Lacy is concerned about my absence, why are you here instead of him?"

Jourdain squared his shoulders. "Personal business, and told him I would inquire."

"What business?" Dominic tried to restrain the crossness creeping into his voice and continue in his invalid role.

"To gain your reassurance that nothing will disrupt the wedding."

When Dominic stirred with anger, Adele laid hold of his arm to forestall any reply. "Monsieur, Dominic has made no action to interfere. At present he needs rest to regain his strength if he is even to attend the wedding."

"I wish to hear it from his lips."

"Is that necessary? He is ill," said Madeline in dispute.

Jourdain's response to his wife was a snarl of disapproval from which she recoiled.

Dominic spoke in a level voice. "I do not condone this marriage. Yet for Sabrina's sake, I will not interfere and draw further shame upon her."

Jourdain's temper flared. "Mind your tongue! This marriage is a good one!"

"This marriage should not take place!" Realizing he sounded and moved to quick for his condition, Dominic collapsed onto the cushions. "Forgive me, I am weak and dizzy."

"Your word."

"Dominic, please," his mother urged.

How fragile and old she appeared to him. "My word," he said in painful sobriety.

Jourdain left with Madeline obediently following.

Two days later in the early afternoon, the wedding bells of Notre Dame struck. The noble and eloquent Gothic architecture took over two hundred years to complete. On the nave and choir, slender tall spires rose to the heavens with magnificent flying buttresses as support. The north and south facades were designed in the true Gothic manner with a large pediment flanked by two small portals. Above the north jamb stood the graceful Virgin greeting all who entered.

The bride and her family arrived at noon. No expense was spared in adorning the Marquis de Charbonier's niece for this day. Long tedious hours were spent on the shimmering white satin gown with painstaking lace at the collar and sleeves. Diamonds and pearls from the Orient were incorporated into the dress to add glimmer and shine. The long train would be held by two pageboys while four petticoats gave the skirt its ruffle and body. A veil of Venetian lace covered Sabrina's head. The marquis considered the dress a work of art, but to Sabrina it was a shroud rather than a glamorous gown for a happy occasion.

Adele and Madeline were also beautifully gowned and jeweled for the occasion. They escorted Sabrina to a chamber left of the nave. Sabrina battled to maintain an outward appearance of indifference as she sat with hands folded in her lap. Though her manner appeared quiet and aloof, her countenance barely masked her inner turmoil. Her features were pale, lips pressed together and her eyes lackluster.

Madeline knelt beside her niece. "I must take my place to greet the guests. Try to understand, Jourdain believes he is doing right." Sabrina did not respond, or even look at her. Madeline kissed her niece's cheek and left

Adele remained. "What can I say? I love you like a sister and will always be there when you need me."

Sabrina didn't look up and muttered, "Thank you."

A quick knock was followed by Dominic's entrance.

Sabrina rose. They had not seen each other since her visit. His new suit of plain brown velvet shone forth with the riches and taste of his station. The color was more somber than fashionable for such a celebration, but matched the dark mood she saw on his face. She bit her lip to maintain her composure.

He took her hands, which were cool and trembling. "I came to give you encouragement, but seeing you, I find myself at a loss for such words."

Emotions overwhelmed her and she turned away.

He drew her back to face him. "You think of Arsène. I promise, no harm shall ever befall him. If that is all I can do to bring you some peace and happiness, I will gladly do so."

Another knock at the door and Jourdain entered.

"I came to wish my cousin well," said Dominic to his father's displeasure. He kissed Sabrina's forehead and left.

Jourdain spoke after Dominic departed. "The King, Queen, Prince and Cardinal are present. A wedding fit for a princess. Rightly so, a Charbonier is getting married."

"How convenient that I'm a Charbonier today when for years you hid my existence from the world."

"You may find this hard to believe, but this decision is not totally to my liking. I wish you could understand."

"I understand more than you know."

"Then take my arm, for that knock means it is time."

She stared at him, hardness about her eyes and mouth. "I will walk beside you, but I will not take your arm." She turned to Adele, who pulled the bridal veil over her face.

Adele led the way from the room to the aisle for the long, agonizing walk to the altar. Jourdain escorted Sabrina, distance between them.

From under the veil Sabrina's eyes swept over the crowded cathedral. In front, the King, Queen, and Prince Gaston sat. The Queen appeared tired while Louis enjoyed himself. Gaston sat rather sedate in his mood. Since Jourdain was a royal favorite, Gaston was ordered to attend. He also avoided Sabrina after learning of her marriage. This confirmed the truth of his attention being purely political and not true interest.

Richelieu sat opposite the Royal Family and the Charboniers. He was most piously dressed in his rich red velvet robes. He fingered the heavy gold cross about his neck. To the causal observer the Cardinal appeared bored, when in fact it was the opposite. He was delighted, only his self-restraint kept him from manifesting his glee.

Dominic sat beside his mother, his face void of expression. Other higher nobles present included, the Prince de Condé, Ducs de Bouillon, Franchot, Longueville, the Marquis d'Avallon and the Comtes de Reynard. Lesser noblemen and women made up the remainder of the guests.

Before the altar stood the Comte de Borchard dressed in white and gold brocade. The buttons of the doublet were diamonds set in real gold. He wore no sword, just the matching cloak and gleaming white hat with yellow dyed ostrich feathers. The count spared no expense in adorning himself with gold, diamonds and the finest perfume money could buy. He appeared almost ten years younger, but nonetheless fat in Sabrina's estimation.

The Bishop of Lyons waited at the altar, his aides in place around him. They were all dressed in ceremonial attire of the Church.

Each nerve-racking step brought Sabrina closer to her fate. She clenched her hands and forced herself not to look at Dominic when she passed the family pew. For if she did then she would not be able to continue.

She stopped and Borchard smiled at her, eager. She faced forward, her clenched hands now visibly trembled. To her, the Latin phrases meant nothing but she followed the bishop's instructions. All the while her heart cried out to God for strength. The ceremony ended with the Comte de Borchard walking down the aisle with his new countess, smiling large and proud.

Richelieu insisted on hosting the celebration. His taste of luxury shone in his design of the ballroom. On a large platform cordoned off by a gold railing, an ensemble of musicians played. The well-designed dance floor appeared to be one solid sheet of rose color marble. The white walls decorated with mahogany panels upon which hung paintings of famous scenes in church history. Marble statues of Christian martyrs stood beneath their respective paintings. Between each section of mahogany stood a window with maroon drapes. Windows on one side opened to the beautifully landscaped garden, while the other, to the private courtyard. In the banqueting hall a sumptuous feast awaited.

The King and Queen were announced, and all pomp and circumstance were given the Royal couple. The count and countess bowed before their Majesties.

"You are a lucky man, monsieur," said Louis. "You now have lovely new countess and connected in-laws."

"Thank you, Sire."

"I hope this will not stop you from attending court," said the Queen to Sabrina.

"I must see what duties my new station brings, Your Majesty."

The Queen solemnly nodded with understanding.

"Come, Madame. I wish to speak to Jourdain."

Richelieu appeared. With a large smile, he accepted the kiss Sabrina placed upon his ring of office. "Congratulations, madame and monsieur."

"Thank you, Eminence. Your selection of the Bishop of Lyons was excellent. I am in your debt," replied Borchard.

"By the way, I did not see the Duc de Trudeau or the Duc de Rohan."

"Both were indisposed, Eminence."

"I hope nothing serious."

Borchard smiled. "My sources say nothing that cannot be remedied, Eminence."

"As you say, for you are familiar with the situation," said Richelieu with a toothy grin, which made Borchard's smile fade.

Sabrina's gaze shifted between them, wishing ignorance of intrigues.

Dominic did not feel well after the wedding and wandered the palais before entering the ballroom. His illness of heart troubled him, not his wound. Despite his physical strength, intelligence and resources, he was forced to watch his beloved cousin manipulated by malevolent forces. Was he being a coward or prudent? The question plagued him. Still, he would not abandon Sabrina, but he needed to gather his emotions after the ceremony.

Gather my emotions? He scoffed to himself. *She trembled walking down the aisle and looked so pale and fragile when the veil was lifted.*

Never did he suspect such a tragic turn of events when she arrived in Paris. Prudence convinced him it was more dangerous for her to leave. Alas, hindsight showed differently. He should have sent her to Trèvoux instead of attending the Spring Festival and followed his resolve of not involving her in their deadly game of intrigue.

"Dominic," said Adele, appearing beside him and taking his arm. "Where have you been?"

"Clearing my head."

"Of the wedding or the journey?"

189

"Both."

"Brooding won't help them, but your presence will bolster her. So, come. At least eat something. I know you had no breakfast." She pulled on his hand to lead him to a table.

In the dining room, Louis, Richelieu and Jourdain sat to eat. Most of the table's occupants were dancing. The Queen and marquise were partnered with Condè and the Duc de Lyunes, son of the former Prime Minister, d'Albert. Sabrina danced with Gaston. Several guests detained Borchard.

Richelieu noticed Dominic and Adele take a seat at a table across the room. He spoke to Jourdain. "Dominic has been distracted from his duties of late."

The King spied the couple. "That's natural after the tragic loss of their child."

Jourdain choked on the wine.

Richelieu helped Jourdain recover by slapping him on the back. "Are you all right, Jourdain?"

"Yes, Eminence, thank you," his voice was strained in recovery. "What about the child, Sire?"

"Did he not tell you? Well, you've just arrived in Paris and for the happy occasion of your niece's wedding," said Louis matter-of-factly. "Your daughter-in-law was set upon by brigands, and as a result, lost the child she carried."

Jourdain took a drink, using the dodge to glare over the rim at his son.

Richelieu spoke to the reaction. "Strange he did not tell you."

Jourdian spoke after swallowing, or rather pretending. "Perhaps he did not want to upset my wife. She does not take bad news well."

"That could possibly be the reason."

"Bah!" interjected Louis, a rough wave at Richelieu. "Must you always be suspicious of people? The Charboniers have done France a service. I will hear none of your unpleasant speculations."

Richelieu fell silent to the reproach, fingers tugging at the cross about his neck. De Lacy enter the ballroom. "Excuse me, Sire. Captain de Lacy appears agitated."

"Go. Tend to your precious Guards."

Richelieu met de Lacy on the far side of the room. "Any news?"

"Two Musketeers left Paris a few days ago. One was Rohan's protégé. It appears Father Joseph learned before I. He alerted our agents and offered a handsome reward, but so far no news of them or the dukes."

"So that's where he's been. He knew I did not want to be involved." Richelieu cynically smiled. "Tréville will not be so arrogant on my next visit."

"There is more. The Duc de Bouillon departed Paris immediately after the wedding, heading south."

"South? Langerdoc, perhaps," mused Richelieu in thought.

"I thought the Huguenot army was destroyed?"

Richelieu shook his head. "I always suspected Rohan had some reinforcements hidden. I do not like to admit being wrong, but Tréville may be right. Rohan and Bouillon are too dangerous to be running around the country. Set the night watch and keep me informed."

After de Lacy withdrew, Richelieu was not ready to return to the table where Jourdain and the King sat chatting, so he decided to mingle.

At ten-thirty in the evening, Borchard made excuse for departure and thanked Richelieu for his hospitality. Sabrina only smiled when Richelieu gave them a blessing before leaving.

Despite fatigue from the long day, she grew nervous upon entering the carriage. Borchard sat close to her, pressing her hand to his lips. She repined at his kiss, yet he held onto her hand. She turned to the window, biting a lower trembling lip at the frightening realization she was now his wife. She knew she spoke words to that effect, but the public ceremony and reception provided a surreal aspect. Now, alone in the carriage and en route to his home, reality struck in full force.

He tried to engage her in small talk during the ride, but she didn't respond, gathering her courage for what was to come; the wedding night.

No, she would withstand him. After all, this was just a show to cover his treachery not a real marriage. Armed with that resolve, she left the carriage to enter the house. But once inside, a deep, disturbing coldness overcame her. She forced herself to speak.

"I wish to be shown to my apartment. I am fatigued and wish to rest."

"Indeed," said Borchard with a lewd smile. " René will show you to your rooms at once."

René, a small thin man with coarse brown hair, proved pleasant when showing the amenities of her apartment, but she didn't really listen.

"Has Angela arrived yet?" she asked, interrupting René.

"Yes, madame. I shall send her to you directly if you wish."

"Do so." She turned her back to the chamberlain, who left.

Moving further into the room she found herself in front of the vanity mirror. Staring back at her was the reflection of young woman in her wedding gown. A radiant gown dulled by a despondent expression. Not what she dreamt as a child of a princess marrying a handsome prince to live happily ever after. Dreaming proved a way of escaping the dreariness of her cloistered life in Reims. When Arsène came along she thought her childhood fantasy came true. This reflection showed reality not a dream. She collapsed into the chair before the mirror, weeping. Tears fell but her eyes were closed and hands clenched in prayer. Her lips moved, but the words were uttered from a broken heart and not her voice.

The door opened and she sat up expecting Angela, but instead saw Borchard. "Do you not knock, monsieur?"

"I did, but received no response." He made no comment to her tears, his gaze wanton. "You are beautiful, dear wife." He took her hands. "I dismissed your maid, you will not need her." He pressed her fingers to his lips. "This is our wedding night."

His vulgar desire was terrifying, but she must not repine. "Let us end this feeble pretense! We both know you received your treacherous payment! Be good enough to withdraw."

He laughed in haughty mockery. " I have no intention of leaving until I tasted the fruits of my payment."

This time she jerked her hands away but he seized her and kissed her. She kicked him in the shin, and tore herself away. "Vile beast! Your touch is base and disgusting!"

He straightened, anger on his face and in his voice. "As my wife, you will learn to tolerate it. Only after I feasting will my victory be complete."

"Do you not fear my uncle if this falsehood be discovered?"

"Jourdain could not refuse a Royal Command of the Queen in choosing a suitable husband for his niece. As for Dominic and Lamonreaux, there is too much danger to them if you refuse."

She gaped at him, horrified at the scope of the scheme.

"You understand. Good. The continuation of your understanding will keep the Gascon alive and your cousin from facing disgrace."

Fear and emotion made her whirl about, seizing the bedpost to keep from fainting. She hoped the fact of her marrying him would be enough. Only, now he made new threats against those she loved for her total surrender as his wife. *Oh, Lord! How foolish and naive I am!*

From behind a hand touched her hair and removed the hairpiece. The hand began caressing the back of her neck. He whispered in her ear. "You are all I wanted since the Spring Festival. Such a noble and delicate prize can only be admired by your equal, not some uncouth country bumpkin."

She bit her lip to stifle a sob and went rigid.

"Lack understanding so soon?"

Taking a deep breath, she forced herself to relax and when Borchard tried again to turn her, yielded. Borchard would have his reward.

✣ Chapter 16 ✣

TWO DAYS AFTER THE WEDDING, RICHELIEU ENTERED the main audience chamber and sat at his desk, irritated and tugging at the cross about his neck. Father Joseph followed.

"He did it! I truly did not believe he had the courage!" he chided.

"I assume you are referring to the Duc de Trudeau." Father Joseph took a seat in front of the desk. He was a short, stout, balding older man.

Richelieu frowned in deep contemplation. "If only he had delayed Trudeau."

"Perhaps he did not wish to risk possible escape and failure."

The Cardinal challenged the older priest. "You condone this?"

Father Joseph shook his head and spoke in mild responded. "I condone nothing. I'm only taking an objective view. You dealt with men of this ilk before. Are you really surprised?"

"No. Still, I am disturbed by the man's death. Heretic or not, William Trudeau was a good man to have as an ally. I tried to persuade him to denounce the Huguenots, but he was stubborn. Alas, we see the results of that stubbornness."

Father Joseph crossed himself and said a short Latin prayer. "Amen," he and Richelieu said together. Father Joseph continued. "I discovered further facts about the Musketeers. The other is Lieutenant Philipe Bourdias. I assumed they rode to warn Trudeau so I took the liberty of alerting our agents."

"Baron Bourdias' son?"

"The same. Brother-in-law of the Comte de Trèvoux. Whose wife—"

"Mistress of the Queen's Bedchamber," Richelieu finished the sentence. "Perhaps a family affair." He slyly smiled, a gleam in his eyes. "Clever to request Mademoiselle Charbonier's hand in marriage. I mistook it for pure greed. Have our agents located the Musketeers?"

Again Father Joseph crossed himself. "Alas, our agents failed, and at a deadly price. They were in Calais with Trudeau and left after his tragic death. I've received no word since."

Richelieu stroked his goatee in an attempt to stifle a satisfied smile. "Their little charade shall soon be brought to light. Order my carriage. I intend to pay Tréville a visit he shan't forget."

Tréville sat in his office looking over papers and maps of La Rochelle. He muttered and growled in frustration as he worked. The King wanted a second plan if Richelieu's dike failed. "If only I were permitted to lead my men to Ré. I could hold the island. Blast, Richelieu," he swore. "Dam up the harbor indeed!"

Thus far Chevalier Torais was successful, or rather lucky, in Tréville's estimation. The smaller fortress of St. Martin and Le Pree were sufficiently fortified but the islands concerned him, for with them came control of St. Martin's harbor, a key in possibly neutralizing the threat of an English armada. With a critical eye, he surveyed the map. Already in an ill-enough mood, he scowled when a knock disturbed him. He threw open the door intent on confronting his interrupter.

"I left strict orders not—" he stopped, taken back at seeing Richelieu.

"Do you always greet your visitors with such indignation, Captain?"

"No, Eminence. Forgive me, I was not expecting you." He moved aside in a humble bow to allow Richelieu to enter, yet quizzically stared after the priest. "To what do I owe the honor of this visit?"

Richelieu waved for the door to be closed. "I came to inquire after your Musketeers."

Tréville closed the door and crossed to the desk, his suspicion growing. "Were they baited into another quarrel by your Guards?"

"No, Captain. I came to inquire if they are ready for a campaign?"

"To La Rochelle? Of course, whenever the King wishes."

"The King gave command to Prince Gaston and asked me to finalize plans on the dike. We leave in ten days. Is that sufficient time for your infallible Musketeers?"

With wounded pride Tréville counter-parried. "Ten days is plenty of time, Eminence. What impossible task do you wish my men to accomplish? The entire siege of La Rochelle?"

"You will relieve the garrison on Ré."

Tréville's eyes lit up in a mixture of disbelief and pleasure. *No, he could not know! That's impossible!* He had to sit.

Richelieu continued, "There is another matter to bring to your attention, Captain."

"Oh?" asked Tréville, as if waking from a trance.

"Information concerning Lieutenant Bourdias and Sergeant Lamonreaux. I believe they are in your personal company."

"Lamonreaux and Bourdias?" echoed Tréville in confusion.

"Where are they?"

"Where are they, Eminence?"

"Yes, Captain! Must you repeat everything I say? Or are you now deaf?"

Tréville contained himself by gripping the arms of the chair until the knuckles turned white. "They are with their company on the practice range."

"Are you certain?"

"Are you insinuating I do not know the whereabouts of my men?"

"Not at all. I assume you have spoken to Sergeant Lamonreaux about our recent conversation."

"Yes, and he knew nothing of your plans, Eminence."

Richelieu eyes blazed with anger. "You were indiscreet concerning me?"

"Since you were ambiguous there is no other way for me to determine the meaning of the whole affair."

"Captain Tréville, I should not need to instruct you in the ways of Court policy in dealing with matters of State!"

Tréville bolted to his feet. "Neither do you need to instruct me on how to deal with my men! I asked for specifics, you gave none. As for my handling of the situation, neither do you require specifics. Yet if you wish to press the matter, we can bring it before His Majesty for judgment!"

Richelieu scowled with exceeding wrath, yet in arrogant dignity replied. "Burdening His Majesty is not necessary. However, when next you see Lamonreaux and Bourdias inform me."

"If you have anything against these men I want to know."

"Yes, Captain, when you do as I ask, you shall. But," he said with a shrug, "I don't believe you shall see them again."

Tréville intercepted Richelieu at the door. "I demand an answer!"

Richelieu stiffened. "You demand nothing of me." He pushed past the captain in leaving.

Tréville trembled in rage at realizing he played right into Richelieu's hands. Slapping the hilt of his sword, he strode to the window and looked down into the courtyard to some sparring Musketeers. "Lamonreaux and Bourdias, if you are involved with some scheme Richelieu has discovered, I hope to God you confide in me; otherwise I can do nothing to help you."

He returned to his desk, rang for his secretary and issued the order to make ready for a campaign. He also ordered Lamonreaux and Bourdias to report to him immediately.

Arsène and Philipe returned to Paris and the Bourdias chateau after parting from Rohan on the outskirts of Paris. They timed their arrival thirty minutes apart and came from different directions. They discovered a message summoning them to Tréville's office. Not bothering to clean up from their journey to facilitate their story, they made haste to headquarters. Arsène no longer needed a bandage on his head while the daily draught helped Philipe's pain but total recovery of the cracked ribs would take time.

Tréville sat at his desk buried in maps when they entered his office. For a long moment it seemed they were forgotten, but that was hardly the case when Tréville cast an angry glance upwards, sharply clearing his throat and leaning back in his chair.

"You two seemed to have taken a journey."

"We did, Captain, to Reims," said Arsène.

"Reims, Sergeant? Bourdias looks more like he had an encounter with the Cardinal's Guards." Tréville rose, walked to the front of the desk and stood before Arsène. "Speaking of the Cardinal. He knows more about my men than I." He watched them exchange perplexed glances. "Yes, gentlemen. His Eminence paid me a call earlier, and particularly interested in the two of you. Why? I asked myself. Now I ask you! Why?"

Arsène felt a lump rise in his throat and his pulse quicken. Philipe appeared incommode perhaps due to pain. Still, he was not good at lying, keeping confidence yes, but not verbal deception. And this excuse must be convincing for Tréville was too shrewd in matters of intrigue. Thus Arsène looked directly at the captain to speak.

"Over a week ago, Philipe learned of his dear grandmother's illness. According to his mother's letter, the old woman lay on her deathbed and she wanted to see him before she died. Not wanting him to ride alone I accompanied him to Reims. Alas, she died before we arrived. We stayed for the funeral. But en route back to Paris, we were set upon."

"Set upon?" Tréville cross-examined with a dubious expression.

"Yes, Captain. We suspect some of the Cardinal's men. If you recall, he inquired about me not too long ago. My innocence is not changed. The strangest part is a letter signed by Father Joseph, instructing them to kill us. Lieutenant Bourdias took the liberty of relieving one of them of it." Arsène pulled out the paper and handed it to Tréville.

"Along with his life I'm sure," said Tréville, a side-glance to Philipe, who still did not speak and appeared even paler. Tréville read the letter. "This is Father Joseph's hand, but this should have been destroyed. What mystery are you two involved with? Answer me truthfully, Lamonreaux. What is this affair of State?"

"Soothe, Captain, I already told you my association with a certain lady had nothing to do with an affair of state. Any interference was unintentional."

"Sergeant, you captured Richelieu's interest." Tréville raised a hand to quell a protest. "You gave ample excuses, but I warn you. This latest affair better have a good explanation or I shall do as the Cardinal bids, and send you to him!"

Arsène was made mute. Rarely did a hint of doubt or fear appear on his face in such situations.

Philipe spoke. "Captain, Sergeant Lamonreaux's association with the lady in question was exactly as he told you. Her cousin, the Comte de Trèvoux, did not know of this until his father, the marquis, made the announcement. As for our journey, you of all people know the Bourdias reputation, having served with my father." His voice halted slightly when mentioning his father, but the rest he spoke strong and sure for it was true.

"Can your story be proven?"

"We obtained leaves from Captain du Pree," said Arsène, recovering his voice.

"That's another thing! Why was I not informed of this?"

"You were in audience with the King."

"Here are leaves and a letter from my father." Philipe tried to maintain a calm exterior when pulling out three wrinkled parchments from his pockets.

Tréville took the papers and read the forged letter first.

> *My Old Friend and Comrade,*
>
> *I write in hopes of curbing your anger against Philipe and his companion, Sergeant Lamonreaux. He told me of the dilemma that delayed his arrival to Reims. I'm sorry to say my mother-in-law died before her wish was fulfilled. Accept my apologies if the summons of my son inconvenienced you.*
>
> *Take care, my friend, and go easy on the boy for my sake.*
>
> *Deepest regards,*
> *Jean-Claude*

The brief time it took Tréville to read, Arsène and Philipe barely breathed. If Tréville did not believe them, they would be lost!

Before Tréville could read the leaves of absence, du Pree arrived. "Ah, du Pree! Bourdias and Lamonreaux have returned."

"They appear rather hurt and disheveled for such a sorrowful journey."

"You remember?" said Tréville, hopeful.

"Of course. But what happened to them?"

"That is what I'm trying to determine." Tréville gave Father Joseph's letter to du Pree.

"I thought you went to Reims?" du Pree asked Philipe after reading.

"We did. My grandmother died shortly before we arrived."

Tréville handed du Pree the forged letter to read.

"Strange, but not surprising," said du Pree.

"Why do you say that?"

"Father Joseph is a fanatic with rarely any rhyme or reason to his actions. If the Cardinal had anything to do with this, he would not be so careless. Why tell you to warn Lamonreaux if he planned to assassinate him? No, Richelieu is more cunning and intelligent compared to Father Joseph's reckless destructive nature. Perhaps he thought to serve Richelieu where Lamonreaux is concerned."

Tréville snorted with irony. "I believe he's as mad as a loon. What of Bourdias?"

"He is my good friend," Arsène ventured an answer. Thus far he and Philipe listened as their fate hung on every word, though the conversation was carried on as if they were not present.

"Eliminate the possibility of vengeance?"

Du Pree shrugged. "Would be a futile attempt on Bourdias' part, but honor would be served. Also, I verified Lamonreaux's story at your request. The *affair d' amour* is purely that and not political intrigue."

Arsène felt a shiver shake the very marrow of his bones. Du Pree spoke to Sabrina! She is the last person he ever wanted his past to tarnish. He sensed Philipe's concern and briefly met his friend's stare. The eyes were nearly all brown and heavy with worry.

Tréville's abrupt clearing of his throat made them look forward again. "Have you been truthful in respect to this affair, Sergeant? Mind how you answer, for it could mean your life as far as the Cardinal is concerned."

Arsène clenched his fists for strength. "Yes, Captain."

"Bourdias?"

"I only support my friend faithfully and do not abandon him, even when sorely threatened by one such as Father Joseph."

Tréville gave Philipe a partial smile. "You are much like your father, a good and loyal friend. However," he said with a sign of resignation, "since Father Joseph is involved there will be further investigation lest Richelieu accuse me of being soft-hearted. Mind you, I believe you are innocent. Until this inquiry is completed you will both confine your activities to a minimum. And for heaven's sake, stay clear of the Cardinal, Father Joseph, de Lacy, or any of His Eminence's Guards! About your grandmother, Bourdias; my deepest condolences." He picked up the forged letter, a fond smile of remembrance appearing. "It has been too long since your father and I corresponded. Perhaps I shall write him soon."

"Meanwhile, stay out of trouble for the next ten days," said du Pree.

"Why ten days?" asked Arsène.

"A campaign leaves for La Rochelle under Gaston's command. In actuality, Richelieu will be in charge. Now return to your men, Lieutenant. And mind what I said! Both of you." Tréville dismissed them.

Once in the plaza, Philipe drew Arsène into the shadow of the building. "Our secret can't be kept if Tréville writes my father."

"No time with the campaign only ten days away. If he does, we'll deal with it then. This time your letter and speech saved us."

"I'm grateful for one opportunity to repay the debts I owe you for quick thinking."

Arsène chuckled, but hollow and humorless. "In celebration of your departure from untainted pragmatist to Machiavellian, the drinks are on me. I know just the place where the greeting will be warm and the wine, bottomless."

"No. Go home, Arsène. I will speak to Dominic. We are at a critical juncture, even a minor mistake can cost our lives."

Arsène scowled and chided, "I'm not a fool!"

"No, stubborn."

"As you are irksome! I will behave. Only do not be tedious and remind me of my every action." Arsène stormed off.

"Meet me at platoon in two hours!" called Philipe.

"I have to meet a special friend!" Arsène kept walking as he replied.

"Three hours," Philipe amended the time understanding Arsène's code sentence for calling upon Rohan.

In his fuming state, Arsène made his way toward his apartment. The jolting of a nearby harness startled him. A carriage stopped before Borchard's chateau, so he paused unseen at the corner, watching in dreaded anticipation. Borchard alighted first then came Sabrina. He knew he would see her at Court, but he never anticipated such a paralyzing reaction and his heart seemed to stop beating. She turned to the coachman, who spoke to her. Arsène ducked behind the corner to avoid being seen. His breathing labored and he trembled. The thought of Sabrina as another man's wife disturbed him, but the reality of seeing it tore at every fiber of his being. Gritting his teeth against the pain, he ran off.

Philipe's visit with Dominic proved disheartening. Each shared what happened but Dominic's poignant lament for Sabrina disturbed Philipe.

"Never in my wildest imagination did I anticipate anything like this. Arsène blundered with a few heated words, but father's actions stem from a deep-seated hatred that places us in peril. Oh, Philipe, if you saw her that day. God in heaven only knows how Arsène would have acted if he were there. I barely kept my wits."

Philipe listened with tight jowls and darkened eyes. "Where is she now?"

Dominic shrugged since he took a drink. "I don't know. She was not at his chateau when I sent André with a note, hoping for a visit."

"With the campaign a reality, I wonder what Borchard will do?"

"Who knows? What about Arsène? Did he said anything about marching against Rohan?"

"No, we parted after leaving Tréville's office. Perhaps when we meet at the platoon, I can coax him into speaking."

Dominic took careful note of Philipe's tone and worried features. "Do you think he will act rashly?"

"I'm not sure." Philipe finished his drink. "I better not keep him waiting."

Philipe arrived at headquarters to discover Arsène was not there and no one had seen him. This was odd, since he was never absent from duty. By late afternoon, Arsène had still not reported and Philipe became worried. He posted watches before leaving headquarters to head for Arsène's apartment.

He didn't see the turned drape, a signal that Arsène wasn't home. Using his key, Philipe entered, calling his friend's name. No response and no sign Arsène had been there. He may still be with Rohan.

Leaving the apartment, he proceeded to the duke's chateau and used the back entrance. The maid gave him a note saying the duke left it for the sergeant, but he hadn't arrived. The note was written in coded phrases, but Philipe wasn't surprised to learn the duke left Paris again due to the campaign. Arsène's absence from duty and neglect of the duke made the mystery more alarming.

He searched every place he and Arsène frequented over the years determined to find the Gascon, hopefully in one piece. He couldn't image what would delay Arsène save injury or worse.

Notre Dame's bell rang eight o'clock at night when Philipe paused by Le Pont-Neuf frustrated by a fruitless search. "Blasted, Gascon! What folly have you stumbled into this time?"

Hearing familiar laughter, he turned to see an inebriated Arsène emerge from a tavern and leaning upon a barmaid.

"I appreciate your concern, but I am well," he slurred.

"Go home, monsieur." The girl pushed him off her shoulder.

"Arsène!"

Startled, Arsène stumbled, trying to draw his sword. "Wanna fight?"

Philipe caught Arsène's arm. "No. It's me, Philipe."

He squinted to focus. "Who's the fellow with you?"

"Is he a friend of yours, monsieur?" the girl asked.

"Yes, and I'll take care of him. Does he owe you money?"

"No. But he wanted more than drink." The girl left.

"Where are you going?" Arsène asked after the girl.

"Come, I'll take you home."

"Leave off!" Arsène jerked away. In doing so, he stumbled and fell backward into the wall separating the street from the river.

"You don't mean that."

"How do you know what I mean? I'm not your twin. You can't read my mind!"

"It doesn't take a mind reader to see you are troubled. I've never seen you so drunk."

"Sorry to disappoint you, but I'm not as drunk as I'd like to be." Arsène tried to stand. "Where did the wench go?"

"Enough, I'm taking you home." Philipe took Arsène by the arm.

"I said leave off!" This time Arsène did not jerk away, instead he punched Philipe in the face.

The unexpected blow sent Philipe backwards, tearing a piece of Arsène's sleeve. The blue eyes became enraged at seeing the tear. Philipe gaped, stupefied by the unusual violent look directed at him. Before he could utter a word, Arsène attacked. Fortunately in his drunken state, he proved clumsy. Philipe didn't want to hurt Arsène in his attempt to contain the hotheaded Gascon, but Arsène managed to punch him in the stomach. Another blow to the jaw sent him sprawling to the street. Arsène went to leap upon Philipe when massive arms caught him from behind.

"Stop it!" snapped Dominic, fighting to restrain Arsène, who cried out in fury. "I don't want to hurt you so stop struggling!"

Philipe got to his feet, but remained bent over in pain and holding his stomach. "What's come over you? Perhaps I should let Dominic toss you in the river to cool your hot head and sober you up!"

Arsène ceased his struggle at seeing Philipe's injuries, a bruised jaw and blood oozing from a cut lip. In remorseful befuddlement he stammered; "Philipe! I'm sorry. You can let me loose, Dominic. I won't do anything else."

For a moment Dominic hesitated but released Arsène after an assenting nod from Philipe.

Utterly ashamed, Arsène staggered off.

"Where are you going?" asked Philipe.

"Does it matter?" replied Arsène over his shoulder.

"Of course it does."

Arsène paused and glanced back. "I'm going to find a nice soft place to lie down. I mean my bed. You can both go home and forget this happened." Once more he moved off.

"I know about Sabrina," said Dominic.

Arsène pulled up short, but did not turn.

Philipe's quizzically glance found Dominic. "Sabrina?"

"She returned earlier today," he explained, but watched Arsène.

Arsène's back remained turned to them, but his voice was hoarse. "I saw her with Borchard at his chateau. I never knew anything could hurt so much! If I hadn't left, I would have killed him!"

"She saw you and asked me to seek you out."

Arsène turned, his face wretched and eyes moist. "Don't tell her how you found me. The pain is bad enough, I cannot bear her pity!" He ran off.

Dominic stopped Philipe from following. "He must deal with this himself."

✤ Chapter 17 ✤

URING THE DAYS OF CAMPAIGN PREPARATIONS, Philipe sensed a distancing between himself and Arsène. Not that Arsène acted moody or unsociable, quite the contrary. A troublesome arrogant cavalier attitude developed. When he tried to speak to Arsène about the Huguenots and the campaign, the Gascon either dismissed the importance or avoided it. He thought about speaking to Dominic concerning Arsène's changed behavior, but with all under heavy scrutiny and surveillance, Dominic could offer little help. Thus he considered any options singularly.

Going on the campaign helped with leaving Paris, but what were odds of arriving safe to La Rochelle if discovered? What about deserting at La Rochelle? He knew Arsène wouldn't raise a hand against Rohan, but what about against his own company? How would Arsène respond when the time came? How would he respond to turning against the men under his command? Philipe cringed at realizing the moment of decision was at hand.

True they preformed their clandestine Huguenot activities under the guise of loyal Musketeers, but they had never turned against their own men. All their covert encounters were with de Lacy and the Cardinal's Guards. Yet too much had been sacrificed to turn back now. He pushed his mind down any avenue of thought in hopes of finding a satisfactory plan.

Alas, by the afternoon of the day prior to departure, he was frustrated by the gnawing question regarding Arsène's frame of mind when action was needed. Never before had he doubted or even felt a twinge of uncertainty. He brooded all the way to the company stables where he and Arsène agreed to meet to make a last inspection of the horses for the journey.

Rounding the corner, he spied Arsène speaking to a woman in a cape with the hood up to conceal her identity. This was obviously a private

206

rendezvous by the location. Arsène kissed her, and the hood fell back. Jeanette Charise!

Philipe accosted his friend. "Arsène, why are you debasing yourself by succumbing to this wench?"

Jeanette's eyes narrowed at Philipe. "Debase?" She turned to Arsène and demanded, "Will you allow him to insult me?"

"What? You want I should draw on him?"

"I want you to behave like a gentlemen and defend a lady's honor!"

"What lady?" chided Philipe.

Jeanette slapped Philipe and stormed off.

Arsène made no comment to Jeanette's action or Philipe's glowering rather moved to tend the horses. Philipe followed, annoyed and let Arsène know it.

"I don't believe you! Have you thought about Sabrina and how she would feel? She married to save you not to see you ruin yourself."

Arsène seized Philipe. "Keep her out of this."

"Impossible. We leave for La Rochelle tomorrow. I hope and pray the Gascon I've come to know and love can face the challenge and be depended upon and not this stranger I now see!"

Stunned, Arsène loosed Philipe. "I would not forsake you for any reason, and grieved you would even question me."

For the first time since returning, Philipe saw a crack in the façade. "Then dine with Dominic and me at the Café de Halles this evening." There was the briefest of hesitation, but he wouldn't allow the crack to close and made Arsène look at him by taking his face in his hands. "Please, *mon fere esprit*. You can't fail us now."

A faint smile appeared and Arsène nodded. "I'll be there."

Once around the corner from them, Jeanette paused and listened to the conversation. She scowled when Arsène agreed to meet for dinner. Suddenly a hand jerked her around bringing her face-to-face with de Lacy, who was in a foul mood.

"You're taking your time, my dear."

With wounded pride, she regained her composure and shook off his hold. "Tonight I have a rendezvous with him, but need your help."

"My help? You can't work your wiles on a simple Gascon?"

"Not the Gascon. His arrogant friend Bourdias invited him to dine with him and Charbonier to avoid our rendezvous."

"I can take care of Charbonier. Bourdias, not so easy."

Jeanette slyly smiled. "Never mind. I thought of the perfect person to employ and teach the interfering cur a lesson."

"You better, my dear," he said with a hard warning. "I know Lamonreaux is somehow involved with the Huguenots. I want specifics, names and such. Do you understand?"

"Do you want only the information, or Lamonreaux as well?"

"Information for now. If action is to be taken, have no fear. You will not be involved. I can handle one Gascon."

"Then why do you need my help now?"

He snarled. "Complete your task tonight or the visit I promised you will not be one of gratitude." He gave a faint sigh of displeasure, caressing her shoulder and up her neck. "It would be a shame to wring such a lovely neck." Upon pronouncing the last sentence the caress became a hard grasp about her throat. She gasped and became frightened. He shoved her away. "Now go, and produce results."

That evening, Philipe placed the finishing touches on his suit, a blue and gold brocade with all the trimmings of gentry. For the length of the campaign he would be in uniform, thus decided to forego it for more suitable attire for an evening out.

Roger entered. "Master, Mademoiselle Pontinière is here."

"Elizabeth." Philipe privately smiled. "Admit her to the salon and tell her I shall be down presently."

He looked in the mirror for one last inspection. The bruise on his jaw from Arsène's blow was barely visible, and the cut a pale pink line. Pleased, he fetched his hat, cloak and gloves and proceeded downstairs to the salon.

"Elizabeth," he greeted. For an impromptu visit she was finely dressed in a cream colored silk gown and smelled of sweet roses. Her cloak lay over the back of a chair.

She indicated the glass of port she held. "I hope you don't mind. Your man said to make myself comfortable."

"No. Unfortunately, I have an appointment."

"Oh," she said in visible despondency. "I supposed I should have sent a message, but I miss you so." Her lower lip pouted.

"I fear campaign preparations have kept me busy."

She gave an extreme sigh of melancholy. "My improvement of your disposition was not sufficient to warrant further alteration?"

"Your alteration was exactly what I needed."

A brooding cloud passed over her face and she placed a delicate hand to her bosom. "Only for one night. It is the nature of men and women. For a man temporary, for a woman much deeper." She placed down her glass. "I don't blame you for not finding me attractive."

"No." Philipe tossed aside his cloak, hat and gloves and crossed to her. "You are a very pleasing woman, Elizabeth."

She looked at him with soft eyes. "Do not try to soothe me. I made a fool of myself coming here." Overcome, she took a deep breath. "I feel warm and faint!"

He helped her to the sofa and fetched her glass of port. "This will help."

She took a sip in an attempt to calm herself. "Forgive my display."

"There is nothing to forgive."

"You're so kind. But I'm keeping you from your appointment."

"No need to rush. Finish your drink and regain your strength."

Her smiled turned plaintive. "Will you join me in a farewell drink?"

"Of course. Only not farewell." Philipe poured a glass of port. Upon returning to sit beside her, he raised the glass in salute. "To another time, and very soon."

"Very soon," she echoed and drank.

He drained the glass and frowned. "Must be the Italian brand. Spanish is much sweeter."

"I find it marvelous." She took a hearty sip.

"Would you care for another glass?"

"Too much port makes me giddy. I prefer burgundy for drinking. Please, help yourself. When I'm finished I shall leave."

Philipe poured himself another glass and sat again. Elizabeth raised her glass in a mild salute and took a sip. He drank another half a glass.

"I hope whomever your appointment is with will not be too disturbed by your tardiness on my behalf."

He laughed. "No need to fear. A few moments will not matter too greatly." He balked at a sudden strange sensation. His expression turning sour yet confused.

"Is something wrong?" she inquired, batting her blue eyes.

"Er, no. What did you say?"

"I hope your friend will not be too put out by my delaying you."

"He shouldn't be," he nonchalantly said, taking another drink.

"He?" She feigned annoyance, watching him. "You would leave me to keep an appointment with him?" her voice throaty and sensuous.

His perception became fuzzy and she appeared different, hazy and surreal. Her clear blue eyes alluring and her round, rich lips inviting. "An important appointment," he said, confused by the growing sensation.

"Very important?" she breathed in his ear.

An overwhelming suffusion ran the length of his body. It coursed through his veins, tingling his senses and clouding his mind. The sensation intensified when she began kissing his neck. The scent of roses filled the air about him. "I can't be too late," he heard himself protest, but it didn't sound like his voice. It was distant and abstract.

Elizabeth became bolder, moving from his ear and to kiss his mouth. A low moan escaped Philipe's lips. Everything was disjointed; everything became warm. He felt himself falling, and then all went black.

Arsène decided to pack his saddlebags and ready his equipment before heading to the rendezvous with Philipe and Dominic. As he knelt before the trunk to pack the saddlebags, he laid the Bible on the floor. Once he was finished packing, he replaced any unnecessary items into the trunk. Picking up the Bible, he hesitated. So much heartache and danger happened he didn't return for further reading. Would it help? What could it hurt? He stuffed the Bible into the saddlebag. He closed and locked the trunk. He placed the saddlebag on the floor next to his musket at the door to his bedchamber for easier gathering in the morning. Grabbing his hat, he left the apartment.

He just arrived at the rendezvous when a boy came running up to him. "Sergeant Lamonreaux." The boy gave him a note and ran off.

The note was from Dominic saying he was detained indefinitely and Philipe sent to Vincennes on military business and would not return until after midnight. Arsène crumpled the paper. He came to this meeting reluctantly only to find it was canceled. A nearby group of soldiers laughed in camaraderie. He threw the crumpled note into the river.

Uncertain of what to do, he began to wander the streets. Many different scenes came into view. The city was filled with soldiers all making the most of their last evening in Paris before a major campaign. Some kept company with sweethearts or wives, others with cheerful comrades.

Arsène watched a couple, lovers by their cooing and endearing words. He breathed a heartsick sigh and moved off. If he asserted himself he and Sabrina could become lovers, but deep in his heart that would not satisfy. She touched his soul and he wanted more from their relationship; he wanted her as his wife, his life's helpmate.

A few times a fellow Musketeer shouted a greeting to him. One even asked after Philipe since he was alone. To them, Arsène acted cavalier and merry, replying that he was on his way to meet Bourdias. He didn't blame Philipe, duty was duty; but that didn't ease the sense of abandonment and hurt. Deprived of his love, he at least wanted the support and comradeship of a dear friend.

After three hours of aimless wandering, he arrived home. To his surprise, the table candle was lit and an inside shadow moved. He drew his sword.

"No need for violence, Arsène," said a female. She threw back her hood and stepped into the candlelight.

He snarled at Jeanette. "How did you get in?"

"It was not too difficult convincing your landlady with *l'amour* in the air tonight," she said with a wide smile. "Why are you late in coming to me?"

"I was detained," he said flatly, sheathing his sword.

"Are you available now?"

"Available, yes. In the mood, no."

She moved to his side and caressed his face. "This is your last night in Paris before going to war. Remember the kiss I gave you earlier as a sample," she whispered and began undoing his doublet.

Arsène remained motionless in vexation. Her advances made his senses come alive. It had been a long time since he took pleasure with a woman, especially one of such alluring beauty. Her hand caressed his chest and her mouth was warm on his cheek. "I cannot!" he said, the words forced and difficult to speak.

"Pretend I am she."

He was losing his self-restraint, and when she pressed her whole body against him, it was too much. He took her in his arms and kissed her. Whereas Jeanette aroused his physical desire, her kiss was different then Sabrina and he tore himself away.

"You kissed me. Why resist now?"

"You don't understand fidelity do you?"

"Your reputation is far from spotless!"

"I know," he murmured.

"Arsène, there is no need to play the gallant. Our emotions for someone else have nothing to do with our desires. I do not want your heart, so you need not fear."

"No, you want revenge."

"Men avenge themselves by the sword. Women have only ourselves to use to such ends."

With a disgruntled growl, he began heading for the door.

Panic set in and she said, "I promise, once I have answers to my questions—"

"Answers?" he interrupted, a harsh level glance at her.

She flashed a nervous smile and heaved an uneven shrug. "Answers as to why you refused my mother, but more importantly," she tried assuming her earlier seductress role, drawing close to him, "how you are in bed."

He stopped her approach as nervousness filled her expression, despite her attempt to hide it. "Why do I suddenly suspect revenge for your mother is not the reason for your visit? What trickery is this?"

"No, trickery," she said, a laugh feeble in attempted joviality.

He flashed a hard, cynical smile. "You are trying very hard to be the intriguer, but in that respect I'm better than you. So you may ask your questions, my little vixen, for by them I will learn what this is about." His grip on her arm was painful and she winced, trying to get free but he held fast. "Well, girl, speak! Who put you up to this?

She stood mute and no longer the temptress, but a frightened girl of fifteen.

"Your mother?" he pressed.

She shook her head, unable to speak.

"Not your mother. The Comte de Borchard?"

"No," she clamored.

"De Lacy?"

A muted cry of terror escaped her compressed lips.

"Zut!" He shoved her away, turning aside to regain his composure and not realizing he pushed so hard that she fell to the floor. Snatching his hat, he departed.

"Arsène! Gascon cur! He'll kill me!" she called frantic, but ignored.

He ran across the street and around the corner. Learning of de Lacy's involvement could make his latest folly dangerous for all. He considered sneaking out of Paris, but no. He would not abandon Philipe and Dominic. If he survived the night unscathed and arrived at the parade ground in the morning, de Lacy would be thwarted. Thus he made his way to a hiding spot he utilized before, a small tack room in an abandoned stable on the far bank.

He settled into a cozy corner of the tack room. The chiming of a church bell sounded the hour of two o'clock. Four hours until dawn. He drew his sword and laid it across his lap for quick access should anyone wander inside. He considered the entire situation since Sabrina fled to Paris. Every memory and emotion attached to the relationship stabbed at his heart. Now, come morning, he was to leave on a campaign against Rohan. He couldn't do that! But what were his options? Perhaps after using the campaign to safely reach La Rochelle, they could discover a way to desert and reach the city. How? The noise and clamor of an encampment and battlefield often brings confusion. Ah, confusion, his constant companion of late. It mocked him, hounded him and now threatened his ability to reason. But he knew it wasn't his lack of rationality causing his tumult. The answer lay in his heart and spirit.

"Lord, please, some how, some way help me to see my way clear in all this. My heart and mind have failed under this unbearable weight! You need to do something, for I am at a loss."

He wiped his eyes and leaned back against the wall, listening and waiting both for the physical and the spiritual; physical in the form of any intruder and spiritual in longing for an answer and some peace.

A rooster crowing startled him. He fell asleep as told by the shafts of gray light filtering through the slats. Not what he wanted to do and moved to the slats to get a better view of the light. Dawn. He passed the night safely and felt a measure of relief.

"Thank you, Lord, for one challenge met."

He stood, sheathed his sword and stretched out the kinks in his muscles before emerging from the tack room. Not many people were up and about yet, but would be soon. If they weren't connected to the campaign they wanted to see the military on parade.

He reached the main boulevard to turn for headquarters when someone called him.

"Sergeant! Sergeant Lamonreaux!" A worried Roger came running. "Thank the Lord!" he said in breathless relief. "My master—is just lying there. I don't know if he's alive."

Arsène ran to Philipe's home, a winded and worried Roger following.

"The drawing room!" said Roger.

Philipe lay face down on the floor. Arsène felt for a pulse, an anxious Roger hovering over his shoulder. "He's alive." He turned Philipe over and opened the doublet searching for wounds but found none. He opened Philipe's eyes. The pupils were glossy and slow to respond to light. "Help me get him on the sofa."

Roger did as bade. "Will he live?"

Arsène did not answer, looking for signs of what happened. A spilt glass of port lay on the floor near when he found Philipe. Another glass sat on the table next to a half empty bottle. He picked up the fallen glass and sniffed. He crossed to the table and smelled the half empty bottle then took a cautious sip, grimaced and spit out the port.

"What is this?" he demanded.

"Spanish port. The bottle you gave him for his birthday. Has he been poisoned?"

"Drugged, and very potent, I still taste the bitterness." Arsène returned to further examined Philipe, who's breathing was steady and he did not appear to be in distress. "Did he have a visitor last night?"

"A woman I didn't recognize, but the lieutenant knew her."

"What was her name?"

"Pontinière."

"Elizabeth Pontinière? Strange. Why would she drug Philipe?"

"She arrived just before he left for your rendezvous."

"You didn't notice her departure or that he was still home?"

"She told me he left for his appointment. At the time I had no reason to doubt her. Earlier he generously gave me the night off."

Philipe began to stir from his stupor, so Arsène encouraged the rousing by gently shaking him. "Wake up, Philipe. We have a campaign to attend." He fought the prodding with an annoyed grunt but Arsène tapped his face. "Come, Philipe! Up!"

Philipe awoke with a start then glanced about in confusion. "Arsène? Oh! My head." He noticed the lightness of the room. "*Ma foi*, it is tomorrow? I mean, morning?"

"I'm afraid so." Arsène helped Philipe sit.

"Can I get you anything, master?" asked Roger with concern.

Philipe blinked several times to focus on Roger. "Something for a splitting headache." He held his head. "I can't be drunk. I only had a few glasses of terrible Italian port."

"You had more than that. The port was the Spanish bottle I gave you, only drugged by Elizabeth Pontinière."

"What? Talk sense, man. Why would she drug me?"

"This is where I come into this plot of revenge."

Philipe frowned in annoyance and pain, his eyes dull and heavy. "Take pity on my condition and be more specific."

Arsène waved his hands in frustration. "A bit sordid and confusing but it began with Dominic's note informing me he was detained and you sent to Vincennes on a military mission."

"Dominic wrote that?"

"It was in his hand. More disturbing is who is behind this orchestrated effort and why. I found out the answers at my apartment."

Philipe went to question Arsène's further when Roger returned and handed him a cup. He looked inside the cup and took a whiff. "Buttermilk?"

"With some of the sergeant's herbal headache remedy," said Roger.

Philipe hesitated to drink long enough to and ask, "Why would Dominic write you such a note? And what does this have to do with Elizabeth?"

"Jeanette somehow learned you persuaded me to avoid our rendezvous and meet with you and Dominic."

"So she planned revenge on you by convincing Elizabeth to drug me and prevent our meeting?" he asked after the second sip.

Arsène glanced along his shoulder at Philipe. "De Lacy sent Jeanette to pry me for information."

Philipe nearly gagged as he finished the buttermilk. "What? You didn't fall for it, did you?"

216

Arsène became offended. "My flesh may be weak at times, by my mind is still quick. I manage to get the truth without succumbing to her."

"Where's she now?"

"I don't know. I left her pronouncing curses upon Gascons."

"And de Lacy?"

"I've not seen him, but it would be unwise to act directly against us this morning. I think we may be safer on the battlefield than in Paris."

Philipe began to laugh, but stopped when his head hurt.

"Are you well enough for the campaign, master?" asked Roger.

"I have little choice." He handed the cup back to Roger before trying to stand. Once on his feet, he swayed slightly, but waved off help from both Arsène and Roger.

❧ Chapter 18 ❧

URIOUS OF THE REASON FOR THE HIVE OF ACTIVITY IN THE HOUSE, Sabrina made her way downstairs. Her curiosity increased at finding Borchard inspecting military equipment in the foyer.

"Monsieur, what is all this?" she asked.

"Ah, madame. I have some business to discuss with you."

"Does it concern these items?"

"It does. I'm sure you're aware of the campaign leaving for La Rochelle this morning?"

"Of course."

He smiled, looking at her in the way she came to know he meant for affection. For an older man, he fancied himself a great lover. She inwardly shivered with repulsion when he spoke.

"You are beautiful and it grieves me to leave you so soon."

"Leave?" she heard herself ask, still shaking off his look.

"His Eminence asked me to be a part of the entourage to La Rochelle."

Her ire rose. "You will openly betray the Huguenots by marching against them?"

His features grew firm. "I knew my announcement would disturb you, which is why I waited until this morning. I was forced to make a decision. Either continue in this dangerous charade or to cut my way clear to the side of victory. I achieved what I desired. Now the final cord can be severed."

Outraged, she clenched her hands. "What is the purpose of telling me? To torment me?"

"I tell you because today you shall join Their Majesties and other families of the entourage in reviewing the parade." His eyes narrowed and voice dropped in tone. "As my wife I depend upon your obedience and silence in this matter. Be good enough to be ready to depart in an hour." He turned on his heels and left the house.

For a moment Sabrina stood stunned. Her marriage and submission were not enough, now he would raise arms against her people! Intense anger spilled over into tears and she ran upstairs, burst into her chamber, startling Angela.

Sabrina paced the room trying to calm down and concentrate. "I must do something! I cannot live with such a beast," she spoke aloud then seeing her maid she stopped. "Angela, faithful servant of my youth! I will go to Trèvoux. Uncle rarely visits and Dominic will not mind."

"What?" squealed Angela, confused and concerned.

Sabrina continued speaking, bolstered with confidence of her decision. "After the count and I leave for the ceremony, pack what you can. Wait for me in the carriage behind the palace. We leave for Trèvoux when I can get away. Now fetch my gold and green dress. I have a Royal ceremony to attend."

All manner of banners and pageantry decorated the palace plaza. Each division was assigned a place. To the far right stood the cavalry, who would lead the procession. Behind them came the Swiss Guards and Pikemen. On the far left assembled the artillery and Cardinal's Guards. The center position on the plaza was reserved for the King's Musketeers.

Captain Tréville barked orders from astride his stallion. His campaign uniform consisted of a plainer doublet designed to accommodate the shiny and elaborate cuirass. A large crimson sash replaced the baldric. The boots were those made for a cavalry soldier, heavy leather and reaching to the knees. It was too warm for a cloak, but the cuirass was fashioned to accept one when needed.

Like the rest of the soldiers, Arsène and Philipe played their roles in following Tréville's orders. Philipe still appeared tired about the eyes, but his mind clearer. Unlike Arsène, he wore no tunic, as officers did not do so. Neither did he wear the cuirass or sash of the senior officers, rather the plain silver gorget about his shoulders and epaulets of a junior officer. His gloves were light gray rather than the common black, another identification of his rank. He noticed Arsène fidget with Ranger's bridle but made no comment. What could he say that wouldn't be misconstrued or overheard?

The sounding of trumpets and drums beating drew their attention forward.

Richelieu descended the palace steps to his horse, a beautiful white Andalusia stallion. The Cardinal placed aside his robe of office and wore a crimson and gold doublet and breeches. The gold cuirass shimmered in the sunlight. The hilt of an elaborately carved sword swung from a black sash. The polished cavalry boots shone with each step and the spurs clanked. The crowd cheered and waved. He acknowledged the masses with a wave and made the sign of the cross with some mumbled Latin phrases before mounting.

Father Joseph sat mounted upon a mule, waiting for Richelieu. Unusual for a Capuchin, pledged to poverty, to be seen riding any type of beast, but under the circumstances, Richelieu insisted. What a contrast the two priests made. One all resplendent and seated upon a magnificent steed, the other humble and mounted upon a mule.

Richelieu beckoned de Lacy to him. The captain pulled his mare beside the Cardinal's horse. "I do not appreciate my captain being late for such an significant event."

"My apologies, Eminence. I had important business."

"Your personal affair with Mademoiselle Charise is of no importance to me, Captain! This campaign is."

"I have no personal business, save to serve Your Eminence."

With cold and calculating eyes, Richelieu stared de Lacy. "Did this business have favorable results?"

"Alas, I fear not, Eminence."

"You know the price for failure, Captain."

"Yes, Eminence, only I was not the one to fail."

"That does not change the price. The piper needs to be paid."

"By an anonymous source, it is paid in full."

For a moment, the Cardinal said nothing, then made a curt wave. "See to the men, Captain."

After he dismissed de Lacy, another trumpet sounded.

Gaston appeared, radiating the glory and majesty befitting his station. Upon his cuirass hung a cross of the Knights of the Holy Ghost. A large scarlet sash encompassed his waist. Gaston wore no cloak and a plumed helmet replaced his cavalier hat. In his right hand he carried a baton of a *maréchal* of France. Most considered Gaston a formidable military leader, whose capabilities were overshadowed by Louis' exploits. At the bottom of the steps, he mounted a magnificent white Lipizzan stallion.

Richelieu saluted the Prince. "All is ready, Monsieur."

Gaston turned the horse to inspect the nobles in his entourage. Present in the party were the Prince de Condé, Duc d'Angoulême, Duc de Luynes, his two brothers, Baron du Modence, Admiral Montmorency, who commanded of the Royal Navy; and of course, the Comte de Borchard.

The trumpets blew a third time. The King and Queen appeared on a balcony overlooking the courtyard. The wives and families of the entourage and the Queen's ladies accompanied the royal couple.

All eyes gazed on the sovereigns. Arsène's heart skipped a beat at seeing Sabrina amongst the nobles. How beautiful she appeared and sweet memories flooded his mind as she wore the same gown as the night at Saint Germain-En-Laye. So much happened to change both of them since the terrace meeting. Yet no length of time could quench the burning on his lips at remembering their first kiss. He shuddered at the thought this may be the last time he would ever see her. Her discreet glance scanned the parade ground, but in the mass of military personal, doubtful she would see him. He felt Philipe's supportive hand on his shoulder, but dare not look at his friend.

In another part of the courtyard, Dominic also noticed Sabrina standing with Adele near the Queen. Somehow Sabrina appeared different and he became uneasy. In such a short time she changed. He attempted to communicate with her before the campaign left Paris, but to no avail.

His gaze shifted to Adele, so beautiful and he would have to carry this last sight of her to an uncertain future. She behaved bravely at their earlier parting. A proud smile appeared in deeper appreciation for the stalwart side of her character. The smile faded when the King raised his arms and the massive crowd gathered to see the royals and military parade grew quiet.

"Ride to La Rochelle and victory for France! May God be with you!" said Louis.

After saluting to Their Majesties, Gaston began the parade that would first pass by the balcony, through the gates and out into the city.

When the last company of the Cardinal's Guards left the courtyard, the King and Queen withdrew from the balcony. Those in attendance followed to a reception in honor of the campaign. Before Adele could take two steps, Sabrina detained her using a discreet hand, but said nothing until the balcony was clear.

"I leave Paris, but no one must know."

"Why?"

Cautious, Sabrina glanced about for anyone nearby before answering. "The count left with Richelieu. He admitted his treachery this morning. He is a vile man—" she balked, seized by discomposure, turning from Adele.

Disturbed by the action and implication, Adele drew near and asked, "Has he used threats to force you into consummating the marriage?"

"What else could I do?" Sabrina wept.

Adele held Sabrina in sympathetic comfort. "Poor child. I understand your desire to leave, but where will you go?"

Sabrina composed herself enough to answer. "Trèvoux."

"Trèvoux?" echoed Adele, stunned.

"Only for a short time, so I can think clearly. Dominic would allow it. Will you?"

A hint of distress crossed Adele's feature. "Naturally. My only concern is for you should the marquis discover you are there. He agreed to this marriage."

"The count claimed he was commanded to do so."

Adele smiled gentle and kind. "Still wanting to believe in good. What if it was his revenge for you running away?"

Sabrina sighed in weary lament. "Then, with God's help, I will use my independence to whatever means necessary to protect myself."

Adele became somber, flashing a pondering glance at Sabrina. "Trèvoux rightfully belongs to you as it did your father."

"I would never displace you and Dominic. I only need a place to think."

"I will come with you."

Sabrina made a grateful smile at the offer yet shook her head. "I must do this alone. But will you see me off? Angela is waiting around back."

Adele took Sabrina's arm and they made their way to the back of the palace and the awaiting carriage. She embraced Sabrina. "Please, write. I shall know what happened by where you are. Then I shall come as quickly as I can."

Sabrina entered the carriage. With a knock on the roof, the driver was off.

For the next two days, Sabrina pressed the journey and by late afternoon of the third day the carriage drew near her ancestral home. In anticipation, she looked out the window at the massive château standing within a dry moat across a bridge. A flutter of nerves rose in her stomach when the carriage drove through the wrought iron-gate and into the courtyard.

Not waiting for the footmen, Sabrina alighted from the carriage when it stopped. The château's three pavilions connected in a horseshoe shape about the courtyard. A long galley way attached to the outer pavilions served to separate the château from the moat bridge. Massive columns marked the entrances to each pavilion. The center was the main house with the

Charbonier coat of arms etched over the portal. Tears swelled, taking in every detail of the Renaissance architecture. The slate roof showed signs of needed repair.

A gray haired man of sixty years of age hurried from the house. "Madame?"

"Are you Monsieur Tullies?"

"Yes, madame. And you?" he asked in guarded inquiry.

"The Comtesse de Borchard, formerly Sabrina Charbonier. My father Michael once bore the title of Comte de Trèvoux."

The man smiled, his eyes growing misty. "Dear master Michael." He then grew concerned. "You mustn't stay, madame. The marquis and marquise are here."

Sabrina knees quaked at his statement, but she could not repine, not with so much at stake. She drew herself upright. "Monsieur Tullies, I traveled all this way to see Trèvoux, my father's home. I will not get into my carriage and drive away."

Passing the fretting Tullies, she entered the château. The interior was as marvelous and large as the exterior with vast columns rising to ceiling with pilasters and wood paneling richly carved, gilded and decorated.

Tullies hastened to follow. "The marquis shall be back shortly from the vineyard. The marquise is in the Red Salon. A room that used to be Master Michael's favorite," he said with tremor of fondness.

With so many rooms in the château, color played an important part in distinguishing them. The furnishings of the Red Salon were covered with sheets and the windows bare of drapes but no sign of her aunt or any workers. She walked around the room as if trying to get a sense of it.

"What made this his favorite room?" she asked.

"The view." Tullies motioned to the doors and terrace windows.

Sabrina moved to the terrace door. Indeed, it was grand view into the garden and the countryside beyond.

"Truly, madame, you should not be here when the marquis returns."

As she turned from the door she noticed a painting partially hidden behind a large display case, the sheet dangling to reveal part of what

224

appeared to be a portrait of a young man. "Who is this?" she asked, crossing to the painting. She began to pull off the sheet when Tullies snatched it from her to cover the picture.

"Please, madame, you must leave!"

"I will not simply turn and go! Now, whose portrait is this?" She grabbed the sheet and yanked it off, but the case blocked a complete view. "Tullies?"

"Your father as a young man."

"Move it out where I can see it clearly."

Tullies complied, but only far enough so it could be slipped back behind the case where it was hidden.

The picture did not seem startling in itself until one looked at the face of the tall brawny young man. Sabrina moved closer to observe the portrait. A smiling pair of chestnut eyes gazed out from the portrait. The hair was the same fawn color as hers. Like most of the Charbonier men, the rugged features were tempered by the healthy youthful countenance.

"Father," she muttered, covering her mouth to contain her emotions.

"The portrait was painted on Master Michael's eighteenth birthday, a week before he married your mother. I see a resemblance to both your parents."

"I see Jacques—and Dominic."

"Yes, the marquis noticed the same with his son. Who is Jacques?"

"Jacques *was*," she corrected with a slight quiver to her voice, "my eldest brother. I am the only survivor of the fire."

"Sabrina!" exclaimed Madeline in alarm. She rushed from the threshold into the room. "What are you doing here? Does your uncle know?"

"An unexpected trip, Aunt Madeline."

Madeline trembled and grew pale. "Oh, Tullies, cover the painting and put it back. Your uncle must not find you here."

"I tried to tell her, madame," insisted Tullies. He rushed to follow her instructions.

"Too late," Jourdain's hard voice announced. "Why are you here?"

His harsh piercing expression almost caused Sabrina to lose her resolve. In the past she retreated to her chamber to find some peace but since fleeing Reims in desperation, she found a new courage. Her trip to Trèvoux put her courage to the test. "To see what you denied me all these years. More so now since I married without a proper dowry."

"I gave the count money to atone for Trèvoux."

Her courage waning, Sabrina glanced about the salon as if drawing strength from the surroundings. "Money and dowry are not the real the issue, are they, Uncle?"

"What would you know about the real issue?"

Sabrina resisted the impulse to withdraw from his bitter scoffing. She needed to know the truth. "Lord, give me strength," she whispered in prayer then spoke aloud. "A conspiracy lay behind my marriage in which I was used as a reward for services rendered to the Crown. Those services being betrayal and murder!"

Jourdain snarled in great annoyance. "Who told you? Borchard? I told the fool to keep his mouth shut."

Her eyes widened in momentary incredulity. "You did know!" Her emotions turned to hurt and anger. "How could you use me to further such a loathsome beast?

Ashen with fright at the accusation, Madeline stared at her husband. "Jourdain, what is she saying? You told me the marriage was for her benefit."

"It was for the good of France!"

"For the good of France?" echoed Sabrina with discomposure. "To be used as a reward for a traitor and murderer of my own people?"

"The Protestants are a thorn in the flesh of France since their heretical inception! All should have been killed on Saint Bartholomew's Day and put an end to the idolatry that has poisoned France ever since!"

Despite her rising emotion, she glared at him. "How cruel you treated my father when he came to see you at Reims to make amends."

His fury exploded and seized her. "Get out!" He threw her toward the door.

She stumbled, catching herself on the door handle to keep from falling. "If you ever set foot in this house again, you will be destroyed!"

At his declaration, Madeline gasped in horror and fainted.

Terrified, Sabrina raced from the house, tears blurring her vision. She shouted for her driver to go! For miles she fought to bring her emotions under control. Borchard proved difficult enough with losing a part of herself to him, but this was nearly inconsolable. To be betrayed and used as pawn in a political chess match by her uncle then cast out like her father. What now? Returning to Paris and Reims were out of the question. It came down to the only place she was mistress, to Borchard's home in Brittany.

✤ Chapter 19 ✤

THE FRENCH FORCES REACHED LA ROCHELLE to find the English Navy waiting with eighty ships and ten thousand marines and sailors. The situation for French troops on the small islands of Ré and d'Oléron proved worse than expected. Not only did they face heavy English bombardment, the English managed to land a force of several thousand men, forcing the French forces to barricade the citadel. Eight hundred Huguenots took advantage of the French garrison's weakened situation and the English taking Ré to strengthen La Rochelle.

After observing the situation and reviewing reports, Richelieu advised Gaston to send the Duc d'Angoulême with a division to blockade all roads to La Rochelle. He assigned Father Joseph to secure a line of communication with the Catholics inside the city and ordered Captain Tréville's regiment to make ready to cross the harbor and relieve the garrison on Ré. This would be a most difficult task with the English Man O' Wars standing like menacing harbor sentinels.

At news of the regiment's assignment, Arsène felt smothered beneath the weight of his conscience. He could not fight against Rohan! Yet they were under constant watch by de Lacy or some other of the Cardinal's men. In fact they had not seen Dominic since leaving Paris and Arsène began to lose hope being away from Paris would clear his mind. Thus he met the dawn of departure with a gloom as dark and real as the storm clouds.

Thunder clapped and lightning streaked making it hard to tell morning from night, save for a watch. The howling winds caused fierce waves to crash upon the rocks spraying the soldiers trying to enter the boats bouncing like balls at the end of large ropes. Some boats would haul supplies while others would carry the men. It was a treacherous morning for crossing the harbor, but somewhere in the torrential sheet of darkness covering the sea, stood the English fleet.

Soaked to the skin, Arsène and Philipe awaited orders to board. Each clenched a musket, their hats pulled down low and collars turned up in a futile protection from the storm.

"When?" asked Arsène asked, leaning close to Philipe's ear, since shouts were barely audible through the driving rain.

"Patience. Tréville will call off this insane venture."

"With the English offshore? Never!"

"Bourdias, your platoon is next!" an officer shouted.

Arsène hesitated, actually taking a couple of steps backwards.

Philipe stopped his retreat. "We must cross."

Arsène grew stiff in fear, staring at the dark, churning water.

Philipe leaned closer and asked, "Can you swim?"

Arsène shook his head, still staring at the water.

"Bourdias!" came the second call for boarding.

"Sit in the middle. I'll sit on the side and help row." Philipe nudged Arsène into the boat.

Eight Musketeers boarded the rocking boat. Six men took an oar to row including Philipe. Arsène become seasick almost immediately, pressing his lips together and tightening his grip on his musket.

Waves lashed at the boat and the saltwater stung men's eyes. For a moment Philipe was blinded and began to wipe his eyes clear. His oar broke. He reached for the oar, but the boat pitched, throwing him overboard.

Arsène grabbed for Philipe, but a hand pulled him back and the man scolded, "You want to get us all killed?"

Arsène jerked away. He forgot his sickness and scanned the surface anxious for Philipe. A head pushed through the waves on the opposite side of the boat. "Philipe! Over here!"

In desperation, Philipe tried to keep his head above the surface and began swimming toward Arsène. The boat began drifting, taking it away from Philipe.

"Steady! He's getting closer," Arsène commanded to the pilot, a brief glance over his shoulder. When he looked back, Philipe disappeared below the waves. He held his breath, watching the raging surface. A sudden cry caught his attention. Philipe resurfaced within arms reach. Seizing him by the collar, Arsène began pulling him to the boat. Philipe grabbed Arsène's arm, but instead of moving toward the boat, he pulled Arsène off balance and into the water. The boat became caught in the tide and the pilot could not keep the boat steady and it drifted away from them.

Arsène broke the surface, frantically gasping for air and trying to keep his head above water. Philipe appeared beside him. "Hook your arm through my baldric and we'll swim for shore!"

Arsène did as instructed and tried to swim, but it was a feeble attempt, more slapping at the water than effective strokes. He gagged on seawater and coughed for air as waves kept hitting him in the face.

"Stop thrashing! Just use your legs and let me swim for both of us!"

Luckily they were within a hundred yards of shore. However, the tide swept them down the coast away from the launch area and La Rochelle. Once near shore, the waves assisted them onto the beach. Aiding each other further onto land, they collapsed.

After several moment of catching his breath, Arsène pushed himself to his hands and knees, glaring at Philipe, who remained lying on his stomach exhausted. "Why did you pull me in? I told you I couldn't swim!"

Philipe took a deep breath before replying. "To get back to shore, of course. We either die trying or be killed by English cannons."

"Drowning is hardly a way I want to die." He coughed, spitting up some more muck. "Aggh, seawater tastes awful." The sound of nearby voices alerted him. "The coast watchers. Pretend you're injured." He pulled Philipe to his feet and began dragging him up an incline.

The two men saw them. "What happened?"

"He almost drowned. I'm taking him back to camp to see the surgeon."

"Need help?" asked one soldier.

"No, the ground's flat. I can manage. Your duties are pressing this morning." Arsène readjusted Philipe, who leaned on him as if unconscious.

The coast watchers moved south while Arsène headed northeast. Once behind some rocks he jabbed Philipe in the ribs. "You can get up now."

Philipe straightened and looked to get his bearings. "We're south of camp and La Rochelle is north. We'll go east around camp then north."

Twice they stopped to allow sentries to pass on patrol, but with the fierceness of the storm, no one wanted to stay out in the foul weather for long and quickly went about their business before dashing for shelter. Stopping a third time, Philipe slapped Arsène's arm and pointed to something out of the bushes. Borchard entered a tent at the edge of camp.

Arsène moved for a better view, Philipe at his heels. They reached the undergrowth near the tent and concealed themselves when someone from inside spoke.

"Please, be seated, Count," said Richelieu. "I have sent for Captain Tréville, but I'm afraid he will be very upset at the discovery."

"Indeed, considering he too was fooled by their appearance."

Philipe went to speak when Arsène covered his mouth at hearing Richelieu greet Tréville.

"Good of you to be so prompt, Captain," said Richelieu.

"I pray this is brief, Eminence. I was about to disembark and join my men," said Tréville with annoyance.

"All is going splendidly. The first garrison is in camp. Be seated."

"Thank you, but I prefer to stand."

"As you wish," said Richelieu, flashing an unusually pleasant smile.

At the Cardinal's mood change, Tréville surmised some treachery was afoot. Borchard sat in the corner, and in curiosity he turned from Borchard to Richelieu. "Why have you summoned me, Eminence?"

Richelieu casually rested his elbows on the arms of the chair. "This concerns two of your men. Again I refer to Lamonreaux and Bourdias, and very annoyed to discover they returned and you did not inform me."

"They gave account of themselves to me so I saw no reason—"

"No reason to do as ordered?"

"An order, Eminence? You made it sound like an inquiry."

Richelieu agreeability began to change to firm rebuke. "With all your years of service, you need to be instructed in the ways of politics? I'm afraid you gave aid to wolves in sheep's clothing. Whatever account they gave you, and you've verified," he stopped a protest by raising a hand, "was false. They are members of that infamous group The Huguenot Sword."

"Impossible!"

"It is true, captain," said Borchard.

Tréville could no longer contain his indignation at Borchard or his implicating two of his men as traitors. "What do you know of this, Huguenot?"

"Captain Tréville!" snapped Richelieu.

"I understand the captain's anger, Eminence. He is ignorant of my actions."

"But I will not tolerate it! Captain, hold your tongue and listen."

Tréville stiffened and straightened to the reproof as the Cardinal continued.

"The count can confirm this because he infiltrated the Huguenot high command. Done with the King's knowledge and permission, of course. Lamonreaux and Bourdias used the uniform of His Majesty's Musketeers for their treasonous acts. You doubtless know Lamonreaux's benefactor, the Duc de Rohan. I spoke to you upon this matter, and an affair of state. Or did you forget that also?"

The only visible displays of Tréville's fury were the hard-set eyes and twitching upper lip.

"Their trip to Reims was actually to Calais as escort of the Duc de Trudeau," began Borchard. "The duke was on his way to England to deal with Buckingham for the ships you now see in the harbor. Unfortunately, he met with an timely end."

"A pity." Richelieu crossed himself.

"This is fantastic!" exclaimed Tréville. "I am aware of Lamonreaux's benefactor, and his reputation, but he is one of my best men. As for Bourdias, I am personally well acquainted with the baron. His son has never been disobedient to me or any other commander. What of the letter from him verifying his son's trip to Reims? Do you call him traitor also?"

"A forgery. The baron is an honorable man, so be easy on his account," answered Richelieu. "I realize this is a surprise, but remember, I approached you on the matter."

During a brief silence, Tréville considered everything. Images and snippets of conversation with Lamonreaux singularly, and most recently with Bourdias, flashed through his mind. It galled him to learn how they duped him all these years, and how he fell for their lies. No one makes a fool of François Tréville! He clasped the hilt of his sword snapping to attention. "I'm at your command, Eminence."

Richelieu reached over to the corner of the table for two folded pieces of paper. "These are warrants for the arrest of Arsène Lamonreaux and Philipe Bourdias. The charge: high treason with a sentence to match." He paused in handing the paper to Tréville. "Death by hanging."

Receiving the papers, Tréville saluted. "I shall tend to it personally, Eminence."

Arsène and Philipe buried themselves in the bushes when Tréville emerged and marched past them. "We best leave." Arsène touched Philipe's arm, the latter remained focused on the tent with deadly intent. "Philipe?"

"Yes, yes, but separately. This way if one is captured the other will be safe."

Arsène balked, shaking his head. "No. It doesn't feel right."

"I don't care what you feel! We separate. You go that way." Philipe pointed in the direction they headed. "We'll meet just outside La Rochelle."

Arsène hesitated in complying, but Philipe would accept no delay or opposition.

"Go! Before I forget myself and make you go!" Philipe clenched a fist.

Wary, Arsène looked from the fist to Philipe's determined face. "Very well, but be careful, *mon ami.*"

Philipe flashed a smile and nudged Arsène on his way. After waiting a moment for Arsène to disappear into darkness, he proceeded in the opposite direction.

From out of the shadows someone seized Borchard. One hand covered this mouth and the other pressed a dagger to his throat. A voice hissed in his ear. "Good evening, *Monsieur le Traître*! I advise you to remain still and silent, lest my hand slip." The blade pressed closer.

Borchard tried to glance over his shoulder but the pressing dagger prevented him

"My voice is familiar, isn't it?"

Borchard made a careful nod, mindful of the dangerous dagger.

"It should be. As should the face of man who is about to kill you!"

Borchard wrenched free. "Guard—!" his cry stifled when the dagger plunged deep into his left breast. He managed to catch of glimpse of his murderer, widening in surprise. "You?" he gasped.

Philipe withdrew the blade and Borchard sank to the ground. Not far off, he heard a commotion but he had to make certain Borchard was dead and felt for a pulse. None. Nervous, he rushed to make his escape, the bloody dagger clenched in his fist.

Several times he tossed anxious glances over his shoulder, but so far no outcry of discovery of Borchard's body. He pushed through a thicket and was about to pass several boulders when a hand grabbed his right arm. Instinctively, he whirled about dagger first.

"Philipe!" Arsène barely avoided the face-high slash.

Philipe gaped in surprised horror. "Did I cut you?"

"No, thank heavens! Did you meet with trouble?" He indicated the bloodstained knife.

"A little," he said in nervous replied. "We better leave quickly." He nudged Arsène forward and looked back the direction he came, but still no signs of discovery. He trembled as he followed Arsène. In all his years of intrigue he never killed in cold blood. By the same token, there was not a person more deserving of death than Borchard. He wondered if he should say anything to Arsène. *No, too heavy a burden, and you should have no part of this.*

Philipe constantly looked back, staying alert to every sight and sound. Once a safe distance from camp, they paused to catch their breath. Philipe wrung his hands together, not from the cool weather, but internal uneasiness. He complained when Arsène regarded his actions.

"Plague take this wind and rain! We've got to get out of these wet uniforms before we die of exposure."

Arsène sat on a large boulder and shivered, the wet clothes chilly and he tried to rub his legs. "What a cheery thought. We either die by hanging or from exposure. At least those are better choices than drowning."

"Perhaps, but we can't stay here." Philipe took the lead.

After a short distance, Philipe tripped over something unseen, fell forward and landed on a large, soft object. Startled by the sight of a dead man beneath him, he pushed himself to his knees. Ashen and trembling, he stared at the body. A waved of nausea struck and he screwed his eyes shut, swallowing back the sickness.

Arsène stood next to what Philipe tripped over: another dead man. Both were civilians and not long dead. One's throat was cut; the other killed by musket fire to the forehead. He knelt beside Philipe, who was slow to recover. "This might sound inhuman, but they're dead and—well, no longer in need of their clothes."

Philipe shook his head, still trying to quell the queasiness.

"This would give us more time to escape once we shed these uniforms," Arsène continued his argument then became concerned. "Philipe?"

He waved the matter aside. "Startled by the sight. I don't fall on top of dead men everyday. Let's do as you suggest."

Not a perfect fit, but neither cared about appearance. Once dressed in civilian clothes and the dead men in Musketeer uniforms, they moved on.

Over the next hill, La Rochelle loomed before them. At the sounds of hooves and cartwheels they hid in the shelter of some trees. A heavily laden cart pulled by a large horse came into view. A group of armed men dressed in civilian clothes surrounded the cart but no banners or colors displayed for identification.

"Must be a smuggling party," said Arsène. "We'll join them and slip into La Rochelle."

Cautious, they positioned themselves at the rear of the smugglers. No one seemed wise to the addition, more concerned for moving the cart and getting out of the foul weather judging by the chatter. When the group paused at smaller city gate, Arsène and Philipe huddled together, wary and ready to make a quick move if discovered. Fortunately, they were admitted with the group, no questions or suspicion.

Being unfamiliar with La Rochelle, they made discreet inquiry if the Duc de Rohan was in the city and learned he had taken up residence in the grand château not far from the mayor's house. It was a fourteenth century building that sat on a knoll overlooking La Rochelle. Four separate lodgings encompassing a tiny courtyard. Each had its own staircase and turret. Cold and impatient, they waited for an answer to their knock.

The door opened, and Chandler grew wide-eyed in astonishment. "Sergeant! Lieutenant! How on earth?"

Arsène cocked a smile. "After all these years, are you really surprised?"

"You've outdone yourself this time! The duke will be overjoyed. He is in the study, second door on your right." Chandler pointed down the hall.

Rohan stood at the back of the room reading some papers and so engrossed he didn't notice anyone enter. For a moment, they waited to be recognized. Finally Arsène cleared his throat.

"Monsieur."

Rohan glanced up from reading. "Arsène!" The papers fell onto a nearby table, and he engulfed Arsène in a bear hug and kissed him on both cheeks. He greeted Philipe. "How did you get here?"

"It wasn't easy."

"Indeed! Since the army arrived, I wondered if we would ever meet again."

"Nothing could keep me from you."

Rohan smiled, large and proud at his protégé. "What of Dominic?"

"Still at camp."

"We barely escaped. Especially considering our death warrants," said Philipe.

"Borchard exposed us as The Huguenot Sword. Richelieu acted and charged Tréville with warrants for our arrest as traitors," Arsène explained to Rohan's befuddlement.

"Not Dominic?"

"Not that we know of."

Rohan tugged at his bread in thought. "Let's hope Richelieu will not choose to act against him because of your escape. "

"We fled out of desperation with no chance to get to him," said Philipe with regret.

"Dominic's name and position may be his saving grace."

"With the marquis' actions of late, I doubt it," groused Arsène.

"If not Jourdain, then the King. With the marriage contract, strong proof will be needed against him. Besides, Borchard would be foolish to betray his new family."

"I hope you're right, monsieur. I hate the thought of Dominic standing alone against Richelieu and de Lacy," chided Philipe.

"We shall pray for his deliverance since we are helpless to aid him in other ways."

Philipe said nothing. His disbelieving smirk spoke enough.

Rohan's expression grew troubled at Philipe's scoffing, so Arsène changed the subject. "Since we are here, what can we do to help, monsieur?"

Rohan was slow to change his focus from Philipe. "Much. The people itch to fight and I'm in need of good loyal men to keep the peace. The Catholics constantly make trouble. We've captured a number of spies. Philipe, you shall be an officer in the militia. Your knowledge and skill is needed."

"I'm at your service, monsieur."

"You, my ingenious Gascon, will aid both the military and medical. I still use the herbal remedy you gave Chandler for my stomach pains, more so now than ever. Both of you will receive commissions to the rank of captain. As for lodging," he paused in consideration. "The château is filled to the rafters, but I'll instruct Chandler to secure a room. Meanwhile, you are welcome to a pallet by the fire in here. The study is the last room unoccupied, and my only place of solace during the day. At night, it is yours until other arrangements are made."

"Thank you, monsieur. We leave you to your solace," said Arsène with a smile.

Rohan laughed. "Not for long. You shall both join me for dinner at eight. I want to hear of your latest escapades and anything you know of the King and Cardinal's plans."

✣ Chapter 20 ✣

THE FRENCH MANAGED TO LAND REINFORCEMENTS ON RÉ and send the English retreating back into the sea. Buckingham ordered another bombardment of the islands to be preceded by a second invasion. Three different times the English tried to land on Ré only to be repelled. The cost proved great for the French. A third of Tréville's company lay dead or wounded and only managed to cripple four English ships.

On shore, Richelieu and Gaston kept abreast of the battle; only Richelieu wondered how long the tough Tréville could be successful. Gaston argued the captain's merit, but Richelieu did not wish to take chances under the circumstances. Construction on the dike had only begun. Thus, against Gaston's wishes, Richelieu wrote the King, imploring him to hurry with reinforcements. Of course hurry was a relative word to royals as the storms of July gave way to the heat of August and no word from Paris.

September brought the most determined English offensive. Through dense fog and hazardous tides they attacked Ré. During the ensuing battle, the English lost six minor vessels and one Man O' War. By October, both sides were licking their wounds but unwilling to give ground or yield to the deteriorating elements of autumn.

In early November, Louis finally arrived at camp with the needed reinforcements. Even on the battlefield, the pomp and circumstances of royalty were displayed. Among his entourage were the Marquis de Charbonier and the Baron Bourdias.

Dressed as a warrior king, Louis wore all the armor and trappings. Upon the gold cuirass was the Royal Cross embellished by tongues of fire and lilies. The regal purple cloak and matching gloves were fur-lined against the cold. The gold hilt of a wonderfully crafted sword swung at his hip. He drew rein and waited for a servant to hold the stirrup before dismounting.

Gaston, Richelieu and all commanders assembled before the Royal Tent.

"Welcome, Sire," said Gaston, but Louis ignored his brother, focusing on Richelieu.

"How goes it, Cardinal?"

"As well as can be expected, Sire."

"It goes well," said Gaston, imposing himself between the King and Cardinal. "The Musketeers continue to hold the island and keep the English at bay."

Louis didn't even look at Gaston, rather headed for the tent. Dutifully, the rest followed.

A hand detained Richelieu from proceeding. To his surprise, the hand belonged to Reynard. "Monsieur le Comte."

"My presence surprises you, Eminence? Given the situation, to continue in my former employ would have been more hazardous than to discard it. The King was gracious in allowing me to accompany him. Or rather, accommodating the Queen's request on my behalf."

Recovered from his initial surprise, Richelieu spoke with cool indifference. "Indeed. You heard of the fate of your companion?"

Reynard smiled with indifference. "Borchard played his scapegoat role to the end."

"I compliment you on the success of your scheme, but be warned. With your scapegoat gone, the truth about the Duc de Trudeau and Mademoiselle Charbonier may be revealed."

Reynard stiffened in concern at the warning. "Why should that happen, Eminence? Have I not proven myself of service to you?"

"Your service to the State," Richelieu coolly corrected, "has been appreciated. Yet since the State no longer requires your services, your well-being is your own affair." He made his meaning clear with a cold stare, but the expression vanished when he spoke again. "Yet I will tell you certain Musketeers died in an attempt to desert and their comrade was not happy to hear of it, though he has made no move to reveal himself. Your presence may incite him."

Reynard straightened his shoulders, pride in face and voice. "I assure you, Eminence, I can handle my own affairs."

"Beware of who he is and how you deal with him. I will not intervene if you fail. Take well note of this last warning extended you." Richelieu entered the tent.

"What did you speak to Richelieu about?" asked Jourdain. He was also dressed for battle. The Baron Bourdias accompanied him. Philipe bore a strong resemblance to his father, forty-three-year-old Jean-Claude.

"Something you will find interesting. The rumors about Borchard are true. He is dead. Along with those two meddlesome Musketeers." Reynard's eyes flashed to Jean-Claude while speaking.

Jean-Claude's jowls tightened in rage, clasping his sword.

Jourdain spoke to forestall any further reaction by Jean-Claude. "It is a shock," he said to Reynard.

"Perhaps to the baron, but I thought you knew of his involvement with the Huguenots?"

Jean-Claude's lashed out, "Why would Richelieu tell you and not us?"

"I'm afraid I cannot answer your question—" His reply became cut short when Jean-Claude lunged and seized him about the throat.

Jourdain intervened to prevent Jean-Claude from choking Reynard, but the baron was not easily subdued. He engulfed Jean-Claude in a bear hold, and Reynard broke free. "Go!" he snapped to Reynard.

"And stay out of our sight!" shouted Jean-Claude, struggling to be free but Jourdain was bigger and stronger.

"Enough! We shall learn the truth or if Reynard is saying that only to save himself from a charge of treason."

"What do you mean?"

"Come. We need to talk in private."

Dominic sat in his tent composing a letter to Adele when someone entered, brisk and sharp. He started at seeing his father and Jean-Claude, both looking grim. "Father. Baron. When did you both arrive?"

241

"We accompanied the King. Since arriving we heard from a reliable source some distressing news concerning Philipe. We came to learn if is true?" said Jourdain.

Dominic's momentary surprise turned to a mixture of lament and irritation. "That he is dead? Unfortunately, yes. I'm trying to compose a letter to Adele. I'm sorry, monsieur," he said to Jean-Claude.

"Sorry does not begin to make amends for dishonor!"

Dominic jowls tightened but tempered his response. "What do mean?"

Jourdain scowled in disbelief. "Don't play the Judas! I told Jean-Claude everything about you, Sabrina and that cursed Lamonreaux. Was Philipe involved with the Huguenots?"

Dominic's wary gaze shifted between them. "If your source is reliable, why ask me?"

"Because I suspect your involvement!"

His father finally admitted it, yet at the moment he was uncertain whether to be relieved or outraged. Jourdain's prompting glare required an answer. "If I were involved with the Huguenots, why am I here instead of at La Rochelle?"

"Some intrigue no doubt. You cannot embrace such a heretical religion without accepting its rebellion. Just like your uncle!"

That stung and Dominic rebuffed. "You can't leave the past alone, can you? First Michael, Sabrina and now Philipe."

"So you admit it!"

"I admit nothing, you accuse!"

"With good reason. You became a heretic!"

The statement struck Dominic with a sudden thought. This was not just about Philipe, rather goading, hoping to vindicate suspicions by forcing an admission.

Jean-Claude stepped forward to confront Dominic. "Did Philipe become a Huguenot?"

Dominic stood his ground, clenching his fists while looking down at his father-in-law. "I give you the same answer. Why was he here fighting under the King's banner rather than at La Rochelle?"

Jean-Claude regarded Dominic with perplexed suspicion as he asked, "Have you heard about what this scandal did to Adele's position at Court?"

The question stunned Dominic. "No. Has something happened to her?"

Jean-Claude's jowls tightened and his voice thick in reply. "The Queen asked her to retire after learning Philipe and Lamonreaux were shot while deserting because of warrants issued for their arrest for treason."

Dominic clenched the hilt of his sword to steady his rage. "Philipe drowned during the dangerous crossing of his platoon from shore to Ré. A crossing ordered by Richelieu. Does that sound like a traitor?"

"We heard he was shot by the shore for desertion."

Anger turned Dominic's countenance fierce and intimidating. "Then you were told something different than I by Prince Gaston." He snatched up the letter he composed and waved it in Jean-Claude's face. "Which version should I tell Adele? Honor or disgrace?"

"Gaston?"

"Yes, the Prince told me. Who is your reliable source?"

Jean-Claude stepped back, his posture becoming thoughtful. "Maybe we acted in haste," he said to Jourdain before leaving.

Jourdain didn't immediately follow Jean-Claude. "You may have convinced him, but I know better."

Apprehensive, Dominic stared at his father. "What do you want of me?"

Jourdain's answer was direct and harsh. "What I always wanted, to save the family name. To do so, you must renounce the Huguenots."

"Is this how you treated Michael? Demand he bend to your will rather than listen to reason and hear his heart?"

"What about scandal and your wife?"

Dominic fought to keep his temper from exploring at the threat. "You fight with weapons I cannot counter. If I agree to your demands, I could lose the respect and love of my wife and cousin."

Jourdain's tone and demeanor softened. "Yet win back the love and respect of your father. Who can do more for you than they."

Dominic sighed and made a doleful shake of his head. "No one can do for me what I desire most."

243

"What is that?" A hint of kindness found its way into Jourdain's voice. He squared his shoulder and declared, "To bring my friends back to life."

Jourdian's kindness vanished. "You accused me of being unable to leave the past buried with the dead! Even from the grave their hold on you is strong. I have spoken my peace and will make no other overture for reconciliation. The choice is yours." He stormed out.

Nearing the tent he shared with Jean-Claude, Jourdian heard angry words and blows. He drew his sword and rushed inside. Jean-Claude viciously attacked Roger.

"Filthy liar!" shouted Jean-Claude.

Bloodied and unable to give any defense, Roger tried desperately to stay the blows while whimpering. "No, it can't be true—" his words cut short when Jean-Claude threw him across the tent and he landed in a crumpled, painful heap.

"Jean-Claude!" said Jourdain.

Laboring with angry breath, Jean-Claude bellowed, "Get out of my sight, you worthless cur! I curse the day I hired you."

Painful and gasping for air, Roger stumbled out of the tent.

"Did beating him help?" asked Jourdain.

Jean-Claude scowled in anger, but didn't reply as an officer arrived to inform them the King ordered his staff to assemble on shore.

Jean-Claude took a moment to regain his composure before he and Jourdian proceeded to join those of royal entourage: Gaston, Duc d'Angoulême, Marquis de Feuquières, Marèchals de Marillac and Schomberg, Captain DuBorcy of the Royal Guards, Captain de Lacy, Chevalier Torais, and Admiral Montmorency.

Exhaled breath chilled into white smoke as all stood on a mound at the edge of camp to view the harbor. All listened to Richelieu explain the dike's progress to Louis.

Giant oak trees protruded from the water halfway across the harbor. For construction purposes, there was scaffolding about the trees. Richelieu used the largest and heaviest oak trees found in the area. Oak was strong and formidable when hewed together. The trunks were stripped of leaves and branches, while the tops carved to a point like a gigantic spear. Any ship attempting to cross the barricade would be impaled like a helpless fish swimming into the range of a harpoon.

"By my faith, I had not envisioned it so!" said Louis in wonder.

"I'm glad you are pleased, Sire." Richelieu smiled.

"Magnificent!" Louis placed hands upon his hips and scanned the length of the dike. "To think, Tréville and I privately joked about this wooden oddity."

Richelieu let the slight pass. "It will be a long siege, Sire. The dike will block the main source of water for commerce and the Royal Army will surround the rest of the city. By spring the Huguenots will be ready to surrender."

"Yes, I see it now. Excellent." Louis patted Richelieu's arm. "You've outdone yourself this time, Cardinal. Come, let us toast the forthcoming victory!" He led the group back to the royal tent.

"Despite the Cardinal's great advances, Tréville has taken refuge in the fortress the past several month as the English lay siege to the islands," said Gaston, once all were assembled inside.

"You reported he successfully holds the island," scolded Louis.

"He does. Your Musketeers are expert marksmen. To venture anywhere near the fortress proves fatal. Artillery has been placed near the shore to serve as a warning to Buckingham. If he dares to make a full scale effort to invade Ré, he places his fleet within cannon range."

"You seem to have taken many liberties with my army. Most of which have cost lives, yet still the enemy is here!"

"I have done what I thought best under the circumstances!"

"Then your judgment leaves much to be desired!"

"Sire," Richelieu intervened before an angry Gaston could respond again. "The Prince has given an adequate account of himself these past few months."

"Adequate is not good enough for a Royal Prince. Especially when the fate of France depends heavily upon the outcome of this confrontation,"

Louis harshly spoke then turned to Gaston. "As of this moment I am assuming supreme command."

Gaston's shoulders heaved in contempt. He not only felt the sting of the King's cruel rebuke, but all eyes were upon him. "Then I withdraw from this campaign!" He stormed out.

Ignoring his brother, Louis turned to Chevalier Torais. "If I were you, I would be grateful for such brave men as Captain Tréville and his company; and pray they come out of these as unscathed as possible."

Torais deeply bowed to the reproach. "My prayers are with him, Sire. Might I add, I also pray I may redeem myself in whatever way Your Majesty wishes."

Louis cocked a conceited smile. "Well spoken, Chevalier. I shall consider the possibility. Now, go; and await my orders." Torais saluted and left and the King grumbled, "I should have dismissed him long ago."

It suddenly became evident to all that Louis was in a foul mood, for Torais was a favorite. All would tread lightly in speech. DuBorcy snapped to attention when the King turned to address him.

"See the Guards are ready for inspection in the morning."

After a silent, reverent bow, DuBorcy departed.

"How long can the English hold out, Eminence?"

Richelieu paced a bit before answering. "Difficult to say, Sire. They are a stubborn people, too proud for their own good. They do not take defeat lightly. Judging by the reports and my observations, I would guess a few weeks."

Louis rubbed his chin as he studied the map. "What would be the most expedient way to defeat the English?"

"Meet them on their own terms, Sire," said Admiral Montmorency.

From under displeased brows the King glanced up. "A sea battle? Do you remember what happened last time, Admiral? The Royal fleet towed to La Rochelle harbor in disgrace!"

"Aye, Sire," he solemnly answered. At age thirty-two, Henri Montmorency made a name for himself as commander of the Royal Navy. Much was expected of him since his sister was married to the Prince de

Condé, the King's cousin. "If Your Majesty will consider, the ships that now constitute the Royal Navy are of better quality and equal to the English, being originally their vessels."

"Bravely spoken, Admiral. Cardinal?"

"I agreed with Monsieur l'Admiral. Buckingham would not be expecting us to use our navy against him. It could work this time."

Louis shifted focus back to Montmorency. "What do you propose?"

"The ships are anchored ten miles south of St. Martin." He pointed to the exact spot on the map. "The English have been fighting since summer. They are tired and their vessels battered. In two days I could sail up the coast and outflank them, here."

"How many ships are under your command at present?"

He made a slightest hesitation in answering; "Roughly forty, Sire."

"To how many English ships?"

"Down from eighty, but I don't have an exact count."

"Almost two to one? What about troops? Do you know the English strength?"

"Buckingham began with a little more than ten thousand, roughly half landed on Ré but hundreds died from disease and battle, reducing his numbers to around seven or eight thousand."

"And those of your command?"

"Over four thousand."

"Again nearly two to one!"

"Sire, our troops are fresh and ships ready! Buckingham can't maintain an assault on the islands if he must meet out cannons."

Louis regarded Montmorency. There was no denying the admiral's enthusiasm or his passion. He caught a short nod from Richelieu and spoke. "Very well, Admiral. You may leave at your convenience."

Montmorency snapped to attention and saluted Louis, nodding to the Cardinal before leaving.

With one of their numbers succeeding with the King, the air was a bit more relaxed thus d'Angoulême spoke. "Sire, I believe the defeat of the English is at hand, yet we must be patient."

"You don't believe the Rochellias' will surrender after the English are driven off?"

"No, Sire. They will put up resistance, but victory will come in time."

Louis picked up a ruler and tapped it in his palm. "Explain yourself."

D'Angoulême stood at the other end of the table. "Victory over the English will eventually lead to the demise of La Rochelle. The city, as Your Majesty is well acquainted, is of ingenuous engineering. It cannot be won in battle. It must be won by siege."

Richelieu picked up the explanation. "Once surrounded, the inhabitants must rely on the outside world for supplies."

"Are you forgetting the city has four sides? One is the harbor. What about that?"

"That is where the dike comes in, Sire," said Richelieu with a slight tone of pride.

There was a pause of a few moments in which the King studied the map. Louis allowed the ruler to slip from his fingers to the table. "We defeat the English navy with our navy, which is composed of English ships. Then we starve the inhabitants of La Rochelle by plugging up the harbor and laying siege to the city. If this all comes to pass, it will go down in history as one of France's greatest triumphs."

Richelieu frowned. "I fear it is France's darkest hour. To spill the blood of ones' own countrymen could hardly be considered a victory."

"Plague take your condescension! These Protestants defied me shamefully! Not to mention Buckingham's repeated insolent advances toward the Queen!"

"Sire," began Richelieu, lowering his voice. "The Queen is in full agreement with this campaign. Do not shame her with such public accusations. You have already rebuked your brother and sent him scurrying from camp in anger."

"Sire!" Captain duBorcy returned and with a rather dusty looking gentleman.

"What?" snapped Louis.

248

"Sieur de Lizon escaped from La Rochelle with important information that may help an invasion."

"Really?"

"Yes, Sire," said Lizon, bowing. "If I may see a map, I can provide you an exact location suitable for invasion."

Louis waved Lizon to the table. "Will this do?"

"Indeed, Sire." Lizon pointed on the map of La Rochelle. "On the east side lies a canal which small boats use to gather salt from the marshes. It is accessed by a grilled water gate. In the middle of the moat is a stone pylon, which is connected by a drawbridge with a barbican at one end. The canal is not too deep, three feet at low tide. The grille is made of wood and can easily be destroyed by a petard. A small assault party could sabotage the grille and make way for a cavalry invasion by either this gate or the main gate."

Louis smiled with immense pleasure. "Gentlemen, I am open to suggestions on how to best utilize this information.

The debate and formulating lasted until midnight when a course of action was finally decided. The assault party would do as Lizon suggested while an invasion force would be concealed outside the main gate of La Rochelle. Maréchal de Marcillac would lead the assault force of five hundred men, with Maréchal de Schomberg waiting with fifteen hundred men as the invasion force.

"Who will lead sabotage mission, Sire?" asked Richelieu.

"I leave the choice to your discretion, for you know the mettle of men in this campaign better than I."

Richelieu turned to de Lacy. "Fetch the Marquis de Feuquières and the Comte de Reynard. As for the rest of you, good-night."

Neither Louis nor Richelieu spoke until the others departed.

"Feuquières is a good man, but why Reynard?" asked Louis

"He is loyal to Your Majesty. Consider it a token of your gratitude."

A few moments later, de Lacy returned with Feuquières and Reynard. They listened closely to the King and Cardinal.

"Ten men should be sufficient for the sabotage party. DuBorcy and Captain de Lacy will select the men. Sieur de Lizon was the bearer of this information, and will be at your disposal for briefing. Maréchal de Marillac is in command of the invasion force so coordinate your efforts with him. Tonight should be sufficient for preparation. You will leave by dawn."

"You may depend upon us, Sire," said Feuquières.

"Gentlemen, if you succeed, you will have the gratitude of France."

"Sire," began Richelieu after the nobles were gone. "If you permit me, I am greatly fatigued and wish to retire."

"Of course. How thoughtless to keep you up so late."

Richelieu left with de Lacy. Once outside, he breathed a weary sigh of relief and lumbered to his tent.

"Do you think they will succeed?" asked de Lacy.

"No, which is why you will assign Trèvoux to the mission. It should be interesting to see whether he chooses to serve the King like a good soldier or desert and be branded a traitor to France. Instruct two of your men to keep a close watch on him. If an opportunity arises, a stray blade or ball would not be suspected as anything but the unfortunate fate of a soldier."

De Lacy wickedly smiled. "With pleasure. Good-night, Eminence."

Dominic went about the rest of his duties upset at the encounter with his father and Jean-Claude. It was difficult enough dealing with the deaths of Arsène and Philipe, but his father's threat to Adele and Sabrina posed a challenge he did not expect. To betray the memory of his friends by renouncing the Huguenots and all they fought and died for was unthinkable. However, any hasty or ill-conceived action would expose his wife and cousin to his father's spleen. Thus by the end of the long hard day, he looked forward to retiring and getting some rest.

He went to enter his tent when a hoarse weak voice call, "Monsieur le Comte!" For a moment he looked about, then a second call. "Over here, monsieur." A hand waved from behind a bush a few yards from the tent. Ready to draw his sword, Dominic approached the bush.

"It is I, Roger, monsieur." He carefully poked his head out. His face bruised, one eye swollen shut, the other puffy and his upper lip also swollen and caked with dry blood.

"*Mon dieu!* Where did you come from and what happened to you?"

Roger waved Dominic behind the bush. "I accompanied the baron and marquis in hopes of reaching my master. But when the baron returned to the tent he was enraged." He flinched when Dominic examined his wounds.

"He did this?"

Roger nodded, gritting his teeth against the pain in his right side. "And cast me out."

"What did he say?"

"Something about warrants and dishonor. I didn't understand, but he said the lieutenant," he voice grew choked with grief, "is dead. Is it true? Are he and Sergeant Lamonreaux dead?"

"I'm afraid so."

Roger began to weep. "I didn't want to believe it."

"Neither did I and loathed writing Adele. I have yet to dispatch the letter …" he stopped and stared at Roger. "Are you well enough to travel?"

"I could, I suppose. Why?"

"Wait a moment."

Dominic went to his tent, fetched the letter, a purse and a small leather book that he quickly wrapped in one of his handkerchiefs and tied close with a piece of string. He pocketed the book to fetch a wooden box. He was about to leave when he went to his writing desk, grabbed a piece of paper and wrote a quick note. He returned to Roger.

"Give this to Adele and stay with her. I don't know what repercussion will come from this, so I trust you, as Philipe did, to keep her safe."

Roger put the letter in a pocket on the inside of his doublet. "I will, monsieur, only I have no means to get back to Paris."

Dominic handed Roger the purse. "This should be enough. And this is a pass I wrote stating you are Corporal Neville on medical leave from my regiment to return to home to Paris to convalesce." He gave the pass to Roger, who put it in his outer doublet pocket. "I managed to get Arsène's box of herbs before they confiscated his belongings. I'll tend your wounds then you can take the box for use on the road. Also," he paused to pull out the wrapped book from his pocket, "tell Adele to give this to Sabrina. It was among Arsène's possessions."

Roger took it and placed it in his pocket, not asking what it was.

Dominic proceeded to tend Roger's wounds. When finished, he said, "Your loyalty to Philipe and your aid to me and my family is something I will not forget. Godspeed."

Roger flinched when standing, but once on his feet, smiled. "God keep you safe until we meet again, monsieur."

For a few moments, Dominic watched Roger until he disappeared into the darkness then returned to his tent. He didn't feel it necessary to tell the loyal valet he suspected his encounter with Jean-Claude pushed the baron to rage resulting in the assault.

He tried to get some rest for his perturbed spirit, heart, and mind. Alas, an unwelcome visitor brought more bad tidings. De Lacy burst in upon him.

"How dare you?"

"Do not scold me, Monsieur le Comte. Despite your rank, you are still a soldier under my command."

For several months he thought he was forgotten. Perhaps he was now to be immobilized. The sheepish grin on de Lacy's lips roused his suspicion. "Mind you, Captain. This better be military business. If not, your rank means nothing."

De Lacy appeared unaffected by the threat. "I have a special assignment for you, Monsieur le Comte. You are to be involved in a secret mission to La Rochelle, under the command of the Marquis de Feuquières and the Comte de Reynard."

Stunned, Dominic repeated, "Reynard?"

De Lacy noted Dominic's questioning tone. "You seem uneasy, Count."

Dominic recovered himself. "I don't recall seeing him in camp."

"He arrived with the King. I thought you would be pleased by the assignment. But you haven't said a word. I'm sure His Eminence would appreciate your gratitude. You still tread on dangerous ground."

With clenched teeth Dominic leaned closer de Lacy, his eyes ablaze with rancor. "Beware of shadows, de Lacy."

"Do you threaten an officer of the Cardinal?"

"No, a warning."

De Lacy cynically snickered. "Don't make threats you can't fulfill. Be ready at dawn." He marched off.

Dominic's thoughts shifted from de Lacy to Reynard. *He must be the other traitor!* The more he thought about the situation the more pieces of the puzzle began to fit. Reynard was more powerful than Borchard thus his risk greater. He wondered if Reynard had anything to do with the marriage contract, or if Borchard act singularly. He winced thinking of his cousin now a widow and Arsène dead.

"If you did use my cousin, you will regret it," he swore. "Yet you too go to La Rochelle. My guess is our involvement in this was Richelieu's doing. This shall be interesting."

In the cold stillness of the early frosty morning, the members of the assault team gathered. The horses stomped their hooves, billowing white breath came from their nostrils. The woolen cloak did not help to ward off the chill of the metal cuirass as Dominic wore full battle dress. He scowled when his father and Jean-Claude appeared on horseback next to him.

Jourdain regarded his son with cold indifference. "Your mettle will be tested this day and determine if what you claim is true or not."

"Is this your way of wishing me God-speed by questioning my valor?"

"No, my way of telling you we will be with the invasion force and see for ourselves your true heart in this business."

"Will nothing short of my death still your doubts?"

"We do not wish that," said Jean-Claude in dispute.

"Maybe you don't." With a last glare at his father, Dominic moved his horse away from them to the rear of the assault column. He was alone for only a moment when Reynard appeared beside him.

"A surprising turn of events? I don't think we expected to see each other again."

"Had you thought I too was dead?" he said, his patience thin.

"Mind your tongue! I could have you arrested and shot as a traitor."

"What will happen when my father discovers the truth about your treachery? Will Richelieu shield you from the wrath of the Marquis de Charbonier? But I don't think going on this mission was your idea."

"What I've done, and do, I do for France. Your father is well aware of my action, as witnessed by our dealings with the marriage contract."

"You were responsible?" hissed Dominic, his blood boiling. "Why Borchard? Why not take Sabrina for yourself?"

"And risk exposure? Borchard was the man for that," he replied with chuckle of cold malice. "Yet I will tell you this. An old law of chivalry states, when a man deprives a lady of her support he is bound to provide for her."

The cryptic statement momentarily stymied Dominic before his eyes narrowed upon Reynard. "If I learn you had a hand in the deaths of Arsène and Philipe, there won't be a hole big enough for you to crawl into!"

He kicked his horse and caught up to his men a few yards ahead. He snarled in abhorrence and sorrow enraging his mind and spirit. *Wait! He didn't mean Arsène and Philipe he meant the fire! It was Borchard all those years ago. I thank Providence for the hand that struck you down, for if it hadn't, I would.*

He gritted his teeth and continued the ride to La Rochelle.

✦ Chapter 21 ✦

I N THE MIDDLE OF THE NIGHT, ARSÈNE AND PHILIPE were summoned to Rohan's quarters. Mayor Geriton was with the duke when they arrived.

Rohan explained, "Lizon escaped and went straight to the King and Cardinal. We couldn't learn anything from our spies of what he told them, but we cannot take any chances, he knows La Rochelle too well." He beckoned them to the table of maps.

"All evening we dispatched soldiers and police to secure every part of the city. Only this assignment requires cunning and planning which is why I summoned both of you." He pointed to the map of the area surrounding La Rochelle. "A small canal on the eastern side of the city. The grille water gate is wood, and shallow enough at low tide for men to cross on foot or horseback. They may try to enter through the grille, or some how lower the drawbridge and bring cavalry across and into the city."

"Is this a bastion?" asked Philipe concerning a marking on the map.

"Yes, only the grille is obscured from full view. We must place someone between the bastion and grille to draw attention."

"I will take the position and Philipe organize musketeers on the bastion to provide cover," said Arsène.

"Take what you need from the armory and make ready. We wasted an entire day already."

Within an hour Philipe gathered thirty men. Ten he sent with Arsène for planning, while the remaining twenty he ordered armed with harquebusiers and pistols. The former weapon was more adequate for an ambuscade than a long barrel musket requiring support. The harquebus was heavier and fired by matchlock rather than flintlock, but at close quarters wreaked more havoc and damage than a musket. The pistols added another shot. Of course each man had a sword, but Philipe hoped with a well-planned ambuscade close combat would not be necessary.

The bastion had been reduced by cannonade to a heap of rubble but enough of it remained to hide twenty men and weapons. He dispatched a scout to watch for enemy soldiers.

He became concerned, wondering what kept Arsène so long. Then again, he wondered about Arsène's behavior for months. The situation was precarious at best, and though he understood the reason for Arsène's agitation, he was uncertain of how to deal with it. During heated arguments, Arsène criticized him for any number of reasons, all negligible in the scheme of things. He thought of revealing the truth of Borchard's death and easing the tension. Yet, what good would it do in such a volatile situation? With these thoughts, he wrestled but until he could decide, he had a promise to fulfill no matter how difficult Arsène made it with his rash behavior.

When Arsène and his men finally arrived at the bastion, he wore the uniform of an officer in the King's Musketeers.

"A little dangerous, don't you think?" chided Philipe.

"More for them than me, I hope. The men are dressed as infantry. A work detail should draw their attention. Also, I gave the gatekeeper a sign and countersign," he replied in a manner too casual for Philipe's agitated mind.

"When will we know to fire?"

"I'll signal you somehow, but keep a sharp eye out and a steady trigger finger, and pray the uniforms don't get mixed up."

Philipe grabbed Arsène's arm when the latter began to move off. "Don't throw your life away on some silly escapade!"

Arsène shrugged, continuing in his flippant attitude. "What is life, but one big game of winning and losing? How often have we lived through events like this?"

"I stopped counting. Only this feels different."

Arsène laughed. "Since when did the practical Philipe Bourdias start having perception?"

"Since my reckless Gascon friend lost it!"

"I hadn't realized I lost anything. I am simply helping Rohan."

Philipe shook his head. "Not what you do rather how; rash and cavalier. Where is the Gascon who thinks and perceives? Unless he wants to get killed."

Arsène became perplexed. "You think I'm trying to die?"

"Yes! You don't know what the future holds. None of us do. But to continue in this way can only lead to self-destruction! Did you not heed what I said in Paris?"

The reply was subdued. "In Paris I left my heart, the one that feels and perceives. The one beating in my chest only keeps me alive. So no more counsel on my actions." At Philipe's despondency, he added, "I don't want to die, and I apologize for giving you the impression. It was not a conscious effort, I assure you."

Philipe chewed on his mustache once more wrestling on whether to tell Arsène about Borchard.

"Now, we have a task to do. I shall do my best with great caution, I promise."

Philipe gave a disgruntled snort at seeing the eastern skyline grow lighter. "Let's be quick about this business." He moved behind the bastion to finish positioning his men while Arsène joined his group.

The scout returned and reported to Philipe. "A small mounted troop of twelve is heading this way, Captain. One rode ahead, probably to scout so I returned. I don't think he saw me."

"Very well. Get in position."

Philipe watched Arsène place the phony work detail directly in front of the bastion. The canal was a hundred yards behind them and slightly down hill. He was about to call to Arsène, when he caught sight of riders and slipped back behind the wall.

"If one of them lays a finger on Captain Lamonreaux, he's mine," said Philipe and readied his musket. He rested the barrel of the harquebus on the wall for accuracy. With the butt nestled in his shoulder, he pressed his left cheek against the cold stock, keeping careful aim on the advancing enemy. One hand held the weapon steady; his trigger finger ready. The men of the bastion held the same ramrod-still position as their captain.

Feuquières stopped his men a quarter mile from the work detail when the royal scout returned and saluted the marquis. Reynard and Dominic rode with Feuquières.

"King's men by their uniforms, monsieur. The officer is a Musketeer."

"Strange to find a detail out at this earlier hour," said Reynard.

"They may be planning to use that bastion," said Feuquières, pointing ahead. "Perhaps the King sent them to be of assistance."

"No armed guards, monsieur."

"Stranger still," mused Reynard, eying the work detail.

"Must be safe if Musketeers don't use guards."

"Musketeers would rather die than have their pride wounded by the appearance of guards," said Dominic. "He's seen us. Best make a decision, lest we give him cause for alarm."

At the approach of the royal scout, Arsène raised a warning hand. "Close enough."

"You are King's men?" asked the scout.

"If not, would we be insane enough to be out in this intolerable cold in plain sight of the enemy?" said Arsène with an ironic chuckle. "What business have you here?"

"King's business, if you'll permit, sir."

"Who am I to interfere in the King's business? Do your duty. We will help if we can."

The scout saluted and rode back to the troop.

Arsène sent a careful side-glance to the bastion. He was unable to see Philipe, but knew Philipe watched the events. Two noblemen joined the scout and rode toward him. They were within a hundred feet of the work detail when suddenly; his heart skipped a beat.

Reynard! If he recognizes me—too late!

Reynard gave the alarm. "It's a trap!" he shouted and drew his pistol.

In a thunderous roar, twenty harquebusiers opened fire upon the royal troop from the bastion. Six soldiers fell. Feuquières' horse was killed, sending him hard to the ground. Two Huguenots from the work detail placed muskets to Feuquières' chest, forcing his surrender.

To save himself from the hail of balls, Dominic made his horse fall, rolled off the animal and partly slid down the embankment into the icy water of the canal.

A Cardinal's Guard suffered a left shoulder wound when unhorsed. He saw Dominic scramble up the embankment toward the bastion. He unsheathed his dagger and went after Dominic from behind.

At the sound of the shot close by his ear and an agonizing groan, Dominic whirled about. The guard, a raised dagger clenched in his hand, his face bloody from shot that sent him into the canal. Before Dominic could react, a Huguenot cold-cocked him from behind and he collapsed to the ground unconscious.

Reynard killed a Huguenot with pistol shot, but further heroics were quelled by the addition of twenty men from the bastion.

Surrounded, Feuquières ordered his men to yield.

Philipe came alongside Arsène just as two soldiers drug the unconscious Dominic to where the royalists were being assembled. Face down Dominic lay before Philipe and Arsène. The back of his head was very bloody. Philipe moved to help him, but was stopped by Arsène.

"That's all of them, Captain," a soldier said to Arsène.

"For your sake, Captain, I hope my companion is not dead," began Feuquières. "His father is a powerful lord and would not take kindly to his son dying in such a dishonorable manner."

Arsène knelt to examine Dominic's head wound. He turned Dominic's head to see his friend's face. There was no response to the movement and the features were pale. He sent a scowl to Reynard before turning to Feuquières. "After such a nasty blow, recovery is doubtful."

Philipe clenched his fists, angry eyes finding Reynard.

Reynard turned from Philipe to Arsène, who remained beside Dominic. "A rather surprising end to your little intrigues, eh Lamonreaux?"

Feuquières knitted his brows at the exchange but Arsène's menacing eyes and harsh response to Reynard, stopped any words.

"You, *Monsieur le Traître*, are my prisoner!" Arsène felt a stirring beneath the hand he held on Dominic's shoulder. He pressed down to restrain the movement and looked to Philipe, his focus upon Reynard. "Captain Bourdias, alert the gatekeeper. Sergeant le Croix, take charge of the prisoners and make them comfortable in their new home."

At further movement from Dominic, Arsène strengthened his restraint. While the soldiers carried out the orders, he pretended to examine the wound again. "For your life's sake, stay still," he whispered to Dominic. The latter ceased moving.

Straightening to view how his orders were being carried out, he saw Philipe beside the gate wearing a worried expression. "Close the gate!" he called. After Philipe did so, he leaned down to Dominic. "You can sit up now."

Philipe raced over and fell to his knees. "You said he was dying!"

Arsène grinned. "Not with his thick skull. I wanted Reynard to think so."

Dominic looked at them in wondrous relief. "God be praised! Seeing you both alive cures any pains I have endured!" He embraced Philipe and Arsène in turn. "When I heard your voice, I thought I too must be dead, but when you spoke to Philipe—this is a miracle!"

"You thought we were dead?" asked Arsène in confusion.

"Killed the day of the crossing."

"Ah! The dead civilians we changed clothes with."

"Drowning was the official report. Either way, I could not believe my childhood friend and Gascon were gone. How bitterly my heart grieved." He swallowed back a wave of tears. "To find you both alive, pieces of my soul are restored."

"I'm sorry, old friend. We only thought to escape," said Philipe.

"All is forgiven." Dominic laughed, but then became sullen. "I wrote Adele and I'm certain she told Sabrina."

Arsène looked to the ground, murmuring, "Oh, Sabrina."

Dominic placed a hand on Arsène's shoulder. "Do not fret. All will be well when we return alive. Especially with Borchard dead."

Arsène's head snapped up. "What?"

Philipe squirmed at the mention of Borchard.

"You don't know?" asked Dominic, surprised by the reaction. "He was killed by some assailant a few months ago."

"Murdered?" Arsène was still stunned and perplexed.

"By Huguenots or rogue smugglers perhaps."

"What difference does it make? He's paid the price for his treachery," chided Philipe. "Our concern now is for Dominic. Sight of that uniform can be just as dangerous as a renegade's knife."

"How did you know it was a knife? Dominic didn't mention it," asked Arsène, coming out of his benumbed stupor.

Philipe shrugged, trying to think of an answer. He was not a good liar, and Arsène was seldom fooled. "I can't picture Borchard's fat frame dueling. How else?"

"Shot," said Arsène, watching Philipe.

"No, a knife," said Dominic, his curious gaze shifting between them.

"A lucky guess," said Philipe, trying to be casual. "Now, let's get Dominic to safety, tend to his wound and find him some new clothes."

"What time is it?" asked Dominic, anxious.

Arsène pulled out his watch and read. "Half past seven."

"Quick! An invasion force waits just outside the main gate."

Rohan and Geriton worked in the duke's study when Arsène, Philipe and Dominic burst in on them. "Has something hap—Dominic? What fantastic turn of events is this?"

"The grille," said Philipe, indicating Dominic, who took up the explanation.

"The King dispatched an assault party to breach the grille and open the main gate for a cavalry invasion. Marillac and Schombreg wait with two thousand men. However, if it was not accomplished by eight o'clock the mission would be abandoned."

The clock on mantle showed seven forty-five. "We can't take a chance. Philipe, tell Major Le Strade to secure the gate. Arsène, inform Major Éraste to have the artillery stand by. Dominic, stay and rest. I'll send Chandler for a surgeon to tend your wound," said Rohan.

Arsène laid hold of Philipe's arm to stop him from leaving, but spoke to Rohan. "We took prisoners. One is the Marquis de Feuquières, the other, our second traitor—Reynard."

Rohan was thunderstruck into a moment of silence. "Reynard? This is incredible!"

"Shall I send them to you for an interview?"

Rohan absentmindedly nodded still pondering the revelation. After Arsène and Philipe left, he sent Dominic with Chandler to see the surgeon for medical attention. Geriton remained.

Rohan's difficultly in accepting the betrayal was evident by the visible conflict on his face at seeing Reynard. "I knew of Borchard, but when Arsène mentioned you, I could barely believe the news. Why, Maurice?"

Reynard acted unconcerned almost boarding on arrogant indifference. "The same reason you do this, Henri. For France."

The impudent way Reynard looked and spoke, infuriated Rohan. "A patriot does not betray his faith or his friends, Monsieur le Comte!"

"For one's country any price is worth paying."

"What was your price? Was it any better than Borchard or Condé? Did it gain you equal status to me or the Bouillon?" His speech grew bitter with each word.

"Why don't you ask your protégé?"

Fire rose in Rohan's eyes. "A blow struck at Arsène is a blow struck at me!" He added emphasis in striking his chest.

"Only when the blow strikes the heart of the enemy does it stop him."

Furious at the implication, he seized Reynard. "You, and not Borchard, tore his heart apart!"

Geriton rushed to physically intervene. "Monsieur! If this was only a personal blow then let him answer to your sword. But his actions injured all Huguenots. Let him answer to the Council and receive his just punishment."

"Indeed, his crimes are great, including the assassination of the Duc de Trudeau." Rohan fiercely snarled and shoved Reynard away. "You will stand before the city elders charged with treason and murder."

"I protest! I am of noble blood and commissioned by His Majesty for this mission."

"You are a traitor! The place upon which you stand is the sovereign city against which you committed your crimes! Prepare what defense you can. May God have mercy on your soul, I cannot!" He waved for Geriton to remove Reynard.

Rohan paced in an attempt to bring his emotions under control before the next interview. The fact that a man he trusted was responsible for the assassination of his dear friend William and caused heartache to Arsène grieved him. If he had the slightest suspicions of Reynard, he would have taken great pains to prevent the unfortunate events. He became so caught up in his personal turmoil he didn't realize Geriton returned until the mayor spoke.

"Fear not, monsieur. If the Council finds him guilty, judgment will be just and swift."

"There is no question of his guilt!"

"Then he shall soon stand before God to eternally answer for his crimes. Shall I bring in the marquis?"

Rohan nodded and took the time Geriton went to fetch Feuquières to bring his attention back to the situation at hand. Fortunately this interview proved more civil and he informed the marquis he would remain a prisoner until the conflict resolved. Feuquières expected nothing less, and as long as his treatment was favorable he would act according to the laws governing prisoners of war. Rohan did not press Feuquières for information when the marquis politely refused to answer. Dominic would be more willing to talk.

Le Strade and Philipe watched the horizon and the advancing invasion force. Le Strade grumbled under his breath. "You're friend had wrong information. They aren't going to withdraw."

Philipe glanced to Arsène and Éraste. They stood some distance away and appeared to be arguing. Eraste hastened from Arsène to the artillery crews and began yelling. Philipe slapped Le Strade's arm upon seeing the cannons being prepared to fire. "Major!"

La Strade swore and raced toward the artillery but Arsène met them halfway. "Who gave the order to fire?" he demanded.

"Movement from the force. I told him they appeared to be runners, but he wouldn't listen."

"Blasted fool!" swore Le Strade. He, Philipe and Arsène raced up to the battlement to view the results of the cannon fire. The volley cut down the invasion force. "Maybe they will withdraw without a response from their cannons. Bourdias, have the man stand ready should they response. Lamonreaux, go back and tell Eraste: *I* give the order to cease firing."

Schomberg and the invasion force were unprepared for the cannonade. Confusion spread through the ranks about what to do in response.

"Monsieur, shouldn't we charge?" asked another aide.

"Feuquiéres hasn't secured the gate. It would be suicide."

"We're being cut down now!"

Schomberg snarled, his eyes scanning the line of death and injury. "Tell the men to fall back and take cover."

The aide did as ordered and the force scrambled to take cover.

Jourdain and Jean-Claude became separated, trying to bring some order to the chaos among their men. One cannon ball landed beside Jourdain's horse, killing the animal and tossing him some ten feet into the air and backwards.

"Jourdain!" Jean-Claude pressed his mount toward his fallen friend, and leapt from the saddle before the horse stopped. Blood covered the entire front of Jourdain's doublet and ran down his face. With so much blood it was hard to tell the location of the wound, but serious enough for Jean-Claude to feel and find a pulse. "Sergeant Gilliam! A litter for the marquis and hurry!"

Schomberg appeared beside Jean-Claude, still on horseback. "How bad is he?"

"Very bad."

Schomberg swore and called, "Major Bernard! Sound retreat. Feuquiéres has failed."

"Wait!" Jean-Claude bolted up and snatched the horse's bridle. "The Comte de Trévoux?"

"We can't wait to find out his fate." Schomberg rode off to take command of the retreat.

Arsène arrived returned to the artillery line in time to witness Schomberg's retreat. "Cease fire! Cease fire!"

"I give the orders here!" snapped Éraste.

"The order comes from Major Le Strade. And they are in retreat. No need for unnecessary killing."

Éraste snarled at Arsène. "I will mark your insubordination, Captain."

"And I will mark your disobedience of the duke's order!"

Éraste scowled at the rebuff then shouted. "Cease fire!"

A cleaned and bandaged Dominic arrived at the duke's quarters only a moment before Arsène and Philipe returned.

"You look better," said Philipe.

Dominic just shrugged, appearing fatigued.

"What happened?" asked Rohan. "I thought I heard cannon fire."

"You did," began Arsène. "Éraste ordered the artillery to fire upon some movement from the invasion force. I tried to convince him to wait since the two riders appeared to be runners, but he didn't listen."

"His actions forced Le Strade and I to take up supportive positions," added Philipe. "Fortunately, we received no return fire and the cannons stopped when they retreated."

"By my order. Rather my relaying of Le Strade's order. Éraste said he'll report my insubordination," said Arsène with a wry grin.

"Let him try. I'll have a few words for him." Rohan's focus shifted from them to Dominic. "How are you feeling?"

"Better, monsieur."

"Can you answer some questions?"

"Of course."

"Make yourself comfortable." Rohan sat at his desk and Dominic took a seat in front of the desk. "Was this mission a result of Lizon's information?"

"Yes, monsieur."

"How did Reynard become involved?"

Dominic shifted in the chair, more due to reluctance to answer then discomfort. "You can well imagine our surprise at being thrown together. Through heated words, he confessed his part in the marriage contract."

Arsène straightened and squared his shoulders but said nothing as Dominic continued.

"He is a shrewd man and must have blackmailed Borchard. After speaking to him, I recognized it was his voice I overheard betraying Trudeau to Richelieu."

"Why Borchard for this ruse? Why not marry Sabrina himself?" demanded Arsène.

"Something to do with my uncle's involvement with the Huguenots. By Reynard's admission, the fire was deliberate like Sabrina suspected."

Arsène's expression turned to dreaded anticipation of the answer to his next question. "Borchard?"

"Yes——," Dominic answered.

"No," said Rohan simultaneously.

They turned to the duke, quizzical at the opposing answer.

"Dominic's story, along with my earlier interview, brought back memories of long ago. Borchard did not become involved with us until later. The magistrate of Reims was a young Maurice Reynard."

"Maurice," echoed Dominic. " Sabrina mentioned hearing his name the night before the fire. She also said she heard Henri and William. I concluded she meant you and Monsieur Trudeau, but neither she nor I could determine Maurice's identity."

"Maurice was raised Huguenot. His father was a loyal supporter of our cause. Soothe, Fredrick died during the last conflict."

"I don't understand. Being a magistrate, he was an enemy of the Huguenots," said Dominic in confusion.

"Unlike what most Catholics believe, not all Huguenots are patriots. Maurice possessed a fiery zeal for whatever he embraced. When appointed magistrate, he took his work seriously, as he should. His father's death prompted his enlistment in our ranks."

"Sabrina said a meeting in Reims was interrupted by the arrival of the magistrate and the men scattered. She overheard a row between Uncle Michael and Maurice in which blows were exchanged."

Rohan's brows leveled in recollection. "We were still uncertain about Maurice so for prudence's sake, we dispersed and even Fredrick agreed to the decision. The following morning Michael made no mention of a row nor showed no signs of injury—" he suddenly stopped.

"Monsieur, was Reynard injured?" asked Arsène.

"Yes! Nothing debilitating or life threatening and no one gave it much thought at time."

Dominic snarled trying to contain his emotions. "He quoted an old law of chivalry about a man who deprives a lady of her support is bound to provide for her! At first I thought he meant Borchard, but he meant—" his voice choked. "He killed my family in an act of vengeance!"

Rohan moved from behind the desk to the calm the upset Dominic. "He is to be tried for treason by the city elders. I'm certain he shall be found guilty and meet his long overdue due punishment."

Dominic's respond was a curt nod, conflict visible on his face.

"How did you and Reynard come together on this venture?"

" Richelieu."

"The would-be assassin de Lacy's doing, no doubt," said Philipe.

"Assassin?" asked Arsène.

"You shot him," said Dominic to Philipe, half-smiling. "I believe you're right. He was awfully smug when informing me of the assignment."

"When was this?" Arsène again asked Philipe after being ignored.

"Shortly after the volley. He came at Dominic from behind with a dagger. I didn't have time to aim, I pulled the trigger and hoped for the best."

"What can you tell us about plans for the Royal Army?" asked Rohan.

Dominic shrugged with ignorance. "After hearing the report about Arsène and Philipe's deaths, they kept me busy with unimportant assignments. I wasn't to be trusted. To make matters worse, my father and Baron Bourdias arrived with the King and Reynard."

Philipe grew rigid at hearing of his father. "What did he say? Does he believe we are dead?"

Dominic nodded, reticent in his response. "Shot as traitors while deserting." He stood to comfort Philipe when the latter swore. "I convinced him to tell Adele the official version from Gaston how you and Arsène were killed during the crossing to Ré."

Philipe struggled with the news. "What of Adele?"

Again he hesitated and replied with discretion. "I don't know. I sent Roger with my letter and asked him to stay with her."

"There is more you're not telling us," said Arsène.

"Jean-Claude said Adele was dismissed from Court and he beat poor Roger to the point I hardly recognized him for all the injuries." Dominic made motion to his face. "I treated with medicine from your box I retrieved before they confiscated your belongs."

"Why was Adele dismissed?"

"Because of me," said Philipe when Dominic didn't answer.

"Yes," droned Dominic.

"Jean-Claude may beat a servant, but he will not act against Adele," said Rohan.

"Why not? If he believes I dishonored him!"

Rohan took Philipe by the shoulders to curb the young man's temper. "Because Dominic is still alive. He does not dare act against her or risk invoking his son-in-law's anger."

"I told you, I convinced him about the official version."

"Who told him otherwise?" asked Arsène.

"They said was a reliable source. Reynard would be my guess."

"It would make sense," said Rohan then spoke to Philipe, "Another cruel act of against his former comrades."

Somewhat subdued, Philipe nodded.

Rohan turned back to Dominic. "Any news of army activity would be helpful."

"I learned Admiral Montmorency has permission to sail against the English. You see the harbor. The dike we all laughed at is a reality. Within six months the harbor will be completely dammed, all supplies cut off, and the Royal Forces surrounding the fortress on land."

Rohan pulled at his beard, frowned and crossed to the window overlooking the city. St. Martin's harbor was only partly visible through the gray sky. He spoke to himself. "Lord, when all appeared bleak for Israel you sent Moses. Perhaps we made Buckingham our Moses. Have mercy on us, Lord, and forgive our folly. I realize now how foolish and blind we've been. Grant me the strength and wisdom in this hour of need." With a sigh he returned to speak to them. "I'm afraid we have a long siege ahead of us and must take immediate steps in preparation. All supplies must be rationed." He walked back to the desk and sat.

"There is one ray of hope which may shorten the siege," began Dominic. "Gaston and the King had a falling out and Gaston quit the battlefield. Oh, and Paris is in an uproar. Jeanette Charise was murdered the afternoon the campaign left. The King may have to return to deal with those issues."

Shocked, Arsène paled. A sign from Philipe told him to remain calm.

Rohan was not paying attention, rather contemplating. "We cannot place any hope on what Gaston might do in retaliation or a disturbance at Court. As for our situation, the Council will work out the details of rationing. Until then not a word is to leave this room so we can avoid a panic. In the meantime, you should rest." He looked with a smile of pride and satisfaction at Philipe and Arsène. "Good work this day."

After they took their leave and were outside the chateau, Philipe said, "I hope for our sakes, Rohan knows what he's doing."

Arsène turned his collar against the wind. "He does. Come, let's take Dominic to the apartment so he can rest."

Dominic followed in silence, pondering.

The silence only lasted until they reached the large one room apartment and Philipe spoke to Dominic. "Tell me everything that happened with my father."

Dominic shrugged, obviously not wanting to discuss the matter any further. "We exchanged words. And as I said, I convinced him."

"What exactly did he say? I must know."

"At first, he and my father were fixed in their determination to confront me. Jean-Claude went too far in questioning your honor. That's when I told of my conversation with Gaston and challenged him about which version to tell Adele. He backed down."

Philipe sat in one of the two chairs beside an old table, eyes dark and tugging at his moustache.

Dominic sat in the other chair, but Philipe didn't look at him, rather avoided eye contact. "Whereas I convinced him, I will never be able to convince my father. The entire conversation was an effort to get an admission from me concerning our conversion." He laid a hand on Philipe's arm, to make Philipe look at him. "Dead or alive, I would never betray either of you."

Philipe's voice was thick but confident. "I know."

"I'm sorry, *mes amis*. Sorry for all of you," droned Arsène.

Dominic sat back and heaved a shrug. "We knew the chances of grave consequences for our actions, now we must face them." He flashed a smile. "At least we are alive. And God willing, can return to those who still love and support us."

Arsène nudged Philipe's shoulder. "Write Adele and send it with Rohan's dispatches."

"And tell her what? Father accused me of dishonor?"

"That you're alive! We're both alive, which she in turn will tell Sabrina." Inspired, Arsène crossed to the small three-drawer dresser and began looking for pen and paper. "Nothing! Come, we'll go to headquarters. You can rest," he said to Dominic and pulled Philipe to his feet.

"No. This isn't a good idea."

"Why? Surely you don't want Adele to grieve any longer."

"Of course not, but what if by some misfortune we are really killed. Do you want them to grieve a second time?"

Stymied, Arsène turned from Philipe to Dominic. "Philipe is right," began Dominic. "Although I understand and share your desire, it would be cruel to make them relive such sorrow rather rejoice when we do return."

"Very well," said Arsène, with reluctance. "You still need to rest and we have duties."

❖ Chapter 22 ❖

THE FOLLOWING DAY, PHILIPE, ARSÈNE, DOMINIC AND ROHAN did not attend the trial of Reynard. Dominic avoided it for security sake since Reynard was led to believe he would not recover. Rohan told Philipe and Arsène their sworn affidavits would be enough. As for the duke, he was too passionate about the whole affair, knowing Reynard was responsible for William's assassination.

The trial judges consisted of twelve city elders under the direction of Mayor Geriton. La Rochelle's prosecuting attorney was Marc St. Antoine. Major Le Strade and a squad of soldiers escorted the Comte de Reynard into the courtroom of La Rochelle's judicial building. Although given the normal privileges of prisoners with noble rank, dark circles formed under his eyes from not sleeping well. Despite being disheveled, his cold look of arrogance remained intact.

In his opening statement, St. Antoine spoke of the heinous crimes committed by Reynard, including ordering the death of the Duc de Trudeau. He further said the count flaunted his treachery by being involved in a secret mission to infiltrate La Rochelle with the intent to place it in threat of a Royal invasion. With each charge he referred to affidavits, though careful not to use names, but by the number, more than Philipe and Arsène were included.

When St. Antoine finished, Geriton spoke. "You have heard the charges and evidence against you. What do you to say in your defense, Monsieur le Comte?"

Reynard eyes betrayed no fear or concern, simply noble indifference, but his voice filled with disdain. "I go on record as saying this trial is a mockery of French Justice. The only evidence you present is the words of traitors to France. I demand to be judged by my peers which is the right of every French noble!"

"Monsieur le Comte, La Rochelle is a sovereign city against which you have taken steps to undermine,' began Geriton in rebuke. "You are thereby considered an enemy of this city. The charges of treason only add to your miserable acts of sedition. According to the rules of war, a traitor need not be given a trial; rather can be shot on the spot!"

"Sedition is it! Then, *Monsieur le Hypocrite*, what do you call raising arms against the King?"

"A defense of our rights granted by the Edict of Nantes! But enough! We are not here to debate, but to try a prisoner of war. Since you are vehemently opposed to cooperating, I may, in all good conscience, dismiss this trial and adhere to the rules of war. At dusk you shall be shot as a spy and saboteur!" Geriton beat the gravel on the table and waved for Le Strade to remove the prisoner.

At the abrupt dismissal and death sentence, Reynard balked, shouting objections as he was dragged from the room. His protestations fell on deaf ears and he realized, even if he made defense, the same sentence would have been pronounced.

Le Strade sent for Philipe and Arsène, and when they arrived, he gave Philipe his orders: the execution of the Comte de Reynard. "Since you and Captain Lamonreaux have been so injured, I thought it fitting you should command the execution."

Whereas Arsène received the news with a grim demeanor, Philipe went rigid, and momentarily silent in absorbing the words and implications. His eyes almost immediately turned dark. Still, he tried to sound unaffected as he asked, "When?"

"At the earliest convenience."

Philipe saluted and left, Arsène at his heels.

"This disturbs you?"

Philipe tried to be nonchalant. "Unexpected. By your reaction, you didn't expect it either."

"Perhaps, but I will do it if you wish."

"No!" he snapped, which made Arsène curious and wary, thus he continued more calmly. "This is my charge, and I will follow orders. Le Strade spoke truth; Reynard has caused us great injury."

"I understand. Your honor would rather be avenged by the sword than powder and shot."

Philipe managed a faint smile. "I need to tend to my duties. Alone, please."

"As you wish."

Without another word, Philipe went to make the arrangements. By twilight, all was ready at a secluded part of the eastern wall. The less visible this execution was, the better. Six men stood ready with loaded muskets.

Philipe rubbed his gloved hands together in an attempt to curb his anxiety as they awaited the arrival of the prisoner. His promise to Sabrina, affection for Arsène, thoughts of Adele and Dominic's loss, and present realities weighed heavy on his heart and mind. He chose to kill Borchard, but a choice reached under extreme duress and one causing him many sleepless nights of secret anguish. Now, by fate, the final act of justice for their injuries again fell to him.

He was roused from his musing at hearing the sound of the single somber drum of the final procession. He ordered his men to stand at attention. Although a condemned traitor, a nobleman was about to die and this solemn occasion called for dignity. A lump rose in his throat and he swallowed hard to steady his nerves.

Reynard's eyes fell upon Philipe when the procession halted. "So, it is you and not Lamonreaux."

Philipe fists clenched as Reynard's speech momentarily reminded him of Borchard's surprised utterance upon recognizing him. He forced himself to proceed. "Monsieur, do you have any regrets or sins to confess to God before the sentence is carried out?"

Reynard cynically smiled. "One regret. To observe the look on Lamonreaux's face when I say, I was the puppet master of the innocent damsel, Borchard the scapegoat, and the Gascon the fool!"

"May your soul be damned for it!" Philipe ordered Reynard placed against the wall. "Blindfold, monsieur?"

Reynard refused with a proud shake of his head.

"You have a moment to make peace with your Maker."

"Damn your condescension!"

Philipe stepped back to his place of command. In doing so, he caught sight of Arsène watching a few yards away. Briefly their eyes meet, before he drew his sword and turned back to his task. "Raise your muskets!" He raised the sword above his head.

Reynard stood straight, flashing a scoffing glance from the firing squad to Philipe.

"Fire!" Philipe quickly lowered his sword then winced at the resounding of musket fire off the wall.

Reynard was stuck in twice in the head, three times in the chest, once in the abdomen and made no sound in falling to the ground.

A moment passed during which Philipe stared at Reynard. The man who betrayed them, murdered Trudeau, caused the death of Dominic's child, and endangered Sabrina lay dead. Whoever said vengeance was sweet had never been involved with so contorted a situation.

"Captain?" asked a member of the firing squad.

Philipe made a curt wave. "Remove the body and dismiss the men, Sergeant."

"Yes, Captain."

Arsène joined him. For a moment nothing was said as they regarded each other. What could be said? But he had to speak, thus he asked, "Is Dominic still at the apartment?"

"Yes, but I had to come, even though you disapprove."

"I never said I disapproved."

"You did not want me here. Why?"

Philipe heaved a shrug. "To spare you anymore grief."

Arsène studied Philipe. "So said Dominic when you missed supper. I'm not so sure."

"You expressed grief when I doubted you. Why do you doubt me now?"

"It's been so confusing of late. With your desire to do this yourself and missing supper, I wondered what secret you keep from me."

"Nothing," said Philipe with a forced hollow laugh. "A somber duty I wish to perform singularly. Come, I need some rest."

Jean-Claude couldn't rest, couldn't stop thinking about the uncertainty surrounding Dominic's fate and Jourdain's serious wound. He was surprised to find he lightly dozed in a chair beside the marquis' cot when someone entered. "Sire!" He bolted to his feet in surprise.

"Be at ease, Baron." Louis looked with compassion at Jourdain. He was pale and unconscious, the head wound bandage and the nightshirt barely covered the large bandage around his torso. "Has he awoken yet?"

"No, Sire." He saw the somber way Louis regarded Jourdain. "Despite the seriousness, the surgeon is hopeful since he survived the night."

Louis' sober gaze shifted to Jean-Claude. "The surgeon may be hopeful, but the news I bring may devastate him in his weakened condition."

"What news?"

"A note from Feuquières smuggled out by loyalists contained sad news. The Comte de Trévoux died when the sabotage team was ambushed."

Jean-Claude paled and muttered an oath.

"I'm sorry for the both of you. Especially after learning of the death of your son, Baron."

"Thank you, Sire."

"You are free to leave to console your family."

"I shall wait and be assured of the marquis' recovery."

"As you wish. Again my condolences." Louis left.

Alone, Jean-Claude reflected upon the loss of Philipe and Dominic. His heart stirred with sorrow as he sat back in the chair to watch Jourdain sleep. He felt pain at the initial report of Philipe's death, but his feelings became tempered by Jourdain's belief that Philipe and Dominic converted to the Protestant faith. Adele's dismissal from Court reinforced Jourdain's belief. Still, a part of him resisted accepting the possibility of his son's conversion. However, since being at La Rochelle, the evidence was too compelling to ignore.

How would Jourdain accept this news? He recalled Jourdian mourning his brother's death and guilt prompting him to bring Sabrina into this home. But what was believed of Dominic's activities far exceeded Michael. Everything Jourdain did since Sabrina fled Reims was to preserve the family. A family Dominic was to carry on.

"You already endured much, old friend. What will you do now? What will either of us do without heirs?"

✤ Chapter 23 ✤

UNAWARE OF EVENTS AT LA ROCHELLE, Sabrina attempted to satisfy Borchard's creditors. The count left many unpaid debts and his lawyers advised her to sell everything to satisfy payment. The Paris château sold first. Afterward, she returned to Brittany to settle business accounts in the province.

In the country, labor and material cost less, so Borchard spent more on refurbishing the manor house built in the last century with a square keep flanked by turrets, encircled on top by a parapet. Whereas the outside appeared formidable with a beautiful courtyard and four-arched gallery in the center of the complex, most of the apartments remained unfinished with exposed beams and thick paneling. Borchard started updating the style five years ago. Here Sabrina felt more at ease being away from Paris. Sale of this house even in its present condition would bring in enough money to settle local accounts with a good sum left over to live modestly, yet comfortably for several years.

Not long after Sabrina returned to Brittany, a solemn and weary Adele arrived with Roger. The stalwart valet appeared pale and pensive when Adele handed Sabrina a wrapped item appearing to be the size of a small book. She saw the initials DC on the handkerchief so she knew it was from Dominic, but what the handkerchief held surprised her.

"A Bible? Why send me this?"

"Look inside." Adele's voice was muted.

Sabrina did so and found the inscription. "I didn't know Arsène had a Bible. I still don't understand."

Emotions make her speechless, Adele held out a letter.

Sabrina accepted it with wariness. The seal showed it was also from Dominic. "This is addressed to you," she said.

"Read," was all Adele could say.

A gasp of horror escaped and Sabrina covered her mouth to stifle more outcries, her eyes welling with tears at Dominic's description of how Arsène and Philipe died. She managed to steel her heart against all that happened with her uncle and Borchard. Alas, this horrid news rent the veil and tore her entire being apart! This was the final act of their tragic play, whereas she was free of Borchard, Arsène lay in a cold grave.

Fearing she would faint, Roger helped her to sit on the sofa. Sabrina wept bitter and heart-wrenching tears. Adele sat beside her, tears of empathy visible in an attempt to offer comfort. But all she and Roger could do was wait as Sabrina spent her grief. When the weeping subsided, Roger fetched a glass of port from a decanter on a sideboard to offer her.

After allowing Sabrina to compose herself, Adele spoke. "There was no easy way to tell you. Dominic sent Arsène's Bible as some consolation."

Sabrina noticed Adele was again with child and attempted to put on a brave face. "Oh! I'm sorry, I shouldn't upset you in your condition."

"No, I'm well. Alas, there is more troubling news. If you can bear it."

Sabrina swallowed the rest of the port to steel her nerves to listen. "What?"

"When Father learned of the warrants he beat poor Roger in a state of rage."

"The beating was nothing compared to the heartache upon learning of my dear master's death," said Roger grimly. "The count gave me the letter and charged me with staying near the countess."

Now Sabrina comforted Adele. "Have you spoken to my uncle? Despite everything, he favors you."

"No, and because of what happened in Paris I dare not. When word came concerning Philipe, the Queen requested I retire to Reims, but I cannot! There is no telling how my father will response when he learns I was sent from Court in disgrace. So I came to you, hoping we can remain together until the war is over and Dominic returns."

"Of course. Unfortunately, I can only offer you hospitality for a short time. The sale of the Paris house was not enough to pay all the debts. I must sell this home also."

"With our combined resources we shall have to find a place secluded and away from Court."

"What about Trèvoux?"

"It is the first place my father will look. I want to be away from Court, after danger and intrigue, for the child's sake!" she spoke on the verge of tears.

Sabrina put down the glass to clench Adele's hands. "Hush. We will find such a place."

"I will make certain there are no disturbances," said Roger.

"Yes," said Sabrina with a heartfelt sigh. "Until then, we must rest and gain our strength. You for the child's sake; me, for my own."

The days passed into weeks and then months, but still grief for Arsène overcame Sabrina with thoughts of how she would never again gaze into those endearing blue eyes, hear his melodic laughter or taste his warm kisses. The black widow's dress she wore for public display brought a new private meaning to the word mourning. At those times she was grateful for Adele and Roger and their attempts to divert her.

Roger went from being a valet to estate steward and conducted the more difficult business. He consulted Sabrina only when necessary in dealing with local problems not wanting to burden her. To save on expenses, most of the household staff was dismissed, leaving only Roger and Angela to tend the women. With his help, Sabrina managed to make payment to the creditors from the income of the vineyard and farm. In lieu of payment, farmhands and vineyard workers were given some of the wine and livestock to sell to meet their needs.

Adele used her charm and title on those occasions a creditor tried to bully Roger. From Trèvoux's income, she had more resources than Sabrina, but wanted to be wise in distributing the funds until the outcome of La Rochelle was known and Dominic returned.

Finally the day of birth arrived, but to bittersweet circumstances. Two weeks prior, the manor, farm and vineyard were sold. By the end of the month they were to vacate the property, taking a newborn into the unknown.

Sabrina held the cleaned pink and crying baby boy. She laughed, gazing at the babe. "He's so small."

Angela cared for an exhausted Adele. "And hungry, but I could not find a wet nurse. I'm sorry, madame."

"I shall nurse my child." Adele smiled, reaching for the babe.

Sabrina gently laid the boy in Adele's arms. "What will you name him?"

"I hadn't thought of a name. I hoped Dominic would be present to help me decide." Adele sniffled back a sob. "He may never know his son."

"Don't even think that! Dominic is a strong and determined man. I loved Arsène with all my heart, and Philipe like a dear brother. But Dominic's vigorous constitution has the better chance of surviving this war."

Adele gazed at the child. The beryl green eyes looked up at her. She touched his soft head and the fine blond hair. "He looks like Philipe."

"Then name him so. Dominic would not object."

"Yes. Philipe Charbonier," said Adele with a tearful smile.

The day before they were to leave Brittany a carriage drove up the drive to the château. Angela squealed in dreaded surprise at sight of Marquis de Charbonier's carriage and rushed to find her mistress. Roger stayed out of sight when the marquis and Baron Bourdias arrived.

Sabrina rushed from the back of the house, trying to compose herself to receive the unexpected visitors. Her uncle and the baron stood side-by-side, only Jourdain appeared frail, his face unusually pale and haggard. His clothes hung on him like a scarecrow.

"Uncle. Baron. This is quite a surprise. Is something wrong, Uncle? Are you ill? You look unwell."

"I'm recovering from wounds suffered at the hands of the Huguenots."

"At La Rochelle?"

"You sound surprised. Why? It is the duty of all loyal Frenchmen to defend the King and put down rebellion."

Adele hurried down the stairs to the foyer, interrupting the conversation. "Father? What are you doing here?"

"Since you failed to come home as ordered by the Queen, I came to fetch you. The marquis insisted on coming with me despite his weakened condition."

"You have been ill, monsieur?"

Jourdain waved aside Adele's inquiry to continue speaking to Sabrina. "We have come for two reasons. First to lend you moral support, secondly to offer you a place to live."

Sabrina flashed a cynical smile. "Of course, you still possess Trèvoux, my rightful home. Although Dominic bears the title."

"I meant the offer for Le Château Magnifique. You have a title, but little money and no property. Where else can you live?"

Sabrina stiffened, her eyes narrow and jowls taut. "You would blackmail me again?"

"No, I would strike a bargain. Come back to Reims and live with me until this war is over, and I shall give you Trèvoux, the vineyards, orchards, two properties and twenty thousand *louis d'or* a year pension. Double your original dowry."

"What of Dominic and Adele? You would leave them destitute?"

Her caustic tone brought a sudden flush to his ill features, so Adele intervened. "Monsieur, you said you came to lend me moral support, yet my father would take me back to Reims in disgrace."

"You have wrongly joined the two," began Jean-Claude. "On our journey here we discussed the matter at length. In light of this latest development, he agrees it is best you come with me."

Adele turned to Jourdain. "Because of my dead brother, you too turn against me, monsieur?"

"Given this letter I bring you from the King, it is best." Jourdain reached into his breast pocket for the letter.

Adele took the letter and read. A horrified squeal escaped her lips and she became ashen.

Sabrina moved beside Adele and read over her shoulder. "Dear God, not Dominic!" Upon her utterance, Adele fainted.

Jean-Claude caught her and carried her into the main salon, laying her upon the sofa.

Sabrina knelt beside the sofa awaiting Adele's recovery. She read the letter again. Dominic died honorably in the service of France, on a secret mission to infiltrate La Rochelle. By the compassionate tone of the King's letter, he appeared ignorant of Adele's dismissal. In confusion, she turned upon her uncle.

"I thought this was what you wanted. For your son to die in the King's service. Now, you turn your back on Adele but more sadly, your grandson!"

"What?" said Jourdain in surprise, turning to Jean-Claude, who was also stunned at the news.

"A grandson not two months old. But do you inquire after our health or welfare? No! Rather barge in here spouting accusations and threats, callous when informing her of her beloved husband's death." By now Sabrina was livid, and her voice quivered and tears swelled. "My God, he was your son!"

"This is unforeseen. She can't go to the convent now," said Jean-Claude.

"Convent?" she horrifically echoed.

"Where else would a disgraced widow go?"

Sabrina covered her face with her hands in tremendous dismay. "Lord! Give me strength, for all our sakes," she lowly prayed.

Adele murmured before waking. Sabrina responded to aid her recovery. Adele's gaze shifted between Sabrina, the marquis and her father before sighing. "I hoped it was bad dream."

"I know. Only now we must return to Reims and be separated. I told them of your son."

Grief and anger filled her eyes in turning to her father. "You will accept my son? The son I named Philipe?"

Jean-Claude stiffened at her statement. "A name can be changed."

"But not the father!" chided Sabrina to Jourdain.

"We shall return in the morning for departure." They left.

Sabrina leaned against the sofa weeping. Her whole world came full circle to where it began. Her heart and soul experienced a quandary of extreme happiness and bitter sadness.

There was not much to say so they went about packing for the unpleasant journey. Together, Sabrina and Adele convinced Roger to leave and begin a new life since he could no longer help them. The loyal valet bade the women a tearful farewell.

The following morning, the marquis and baron arrived at eight and in separate carriages. The women would not even be allowed the comfort of riding together. With tears Sabrina and Adele embraced. Sabrina kissed little Philipe. Although a babe, the kiss reminded her of another with the boy's namesake. The remorse of her negative reaction stabbed at her heart. She always loved Philipe for his benevolent nature and noble character. Perhaps, if she had not met Arsène, there might have been hope for them. Now both were dead. She shook herself from the distressing introspection when the Bourdias' carriage left.

Jourdain laid hold of her arm but she refused to move rather confronted him. "Have you no feelings for your innocent grandson? Or does your unreasonable bitterness toward Dominic dampen it?"

"As long as you live under my roof, you shall not question me, nor mention your cousin again."

"Can you not even forgive the dead?"

He snorted a caustic laugh. "Died in His Majesty's service, indeed!"

She gaped in astonishment. "You do not believe the King's letter?"

"Remember I was at La Rochelle and almost killed by your kind!" He swayed and choked on his words, the rush of emotions overcoming him.

"Uncle?"

He waved off her, his voice thick. "Despite what Feuquières' note said no body was recovered or delivered for proper burial. Until I see one I will not be convinced that my son, who betrayed his family, would choose an honorable death." He snatched her arm and began to head for the carriage.

"If you don't believe Dominic is dead you again scheme to use me against him! Only this time it is worse as you include his wife and son."

"If he did what I asked, this circumstance would not happen. But he clings to those schemers he called friends. For Jean-Claude's sake I regret Philipe's death, but never the wretched Gascon!" He fought against his own frail state to thrust open the carriage door. Perspiration formed on his upper lip and his brow.

She watched in apprehension, not so much his condition but his words caused for concern. "What did you ask Dominic to do?"

"To save the family honor and renounce the Huguenots. He did not do so. That leads me to one conclusion; he joined the rebellion." His voice lowered and he swallowed back his visible illness before continuing. "However, since there is a possibility he may be dead I propose this: if he has not returned one year after the war ends, I shall honor our agreement and acknowledge my grandson as the next Marquis de Charbonier."

She stood on the verge of loosing her composure and grappled with the words. "How can you do this to your own flesh and blood?"

"I asked that question of your father and my son when they betrayed the family. You know their answer, and mine!"

Sabrina drew a breath to steady herself. "They chose to live by what they believe. Never did they seek to destroy or hurt you as you do them!"

"Worse, they seek to destroy France!"

Despite his weakened state, by his immovable expression belaboring the point was useless. Her uncle caused her to lose her love and her honor, but if she can regain her rightful property she would be free from him and help Adele and little Philipe. With a new determination, she entered the carriage.

❧ Chapter 24 ❧

O N THE ENGLISH FLAGSHIP, *TRIUMPH*, Buckingham paced the length of his cabin with hands clasped behind his back. He chewed on his lower lip with eyes shaded by drawn brows. The past few months were taxing on the English fleet. Storms ravaged the siege works Buckingham tried to erect while high waves smashed his blockade booms. The French managed to aid their impoverished comrades and fortify both islands. He lost troops and needed military equipment to unsuccessful invasion attempts. Not to mention men dying of disease from contaminated, or as he saw it, poisoned island water. His supply ships were running low, and he received no word from England concerning reinforcement or replenishing of supplies. In short, everything he tried failed miserably and the tide of battle was turning against him.

Those assembled in the wardroom included Benjamin Soubise, Rohan's younger brother by five years. He stood at the end of a sturdy oak table, opposite Buckingham. The resemblance in the Rohan brothers was strong. Benjamin was not as stocky nor his hair as red, more auburn. Yet with the same intense passion for their faith, he worked as tirelessly in England as Henri did in France. Although he found a willing ear and eager heart to help in Buckingham, it was Benjamin's industry that kept the Huguenot hopes alive in respect to English aid. When the fleet sailed, he placed himself at Buckingham's side. He determined to be there when La Rochelle was liberated and greet his brother, mother and sister; all of whom he knew where inside the city.

By the disarray of papers and multiple tankards, they were involved in a long discussion that agitated the duke. Other officers sat about the table when Benjamin rose in abrupt disagreement to a recent argument. Buckingham called for silence at Benjamin's show of displeasure, thus a thick air of uneasiness hung over the wardroom.

Sir Howard Martin sat drumming his fingers on the table. The knowledgeable steel-gray eyes watched the younger Buckingham pace. His experience with the seven seas was uncanny and gained him the post of Vice Admiral, Second-in-Command of the Royal Navy. Martin's patience and thoughtfulness kept the more passionate Buckingham in check.

Next to Sir Howard sat Captain John Farrington, a young graduate of the Royal Naval Academy and admirer of the duke. Major Roger Curtland sat next to Farrington. Last at the table was the weather-beaten face of an old seafarer; a short tempered and bold Irishman, Captain Bruce McNally. These four were the remnants of Buckingham's original campaign cabinet.

"Milord," said McNally. "The men are restless and angry at being forced to persist in this futile battle!"

"Is it futile to help those oppressed by tyrants?" chided Benjamin to McNally.

"Begging your pardon, milord; but we're well aware of Richelieu's dominance of your people. However, we've already gone to great lengths to settle this internal French matter."

Buckingham stopped pacing and spoke before a red-faced Benjamin could utter a word. "We are brethren bound by God! No earthly border will prevent aiding our brothers when called upon!" He leaned on the table, glaring down to the other end where McNally sat.

"Lord Buckingham speaks wisdom. No man who truly calls himself a Christian can walk away from a brother in need," said Farrington.

"Gentlemen," began Sir Howard firm and shifting in his chair to be seen. "Motive for our action is not in question. The problem is how to deal with our situation."

"Since you raised so many objections, Captain, perhaps you can suggest a remedy?" said Buckingham, not hiding his displeasure.

The Irishman colored in anger and turned away. In doing so, he caught Benjamin's rebuking glance.

"The French are more cunning and stronger than we anticipated," said Curtland in his quiet yet authoritative manner.

"We do have some intelligence, Major," said Benjamin.

"The major did not mean to offend you, monsieur," said Buckingham. "Yet no matter how intelligent you French may be, it is one man! Richelieu!" He swore between clenched teeth. "Louis wisely wanted no part of war with England. Soothe, I call his sister my Queen and proudly so. If we could only destroy Richelieu, the French Army would falter and your people liberated."

"Enough of this foolishness!" McNally could no longer contain his fiery temper and slammed his fist on the table. "Let us not continue this insane battle led by false bravado."

Benjamin's chest heaved in contempt. He was thoroughly disgusted with the expedition and personally disliked the Irishman, yet the mission of saving La Rochelle was in jeopardy. He was seasoned enough in battle to realize the situation, and personal satisfaction was placed aside in hopes of salvaging some dignity. Buckingham was not so willing.

"False bravado?" said Buckingham with rage. "Watch your tongue, Captain McNally, or you shall soon find yourself charged with treason if not at the end of my sword!"

McNally bolted to his feet. "Treason? Our losses have been heavy and food grows short! Many men are wounded and dying but still you press battle. You're obsessed with this bloody Cardinal! If you wish to ruin yourself by seeking vengeance on this accursed *Frog* then do so, but not at the expense of the King's Navy!"

"Are you questioning my conduct?"

"Aye!" McNally slapped the hilt of his sword in emphasis.

Farrington groaned in astonishment at the Irishman's brashness.

Buckingham went for his sword, prompting Sir Howard to jump to his feet.

"Gentlemen! Let us not quarrel amongst ourselves! The survival of the fleet depends upon our leadership and cooperation!"

McNally's teeth were set and Buckingham's lips quivered in a snarl.

The first mate rushed in. "Milord! The French have brought their navy against us!"

Buckingham pushed past the man to the quarterdeck. Grabbing the spyglass from the ship's captain, he looked to the horizon.

"What about this fleet, monsieur?" Sir Howard asked of Benjamin.

"I don't know much, save Montmorency is the commander."

"Montmorency!" Buckingham spat out the name while continuing to look through the spyglass. "He is known for being a fierce warrior on land, which is why Louis tapped him for the navy." He lowered the glass to bellow an order. "Battle station! Man all guns and prepare to engage! We shall see how good these French seadogs are against real sailors!"

The other officers scrambled to dinghies in hopes of reaching their ships in time. Benjamin stayed with Buckingham.

"How many ships do you count?" Buckingham called up to the men in the crow's nest.

After a brief pause the answer came, "Forty. With more than half being Man O' War."

Buckingham swore.

"Milord, we can outgun them," said the ship's captain.

"Perhaps if you had heeded my advice—" began Benjamin, only to stop at Buckingham's hot displeasure.

"Would you have us retreat and surrender now? Abandon your people?"

Benjamin stiffened but by his expression the answer was obvious, still he replied. "You know I would not, milord."

The sounds of cannonade made Buckingham return to the rail with spyglass in hand. "He is bold to fire first. Prepare to counter!"

Three French cannonballs fell just short of the *Triumph*. Buckingham grinned at the misses.

"Helmsman, hard to starboard. Return fire once about!"

Buckingham and Benjamin waited for the white smoke to clear and the splashing water to subside. Buckingham cursed at seeing the volley fall terribly short.

Montmorency stood on the quarterdeck of his flagship watching his ships continue a battery of fire on the English vessels. They were returning fire, but not at the rate and accuracy he expected.

"They maybe tired of fighting, Admiral," said his first mate.

Montmorency shook his head. "Buckingham and English pride will keep them in the battle. But to show the great duke we are not as inexperienced as he believes—Execute!" he ordered.

The first mate instructed the signalmen and sent the admiral's orders. Soon the French fleet broke off into flanks, almost continuous in firing. Volleys burst through the air hissing and whistling along the way. The French volley began tearing masts and sails off two English ships.

Montmorency allowed a small smile to appear. "Counter that, milord."

Cannonade came from every direction. The main mast of the *Norfolk* cracked and fell to the deck. The first mate pulled Captain Farrington out of the way and headed for the stairs to the quarterdeck. The sounds of wounded screams followed them as a dozen men suffered various injuries from the downed mast.

"Keep firing! Don't stop!" shouted Farrington. Suddenly, an explosion rocked the ship, sending Farrington and the first mate to the deck. The ship began listing to starboard and they struggled to get to their feet.

"Captain! You're hurt," said first mate upon sight of Farrington's wounded left arm.

Farrington cradled his arm, but ignored the mate's attempt to examine the wound. Instead he called to the sailor peering over the side. "How bad?"

"Holed near the magazine. We're taking on water, Captain!"

"Captain!" a frantic voice called from the port side.

Farrington and the first mate turned to port, the direction of the shout. A sailor them pointed.

"Tis the frigate, *Henry VIII!* She's ablaze and heading for us!"

"Merciful heaven," muttered Farrington before bellowing at the top of his lungs. "Over the starboard side and swim for your lives!"

Farrington and his first mate, never reached the rail. *Henry VIII* crashed into the *Norfolk*. Both magazines exploded and the ships plummeted to a watery grave with all hands.

Buckingham and Benjamin watched the two ships sink.

"Milord!" Benjamin drew Buckingham's attention starboard to the *Dublin*, McNally's ship.

"What is that fool doing?"

He and Benjamin watched the Irishman made a daring attack on the rear of the French Fleet. Several volleys inflicted damage, but a single ship was no match for the counteroffensive the *Dublin* encountered. McNally's ship was soon holed at the stern and taking on water.

"Get out of there! Retreat, McNally!" called Buckingham, despite the distance and knowing full well he couldn't be heard.

Another volley blew a hole through the *Dublin*.

"The damage is too great. He is lost, milord," said Benjamin.

The duke's face grew tight as he screwed his eyes shut in an effort to regain his composure. *Dublin*, *Norfolk* and *Henry VIII* all gone in a matter of moments. Three Man O' War lost and four other vessels crippled or sinking while only destroying one French Man O War, heavily damaging two others and disabling four frigates.

Sir Howard also witnessed McNally's maneuver from his ship *Seahawk*. The *Dublin* was outgunned yet McNally managed to get around them. Sir Howard snapped his fingers.

"That's it! Like the fox with hounds, we'll out maneuver them. Helmsman! Evasive action!"

Progress was slow, but with a thick cloud of smoke from a burning French frigate as cover, the progress improved. Perhaps he hit upon the answer. The only problem was conveying it the rest of the Fleet. Sir Howard summoned the flagman and gave him instructions. He prayed the others would see and understand.

A French ship, *Le Vaillant*, was lining up for a broadside of Curtland's ship, the *Dover Eagle*. The damaged English vessel tried an evasive maneuver, but too late. The cannonade ripped through the rigging, mast and main deck like a knife through butter, killing Curtland. *Le Vaillant's* commander pulled alongside the battered English vessel and boarded. Hand-to-hand combat proved fierce but soon cries went up in proclaiming a French victory. With Curtland dead, the English flag was torn down.

From the *Triumph's quarter*deck, Buckingham observed the horrid scene aboard the *Dover Eagle*. He gritted his teeth when the French colors were raised. He turned his back to the captured ship. For a moment he and Benjamin said nothing, as both knew the end was near.

"Milord! A signal from the *Seahawk!*" called the signalman.

"What does it say?"

"It's hard to read with all the smoke. Something to do with evading the French'."

"Evading?" murmured Buckingham then shouted, "Aye. Evasive action!" He was knocked off-balance when the ship roughly turned to port, but caught himself on the railing.

Suddenly a cannonball sliced the aft mast in half. Benjamin lunged at Buckingham and both went crashing to the deck. The helmsman was crushed to death and the wheel damaged. Buckingham swallowed back a lump when he saw the dead man. His stood, his gaze changing from the dead helmsmen to the main deck then out to sea and the other vessels. The cost was mounting. He swayed and caught himself on the rigging.

"Are you hurt, monsieur?" asked Benjamin, moving to aid the duke.

"No. At least not physically," he spoke the last sentence to himself. "Lieutenant!" he called to a man on the main deck. "Raise the white flag."

"What?" asked the officer, stunned.

Buckingham straightened. "You heard me! Raise the white flag before we all meet a watery grave!" He moved to the rail, his lips curling and eyes narrowing in resentment. "You have won this time, Richelieu! But I swear, there will be another time and place."

Benjamin walked to where he could see La Rochelle off in the smoky distance. Tears welled in his eyes. "I'm sorry, brother. Only God can help you now," he lamented in French.

The French Fleet cheered when the white flag was raised by the *Triumph*. They, a ragtag assembly of misfits and merchant marines had defeated the famed and feared English Navy. To make matters worse, they beaten the English with their own ships! Admiral Montmorency could not have been more pleased and proud of his men. Yes, this was his moment in history. The dove downed the hawk. The King and Cardinal will be at this victory.

✤ Chapter 25 ✤

ORD OF THE FRENCH FLEET DEFEATING THE ENGLISH and sending them into retreat reached La Rochelle. To Catholics loyal to the King, the news was of great relief, while to the Huguenots, a harsh blow. Who would believe the newly reformed French navy capable of defeating the world's most feared naval power? Or the English Man O'War, renowned for its resilience in battle and fierce efficiency of its crew, would be outgunned and out maneuvered by raw recruits? Yet despite the defeat, or Richelieu's completed dike across the harbor, the stubborn Huguenot spirit drove the city to remain in defiance.

Experiencing this first hand brought a different perspective than Dominic ever anticipated. Even with all his clandestine activities and knowing the history of the Protestant cause something troubled him; something he couldn't quite grasp. Regardless of station or rank, those involved were willing to yield their lives to secure their future. In some men, he saw a zealousness bordering on fanaticism. There was a deep-rooted hatred of Richelieu, who represented the Pope and Catholic Church.

He knew the history of the violent persecution against the Huguenots, but the vehement attitude was clearly seen the other way. He began to recognize the slim difference between steadfastness and zealousness. Those who stood fast in their faith often went about their business of rebellion with quiet dignity and would fight if pushed too far. Dominic noticed a peaceful confidence in those who believed in God's revelation of His Divine Will for La Rochelle. Although the desire to avoid bloodshed dimmed when the King's army arrived.

The zealous ones angrily voiced their opinions like the Zealots of Biblical time, the militant Jewish sect who resisted Roman rule. The Zealots used the name of their faith to justify their violent disobedience. Both groups believed in their cause, but the approaches and outcome were very different. Throughout history the pattern repeated itself.

What keenly struck Dominic was that no matter the category one placed oneself in, zealot or peaceful patriot, the result usually came down to bloodshed. Those most fervent could not endure the more patient ones for very long. Cain was ignorant of what chaos he started when he slew his brother Abel over a sacrifice made to God. From that moment, only blood could atone for wickedness. It was this catchphrase that sparked the Crusaders to wipe out the heathens and bring Christianity to the world. Sadly the minor differences within the Christian world soon became a part of that atonement mentality.

Despite the wrestling of mind and soul, Dominic fell into a fitful sleep. He woke around midnight, sweating and trembling. He tried to speak but couldn't utter a word. He gazed about the room looking for someone, but seeing no one.

"Guard duty," he muttered, recalling why Arsène and Philipe were absent.

He rose from bed and he crossed to a window overlooking the city and beyond to the Royal camp. He wore only his breeches and shirt, but ignored the cold floor and the chill of the November night. Lights in the distance dotted the horizon as the royal camp spread out almost as far as the eye could see. Disturbed thoughts and dreams became vocalized in an effort to sort through his feelings.

"Richelieu fights to annihilate the Huguenots while we strive for political recognition and religious freedom. The saddest part is neither side is willing to compromise even though we worship the same God!" He drew a deep breath and sighed. "What foolishness! To tear apart an entire country for the total destruction of one people and one belief."

He shuddered at the realization he was a part a grand senseless folly. As a soldier he had killed, and as a boy he lied and stole. Although in his youth he considered them harmless pranks. Perhaps serving an earthly King was wrong. Does not God appoint the Royal family? Intrigue abounds at Court with all being done for *the good of the state* as Richelieu claims.

He folded his arms across his chest when struck with another shuddering thought. "Oh, Lord! Are we selfish and shortsighted, acting only upon our impulse and not relying on Your Divine wisdom? I know the Scriptures say you cannot serve two masters: God and money. But now I understand the reference isn't simple coins or paper but anything preventing with total surrender to Your Sovereign Will. Even good causes," his voice trailed off into a deep lamenting sigh.

Tears swelled and he sat on a trunk beside the window. "It's not so much my involvement I regret, for you can chasten me as you will. I weep over the involvement of my wife and cousin! Poor Sabrina. I know he compromised her! I could tell by how different she looked. Please, Lord, if I survive, may it not be too late to change and make amends for what I've done or didn't do within my power to act."

Now shivering from the cold night air, he returned to bed and stared out the window at the stars, his mind drifting between thoughts of Adele, Sabrina and his father's warning. The slamming of the door caused him to awake from a brief unexpected slumber. Arsène and Philipe returned from duty, stomping and clapping for warmth. Snow was brushed off their shoulders and the cloaks shook out.

"Snow already?" he asked.

Arsène brought the small embers in the hearth back to life. "Started an hour ago." He heated the poker to mull the two cups of wine Philipe poured. "You'd think he was tired," he teased when Dominic yawned.

"At least he was snug and warm last night," said Philipe with a chuckle. He sat in a chair on the other side of the hearth to drink.

Arsène rested against the wall with his eyes closed but opened one eye at hearing Dominic ask, "Any news?"

"All's quiet for now. Something must break soon and end this confounded stalemate," replied Philipe.

"Not many ways it can end."

"By some miracle we could still win."

"I thought you didn't believe in miracles."

"I never said that."

"Not in those exact words, but you adhere to practicality. In affairs such as this, faith often plays a more important role than practicality. If not for faith and miracles, there would be no practical purpose for this war. If we die, our deaths would be in vain."

Arsène opened both eyes, confused by Dominic's statement.

Philipe choked on his wine, his voice strained. "Are you saying, after all we've been though, the cause isn't worth fighting for?"

"Practically speaking, yes."

Bewildered, Arsène stared at Dominic, but before he spoke, Philipe lashed out.

"What changed your attitude? Have you spent too much time in the Cardinal's Guards that you now turn coward?"

"Philipe!" rebuffed Arsène, though his eyes darted to Dominic. Even tempered for the most part, Dominic became fiery when provoked. Instead, he pushed the covers aside to sit up.

"What is the purpose of this war?"

"We all know the answer!" Philipe spread his arms in annoyance. "To gain political voice at court, rid France of Richelieu, and practice our beliefs in public."

Dominic shook his head. "Those are the excuses of men to shed blood for personal gains. *For the good of the state*, as Richelieu says. Witness the follies of Borchard and Reynard."

"Are you accusing Rohan of selfish motives also?" asked Arsène.

"I'm accusing no one in particular. We're all guilty at one time or another. Look at history and the mockery we've made of religion. The Romans, Greeks and Crusaders, all fought in the name of religion to fulfill their purposes. Arsène, you know Rohan best. Doesn't any of what he says make sense of this chaos?"

Arsène flashed a guarded glance to Philipe before answering. "Some."

"Being here, I believe we allowed ourselves to be swept away by the desires and greed of those dictating the circumstances. Snared in a web too difficult to cope with alone and contrary to God's practical design. Soothe,

He sent His Son to die so we might be reconciled to Him, not wage war against each other in the name of the Church."

Philipe's patience was exhausted and he made no attempt to hide his disdain. "Your words are spoken like a true apostle! Yet words don't change or help our situation. Practically or miraculously. Perhaps if you talked to the Cardinal with such zealousness you can persuade him to release us and forget the whole thing."

Dominic became frustrated at being misunderstood. "Philipe, please! My words are not meant to offend. I confess many aspects of this are beyond my comprehension. However, I don't believe a benevolent God, who sacrificed His Son, is the author of this confusion. A man must take responsibility at some point in his life for his actions. In my doing so, I say these things to help my understanding as well as yours."

"My understanding seems to be everyone's concern of late. First Trudeau, Rohan and now you!" Philipe bolted to his feet. "I suppose I should be flattered by all this attention."

"Philipe, your anger and sarcasm aren't helping," said Arsène.

"Ha! Sounds funny coming from you, Gascon."

Dominic rose at seeing Arsène stiffen at the ridicule. "Philipe, please."

Dominic's compassionate voice and expression made Philipe scowl. He grabbed his hat and cloak and stormed out.

"Philipe?" called Arsène, but had the door slammed in his face. "*Zut!* What just happened? Why this sudden change in your attitude to cause derision?"

Dominic's shoulders sagged and his sighed with regret. "What more can I say? I only expressed what God has shown me through our situation. I was unprepared for such a strong reaction. Philipe is usually so reasonable."

"Your argument dealt with faith. Something he never likes to discuss." At Dominic's pricked frown, he added, "I'll see what can be done." Arsène left.

Philipe walked nowhere fast, clasping his hands together in an action of frustration. What was this strange phenomenon? Why this sudden interest in him? This change in Dominic's attitude or maybe his attitude? How could he turn against all they fought for and believed in for years? His anger turned to bitterness at feeling betrayed by his oldest friend.

Providence dealt harshly with him. First his love is denied then his sister's unborn child killed. The incident with Borchard sent a shiver through him, while Reynard made his stomach churn. Now he was a rebel confined to a siege of which the outcome looked bleak. To lose in battle is one thing, but he stood a good chance of losing his friend to an unseen foe. He swore beneath his breath at the thought their relationship would never be the same again. Whose fault is it? Is anyone to blame? He would rather suffer the consequences for high treason than experience what happened with Dominic.

Fatigued by physical and emotional exhaustion, he found a secluded spot near the north wall, wrapped his cloak about him and sat in the snow, clenching his knees to his chest. He took no notice of the cold and lowered his head till his forehead rested on his knees.

To Arsène the cold was more annoying and he rubbed his gloved hands together. Philipe's unusual behavior made him reflect on his own recent attitude. He became angry with himself at realizing the anxiety Philipe experienced concerning him these many months. In Philipe's effort to aid him, the once sure-minded and pragmatic Bourdias became abrasive and unsound. His heart ached in regret, and he hurried his steps to find Philipe and apologize.

After an hour of futile searching, Arsène withdrew to a quiet place to think. His heart almost leapt from his chest at spotting a man sitting by the corner of the wall huddled with his head down. He hurried over. "Philipe?"

Looking up and seeing Arsène, Philipe's anger returned. "If Dominic sent you, go back and tell him it won't work!"

"I came of my own accord. Don't reproach me on that."

"I'm sorry."

"No, I ask your forgiveness. You've changed and it's my fault."

Philipe became perplexed. "What gave you that idea?"

Arsène sat next to him. "For the past few months I have not been a good friend, in fact, the opposite. You said yourself the day we captured Reynard."

"I said that to break you from your depression, not to blame you for anything. If I have changed, it is not your fault."

Arsène shook his head. "No. I forced you into positions of choice one should not ask of a dear friend. Many times you yielded to quell my selfish and unfounded demands. With the utmost sincerity I apologize, and wish I could change the past."

"You make yourself sound as bad as the devil himself, but not so! Deep sorrow and grief compelled you. I admit, you sorely tested our friendship at times, but you had nothing to do with what just happened."

"Maybe not, but I know over the years a bond, no, brotherhood, has been forged between you and Dominic. Don't allow the relationship to crumble in a mere few words of passion!"

Philipe rested his chin on his knees as Arsène continued.

"Dominic sounded like Rohan, who has tried for years to counsel me in matters of faith and God. I employ some of his counsel, but to me such faith is for women and old age. Yet," he paused in sober reflection, "many questions fill my mind of late."

"Questions don't concern me, rather—" Philipe stopped, brows level and eyes staring at some unseen spot in the snow.

"What are you afraid of? Religion? God?"

"I fear nothing!" he insisted, looking askew to Arsène.

"You do. I see it in your eyes."

"Enough counsel! And do not press me."

"You are mistaken. I'm asking so I can understand. Besides, I know you too well. There is something you fear," said Arsène with certainty.

Philipe swiped at the snow. "Something has come between Dominic and me I don't understand."

"Sounds more like self-pity. You don't give yourself a chance to understand. You just walk away."

"What is to comprehend? An infinite God?" He grunted a sarcastic chuckle of remembrance. "I suppose my conversion was in the passion of the moment. Caught up in the zealousness of those about me. If what Dominic says is true, then why all these different religions, rites and rituals? Why so complex if so simple? Am I to unlearn in a moment what has taken mankind a thousand years to breed into society as a way of life? Impossible for one person to accomplish such a task!"

"Then in what do you believe?" came Arsène's calm inquiry.

The question was a simple one, yet Philipe was stymied and mused, "I never thought about it." He became frustrated. "Neither do I want to! *Aggh!* Plague take this confusion!"

Arsène laughed and Philipe grew hot, moving to rise. Arsène restrained him. "Stay. I was remembering all those times I sat where you are with the same staunch and obstinate expression while you counseled me with words of wisdom, which I now find lacking. You, who through hell and high water are a pillar of confidence and strength. You, my friend, who by a mere word, would sacrifice all he had for either I or Dominic; your life included."

"Are you trying to make me feel guilty?"

"No! I'm doing a poor attempt to give back to you some of the confidence and strength you've given me."

Already frustrated, Philipe stood. "Plague again on these feeble words of counsel and tranquility when all about us is danger and unrest!"

"Confound it, Philipe!" Arsène rose to confront his friend. "You can be as stubborn and pigheaded as a mule! Dominic loves you and only meant good by what he said. Can't you see, or is your wounded pride blinding you?"

"Pride is a funny word coming from a thickheaded Gascon! Oh, you were right in saying you lack words of wisdom!" He stormed down the alley.

Arsène swallowed back the painful sting of insult and sight of Philipe walking away. He ran and grabbed Philipe by the shoulders and forced him to stop. "Please! For the love of our friendship don't walk away from me! Forgive my temper and harsh words and let us quarrel no more, rather speak soft and honest words."

For a moment Philipe remained silent, regarding Arsène. "Very well. But I must come to terms with my feelings in this matter as you did about Sabrina. Agreed?"

Arsène bit his lip at the mention of Sabrina but nodded. "Agreed."

Philipe's expression softened and he patted Arsène's arm. "Come. Let us eat and speak no more of this matter until I have thought long and hard."

The weeks passed and snow continued falling until three feet in depth was the shallowest part of a snowdrift. Being a coastal city the Rochellias were unprepared for such a devastating winter. Warm clothing and fuel for fires were scarce. The dike foiled attempts to replenish the city's supplies and over a hundred and fifty died in the first four weeks of winter.

The new year of 1628 slipped by and the next thing anyone realized, mid-March arrived. The people became desperate and hungry, yet never did the mention of surrender cross their lips. Those few dissidents who suggested such a thing were beaten or killed.

Spring gave way to summer's blistering heat and for two months the sky remained cloudless and bright. Water became rationed and rain fervently prayed for. Of those who survived the harsh winter many became ill from eating the rotten food, spoiled by the heat.

One day, after dismissing men to their daily assignments, including Philipe, Arsène and Dominic, Rohan sat in his chamber. Dark pronounced circles were etched under his eyes from weeks of difficulty sleeping, his mind burdened with worry and guilt. Each passing week the mounting total of dead and thought of failure weighed heavy upon him.

Geriton entered and approached Rohan. The once healthy-looking mayor lost a considerable amount of weight for his large frame. His face grew long and thin, with pale cheeks and tired eyes.

"Monsieur, I hate to disturb you, but we must do something. The city is dying!"

"What? Ration food further?" a weary Rohan chided.

"The people already eat grass off the streets and leaves from the trees! They boil their boots and other leather for sustenance. Several have died of the bites received from the rats they captured to eat! We have only enough food for a thousand militia, two hundred garrisoned troops and five hundred people! There are eight thousand left from the twenty-eight thousand who began the siege. My God, twenty thousand have died! At this rate there will be scarcely anyone left."

"Enough!" Rohan slammed his fists on the table and rising. "Don't you think I know what is happening? My mother and sister wither away with starvation!"

"Petition Richelieu to allow us to spare the women and children and let them leave the city."

Rohan snatch a piece of paper off his desk and gave it to Geriton. "I did! Here is his answer."

Geriton read the disturbing statement aloud. "*Everyone leaves together in surrender or none leave until that time.*" The paper slipped from the mayor hands and settled on the corner of the desk. "There must be something you can do." He then spoke with urgency. "Leave and go to England and your brother, beg them for more aid."

"Three times the English have tried to free us and each time suffered a worse defeat. No," said Rohan with a certainty. "There is no help coming. And I will not leave until I see the King and Cardinal ride through the gate!" He gestured to the window.

Geriton shook his head, sobriety on his face and in his voice. "Don't allow yourself to be swept into self-destruction by this. You did all you could and no one here followed you blindly. Our eyes were open. We knew the possible consequences of defeat, and this only hinders our ultimate freedom. A lost battle does not mean the war is over! Have you ever noticed that when Richelieu is certain of victory he excels, but when he doubts he withdraws to reevaluate? He is a man much like us. Perhaps you should retreat and reevaluate. The people know the end is near. For a while you will feel guilty and that is natural. Yet will pass when you find another way to help these people you love so dearly. If you knew of an alternative, would you hesitate to leave?"

"Well, no—" Rohan stopped when the mayor clasped his shoulder.

"This may be your only opportunity. I can do what work remains. I am the mayor."

Rohan sighed in resignation. "You present a good case, Jean. I shall consider it."

Unfortunately, Rohan took his time in consideration and the summer wore on. The situation became more demoralizing than Geriton's vivid description. Driving almost everyone beyond all physical strength and endurance, each day the struggle for survival became more difficult. Soon talk of surrender grew rampant. Perhaps living under the rule of the King and Cardinal would be better.

The morale of the garrison and militia almost disappeared and only a handful of loyal men could Rohan employ to keep the peace. Arsène, Philipe and Dominic were among those. Dominic grew so thin he was almost unrecognizable, his clothes old, dirty and baggy. Arsène's healthy amber complexion now pale and haggard while Philipe's lackluster mood reflected in his darkened eyes and constant forlorn expression.

Crime became a nuisance and Philipe's militia duties doubled when promoted to the rank of major to assumed Le Strade's command upon the latter's death. Arsène volunteered for extra hospital duty and Dominic helped guard the critical storehouses. The friendship between Philipe and Dominic remained strained. Any conversation was casual, and remaining together was out of lifelong habit.

At first Arsène spent more time with Philipe than Dominic, and he feared more for the former. What he feared he didn't know, but his instincts guided him and not often did his intuitions fool him. The time he spent with Dominic became precious having so many things to talk about. Sometimes he became angry with Philipe for placing a damper on all their relationships and thought of abandoning him in favor of Dominic. Alas, no, he could no more deny Philipe than deny himself.

Early one warm humid September morning, the Dowager Duchess Rohan sent urgent word to Arsène that Rohan fell gravely ill during the night. In the back of his mind, he feared something like this would happen to a person close to him. Many already succumbed to illness and disease so it was only a matter of time before it touched someone he knew.

A stately woman in her sixties, the dowager embodied regal grace itself, her shimmering gray hair the envy of many along with strong features. Alas, she too suffered the ill effects of the wretched siege. The hair was dull and brittle while lines of anguish and age formed about her once stalwart features.

Marie, Henri's sister, joined the dowager in Henri's bedchamber. She could be her mother's twin at a younger age. Their strong spirits were tested and tried in full support of Henri.

Arsène approached the bed and balked at sight of Rohan bathed in sweat, his lower lip trembling, ashen countenance and hollow features.

"Henri often praised your stomach remedy, which is why we sent for you. Do you any remedies for such an illness?" asked Marie.

"I shall do what I can." Arsène proceeded to examine Rohan.

Typhoid and malaria reigned among the more serious illnesses at La Rochelle. The two usually went hand-in-hand as typhoid came from a bad water supply and malaria from the mosquitoes infesting stagnate water and mud pits. Rohan did not exhibit the red blotchy patches of typhoid. However, he felt cool and clammy despite shivering and perspiring profusely.

"Has he done or eaten anything unusual of late?"

"I don't recall," said the dowager.

"A few days ago he ventured into the salt marsh to inspect the fortifications," said Marie.

"I remember." Arsène paused in his examination, triumphant in his glance to the women. "I found it."

"What?

"A large infected bite behind his left knee. Malaria."

The Dowager leaned over Arsène's shoulder to view the inflamed culprit.

"Then you can do something?" Marie said hopeful.

"Yes, though I'll need some fever tree. If any remains after the last bout."

"What is fever tree?" asked the dowager.

"A South American remedy the Dutch East India Company brought back ten years ago. The bark is boiled to produce a potent serum excellent at fighting certain fevers."

"I see why Henri praised your skill, but how did you acquire such knowledge?"

"My grandfather served as assistant to a local physician in his younger days. I use his remedies, and by way of observing and speaking with military surgeons over the years I added to that knowledge."

The dowager rang for a servant and instructed him to fetch as much fever tree as possible. "Confiscate it, if need be!"

For the next four days, Arsène kept close vigil of Rohan, administering the serum in small doses at timed intervals. The fever and shivering continued with several fearful bouts of delirium. Finally, the fever broke and the chills stopped, but he had yet to wake.

At twilight of the fifth day, Arsène dozed in the chair next to the bed. A low hoarse voice woke him. He smiled in relief at seeing Rohan awake.

"Monsieur. You gave us a fright."

Rohan cracked a weary grin, indicating his mouth. Arsène helped him drink some wine. "Better. How long have I been home?"

"We're still at La Rochelle."

Rohan groaned. "I hoped it was all a bad dream."

"Don't concern yourself with anything, just rest to regain your strength." Arsène began to tuck the covers around Rohan when the duke gripped his arm, stronger than expected for a man so sick.

"I may be ill, but I'm not a child! I have only to look around and see my failure. I let my foolish human pride and arrogance guide me and not the hand of the Almighty bring us to destruction!" He stirred to rise.

"No." Arsène stopped him, which was easy since Rohan didn't have the strength to fight.

He fell back on the cushions with a loud sigh of lament. "Alas, a great breach in friendship drove the point to my heart."

The statement perplexed Arsène. "You had nothing to do with Dominic and Philipe—"

Rohan stopped Arsène's speech by again gripping his arm. "Allow me to speak! God entrusted not only the survival of the Huguenots, but also three precious souls. I have been remiss in my duty. Yes, I gave words of encouragement and counsel, but never took a stand or set the proper example. Dominic needed help with his father but I allowed circumstances to dictate my action rather than aid him. Dear Philipe. So brave and loyal, yet mysteriously avoiding faith and God. How did I respond to him? By setting it aside, hoping somehow he would see by my example what faith is." His lower lip quivered in regarding Arsène. "But you, my dear son, I wronged the most."

"It's the fever talking."

Rohan shook his head in vehement disagreement. "When we first met, you were so innocent. You matured in stature, intelligence and cunning, but not much in faith. With self-made excuses I allowed you to enjoy your youth while keeping a father's eye out for trouble and an ear open to listen. But when trouble came, you faced it alone without the strong faith needed to withstand the torrent. The evening before I departed for Amiens I began to recognize my folly. The Scriptures say the elders are to teach the younger. I've been a poor teacher!" He sobbed.

"No—"

"Let me finish!" he snapped, despite his fatigue. "I hope one day you will succeed me in leading the Huguenots. For that reason, the Lord brought me this illness. While I lay in fever, my mind was clear and He revealed all. The Lord's mark is upon you, my son. Can you sense it?"

Arsène chewed his lower lip before making a slow, deliberate nod. "I sensed something since … since I met Sabrina," he forced himself to say her name.

"The dear child! I pray I survive to redress myself to her also."

"You will survive. We all will."

"Only God knows the future." He drew Arsène closer and spoke in a husky voice. "What I say now will be most difficult for you to hear and for me to say, but believe me, I do so with love for you and Philipe."

"Philipe?" said Arsène in confusion.

"God blessed you with a unique friendship. But as is the way of things, there is a season and a purpose. Jonathan and David discovered that truth when David fled Saul. He sensed the Lord's calling, but hesitated for reasons of love and loyalty to Jonathan. You have not answered God because you fear losing Philipe as Dominic believes he has done."

Arsène repined at the statement. "I don't have the heart to forsake Philipe."

"Jonathan and David never forsook their friendship. In fact, they flourished. From their friendship they drew strength to go separately to their destinies. Jonathan became a great warrior and hero of Israel, David a mighty king blessed by God to be in the lineage from which the Messiah would come. Don't you understand? God will have you one way or another. You must trust Philipe to His care."

Arsène sat mute, the weight of trying to comprehend on his face. Rohan groaned in weary vexation and fatigue. "You must rest." He placed the cover snugly about the duke but before he finished, Rohan smiled.

"Go back to the apartment. I will be well."

Arsène flashed a plaintive smile of agreement. Rohan closed his eyes. Arsène left the bedchamber to inform the dowager and Marie of the good news before departing the château. Outside, Philipe's voice startled him.

"How's the duke?"

"Better."

"You on the other hand look awful."

Arsène managed a small smile. "This siege is bringing consequences far beyond what my feeble imagination can concoct. I'm going to the apartment to sleep. What about you? Will you return this evening?"

Philipe shifted from one foot to the other. "No."

Arsène frowned. "Not the armory again?"

Philipe nodded. "I'll see you in morning."

For a brief moment Arsène watched Philipe depart before making his way to the apartment. He found Dominic stretched out on the bed not yet asleep.

"How is Rohan?" asked Dominic.

"The fever broke and he awoke this afternoon. He will recover." Arsène sat on the edge of the bed and in a weary voice said, "Philipe sleeps at the armory again."

A pained expression clouded Dominic's brow. "I wish I knew what to do. I have tried approaching him numerous times to resolve the matter, but despite my assurances, he believes I abandoned him in favor of God. In his mind God has never been a practical concept in the events of man. To explain my reasoning is impossible."

"Faith isn't a practical matter."

For a long moment, Dominic regarded Arsène. "After all this, you finally understand what Rohan has been saying?"

"I always understood. I simply didn't apply my understanding. However, because of Sabrina I see things differently." He rose to pace, his usual habit when speaking seriously. "I experienced heartache beyond comprehension when learning of the marriage contract. After the wedding, I became lost, disheartened and confused. In time, I learned to accept reality. Not by faith, rather an act of self-preservation. A well known trait of us Gascons."

"Do you feel different now?"

Arsène again sat on the bed. "The evening before the campaign I prayed God would somehow, some way help me to see my way clear. This afternoon He did. Yet in a manner I never expected." He drew a breath before he spoke again. "Rohan awoke with a great burden for the three of us. In the course of our conversation I saw how foolish I've been. Years ago, when a child of ten, I heard of what a wondrous miracle Christ did on the Cross. How He gave men a reason to live; a reason to hope by reconciling mankind to God and I accepted it, and Him. After coming to Paris, I allowed worldly adventure to take precedence over my faith. This man-made chaos has shown me the true meaning of faith in Christ and how foolishly prideful I've been in trying to survive by my own wit and strength. How feeble is man in his arrogance and pride." He motioned to the window.

"There was a war before this one. I fought in it," said Dominic in painful recollection.

"I didn't. The duke kept me behind the lines as a liaison. Thus I never witnessed mass destruction or chaos. Even though Paris was wroth with danger, my field of vision was limited." In a bashful gesture, he scratched the back of his neck. "I became arrogant and puffed-up in my minuscule role."

"I'd hardly call risking your life on an almost daily basis minuscule."

"Compared to this siege, our exploits were meager. I thought you realized that?"

"I have, but even meager roles have their purpose in the larger scheme. You recognized the faulty way in which you viewed things and placed them in Godly perspective. That is good. Yet, don't debase your contribution. I know the duke would not. Neither would Philipe or myself. You saved our lives on several occasions. And that is no minuscule matter." Dominic flashed a congenial smile.

Arsène grinned. "I yield the point. However, I was narrow-minded. God forced me to see the harsh reality. Not an easy thing to admit to pride, it pains a man's spirit. Pride kept me from practicing my faith. Confound it if I know why, but God in His mercy has been gracious to this thickheaded Gascon. In my brokenness He showed me that no matter how much my heart aches, where there is life, there is hope. Hope is the foundation for faith only we need faith to realize it." He flashed a wry smile. "Philipe once said God could do no wrong as far as Sabrina was concerned, only test and strengthen one's faith. If only he knew how right he was."

Dominic took hold of Arsène's arm, his smile warm. "My heart rejoices at your words. But why your brooding melancholy these last few months?"

"Two reasons. One you know well."

"Philipe. And the other Sabrina?"

"Oh, Lord, how blessed I would be if He allows me to survive and see her again," he said with a catch in his voice then glanced along his shoulder at Dominic, considering his words. "Not only Sabrina. Do you truly believe our deaths here would be in vain?"

Dominic paused a moment before answering. "To rush helter-skelter to one's death for selfish honor and ambition, yes. But for God, the ultimate sacrifice is not in vain. I would yield my life for Him as I would for you or anyone else I love. Besides Rohan, Trudeau and a few others, the motive of Godly justice takes second place to pride and greed."

"Then you believe we should yield to the King's unfairness?"

"No, that would compromise our beliefs. Notwithstanding that righteous indignation gave birth to this rebellion, the pettiness of pride and arrogance soon overshadowed everything. Condé turned against us when he stood in danger of losing his wealth and power. You just said hope is the foundation for faith. Regardless of whether we win or lose, we must stand firm and true to God and our beliefs."

"Then we may have been victorious if we remained faithful."

"Only God can say. Collectively I believe we strayed and assumed our own path to religious freedom. Now, as individuals we must answer and atone for the collective fault."

"So united we stand, but divided we fall."

"Not necessarily, but La Rochelle will fall," said Dominic with certainty.

The statement sent a shiver through Arsène. "If only we could get Philipe to understand before the inevitable happens."

"Perhaps in this, you have more sway than I," said Dominic with a catch in his voice.

Arsène shook his head. "This is one aspect of Philipe I never understood."

"Then all we can do is pray he comes to terms with this on his own. God has done greater feats."

Arsène went to lie on the pallet. Prayer was something he had not done in years, at least not seriously. So much happened he became unsure and even frightened. He prayed for solace, comfort, strength and understanding.

He poured out his heart concerning the duke, Philipe, Dominic and Adele and even the present situation. But his most fervent petition was for Sabrina. Even experiencing immense heartache and facing dangers, his feelings for her had not diminished, quite the opposite. In the bleakest moments he thought of her, their daily walks, sitting together in prayer meetings and her kiss.

How long he prayed, he didn't know but everything in his life was recounted until the prayer of a troubled soul gave way to peaceful slumber.

❧ Chapter 26 ❧

VERYONE AT LA ROCHELLE KNEW THE END WAS NEAR and assembled for the last battle. From his vantage point on the battlements, Rohan watched the royal army draw up in formation. Arsène stood beside him. They watched a group of six horsemen break from the line to approach the city.

"Today it ends. God keep you safe, my dear son."

"And may He protect you, my father."

Their attention was drawn back to the approaching envoy at a hailing call. Arsène jowls tightened and he gripped the hilt of his sword at seeing Tréville leading the envoy. Rohan held Arsène by the shoulder when the envoy stopped twenty yards from the city.

"Monsieur le Duc," began Tréville.

"Captain Tréville."

Tréville's gaze shifted to Arsène. "So, Lamonreaux, you're alive. It took much to convince me of your treachery."

"No harm was ever meant you, Captain. Upon my honor I swear!"

Tréville mockingly snorted. "The honor of a traitor! What of Bourdias? Is he alive and would swear this as well?"

"Captain, I do not believe you came to conduct personal business," said Rohan.

"No, monsieur. His Most Royal Majesty sent me to demand the unconditional surrender of La Rochelle! Lay down your arms and open the gates!"

Philipe placed his men along the battlements, but heard Tréville speak. He began to move for a better view when a hand seized him.

"Stay down. It is bad enough he has seen Arsène," said Dominic.

Shy in meeting Dominic's gaze, Philipe nodded and turned away.

From out of nowhere rocks were hurled at the envoy. One struck Tréville's horse and the animal skidded. Tréville ordered his men to take cover and return fire if necessary.

"Fools!" swore Philipe. "Hand me a—" he began but stopped a seeing Dominic held a musket out to him. "Thanks."

"Don't thank me yet. We only have enough for four shots each."

Philipe settled into position with the musket. A shot struck the battlement near his left ear. With a short cry of surprise, he covered his head.

"Philipe?" Dominic grabbed him, fearful and expectant.

"I'm all right." He brushed the dust from his face and forehead. "No blood. See?"

Not good enough for the anxious Dominic. "Philipe—"

"No time for conversation." He took aim and fired. He ducked back to reload and met Dominic's fretful expression. Philipe rammed the ball into the barrel and took aim a second time. He was about to fire, when something jostled his arm.

Musket fire forced Arsène down. "Did you see Tréville?"

"And DuPree." Philipe took aim but stopped, a tone futility escape as he said, "Cavalry."

The charge caught the attention of others on the battlements. The doom of La Rochelle grew nigh, but they met the charge with a hail of fire.

Arsène, Philipe and Dominic took careful aim for more effective use of the remaining ammunition. Arsène and Philipe were more expert due to their Musketeer training, but Dominic managed well enough.

Philipe fired his last round and cursed. "I have to redeploy the men."

"We'll join you when we can," said Arsène.

Philipe gave Arsène a hearty clasp on the arm. At Dominic's poignant look he knew something had to be said, but he couldn't find the words.

"For friendship," said Dominic.

"For faith," said Arsene.

Philipe flashed a tentative smile. "For freedom." He left.

Dominic and Arsène returned to fire their last round. Arsène cursed at soldiers scaling the wall and motioned for Dominic to retreat from the battlement.

"Help Philipe. I'm going to find Rohan," said Arsène.

"Don't be too long," warned Dominic.

Arsène gave Dominic one of those smiles of confidence before parting.

A sudden noise drew Dominic's attention to the battlements. The walls were breached. A Cardinal's Guard was taking aiming. "Arsène!"

He pulled to a stop at hearing his name but before he could turn someone tackled him and a pistol discharged. For a brief moment he lay stunned, the wind knocked out of him. Beside him on the ground was Dominic with his face covered in blood! Arsène pushed up to knees to determine the problem. A large gash fringed by gunpowder and a friction burn singed both of Dominic's brows and eyelids. Blood flowed down the pale face.

He seized his friend by the shoulders. "Dominic?" At his touch, there was painful moan and some movement. "Thank God you're alive!"

Dominic slowly opened his eyes and called out in fear. "Arsène?" He reached out his hand, which was caught by Arsène.

"I'm right beside you."

"I can't see!"

Arsène was only speechless for a few seconds, but Dominic called again, his grip tightening. "I'm still here. The blindness may be temporary. You were grazed by musket shot, singing your brow and eye lids. Blood covers your face."

Dominic tried to calm himself and moved to sit up. Arsène helped him. "It is blurry."

Commotion of battle drew Arsène's attention. "The walls are breached. We must fly."

Dominic held on tight as Arsène drew him to his feet. Another supporting arm came about his other side, startling him. "Who's there?"

"Easy, it's me."

"Philipe?"

"Yes?" Philipe's quizzical gaze passed from Dominic to Arsène

"The blindness maybe temporary. Powder burns."

"Ah, yes." Philipe tried to sound convincing, but his look to Arsène showed doubt. "Dominic, can you walk? The dowager sends for Arsène."

"I can." Dominic's grip was firm on both Arsène and Philipe.

As quick as they could, they made their way to Rohan's house.

In the study, Geriton tossed papers into a blazing hearth. The dowager and Marie argued with Rohan, who stood near a window overlooking the battle.

"You must leave!" said the dowager.

"What of you and Marie?"

"Richelieu would not dare raise a hand against us. But you, Henri! I fear what he may do if you are found here!"

Arsène left Philipe and Dominic at the door to approach Rohan. "The dowager is correct. Some elders are scrambling out of the city, begging for mercy. Do not give Richelieu the satisfaction of taking you prisoner."

Rohan hesitated only a moment as he looked out to see the truth of Arsène's words. People were fleeing the city as royal forces entered. "Very well, but the three of you will come with me," he said, before seeing Dominic and Philipe. "*Mon dieu*, Dominic. How badly are you hurt?

"I can see dark blurry shapes." Dominic squinted at the duke.

Rohan embrace his mother and sister. "I shall send word when I can." Eyes moist with regret at parting, he left with Arsène, Philipe, and Dominic.

The noise of battle had died and dusk settled in. Once the initial resistance was put down, taking the city was easy. People begged for food and water, thus the posting of guards was minimal since most were more interested in sustenance and tending to the wounded. Still, caution was needed in escaping with the easily recognizable duke.

Arsène stayed closed to Rohan's heels, one hand hovering over the hilt of his sword as they made their way to the postern gate. Dominic held onto

Arsène's baldric to follow. His face was clean and a small bandage was wrapped around his eyebrows. Chandler came behind Dominic with Philipe keeping the rear guard.

Once through the postern gate, they carefully made their way through the dwindling light toward a pre-arranged rendezvous.

"What use am I on this venture without my eyes," chided Dominic.

"At least you're alive," insisted Arsène but suddenly halted.

"What?"

Arsène didn't respond, instead he touched Rohan's arm and pointed ahead. "Someone is there. I can't tell how many."

"I don't see anything."

Dominic grinned. "Even at my best, I could never see what he does."

"Gascons have eyes like cats," said Philipe.

They proceeded with caution to a small grove where they hoped to find horses waiting. A shot rang out and Chandler fell backward into Philipe, knocking him to the ground. Arsène shoved Dominic aside and drew his pistol. In his blindness, Dominic stumbled and fell. Another shot hit the ground not far from him.

"Arsène?" he called in a panic.

"Stay down!" said Arsène and took aim.

Simultaneous to Arsène firing, someone from behind collided with Dominic and both went sprawling. Unaware of what happened behind him, Arsène threw aside his emptied pistol, drew his sword and went to help Rohan.

For Philipe, everything occurred in rapid succession: Chandler mortally wounded, someone collided with Dominic, both tumbling to the ground and Arsène nowhere nearby. The arm of an assailant raised a dagger to strike the helpless Dominic. Philipe pushed aside the dying Chandler and rushed to Dominic's rescue. No time to draw his sword, so he kicked the dagger aside. This left him vulnerable, unable to prevent the repose of a sword thrust up and high into his left breast. He staggered back a step and fell hard to his knees. The man who dealt him the blow—de Lacy!

317

Philipe kept from collapsing to the ground by thrusting out his right hand. He brushed against something metal on the ground, a dagger. The same time he felt the dagger, Dominic snatched de Lacy's leg. De Lacy viciously kicked Dominic. Setting his teeth against the pain, Philipe grabbed the dagger and with every ounce of strength left, leapt upon de Lacy's back, blade first. The weight of his body drove the dagger deep between de Lacy's shoulders. They fell hard to the ground, the impact separating them, but the dagger remained buried hilt deep in de Lacy.

The sound terrified Dominic, and with frantic hands he searched for anything to touch. The first contact was with a leg. His hand moved along the body, pausing in horror at feeling blood at chest level. He then touched the face and facial hair.

"Philipe?" Dominic cradled the head in arms, movement causing a faint groan. Dominic's head snapped up, though he didn't know what direction he face and called, "Arsène!" No response, so he called again then jumped at feeling hand on his shoulder.

"It's me," said Arsène, his voice a bit shaky. He knelt across from Dominic. "What happened to Philipe?"

Frantic, Dominic shook his head. "I don't know! I someone grabbed me and we scuffled. Then I heard blows of some kind—Damn my blindness!"

"Arsène!" called Rohan, vaulting into the saddle. "We must fly!"

Arsène took Dominic's arm to loose his hold of Philipe. "We must go."

"We can't leave Philipe!"

"I have no intention of leaving him, but I'll take you to your horse first." Arsène laid Philipe on the ground before ushering Dominic to the horses and helped him mount.

"Where's Philipe?" asked Rohan.

"Seriously wounded. Take Dominic while I get him." Without waiting for a reply, Arsène handed Rohan the reins of Dominic's horse. He paused at the sight of a person with the dagger in the back. Using his foot, he kicked over the body. De Lacy! Dead by the look of open and vacant eyes. Arsène's jowls tightened and tears of anger welled.

"Arsène!"

He didn't respond to Rohan rather moved to Philipe and gathered him in his arms. Back at the horses, Rohan helped to place the unconscious Philipe in the saddle and held him steady while Arsène mounted. Grabbing the reins in his left hand and bracing Philipe with his right arm, Arsène spurred the horse. Rohan followed with Dominic in tow.

In La Pallice, Rohan roused the farmer responsible for providing the horses. Philipe was still alive when Arsène placed him on a bed in an upstairs room. He examined the wound while the wife readied the necessary items to tend Philipe. The bloody doublet only told part of the danger. Once stripped, Arsène discovers a hole several inches above Philipe's heart and slightly left.

"Must have missed the artery, but a miracle he's still alive," said the wife.

Arsène couldn't respond, taking the bowl and rag she gave him to begin cleaning the wound. He tried to focus on his work and not on Philipe's pale and haggard face. She was right, but for how long would Philipe survive? He couldn't lose his composure, not now. After several unsuccessful attempts to slow the bleeding he swore.

The woman came to his aid. "We need to use cauterize the wound."

"Not with hot elder oil! I've seen men writhe in agony from its usage."

She replied in a calm, sure voice to his outburst. "A remedy I learned years ago from a Flemish physician. A mixture of egg yolk, attar of roses and turpentine. Hold the wound closed while I prepare it."

Arsène relaxed. The wife was a wise woman with knowledge beyond his. He spoke to Philipe. "Your Gascon almost lost his head. Thank God for a levelheaded old woman."

The wife was quick in her business and when she finished applying the paste, he wrapped the wound with fresh bandages.

"If he lives through the night, he may have a chance," she said. "Your friends inquired about you both."

"I'll speak to them. Thank you."

Rohan brought Dominic into the next room and tried to coax him into bed but stopped when Arsène arrived.

"How is Philipe?"

"Still alive. The good wife knows the ways of wounds."

"Thank God," said Dominic with relief.

Rohan grew sympathetic in regard of Dominic. "We must leave before dawn."

Dominic balked at the statement. "Abandon Philipe?"

Rohan gripped Dominic's shoulder. "We have no choice. If Philipe survives, he will face a long recovery from such a near fatal wound."

Arsène sat on the foot of the bed. His own disturbance manifested on his face and in his voice. "How can I leave him?"

"It would be folly for you to stay. He would not want you to jeopardize yourself."

Arsène chewed on his lower lip as Rohan continued.

"I provided them with the funds necessary to give him the best of care, and instructions of where to notify us no matter what. Philipe's fate is in God's hands."

"A God he doesn't believe in," droned Arsène.

"*You* do! Both of you," urged Rohan. "Physically you can do no more than the good wife, whose skills you praise. In spirit and prayer, if God so allows, faith may save him." Arsène didn't respond, so Rohan jerked him by the shoulder to get his attention. "Remember what I said at La Rochelle. God will have you one way or another. Will you take a risk by selfish action?"

For a moment Arsène stared at Rohan in recollection, but the duke's prompting nod to Dominic told him a response was needed. He yielded. "Perhaps it is best—"

"How can you leave Philipe or even consider it?" chided Dominic.

Arsène suffered a sigh at the question. Dominic's face was still marred by the wound, thus he tempered his response. "The duke is right. We must have faith, for nothing else but hope and trust in God will restore Philipe."

"What hope is there in leading a blind man by the hand?"

"Stop it, Dominic!" Arsène snatched Dominic's arm, his breathing labored in his effort to maintain his composure. "Your blindness may only be temporary!"

"If not?"

"You're alive! And with life is hope."

A sudden sob caught in Dominic's throat. "Philipe can't die! What will I tell Adele? My blindness killed him?"

"Or I for causing your blindness."

"No, I acted when—"

"You saw me in danger," said Arsène when Dominic could not finish his statement. "Just like Philipe did for you."

Dominic sobbed, his voice weak. "I don't even know what happened."

"Dominic," began Rohan, "despite the argument and strain, Philipe never stopped loving you and ultimately proved it. That is what you can tell Adele if the unthinkable happens."

"To die not reconciled to God—"

"Philipe's not dead!" Arsène forced himself to keep from shouting.

Dominic sniffled. "I'm just so tired and heartsick."

"I understand."

"No, you can still see. Whether my sight returns or not, blindness is a frightening reality I must deal with at present."

"For now, rest."

Dominic's grip on Arsène's arm was strong and urgent. "Be my eyes tonight and watch over him."

"I will."

A single candle burned next to the bed when Arsène returned.

"I left you a blanket on the chair next to the bed," she said.

"Thank you."

She departed and Arsène approached the bed. Philipe lied so still Arsène wondered if he was dead. Each step closer was more wretched until he finally reached the chair and saw Philipe breathing. Tears blurred his vision and he sat.

"*Mon frère esprit!* To be cut down without even your sword," his choked voice cracked. He wiped the tears from his cheeks, trying to compose himself. He leaned closer and touched Philipe's shoulder. Perhaps it was the dim light or his desperate desire, but he thought Philipe stirred to his touch. He tightened his grip. "I won't leave you tonight; though I must in the morning—" He blinked back the tears. "Lord, you ask the impossible!"

In agitation, he crossed to the window and stared out into the night. Clouds covered the sky, blocking moon and starlight. He could only see as far as the interior light permitted.

"I never noticed before how black the night is without stars or moon. Is that what it is like to be blind? With no hint of light to guide one's steps?" He glanced back at the bed when struck with a sudden thought of new understanding. "Not solely blindness of eyes, but a darkness of a soul without heavenly light for a guide."

"Yet a little while is the light with you," a voice spoke, startling Arsène until he recognized Rohan. "Walk while ye have the light, lest darkness come upon you, for he that walks in darkness knows not where he goes. While ye have light, believe in the light, that ye may be the sons of light."

Arsène was in no mood for a sermon. "If we are supposed to shine our light for others to know the Truth and drive away their darkness, how can I do so for Philipe if I am not here to help him?"

"Why are you still resisting God?"

"He asks me to turn my back upon Philipe!"

"'If any man come to me and hate not his father, and mother, and wife, and children, and brethren and sister, yea and his own life also, he cannot be my disciple.'"

"I can never hate him," he protested, motioning to the bed.

"The Scripture's not speaking of hate as in abhorring, rather in degrees of love. Which do you love more? Ecclesiastes speaks of a season and a time to every purpose under heaven. A time to get and a time to lose, a time to keep and a time to cast away."

Arsène again looked out the window, but the duke was not about to be put off and forced Arsène to face him as he continued. "The time has come to loose yourself from this relationship. For what purpose, only God can reveal, but I'm confident it the best for both. Resist and remain, the outcome may not be as God purposed. Would you risk thwarting His perfect will for you and Philipe by substituting your own will?"

For a long moment of deep silence, Arsène stared at the bed where Philipe lie unconsciousness, his breathing swallow but regular. After years of hardship and suffering, Philipe was horribly thin, his healthy boyish face lean and bleached of complexion. Still the present deepening candescence about his eyes and anguish-lined face were cause for great concern.

"Arsène, there is not much time left. Please, son, trust Philipe to God."

Arsène didn't answer rather sat in the chair beside the bed.

Rohan made himself comfortable in another chair across the room.

He heard Rohan's movement but remained silent. His heart, mind and soul heavy, and though the hour was late and his body fatigued, he didn't expect to fall asleep, but fall asleep he did.

In the quiet of the night, dreams, thoughts and reality come alive. Stark images of those he loved came before his mind's eye just before fading into the oblivion of death. Scene after scene replayed itself with Rohan, Philipe, Dominic, Sabrina, and Adele. The loss of all happened because he remained at La Pallice. He bolted up, laboring for breath, his face covered in sweat, his heart racing. Upon sight of Philipe the discomposure from his nightmare became visible on his face.

Rohan swiftly crossed to Arsène. "Son, what's wrong?"

He couldn't speak, eyes filling with tears of terror.

"A nightmare?"

"More than a nightmare. I remained and lost everyone!" He wiped away the tears, swallowing back a lump in this throat. "I will leave with you. Only allow me a moment to compose myself."

"I'll fetch Dominic and saddle the horses." Rohan left.

Overcome by weakness, Arsène fell to his knees beside the bed. "Lord, I confess I have not been the most faithful and sinless of men, yet I acknowledge Your Divine Sovereignty and ask forgiveness for my years of divergence. Philipe possesses a good, unselfish heart, yet a cynicism I never understood. I pray you overlook that and show him mercy. Help him through the night and in the days to come when I will not be near. Do not let him die without being reconciled. It would tear Dominic apart. My soul loves no man better. Even like this, I can't bring myself to say *adieu*, only *au revoir*, for I pray we shall meet again someday. Amen." Without looking back, Arsène left the room.

In the barn, he found Dominic waiting while Rohan and the farmer finished saddling the horses. Dominic jerked in startled defense when Arsène took hold of his arm.

"Easy, it's me," said Arsène.

"How is Philipe?"

"Alive. Come, the horses are ready." He escorted Dominic to a horse.

"I don't like leaving him."

"Neither do I, but we must. Now, mount." He waited until Dominic was situated before mounting a horse. He took a rein from Dominic. "How far?" he asked the farmer.

"A league north then turn onto a beach road where a boat is waiting. Leave the horses. I'll fetch them later."

Rohan took the lead followed by Arsène with Dominic. The grey light of pre-dawn invaded the eastern sky when they turned west onto the beach road. Soon they heard water breaking on shore.

"We must be near, I can smell the ocean," said Dominic.

"Just the smell make me nauseous," complained Arsène.

"Do you get seasick?"

"I can't swim," he grumbled the admission.

"And I'm blind. What a fine pair we are!"

"Don't worry, I can both see and swim," said Rohan in attempted humor.

On the beach, two men left the rowboat and came to meet them.

"We're not crossing the channel in that are we?" asked Arsène.

"No. We are here to take you to the ship anchored off shore."

Rohan took some coins out of his purse, but the sailors refused.

324

"We've already been paid, monsieur. Now, we must hurry to weigh anchor before sunrise."

In the boat, Arsène sat as close to the middle as possible. He screwed his eyes shut, a lamenting sigh escaping.

"Arsène?" asked Dominic.

"Consider it a blessing you cannot see our departure. Even if Philipe survives, we may never lay eyes on France again."

✦ Chapter 27 ✦

ROHAN'S BROTHER BENJAMIN LIVED IN ST. PANCRAS, a suburb of London's northeast side near St. Paul's mighty cathedral. The Rohan brothers greeted each other though Benjamin was distraught by Henri's thin and grave countenance. After a brief explanation and introduction of Arsène and Dominic, they all retired to the main drawing room. For several hours they conversed about La Rochelle. Benjamin was grieved, but alas, his news was not much better. With the assassination of Buckingham, Parliament voted against further aid for the Huguenots and forced the King to sign a petition never to go to war without Parliament's consent.

"Henri, this new young man Huntingdon sent is hard and shrewd. He inspired Parliament to draw up the Petition of Right. Not since the Magna Carta has an English king waved his rights," said Benjamin.

"What is this Parliament that it can force a king to give up his rightful power?" asked Arsène in amazement.

"This Parliament is not what we know a parliament to be. Ours is strictly administrative. These are the people of England, nobles and commoners alike. They sit together to make laws and enforce those laws. They control vast amounts of wealth."

"What of King Charles?" asked Dominic with confusion.

"Charles is still king, but the will of the people dominates English government."

Arsène shook his head. "He must be some man to persuade Parliament and force a King to sign such a petition."

"I've not seen many like him. He is a Puritan with great moral values and sense of justice. He is keen and forceful in his speech, yet commands respect with his mere presence, however humble in appearance. Mark my words. Oliver Cromwell may only be a junior Member of Parliament now, but someday he will be a man to be reckoned with."

"So then there is nothing that can be done to ease the suffering of those we left behind," droned Rohan.

"At present, no. But at least you survived. What of mother and Marie?"

"I was hoping to get word of them by way of aid. Now all we can do is pray and hope for the best."

Benjamin compassionately regarded Henri and the young men. "You can take the time to recover. None of you should do anything in your present condition. In fact, I know of an excellent physician to treat Dominic's eyes. I'll send for him immediately. For now eat and rest."

The skilled physician not only treated Dominic's eyes, but also prescribed individual diets and exercise for each to aid in their recovery. All the same, Arsène faced each day with fading hope concerning Philipe. But not all was lost. Despite the crushing defeat of La Rochelle, God dealt mercifully in allowing him to survive. Even with miles between them, he and Sabrina were free of Borchard. Thought of her brought joy to his heart and a smile to his lips.

By spring, Arsène gained some weight and his black hair, long neglected, was cut and pampered until the luster returned. When the spring rains permitted, he rode through the countryside, vigorous activity helping his vitality to return. A new maturity showed in his countenance and in his speech. Now, at age twenty-five, the rough youthful edges smoothed to a man of serious consideration, but the blue eyes retained a hint of joviality and self-confidence, severely shaken by the siege. This is not to say he became as dull as a monk. The English gentlewomen found his French charms and good looks irresistible. He behaved courteously in response, but the language barrier provided a good dodge when needed, though Rohan taught him English in order to deal with their allies.

Arsène's new demeanor pleased Rohan. More than anything he did not want the Gascon's formidable spirit quenched, rather molded and sharpened. Their religious conversations were no longer of a father instructing a son, but as mentor and pupil exchanging reason and ideas. Rohan introduced Arsène to many Puritan leaders, Oliver Cromwell, John Pym, John Milton, John Hampden, Sir Thomas Fairfax, and the Earl of Essex. During this time of exposure to strong men of the Protestant faith, he hoped to refine those new attributes of his young protégé much like taking a free-spirited and truehearted stallion, breaking it to the bit and transforming it into a champion thoroughbred. When his time to pass on came, or no longer able to champion his people's cause, he was now confident Arsène would take up the gauntlet and return to France not as a young courtesan, rather a wiser and inspired man.

Dominic also thrived in England, regaining his sight with only a slight blurriness in the corner of the left eye where the shot impacted. He joined Arsène on daily rides and in friendly bouts of swordplay for exercise. Also being from the upper crust of French nobility his name was recognized by English nobles and aided in Arsène's introduction. The fact he risked and lost all for his faith gained him much respect among the Protestant ranks, both noble and common. He, Rohan and Arsène's sacrifice brought tangibility to the situation for the English concerning the Huguenots at La Rochelle. Some still spoke unfavorably of England's assistance in the war but more as internal political matter between Parliament and the King than against their French Protestant brethren.

On a lovely June day, Rohan stood in front of a window in the study. On the terrace, Arsène and Dominic practiced with Benjamin's fencemaster instructing them in new techniques. A valet arrived with a letter for the duke. It bore the seal of Louis XIII. With a mixture of rage, joy and sadness, he read the letter. He looked in empathy to the young men sparring. Opening the window, he beckoned them to join him in the study. He also sent for his brother and did not speak until all were assembled.

"I received this letter today. The hand is that of the Louis, but the contents are Richelieu."

"Good news or bad news?" asked Benjamin.

"Both. I shall tell the good news first since it directly affects our young friends," he said of Arsène and Dominic. "The Cardinal has granted pardon to all Huguenots involved in the rebellion. It is called the Edict of Grace. However, all military and judicial powers are stripped from us as a collective group. I have been sent a copy of the edict you may read later."

"Why would Richelieu do such a thing?" asked Dominic.

"Spain and the Emperor are breathing down his neck while Mantua, Savoy, and Lorraine are causing trouble and may lead to war. Richelieu would be a fool to deal too harshly with us considering the dangerous foreign threat. That is made clear in what I am instructed to do."

"What?" asked Arsène, guarded.

"I am go to Venice and await further instruction."

"Venice? Why not Paris to keep watch of you?"

"Because, my dear Arsène, I'm too dangerous to be allowed back on French soil."

"Exile?"

Rohan nodded.

"You are not bound by this command!" chided Benjamin.

"Yes, I am, brother," said Rohan in solemnity. "Our mother and sister are prisoners. Their release, with return to full rights and privileges, and implementation of the Edict of Grace, depends upon my submitting to this letter and remaining in Venice for the rest of my life."

Fury rose in Benjamin's cheeks. "This is outrageous!"

"Monsieur—" began Arsène in protest.

"No, son! You *will* return to France. The way is clear and I will not have you miss this opportunity." He smiled and placed an arm about Arsène's shoulders. "Just because I can't go to France, doesn't mean you can't come to Venice for a visit. Maybe with your new bride?"

"Yes, monsieur," said Arsène in resignation and a touched smile.

"Good. I'll make arrangements for transportation."

The following the morning, Arsène rose early and made his way to the terrace. His emotions ran the gamut from excitement at returning to France, to sorrow at being parted from his beloved mentor. When he arrived on the terrace, he found Rohan.

"You couldn't sleep either." Rohan smiled. "You are much like me. Once you become attached to something, or someone, you dare not let go and hang on like a tiger. Alas, the world changes, and we tigers are forced to release our hold, at least for a while."

"I know, yet I mourn our parting. I've already lost Philipe."

"You are not losing me. And Philipe was alive when we left France. There has been no word otherwise." He studied his prodigy with an affectionate smile. "I am glad I have a chance to give this to you in private." He pulled out a heavy purse from his doublet. "It is part of the inheritance I promised."

Arsène stood momentarily speechless. "I don't know what to say."

"Embrace me as a son would a father." They stood in a lingering embrace, neither wanting to release the other. Rohan heartily patted Arsène's back. "I hear the others about."

An hour later, a small party left Benjamin's house to journey to the docks. Arsène and Dominic's ship was scheduled to be the first to depart. Rohan clasped Dominic's hand with a strong grip when they bade each other farewell. He took Arsène by the shoulders, embraced him and kissed him on both cheeks.

Once on board and the anchor weighed, Arsène's sadness at parting became replaced by excitement at the prospect of returning to France and being reunited with Sabrina. Only one small detail disturbed him, becoming seasick.

After resting a day from the channel crossing, Arsène felt ready to ride to La Pallice where he and Dominic hoped to learn of Philipe. They heard nothing while in England and were anxious for word. To their disquietude came the news of how the farmer and his family fled from the Cardinal's men during the night some five months ago. At the time, the guards scoured the countryside in search of escaped heretics. No one they questioned had any knowledge of an injured man with the family. By the end of the day, they could only assume the worst; Philipe had died.

His final hope dashed, Arsène allowed himself to weep the bitter tears of mourning. For months he fought his emotions, clinging to a hope against all odds for Philipe's survival. Dominic acted more realistic, but it didn't lessen his grief at losing his childhood friend. They left La Pallice.

Although desperate for news concerning Adele and Sabrina, they circumvented Paris on their journey from La Pallice to Reims. They did pause on the outskirts of the capital for a meal and hopefully gain some news of Court. Most patrons and hosts were willing to speak of the great victory, but specific information was hard to come by and neither wanted to make anyone suspicious with particular questions concerning individuals. They knew Adele was ordered to Reims, but that was almost two years ago. Thus they continued their journey.

Three hundred miles from La Rochelle they reached the crossroads to Reims.

"Why are we stopping?" asked Arsène.

"We dare not go directly to the chateau, and I risk being recognized in the city, which would alert my father if he is home."

"It's been years. You do look slightly different."

Dominic chuckled. "I'm a Charbonier. My height and size alone will be a give away. The Bourdias chateau." He turned his horse to head northwest.

"Oh, and the baron won't recognize you?" said Arsène with wry sarcasm.

"He and the baroness visit relatives in the south this time of year. With any luck, Adele remains or at least we can learn the way of things from the servants without too much risk."

The Bourdias château lay halfway between Reims and Château Magnifique of the Charboniers. The home was a modest two-story château on fifty acres with front facade built of gleaming white interlocking blocks of limestone. The windows were tall and narrow and the personal "B" insignia and crossed swords above each window. Two square corner pavilions were connected by wings to a central pavilion designed similar to a keep. Behind the main château was a private terrace, enclosed by a three-foot tall wrought iron fence. Beyond the fence was the back lawn, and further behind stood the stables, a carriage house, and armory. The armory held a vast collection of weapons not readily displayed in the château.

A few hundred yards from the house, Dominic pulled off the main road and made a wide arch around to the rear. Halfway between the main house and armory they stopped inside the wooded perimeter. Adele sat on a terrace bench speaking to a maid who approached her.

"What luck! We'll wait until she's alone, but let me go first," said Dominic.

"I don't know which will be more shocking, seeing you or me. No, both."

"She's my wife."

A few moments later the maid left so Dominic and Arsène moved forward with Dominic taking the lead and waving Arsène to stay back. Adele's sat facing away from the gate, which squeaked when opened. She bolted up, covered her mouth in surprise at seeing Dominic and swooned. He caught her and lowered her onto the bench. He smiled, caressing her face as she regained her senses.

"You're alive!" She stared in wonderment thought misty eyes.

"Yes, my dear love."

"The King wrote you died at La Rochelle."

"A mistake. Let me look. Magnificent," he said, his eyes drinking in every detail of her lovely face.

She did her own inspection of him, hold his face in her hands. "You've changed.

"Nothing being with you won't cure." He kissed her, long and passionate, but stopped when she wept. For a moment he held her before asking, "Have your parents gone to St. Cloud?"

"Yes. Where have you been? La Rochelle fell last November."

"England. We fled with Rohan."

"We?" she echoed hopeful.

Arsène approached and smiled. "We."

Adele greeted Arsène with an embrace and kiss on his cheek. She turned to her husband. "You wrote that he and—" she stopped at Dominic's muted remorse.

To Adele's whimper, Arsène comforted her. "I'm so sorry," he said.

"Father still grieves. More for dishonor than loss." Her voice cracked.

"Dishonor?" asked Arsène in a strained voice.

"The warrants and my dismissal from Court made him furious. He wanted to be severe with me, but one reason stopped him." She turned from Arsène to Dominic, a tearful smile appearing. "His grandson."

"A son?"

"Who is two years old and I thought would never see his father!"

Dominic embraced her. "My love, you could have taken him and gone to my father. Despite what he thinks of me, he favors you."

"No! The situation is complex and until now, I thought hopeless. No," she stopped his speech. "For now, tell me about Philipe. I need to know."

At Dominic's conflict, Arsène answered. "We all came close to surviving. Philipe," he paused with visible disturbance at speaking his friend's name, "died from a serious wound the day we escaped La Rochelle."

A sob escaped her pressed lips. Dominic tried to comfort her, but she moved away from him in an attempt to regain her composure.

Dominic chided Arsène. "Why did you speak so assuredly of Philipe's death? He may be in hiding, awaiting word that all is safe."

"I would the happiest of men if I were mistaken, but you didn't see … him," said Arsène with halted, strained voice.

The maid returned. "Madame—" She stopped at seeing two men.

"Denise. This is my husband returned from the war and a companion. What is it?"

"Madame Caldias wants to know if you wish her to bring Master Jean-Luc to the garden?"

"Jean-Luc? Is that his name?" asked Dominic.

Adele stayed her answer with a hand at him while speaking to the maid. "Have her bring him." Not until the maid left did she speak. "Father insisted on the name but not the name I gave him. One look of him and you will understand."

Her cryptic statement was not well received. "As much as I want to see my son, there is more to this than you are telling me."

"The situation requires reflection before action, husband. Trust me."

Madame Caldias appeared holding the hand of a fair-haired toddler with beryl green eyes. Dominic and Arsène instantly noticed familiar features.

"Philipe," muttered Dominic.

"Yes, and more now than when I named him so at birth." She picked up little Philipe and presented him to Dominic.

Father and son sat on the bench becoming acquainted. In silent sobriety, Arsène watched. Poor Philipe would never know his nephew, his namesake. He forced a smile each time Dominic showed him the boy.

Adele moved to stand next to Arsène and took hold of his arm. "You miss Philipe terribly. You had difficulty saying his name."

He just nodded.

She leaned her head against his shoulder. "I understand. A part of me misses him also. Yet, Philipe would not us to spend the rest of our lives grieving. Dominic and I are reunited, and with a son. From that I draw strength and comfort. While you," she paused at seeing him grin. "I'm glad to see you still love her. She loves you."

To this news Arsène's smile grew. "I yearn to see her. Is she well?"

"She has been in mourning these many months, in public for the count, but in private for you. Do you know of Borchard's death?" she asked when his expression hardened and his body stiffened. "Arsène?" she pressed.

"Borchard does not concern me rather the marquis. Dominic claims he is ready to face his father no matter the consequences. I'm not so sure. He cannot reproach us concerning La Rochelle due to the pardon, but his hatred is deep and vengeful."

Adele breathed a gloomy sigh. "More so since you left."

He became concerned at her statement. "How so?"

"There is much to tell, but you withstood a siege, and survived an English winter. Will a few more days matter? I'm not unskilled in the area of secret rendezvous." She smiled.

He chuckled, wry and sly. "You are talented, dear Adele; but also avoiding the issue."

She glanced to her husband and son, who sat on the lawn playing with a ball. "Madame, take him inside. It is time for his nap."

"As you wish, Madame," said the nanny.

"Sleep well, my son," said Dominic when he boy went back inside.

Adele led Arsène to the bench to sit. She indicated for Dominic to sit on the other side of her before beginning her explanation. "After the campaign left the parade ground, Sabrina went to Trèvoux, hoping to find a quiet place to think and consider. Alas, the marquis was there and they had a terrible row during which she learned he willingly agreed to the marriage as vengeance against your conversion," she said to Dominic.

Pricked, Dominic scowled in fierce anger.

Arsène stood and slapped the hilt of his sword. "The swine! I shall take her from under his nose!"

Adele rebuked him. "No! You will only make matters worse! He may not be as physically formidable as he once was, but is still powerful."

"What do you mean? Has he been ill?" asked Dominic.

"He suffered near fatal wounds at La Rochelle. Father said something about an invasion and bombardment."

Arsène and Dominic immediately understood what she meant only Dominic signaled Arsène to remain quiet as Adele continued speaking.

"I will make arranges for a secret meeting, flight if you wish, but do not take action and place her in further jeopardy. However, I'm only allowed to visit her once a week, and already did so three days ago. I can get a note to her tomorrow since the marquis has her attending Sunday mass in Reims."

"Why is he so strict with her?" demanded Dominic.

"He doesn't believe you are dead, rather a trick to deceive him and someday you would return."

"I shan't disappoint him!"

"Patience, husband. There is more to tell. Because of the events at Court, I couldn't go to the marquis, so I fled to Sabrina in Brittany. She went there to settle the count's affairs. He left many unpaid debts, forcing her to sell all his assets to pay the creditors."

"Then what could she do to help you?" asked Arsène, confused.

"Sabrina is not the innocent she once was. Confronted by my father and the marquis, she was like a lioness defending her pride. Yet despite her new shrewdness, the marquis purposed a bargain not easily refused. If she returned and remained for one year after the war ended he would give her Trèvoux, prevent me from going to a convent, and acknowledge our son as his heir."

Dominic was beside himself with anger. "Father wanted to send you to a convent?"

Adele fought back tears, shaking her head. "No, my father. After you were reported dead, he sought to shut me away. Sabrina's agreement saved us, else I would separated from our son."

Arsène's jowls tensed and fist clenched the hilt of his sword. "Have these men no honor left?"

"We must act discreetly. Please, be patient for one day," she urged.

Dominic also had difficulty accepting the situation yet added his opinion. "I can deal severely with the baron for his effrontery, but Adele is right. For Sabrina's sake we will arrange a meeting to decide upon a course of action together."

"If Adele's scheme fails, marquis beware, I will fetch her away and fly to Venice."

"The rescue will be a joint effort and we will all leave France."

"Your son and I will be ready for whatever happens. Meanwhile, I shall do my best to secure a rendezvous. Now come inside."

Chapter 28 ✦

ARLY THE FOLLOWING MORNING, Adele began instructing a trusted servant in the delivery of the note, when someone took it from her hand. She whirled around and came face to face with a shabbily dressed, yellow-bearded man. He flashed a cunning smile; the blue eyes keen on her. She waved the servant away, studying the man.

"How?"

"One of your mother's wigs and cosmetics. The clothes came from a stable boy, as you can smell. How do I look?" replied Arsène.

"If I didn't know you were alive and staying here, I would not recognize you."

"What does the note say?"

"To meet me at the stream where we played as children this afternoon at two o'clock. Should the marquis discover the note, I did not mention you or Dominic."

"I'm off to morning mass." Arsène smiled and departed.

Built earlier than Notre Dame the cathedral of Reims was not large as or grand. Still, high Gothic towers rose to the heavens, with stained glass depicting Biblical scenes. The aged gray stones had weathered, smoothing the hard edges.

The marquis' carriage halted before the cathedral. After he alighted, Sabrina appeared. Jourdain aided Madeline to step down when a man, presumably drunk by his swaying movement, stumbled and reached for the person closest to him for support. Sabrina faltered under the unexpected weight, but remained on her feet. The collision jostled the purse from her hand.

"Pardon, sweet lady. I tripped."

337

"You're nothing but a drunken fool," scolded Jourdain.

"No harm done, Uncle."

"You dropped your purse, sweet lady." He got down on his hands and knees in an inebriated state to fetch the purse, shielding it from view. "Here." He stood and placed it back in her hands, holding them for a moment and gazing at her. Their eyes met and he smiled, the blue eyes soft and gentle.

"See your money is safe, Sabrina," said Jourdain.

"I may be drunk, but I'm no thief, monsieur," he insisted in an uneven tone.

"Away with you before I teach you manners!" Jourdain shoved him back.

In compassion, she watched the man stagger away.

"Is it all there?" asked Jourdain.

She opened her purse. Her money remained along with a piece of paper.

"Did he rob you?" asked Madeline.

Sabrina closed the purse before her aunt saw the contents. "No. I just feel sorry for him."

"Such people are unworthy of your pity," scoffed Jourdain.

"Are we not commanded by God to show pity toward the poor and unfortunate, Uncle?"

"No, young lady, you will not bait me into a theological argument this day. Now, let us assume our places, before mass begins."

"Please, Jourdain, do not get upset. Remember what the doctor said about stressing your heart," said Madeline.

Jourdain scowled in resigned annoyance. "Very well. I shall try to stay calm."

Once seated, Sabrina fought her curiosity about the note and the strange tingling sensation when the man touched her and she gazed into his blue eyes. Years passed since experiencing such a sensation, years since she encountered a blue-eyed pauper. *No! It is too fantastic to even consider. He died two years ago. What about the note?*

When the cue came for reciting a prayer from a hymnal, she managed to remove the paper and place it inside the book. After the musical interlude and her aunt and uncle prayed along the bishop in Latin, she read the note. Adele requested a private afternoon rendezvous. *Why would such a man deliver*

338

the note? And why such an unusual request? Struck by a disturbing thought it meant some horrible news, she attempted to quell her reaction by listening to the singing. She managed to replace the note in her purse and assumed a respectful posture in congregational response to the musical benediction.

On the ride back to the chateau, Sabrina gazed out the carriage window. Her mind wandered between the drunken messenger, how to get to the rendezvous with Adele, what could the reason be for the meeting and if there was a connection?

"Still concerned about that drunkard?" Jourdain's harsh voice interrupted her thoughts.

"No, meditating on God's creation. It is a beautiful day. May I go for a ride, Uncle? On the estate, of course."

"With Franchot as escort, yes."

Sabrina sighed and turned back to the window. Not the answer she hoped, though Franchot was a decent man, he was loyal to her uncle.

"Jourdain, when will this stop?" asked Madeline. "Would you turn your niece into a bitter recluse with your unfounded suspicions? Our son is dead and the war long over. Even the Cardinal has forgiven—"

"It is Richelieu's job to forgive!" he snapped but paled and started coughing.

"Now see what you've done." Madeline became upset, fussing over him.

His voice was shallow. "I'm still alive, woman, leave off."

"She is right to be upset, Uncle. You both are in ill health."

Madeline appeared paler than he. He kindly patted his wife's hand. "Very well, my dear. I will recant." He turned to Sabrina and said; "You may ride for one hour. If all goes well, we shall consider other freedoms. Remember, three months remain to our agreement."

Not much of a reprieve, but would serve. "After supper. When the sun is the brightest and warmest."

Jourdain heaved a shrug of indifference, concentrating on Madeline.

The meadow and forest stretched for miles and took twenty minutes for Sabrina to reach the stream. Adele was not present, so she dismounted and sat on a boulder near the water's edge to wait. Although curious about the rendezvous and the beggar, it was good to be alone. Only asleep, did she experience total solitude. She took a moment to banish the thoughts and cares from her mind and listen to the breeze ruffle through the trees and birds singing. The peace and serenity of the surrounding almost made her forget why she came. That was until the sound of hooves pounding on turf made her to turn. She rose slow and deliberate at seeing a male rider approach, two more came up behind but she more focused on the one in the lead. Her uncertainty lasted only a moment when she recognized him but could not utter his name for shock.

"Sabrina!" Arsène drew rein and leapt from the saddle.

"Arsène?" she said in surprise when he caught her in his arms and whirled her about. "I thought you dead!" Through tear-filled eyes she surveyed him, touching his cheek. He was as handsome as she remembered. "You were the man this morning."

"You knew me?"

"I sensed something familiar in the eyes and the touch. Only one man every made me feel so wonderful."

They kissed until she wept, mewing his name. He held her close.

"Didn't I tell you I had a surprise?" said Adele giggling.

Sabrina wiped her eyes before turning to Adele. "Dominic!" From one joy to another, her heart swelled as she embraced him. "You two are here so where is Philipe?" she asked with expectation.

"Alas, my earlier presumption became reality," droned Dominic.

Her sympathetic gaze found Adele.

"At least my husband is alive and has seen his son. How did you manage to come alone?"

"I thank Aunt Madeline. He only permitted an hour before he sends Franchot for me. You and Arsène must not be found here!" she said to Dominic.

"Sabrina, Adele arranged this meeting to take you away," said Arsène.

"He will pursue you with a vengeance!"

"Let him!" declared Dominic. "What action he chooses to take is unimportant. Your happiness and well-being has been sacrificed for too long. Richelieu's pardon makes us free men. Free Huguenots. That is why we returned from England where we've been since November."

"You don't understand! It's not just me—"

Dominic stopped her. "Adele explained everything about Trèvoux, the convent, and little Philipe. Father can threaten all he wants, but nothing changes the fact I am his son, his flesh and only heir. No court will dispute my claim, or yours to Trèvoux."

"Until then, I have money to maintain us in a modest house. Compliments of the duke, who will aid us further if needed," said Arsène with an encouraging smile.

For a moment Sabrina stood stupefied. "Oh, how I prayed this horrible ordeal would end."

Arsène seized her hands, eager and encouraging. "God has answered you; answered both of us. We can finally be together. If you are willing to take the risk and leave the marquis."

"Oh, Arsène, I didn't want to come back. I had no choice, rather no reason to do otherwise. Yes, I'll leave with you!" She hugged him.

The sound of galloping hooves interrupted them. Arsène shielded Sabrina when Jourdain draw his horse to a skidding halt. Franchot accompanied the marquis, pulling up behind him.

Jourdain's countenance was pale, but his cheeks whipped pink by the hard ride. His gaze passed from them to his son. "I hoped you died honorable befitting a Charbonier and Catholic."

A brief pained expression passed on Dominic's features as he replied. "I don't know why I ever thought you would be glad to see me alive."

"This is not the action of a son restored, but more scheming. You didn't have the decency to present yourself to me. Yes, I was told of your return, which why I so easily agreed to let Sabrina ride alone knowing you would seek her out. I never expected to see the cursed Gascon again! My son wasn't enough, now you steal my niece!"

341

Sabrina stepped out from behind Arsène. "No one steals me. Your twisted sense of honor forced us away from you a long time ago. A crueler fate forced me to return."

Arsène observed the proud tilt of her head and fiery eyes. Indeed, she had changed.

"Be mindful of your place, and remember our agreement. Now, come away!"

In defiance, she took Arsène's arm. "You no longer have hold over me."

Arsène grew alert when a flush of rage overcame the marquis' countenance. He assumed a defensive posture in front of Sabrina. Before confrontation could occur, Dominic spoke.

"Sabrina will come with us. Be good enough to abide by her decision. For I warn you, Father, I will not stand by and watch you further debase her or bully my wife and son!"

Jourdain temper exploded. "Son or not, I will not be threatened and insulted!" He dismounted.

"Monsieur!" protested Franchot, who dismounted to intervene.

But Jourdain would not be prevented, shook off his servant and drew his sword.

Adele gasped in horror when Dominic reached for his sword.

Arsène's sword was in hand and knocked apart the blades of father and son. "Satisfy your honor on me and not your son."

"All the better, since you corrupted him!" Jourdain slashed at Arsène.

Sabrina stifled a cry when the sword clashed.

Jourdain gritted his teeth and shoved Arsène's attack aside. Arsène counterattacked but Jourdain continued to advance. To throw Jourdain off balance and back on the defensive, he feinted an offensive move with a shout and forward thrust. Jourdain fell for the deception, which left a clear opening to finish the duel. Yet, Arsène controlled himself and only grazed Jourdain's left side.

"God was merciful in sparing my life, so I spare yours. Let first blood satisfy. Sabrina will leave with us."

Jourdain swayed; laboring for breath, face pale and glistening with heavy perspiration. His eyes narrowed with hate. "I want your death, bâtârd!"

In a wild lunge, he came at Arsène, who easily knocked the attack aside. Jourdain stumbled and Franchot caught him.

"Monsieur, enough, please!" urged Franchot.

Enraged beyond reason, Jourdain shook off Franchot to attack Arsène again. Suddenly, his eyes widened in surprise and he gasped for air. He staggered back and fell to his knees before collapsing. Franchot caught the marquis and gently lowered him to the ground to loosen the doublet and shirt collar for Jourdian to breathe.

"Father?"

"His heart!" said Franchot.

Dominic knelt opposite Franchot. "I'm going to take you home." Jourdain tried to fight him off but in a feeble attempt and soon became still in his son's arms. "Father?" Uncertain, yet fearful, he felt for a pulse. There was none. He lowered his head, fighting back grief.

The sword dropped from Arsène's hand, his eyes filling with tears. "God, forgive me! I didn't want it this way."

"You didn't kill him," insisted Sabrina. "His wound at La Rochelle damaged his heart."

Dominic's voice was strained with emotion. "She's right. Your wound is but a scratch on the ribs."

"Still, he pushed him beyond his strength," said Franchot with a sneer at Arsène.

Dominic seized the servant to get his attention. "This wound did not kill him! And Arsène stopped after drawing first blood. Before God, you know the truth. His heart, you said when he collapsed."

The fierceness on Dominic's face and compelling words made Franchot nod. "Before God, it was his heart and not the wound."

Dominic released Franchot. "Fetch his horse."

At the grand chateau, Dominic bade Arsène, Sabrina and Adele to wait, as only Franchot would accompany him to find his mother. She conducted household business in the study. Her reaction went from shocked to joy at seeing him alive and weeping in his arms. He braced himself for what he must tell her. In words as gentle and honest as possible, he explained what tragedy befell Jourdain. Her painful tears brought him new grief.

"I never wanted to hurt you or Father! Please, believe me," he pleaded, looking to her for reassurance.

"Perhaps to deny and suppress one's feelings is wrong, I don't know. By doing so, you and Michael turned against what your father believed. Do you understand?"

"Yes, but it wasn't a deliberate act. Neither was his death."

She stiffened, incredulity on her face. "You speak of your father's murder as an accident."

"Not murder! Arsène wanted to walk away after drawing first blood, but father would not be satisfied. He tried to attack Arsène but his heart gave out. Franchot knows, he witnessed the incident." He indicated the loyal, yet reluctant servant, who spoke when prompted.

"It is true, marquise. The strain was too much and his heart failed." Franchot fought back tears. "I wish to God it had been different, but I cannot lie before heaven about what I saw."

Madeline's clasped hands were white with effort to withstand the news, and confront Dominic. "Franchot may believe what he saw, but to me, your friend is a murderer. What chance did your ailing father have against a skilled younger soldier?"

Dominic tried to curb his vexation. "Father wanted me dead! He came after me with a naked sword! Arsène intervened to save us from spilling each other's blood. I too am a younger experienced soldier. The outcome would have been same for his heart gave out."

Madeline became ashen and momentarily silent, regarding her son. Sorrow mingled with resolution in her gaze. In a hoarse cracked voice she spoke: "If that is your position, so be it. You are now the Marquis de Charbonier. I shall withdraw to the estate in Lorraine, which is my widow's right." She left.

In a bold gesture of defiance, Franchot addressed Dominic. "I bore true witness as compelled by God, now give me to leave to quit your service to tend the marquise for I cannot stay here."

For a moment Dominic stared at Franchot. "Leave is granted along with my thanks for your service."

"Save your thanks, *Monsieur le Marquis.*" Franchot didn't bother to bow, rather turned on his heels and left.

The door closed and a muffled lament escaped Dominic pressed lips. He did not have time to grieve when Adele entered, sympathetic in her approach. Her eyes asking what her lips did not speak.

"She leaves for Lorraine. I could not convince her his death was natural and that he sought to kill me—" He sank onto the sofa, weeping. Adele sat beside him.

In less than a day his family was destroyed. In truth, his family faced destruction for years.

His mother left for Lorraine. She didn't even attend the interning of Jourdian in the family crypt. In fact, Dominic kept the ceremony small and private only reading a passage of Scripture to the family servants, Adele and Sabrina. Under the circumstances, Arsène did not participate. The exclusivity was much to the chagrin of the Bishop of Reims, who wanted to celebrate a mass for the marquis for all of Reims. Despite Dominic's objections, the bishop informed the new marquis he could not forbid such a mass, and one would be done to honor Jourdain that Sunday.

Over the next three weeks, Dominic took charge. Now he, the Marquis de Charbonier, would be the patriarch of a new generation, who looked to him for guidance. He set right all the estate accounts, local complaints and confusion the war caused Charbonier. He sent our various correspondences, including a short letter to his mother informing her of a monthly allowance. Whereas books could be balanced and complaints of locals handled, soothing the somber atmosphere at the château proved difficult.

In quiet moments when Dominic observed Arsène and Sabrina together, their joy of being reunited was tempered by hardship and loss. He knew the reason for their melancholy, though Arsène said nothing directly to him rather spoke in veiled in comments about getting his life back together. Dominic could, and would, take care of that. When finished with the arrangements, he sent Roger to fetch the others.

Sabrina approached Arsène, who took to sitting on the back terrace during sunny afternoons to read. Sometimes he read the Scriptures, other times scholarly works by renowned theologians and history books he brought from England. She sat in the chair beside him, her smile tender but a bit sheepish.

"I don't know what made me forget or take so long to return this to you." She gave him the Bible.

"Last I saw it was at La Rochelle. How did you get it?"

"Dominic sent it to Adele by way of Roger, along with the sad letter about you and Philipe. He wanted me to have it as some consolation. Once I returned to Reims, I had to keep finding different hiding places for fear of Uncle discovering it and my father's Bible."

He took her hand and kissed the knuckles. "You have nothing more to fear. God has been gracious to us."

"Yes, He has." They kissed. She stopped and laid her head against his shoulder. "When will you speak to Dominic?"

"I plan to after dinner this evening. From all my subtle inquires, I think he is finally ready to discuss it directly. He needed time to grieve and adjust to this new role."

She chuckled. "Silly man, he was born to be the marquis."

"Not under such circumstances."

"True. Aunt Madeline's departure hurt him deeply."

He lifted her chin. "Don't become sad. Not when our future is so close at hand." He kissed her.

The clearing of a throat stopped the kiss. Roger smiled. "Mademoiselle, Sergeant—I mean Captain, the marquis requests you attend him in the private study."

Arsène chuckled. "I'm not in the army any longer, Roger. My name will do just fine."

Roger's smile grew. "Somehow I don't think for long." He escorted them to the study. Adele was already present and Dominic sat at his desk.

"You wanted to see us?" asked Sabrina.

"I did. Please, be seated." He waited a moment as Sabrina sat, but Arsène remained standing next to her chair. "No one feels the loss more keenly than I, but regretting is not the way to spend the rest of our lives. We must put the past behind us and place our faith in God for the future. Therefore, as the Marquis de Charbonier, I made certain arrangements." He turned to Arsène. "Monsieur Lamonreaux, do you still have honorable intentions toward my cousin?"

"More than ever."

Taking pen in hand, Dominic signed a paper, sprinkled it with powder, gently blew off the excess and handed the paper to Arsène. "The dowry my father kept from Sabrina. Upon marriage you become the Comte de Trèvoux with estates in Burgundy, Touraine, and Le Petite Château in Paris along with twenty thousand gold louis a year allowance. I believe the yearly income from the vineyard in Burgundy is around sixty thousand a year, while Touraine is near forty."

Overwhelmed, Arsène stared at the paper. Sabrina was more vocal and demonstrative in reaction, embracing Dominic.

"I grew tried of waiting for one or both of you to approach me on the matter," said Dominic, laughing.

"I never dreamed of anything like this. I only wanted us to be together, not a title," said Arsène finding his voice.

"I know, but it is Sabrina's by right. Besides Charbonier and Trèvoux, there is a lesser baronet in Picardy and Montdidier. In all, the family owns nine estates with various vineyards, dioceses, commerce, etc. Trèvoux gets three, Montdidier two, leaving four to the marquis."

Arsène grew thoughtful in regard to the paper he held. "The amnesty voided my warrant, but won't Richelieu become suspicious with this?"

"The Cardinal stole our happiness once before, don't allow thoughts of him to do so again," said Sabrina.

Arsène shook his head. "Of course not. I'm merely overwhelmed and wondering aloud."

"Stopped wondering. I am held in favor by the King. In fact, I wrote Louis informing him of my father's *natural* death due the wounds he suffered. I told him I survived as a prisoner, and when La Rochelle was liberated, rushed home to reassure my family."

"He wrote my father a similar letter," said Adele.

"How will that help me against the Cardinal?"

"You are marrying into one of the most powerful families in France. Richelieu would need strong evidence to refute the word of the Marquis de Charbonier. Only the Princes are more powerful than I."

Arsène cocked at grin. "A Gascon count?"

"I can think of worse things." The new marquis smiled, rising and walking about the desk to Arsène. "Monsieur le Comte, take your new countess with my blessings." He embraced Arsène, kissing him on both cheeks. "Cousin."

"Now, that is the best title," said Arsène. He turned to Sabrina and bowed. "Your humble servant, Madame." They kissed.

Epilogue

T HE FALL OF LA ROCHELLE LEAD TO THE DECLINE of the political power the Huguenots gained since the Edit of Nantes in 1589. Henri de Rohan's exile to Venice, Italy was to prevent the Huguenots from rallying again as a political force. Only when assured of Rohan's cooperation, did Richelieu allow the Edict of Grace to take effect.

In 1629, Richelieu drafted the Peace of Alais stripping the Huguenots of all political power, razed their fortified towns, including La Rochelle, and annexed all their holdings. Rendered politically ineffective and their income almost totally wiped out, the Huguenot faith began to decline. Many chose to leave France for more friendly Protestant countries like England, the Netherlands and the New World. One of the cities founded by Huguenots is New Rochelle in New York.

In 1633, an ironic turn of events occurred in which Richelieu was forced to call upon Rohan to use his influence with the Protestant princes and lead an army against the Spanish when the Imperial troops threatened to invade France.

But that is another story ...

About the Author

Shawn Lamb lives in Antioch, Tennessee, a suburb of Nashville with her husband Robert Lamb. Married for 26 years they have a daughter, Briana, who is pursuing a career in film.

Shawn began writing in her late teens and kept pursuing a career, eventually writing for the Filmation Studios' 1980s animated series "BraveStarr." She continued honing her craft, winning two awards and earning recognition for screenwriting from the American Screenwriters Association. While pitching historical fiction to various publishers, her daughter asked her if she could write her a fantasy story. It was a challenge switching genres but one she accepted.

Taking the skills learned from writing for children's television along with experience dealing with children in AWANA and during her time in Civil Air Patrol working with teens, she began the Allon fantasy series.

The result are stories of commitment, faith, and endurance; commitment to a cause, the faith to overcome obstacles and the endurance to see it through to the end. Begin the journey of discovering Allon with Ellis and Shannan as they seek to restore hope to the mortals of the kingdom and pave the way for the return of the mighty immortal Guardians.

Allon

Book 1

by

Shawn Lamb

FOR FIVE HUNDRED YEARS THE DARK WAY HAS RULED ALLON, but an ancient prophecy speaks of a time to come when the Guardians will return and Allon will be restored—led by the rightful heir. But sixteen-year-old Prince Ellis must prove himself worthy to be king and able to defeat the evil. Each event tests his character, his wisdom, his courage, and ultimately, his heart.

Allon

Book 2

Insurrection

by

Shawn Lamb

Four years since the defeat of their uncle King Marcellus, sixteen-year-old Wess, his younger brother Bosley and their twin sisters have lived like commoners. When the brothers become caught up in a coup against King Ellis they are faced with a choice: to take advantage of the coup and reclaim their royal heritage or aid Ellis, the man responsible for changing their lives. Their choice could have deadly consequences.

Allon

Book 3

Heir Apparent

by

Shawn Lamb

SHORTLY AFTER A DEFEATED ENEMY ARRIVES IN ALLON with the offer of a royal marriage, strange things begin to happen. What is the connection of four mysterious stones to a jade statue? Are these linked to Prince Nigel's haunting nightmares? The Guardians must learn if this is a marriage for peace or an act of revenge.

Allon

Book 4

A Question of Sovereignty

by

Shawn Lamb

H E SHALL BE ALLON'S GREATEST KING; of such a heritage as to rule Guardian and mortal alike - so says Prophecy of the man to succeed Ellis. He decides upon Prince Sullivan of Gorham to wed his heir, Ellan, unaware that Sullivan's mother is an old enemy. Their arrival allows Ellan's own ambition to blossom. The royal family and Guardians become impacted by dark machinations threatening a coup. Determined to save her father, Tristine meets two unlike allies: a blacksmith and crippled beggar. But how can they help? And what about the Great King?

Explore the Kingdom of Allon

www.allonbooks.com

Featuring

- Read excerpts of Allon books
- Original Character Art
- Interactive Map of Allon
- News and Events
- Photo and Video Gallery
- Links to:
  - o Facebook - The Kingdom of Allon Page
  - o Shawn Lamb's All-On Writing blog
  - o Contact Shawn Lamb